GHOST OF NOSTALGIA

GHOST OF NOSTALGIA

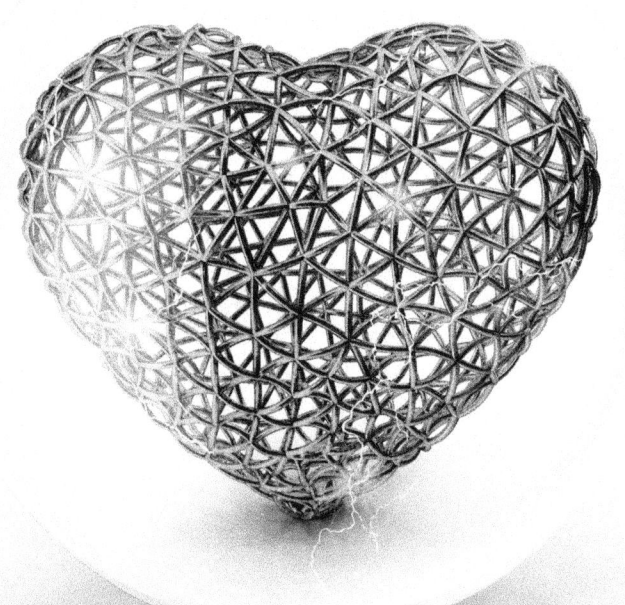

JOANNE HATFIELD

Ghost of Nostalgia

© 2025 by Joanne Hatfield

Editors: Deborah Froese, Noëlla Simmons
Cover and Interior Design: Emma Elzinga

Indigo River Publishing
3 West Garden Street, Ste. 718
Pensacola, FL 32502

www.indigoriverpublishing.com

Ordering Information:

Quantity Sales: Special discounts are available on quantity purchases by corporations, associations, and others. For details, contact the publisher at the address above.

Orders by US trade bookstores and wholesalers: Please contact the publisher at the address above.

Printed in the United States of America

Library of Congress Control Number: 2024919662
ISBN: 978-1-964686-11-0 (paperback)   978-1-964686-12-7 (ebook)

First Edition

With Indigo River Publishing, you can always expect great books, strong voices, and meaningful messages. Most importantly, you'll always find . . . *words worth reading.*

For Elise.
May this novel one day inspire you to reach for the stars.

CONTENTS

GEOGRAPHICAL FEATURES

PREMIER ESPRIT (FIRST SPIRIT)—country founded by Eidolon, the first Suzerain, four thousand years ago. The most powerful country in the world with sovereignty over several other countries. **PREMIER ESPRIT IS DIVIDED INTO EIGHT REGIONS:**

REGION	RELEVANT SETTLEMENTS	LANDFORMS
Tristesse (Sadness)	*Nostalgie* (Nostalgia) *Envie* (Envy) *Jalousie* (Jealousy)–fell 22 years ago	Gentle hills and grassy plains Lake *Oublié* (Forgotten) in *Nostalgie*
Crainte (Fear)	*Remords* (Remorse) *Panique* (Panic)—fell 10 years ago. Located in the *Vallée de la Solitude* (Valley of Loneliness) *Anxiété* (Anxiety)	Mountains, valleys, and rivers *Le Solitaire* (The Lonely) River
Bonheur (Happiness)	*Éthéré Coeur* (Ethereal Heart)—the capital city of Premier Esprit. Nicknamed the "Paramount" because of its great importance. *Calme* (Calm)	Forests, rivers, and gentle rolling hills
Colère (Anger)	*Agacement* (Annoyance)—fell 1 year ago *Honte* (Shame) *Port Refoulé* (Port Repressed)	Flat plains and black sandy beaches
Confiance (Trust)	*Château de Pureté* (Castle of Purity) *Port Espoir* (Port Hope)	Large lakes and highlands
Étonnement (Surprise)	*Extase* (Ecstasy)	Mountains, rivers, and a large island
Excitation (Excitement)	*Plaisir* (Pleasure) *Nerveux* (Nervous)	Black stoney beaches, rivers, grassy plains, and farmlands
Dégoût (Disgust)	*Port Horreur* (Port Horror)	Coastal cliffs, mountains, and caverns

Bassin de la Haine (Pool of Hate)—a restricted area off the northeastern coast of Premier Esprit. It contains the *Île de l'Amour* (Island of Love), Eidolon's homeland.

THE SUZERAIN'S THREE TOWERS OF OPERATION, LOCATED IN ÉTHÉRÉ COEUR:

Résonateur Édifice (Resonator Building)— where Résonateurs are trained, housed, and given assignments.	*Bibliothèque de l'Archiviste* (Archivist Library)—library for all information in Premier Esprit, hub for the relier system, and physical location of the Sommet.	*Pylône de la Science* (Science Pylon)— center for innovation and technology.

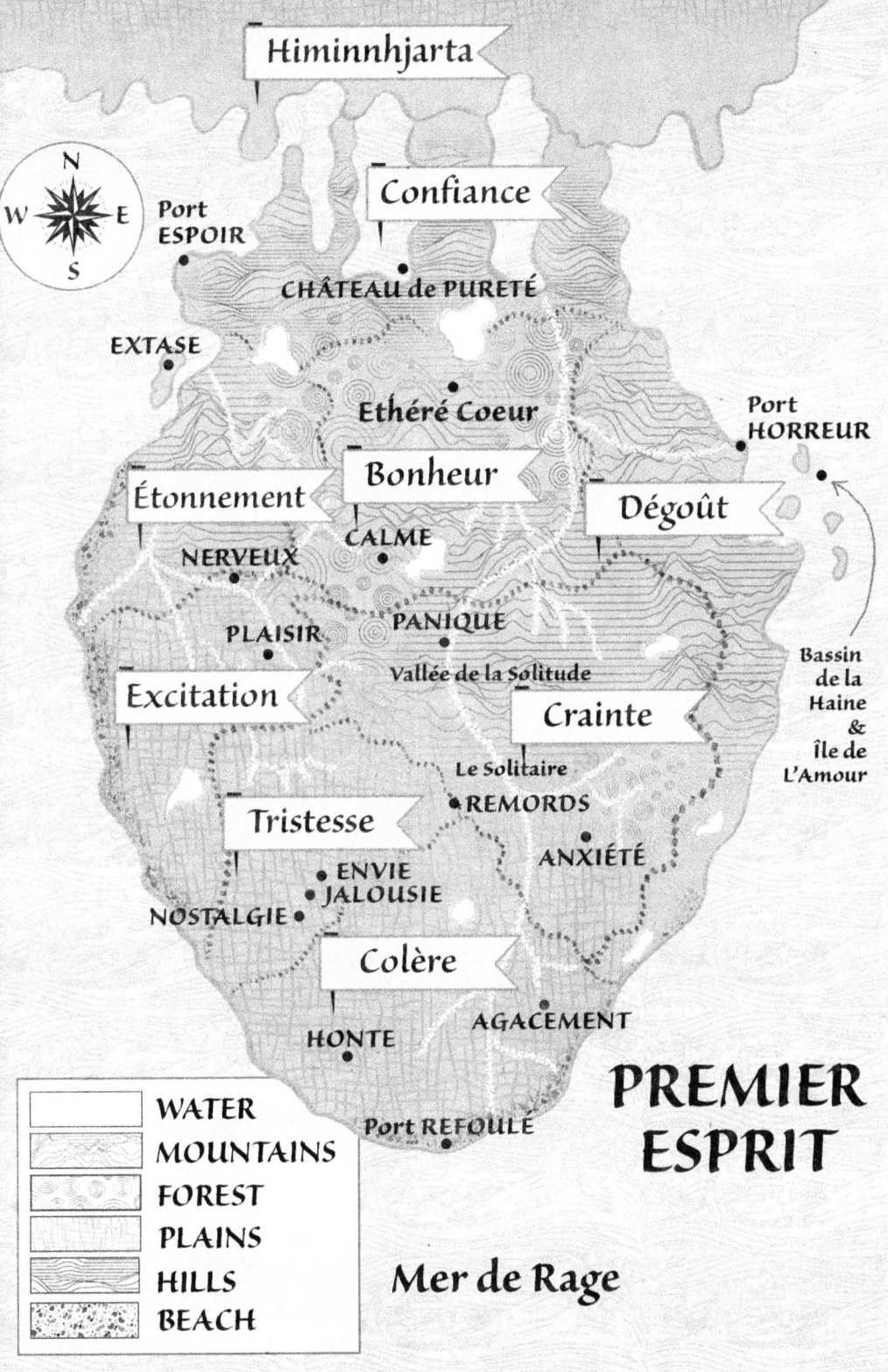

Himinnhjarta

Confiance

Port ESPOIR

CHÂTEAU de PURETÉ

EXTASE

Ethéré Coeur

Port HORREUR

Bonheur

Étonnement

Dégoût

CALME

NERVEUX

PANIQUE

PLAISIR

Vallée de la Solitude

Bassin de la Haine & Île de L'Amour

Excitation

Crainte

Le Solitaire

Tristesse

REMORDS

ANXIÉTÉ

ENVIE
JALOUSIE

NOSTALGIE

Colère

PREMIER
ESPRIT

HONTE

AGACEMENT

Port REFOULÉ

WATER
MOUNTAINS
FOREST
PLAINS
HILLS
BEACH

Mer de Rage

DEAL OF THE HOPELESS

A dark shimmer streaked across the moonlit plains of golden grass, flowing along the rolling hills in a swirl. It stopped, floating like a black cloud glittering with tiny gems.

A lump formed in my throat. I swallowed, and it lodged in my chest like a block of ice. A head of stark white rose from the haze.

A Phase.

The ice in my chest flooded my veins. I was safe here, at the far end of the lake near the barrier's edge. Even with the village on the other side of Lake Oublié, there was no danger. But knowing the Phase was out there—

It suddenly vanished over the hills.

I gasped and put my hand over my heart, its intense rhythm thumping through the rough fabric of my dress. Stop. *Stop.*

I took several deep breaths. *Calm down. Be calm, or the Phase will come back.*

Just a few strides from the lakeshore, I leaned against the thick trunk of the only remaining cork oak near my village. I began twisting fine silver wires together in my fingers with new urgency. The metal was old, frayed, and brittle, but needed. Heart, it was desperately needed to keep the barrier alive. To keep Phases out.

I gazed at the lake, eager for a distraction from the desperation creeping over me. Water lapped against the bank as a cool autumn breeze swept across its surface. Reeds along the lakeshore rustled, and a patch of water lilies bobbed. The reflection of the stars on the water's surface blurred. The only lights found at night outside Nostalgie. Across the lake, my village lay settled in the center of the barrier. It looked like nothing more than a collection of rectangular shadows in the darkness, but Nostalgie was everything to me. To the villagers. Beyond us, nothing but hilly plains stretched as far as the eye could see.

Although other villages were scattered some distance around us, Nostalgie may as well have been alone in the world. We were each trapped inside a wall—a sphere of invisible energy, but still, a wall.

The dark figure streaked along the horizon feeding off my discomfort, sensing my emotions. It was out there waiting, always waiting for its chance to claim a new victim—someone foolish or desperate enough to step outside the barrier and have their heart ripped out.

A chill ran down my spine. The Phases made sure we stayed inside our walls.

A piece of wire splintered and pierced my palm. I hissed. Beads of red dripped down the metal, making it slick. I sighed and set the wires down on the oak's gnarled roots. This was the one tree that hadn't been cut down, the cork from its bark deemed too valuable to lose. The holes in our water barrels grew wider every year, and only cork from this tree could adequately plug them.

As I leaned over to study my palm, wild scarlet curls spilled over my shoulders. The cut was deep enough to form another scar. But scars were good. I ran my finger over the white lines covering my bronze-colored palm. Some of them were straight. Others small and crescent shaped from the times my nails dug into my skin to keep my emotions in control. Scars were reminders to avoid feeling because feeling was death. Emotions called out to the Phases, drawing them like flies to honey. The nature of beings was to seek what they didn't possess. Phases sought hearts, and those of us inside the barrier . . .

I pulled the thin thread of metal from my palm. Wasted. Losing a piece of precious material gave Mayor Edgard another reason to snarl at me through his few remaining teeth. Gavril the constant disappointment. The child of an outsider. The burden.

I dropped the wire to the ground. There was nothing left. All the resources were gone. All the cables and wires and switches—

I drew another deep breath. Calm. I had to stay calm. I stood up and left the edge of Lake Oublié to head for the open plains holding my hands in front of me, feeling for the pulsing energy at the edge of the protective barrier. I took slow steps. I didn't want to move too quickly and accidentally slip outside.

Suddenly, a warm tingling swept over my hand and sent a soothing rush up my arm. I pulled my hand back. Closer. Much closer than last night. The barrier shrank faster each day.

Wind kissed my flesh, and the hair on the back of my neck stood up. I pulled my tattered shawl tightly around my shoulders. The barrier would eventually fall, and no one would know Nostalgie was gone. Only emptiness leftover.

But not right away. I gazed at the pitch-black horizon. If the barrier fell, for a few seconds—maybe more if I weren't the first taken—I would get to breathe the outside air. I would feel the wind on my skin and know I was free. I would be part of the world.

The shimmering mass glinted in the distance. It rolled down the hills and shot into the sky.

A shiver ran down my spine. No. We couldn't give up. I hurried back to the cork oak and retrieved the wires. There had to be some way to save ourselves. Nostalgie wasn't just a village. It was our home—the only place we could live in peace. The only place we could truly call our own. It was my world, the only one I would ever know.

I circled the outer edge of the lake, heading back to the village. The sparse lights of Nostalgie shone dimly through the night as I dodged the rotting tree stumps that marked the skeleton of a once lush forest. There were no shrubs or saplings for miles. Every twig in range of the barrier had been harvested until life was drained from the roots. Only decay remained—a garden for mushrooms we gratefully accepted. Wood was more precious than gold, but the lives we had left were just as precious. Leaving the barrier was not worth the risk of losing any more neighbors or friends.

I entered the village and passed between old patchwork houses and shacks constructed from whatever scraps of wood and sheets of metal villagers could piece together. Only thirty remained. Some families were forced to depend on the charity of their neighbors. All we had was one another. If we didn't work together, the village would fall apart and become a ruin of dust for the wind to carry away.

I followed the worn dirt path to the center of Nostalgie and used my shawl to wipe blood from the wires. Heaps of mechanical junk beyond repair littered the edges of the trail. What spare parts could be utilized were stripped away and the rest tossed aside to be forgotten. As I neared the center toward the hub, the low, ceaseless drone of electricity filled the air. It was dull. Comforting. As long as that hum continued, the Solenoid was keeping the barrier alive.

I passed between two shacks and stepped over a piece of scrap metal, not wanting another hole in my boots. There was barely any leather left—

"Edgard," a hurried whisper drifted through the air from somewhere in front of me. I couldn't see Mathieu, but I recognized the voice of my childhood friend. The mayor's apprentice these days. "Edgard, a word. I need a word with you."

Heart, what did Mathieu want with the mayor this time of night? He rarely stayed up later than a few hours past sunset. I crinkled my nose. When he was awake, he rarely did anything other than follow

Edgard around like a little page. He didn't have time for anyone else.

Curious, I pushed myself against the nearest house, careful not to shift the rusty walls.

"What is it, Mathieu?" the mayor asked sharply.

The clang of tapping metal rang out—another wiring panel being manhandled back into place. Edgard was always looking inside the Solenoid's siphon, prodding the wires and condensers, trying to figure out how it worked. Trying to unlock the secrets of the barrier's creation. Whatever he discovered, he kept close to his heart, guarding the information like a fierce bear. If anyone else dared get close to the hub, he hurled threats of banishment like rocks.

A grunt followed the clatter, and I could picture Edgard's leathery red face wrinkle, his jaw tight. "These repairs won't fix themselves. If we don't maintain the energy pull—"

"Yes, Edgard," Mathieu's voice quivered. "It's exactly that. The limit has receded even more. It's almost to the cork tree near the shore of Lake Oublié. If it continues like this, we won't be able to—"

"Hush, Mathieu," Edgard hissed.

I held my breath, not daring to make a sound.

For a few moments, humming filled the air. Then Edgard's uneven steps rattled on the metal platform of the hub. "Keep your voice down," he said. "Everyone's asleep. We don't need them to wake up and cause a riot."

I bit my lip. Keeping villagers in the dark was better? But coming from Edgard, it wasn't surprising. He would do whatever it took to keep the village's faith in him. I was shocked he even had his apprentice checking the barrier. That required trusting Mathieu not to spread the truth.

"I can tell the energy pull's off," Edgard said in a low voice. "It's so damn hot some of the wires are melting in the siphon's distributor. I need you to make sure the barrier's still up while I patch it. We don't need to run out of energy and have the barrier fall."

"But's that's exactly what's going to happen, Edgard." Mathieu's voice trembled. "We don't have any more time. This is the end."

"It's not the end," Edgard growled. "It will never be the end. Not now. Not under my watch. We survived before." The old man let out a deep breath through his nose. "Though it would be easier if we had a *Résonateur*."

It would be, I thought bitterly. Résonateurs could manifest their emotions to affect the physical world—stifle the air with their contempt or turn their rage into invisible blades. *They can kill Phases.* I looked up at the stars. Résonateurs were the only ones who could pay the price for a new energy source for the barrier. A Solenoid.

They called the price "paying the service," a secretive task ordained to Résonateurs by the governing body of Premier Esprit, the Sommet, in exchange for a Solenoid to power a town's barrier. Everyone had their own idea about what the service entailed, and it was common practice for people to share fantastical stories with the rest of the village about what they read or heard. Edgard once told us that Résonateurs were sent to foreign countries to "deal with" the Sommet's enemies. I asked Mama if that was true. She rolled her eyes and said she wished someone would "deal with" Edgard.

"What about Gavril . . ." Mathieu trailed off.

They couldn't see me, but I still felt like I was being watched. My fingers clenched around the wires.

"I mean Gavril might be a—"

"It's no use," Edgard interrupted. "That one doesn't have a lick of Résonateur in her blood, regardless of what her mother says. Been a burden more than anything."

The wires pinched into my fingers. Burden. The child Mama got stuck with. The extra mouth to split rations with. The constant reminder that Edgard couldn't live up to the memory held in my mother's heart. I pressed my lips together and forced myself to stay calm. Any sustained emotion would draw the attention of that Phase.

Edgard's remark wasn't worth risking the village over.

"Goel. What about him?" Mathieu asked, desperation coating his tone.

"Gavril's supposed father?" Edgard snorted.

"It's been seventeen years since he left to obtain a new Solenoid for our barrier. Surely his service has been paid. Especially since the Solenoid is dying. The Sommet can't expect to keep him away forever."

I looked down at the detritus of Nostalgie cluttered around my feet. My father. The great Résonateur who left and never came back. He was supposed to protect us from Phases. Was his service more important than us?

Edgard let out a low, dismissive chuckle. "Goel? Are you serious? He's never coming back here. If he's not living it up in Éthéré Coeur with the other Résonateurs of the Capital, he returned to that foreign land of his. Fleurette's the only one foolish enough to still hold on to the hope of seeing him again." He snorted again. "Stupid woman needs to give it up and find a new man."

How dare he say those things about Mama? The metal in my hands grew slick again. I controlled my breathing, using the fear of something more terrible than a bitter old drunk to keep me silent. I would not let my emotions call that Phase. I *couldn't*.

"Then we have to find someone else," Mathieu pleaded. "Maybe we can ask for a Résonateur from the Sommet. If the Solenoid fails, and we're left unprotected, only they can save us."

A derisive grunt sounded from our mayor. "Do you really believe they would send a Résonateur here, Mathieu? That the great Suzerain, the ruler of all hearts of the world, would spare a mere fraction of a thought on this little ant nest? We're nothing but a speck to them."

A moment of silence, and Edgard's voice brightened. "But I do have hope, my boy."

I heard a muffled clap and pictured Edgard's hand landing on Mathieu's shoulder.

"We need support. I know that," Edgard continued. "I've already contacted Seigneur Gervais in Envie. He's coming tomorrow. Envie's not so far from here, and they have more supplies than we do. Perhaps we can come up with an agreement. I heard over the *relier* his boy might be looking for a wife."

A wife for Gervais' son Cyril? I fought the urge to gag. What woman would have that misfortune? And from here? Was Envie's stock not good enough for him?

The two men were silent. As moments passed, the constant low hum seemed more deafening with every second.

"I thought I saw one the other day," Mathieu whispered as though the words stifled his breath. "It was horrible—all black and *twisting . . .*"

"Gervais will come, and the matter will be taken care of."

"How can you know that, Edgard? After what happened in Jalousie—"

"That's enough of this talk," Edgard cut the younger man off with a tone as sharp as an ax. "We've gone on about this too long. I will talk with Seigneur Gervais and meet whatever demands he has. We will never have this conversation again." The grating squeaked again. "It's late, boy. Let's retire for the night and get up early. There's a lot to do before the seigneur arrives."

I remained hidden and waited for their footsteps to disappear into the darkness. I pushed away from the house and turned the corner to face the hub and the heart of Nostalgie.

I stood before the great deity. The hub was everything—the fulcrum of our lives comprised by two machines as precious as the sun. A great mechanical barrel perched atop a circular pedestal of metal grating about twenty feet wide, the unabating hum resonating from its metallic body. The siphon. It was as wide as four large casks lined side by side and twice as tall as a man. The once sleek silver surfaces of its curved sides were rusty with age and rough with dented plates. In a few spots, wires had escaped their paneling and sprouted from the barrel like black vines of ivy. At the top of the siphon, a towering metal spire rose up to point at the stars. This was the distributor for the barrier. And in a wide semi-circular indentation that cut to the core of the siphon pulsed the heart. Not an organ of blood, tissue, and mortal life, but an enormous cylinder attached to the siphon by countless electrical veins and arteries. The life source of the barrier. Without it, the siphon had no energy to take and distribute. There was no protection from the Phases beyond. It was our hope, the guardian of our lives.

The Solenoid.

Rapt . . . rapt . . . rapt . . .

My throat tightened. Had anyone else noticed the low taps emitted from the Solenoid? I'd heard them before, several times. They only seemed to rise in the silence of night when I stood nearby. Each time I heard that tapping, the barrier diminished a little.

Was it dying? Was our peace coming to an end?

We needed a new Solenoid, and there was only one way to get one. Edgard was delusional if he thought Gervais, the slick lord of Envie, was going to save us. He only cared for one thing, and we weren't the image he saw in the mirror. We needed to appeal to Éthéré Coeur—the Paramount of the country . . .

A soft crackle and a bright light flashed above me. I looked straight up. A thin line of white rippled along the barrier, spreading out like lightning running along a glass sphere.

. . . and we had to do it before that Phase killed us.

The sun had barely cleared the horizon when Edgard's voice roared through the air, announcing the impending arrival of Envie's seigneur. My fellow villagers bustled around with excitement, gossiping about how brave he was to travel outside the barrier and how they needed to dig out their finest clothes for his first visit in four years. To them, he was a beacon of hope—a kind lord eager to help. They didn't realize his help wouldn't come for free. One of us was going to be traded—sold for promises that were as hollow as Gervais' heart. It made me cringe.

I walked by the old storehouse, a small building that held Nostalgie's food supply. A rusty lock dangled from the door—more a threat than anything. If anyone wanted to steal food, the walls wouldn't put up much of a fight.

A young woman with soft brown curls and a small key tied to her wrist turned the corner of the building and smiled at me. It was Celine. Her father was Edgard's oldest friend and the official lock-keeper of the storehouse—a job he gladly passed onto his child as his knees refused to cooperate with age.

"Exciting, isn't it, Gavril?" she called.

I tried to smile back. "If you like infestations."

She swatted her hand at me and chuckled. "You can't be serious. It's not everyday a seigneur comes to town."

"Thank the Great Heart," I replied and walked on.

Celine was very pretty. She was a few years older than me and had married young—a union that ended suddenly when her groom, a man called Roland, became ill. She was kind and hardworking—a great choice for a wife. But would she leave? Say goodbye to her aging father and never look back?

"Oh, I wouldn't mind running off with him," a smoky voice said.

I turned and saw Bernadette, the local herbalist, standing in the shade of her house with her sister Lucienne. She waved a large lace fan in the air, her graying black hair bouncing back and forth with every flick. Bernadette never bothered to hide her dislike for Mama. Jealousy, my mama would laugh, was an ugly habit. I put my head down and pretended to be interested in a rusty nail in the dirt.

"It's been ten years since his wife keeled over," Bernadette went on. "I'd say Seigneur Gervais could use a good woman to keep him warm at night."

Ugh, disgusting. My stomach lurched.

"I think you're dreaming, Bernadette," Lucienne giggled. "You know he's always had eyes for *his flower*."

"Well, *she's* still pining for a ghost," Bernadette replied. She suddenly let out a bawdy laugh. "All the more reason for me to take his mind off things."

I tried to not let the uninhibited flow of emotions bother me, but when Bernadette began detailing her ideas, it was time to take solace at Lake Oublié.

The golden glow of sunset spread over the lake's surface, making it shimmer like a pool of riches. It was so much more. I settled by the water's edge, letting its tranquility soothe my heart. Slowly the sun dipped down, its rays shooting into the sky for one last dazzling display before it sank into darkness.

"Gavril, they're here," Mathieu said behind me.

My nose crinkled as though I could smell our lordly and lofty guests already. I stood up and turned to face Mathieu. "Then you should go greet them with the others. I'm sure the seigneur won't miss my presence. He's made his distaste for me apparent on more than one occasion."

"About that . . ."

Alarmed at his hesitant tone, I turned to look at the sandy-haired mayor's apprentice. Mathieu's chestnut eyes turned to the ground.

I returned my gaze to the lake and clenched my fists. *Stay calm.* "I think I'll stay here."

"You shouldn't even be out here," he said, voice as taut as a hangman's rope. "It's not safe. We don't even know how much space—"

"I do." The water bobbed up from the wind to lick the toes of my boots, the frigid liquid slipping into holes to nip at my skin. "I come here every day. I know exactly how much space we have left."

"Then you know why you have to come with me," Mathieu replied. "You don't have a choice. Seigneur Gervais demanded your presence." He seized my arm like a rat clinging to its last meal.

I jerked away and shoved him back. "No!"

"Gavril, stop," he grunted, grabbing my arm again.

The threads along the shoulder of my worn dress popped as I tried to pull away once more. "Let go," I hissed.

This time, he held fast. The cloth shredded, and my feet slid on the slick earth. Liquid splashed up around me as I flailed and heaved, falling backward into a shock of icy lake water. It forced the air out of my lungs, but I regained enough sense to push my back from the silt and sat up, shoving the mop of red curls from my eyes.

Mathieu gawked at me, mouth hanging open.

I stood up and looked down at my skirt. Lakebed mud oozed over it. "Does Seigneur Gervais still want to see me now, looking like this?"

Mathieu stared at my filthy attire. "We can fix this," he said, finally finding his words. "We can sneak into your house and have you change."

"Or I could stay here. The mayor prefers I stay out of sight. Why have I suddenly been invited to a soiree with the great seigneur?"

Gervais hated me. He couldn't possibly be considering . . .

Mathieu's eyes shot to the earth again and his hands wrung together, the fingers turning red. "Please, Gavril. The mayor says you might be our only hope."

Every angry word I could think of swelled from the fire in my chest to my tongue, but I swallowed the barrage and took in a deep breath. Calm. "I'm 'hope' now?" I shook my head. "Yesterday I was a burden. Edgard should make up his mind."

"You know he doesn't mean it. The mayor's under a lot of stress—"

"We all are," I said. "The barrier is shrinking, and he keeps pretending nothing's wrong."

"He's not, Gavril," Mathieu replied. "Edgard's well aware of what's happening. That's why he needs you to see the seigneur."

"What makes me so special?"

"You know," Mathieu said. "Your father—"

"Is gone," I finished. "He hasn't been here for a long time."

"But you're here. You're all we have." His voice was weak, pleading for help. The voice of my friend. The voice of Nostalgie.

The fire of my defiance snuffed out in an instant. "All right. I don't know why he wants to see me, but I'll go."

Mathieu smiled and reached for my hand. I hesitated for a second, then slowly took it. No matter our differences, we were in this together.

He led me away from the banks of Lake Oublié. It reminded me of when we were children. When we used to sneak out to the lake and dare each other to step outside the barrier. No one ever won that dare.

"You're not embarrassed to be seen with me? This really is a desperate time," I muttered.

"We're friends, Gavril."

"We haven't been friends since Edgard selected you as his chore boy."

A weary sigh escaped his lips. "You'll always be my friend. It's just . . . well, my duties are important and necessary. I know you don't like Edgard, but he's getting on. Someone will have to take over when he's gone."

"Yes, someone will have to make sure we know who to blame for all our problems. Where is our great Résonateur when we need him?"

"Your father had to pay the service. I don't blame him."

"I do." My insides burned. I pushed my nails into my scraped palms to banish the feeling. "He's made it clear that 'service' is more important than us. Now we are at the mercy of Seigneur Gervais."

Once we reached the edge of the village, Mathieu pushed me against the nearest house. The rusted tin squealed, and a few splinters of wood shook from the patched frame.

"Stay here," he told me and disappeared around the corner.

I waited for a minute, and when he didn't return, I gently pushed away from the wall.

This was absurd. We shouldn't waste our time worrying whether Gervais would be offended by my appearance. If we waited too long, we would be prey for the Phase. It was waiting outside already. And as much as he could ignore a blow to the head, Edgard couldn't turn a blind eye to the ripples and sparks appearing in the barrier at night. A panic needed to be avoided, but—

"There you are," a deep growl rumbled.

I turned my head toward the voice. Edgard marched straight for me, his ratty beard losing gray whiskers with every limped stomp. He roughly snatched my arm in a crushing grip and spun around like a warped cog.

He eyed me up and down. "Disgusting. I don't know what you've gotten into, but our guests want to see you." He buried his fist into his pocket and yanked out a dirty cloth. "Clean up," he hissed, throwing the rag in my face.

I ripped the filthy thing away and threw it to the ground. Edgard paid me no mind and dragged me toward the village center. I stumbled, desperate to keep my feet underneath. I winced as scraps of metal cut through my shoes.

"You're about as useless as that moony mother of yours. I should have kicked the two of you out a long time ago," Edgard grumbled. "Maybe I can finally get rid of one of you. Cut my losses like your father."

A sick feeling churned in my stomach. I wanted to argue with Edgard, but deep down, he was right. He saw it clear as day. My father's absence spoke volumes. It sounded like abandonment.

And now it was Edgard's time to turn his back on me.

The hub was surrounded by people I didn't recognize, though I'd known them my whole life. Costumed for the seigneur, my fellow villagers stared at us and whispered to each other behind tatty gloved hands and patched fans. Some hid their faces behind antiquated, musty masks, while others had matted their faces in layers of white powder thicker than tar.

We made it to the hub, and Edgard threw me down onto the metal grating. My dress tore from a hole around my knee down to the hem as I hit the panels hard enough to set off an echoing thud. A great hush followed the din of the reverberating metal. Still on my knees, I turned from the judgmental eyes keenly locked on me and focused on the constant, dull hum that filled the void and provided my only source of comfort.

Rapt . . . rapt . . . rapt . . .

I stilled when the slow tapping interrupted the hum for a few seconds. I glanced at Edgard. He wiped sweat from his red forehead but didn't appear to notice the strange sound.

My mouth felt like sand.

"I hope this isn't how you treat all of your trade property, Edgard," a voice spoken from the nose said from the side.

A man in the frayed, exhausted silk ruffles of his forefathers sauntered to the front of the Solenoid. He sounded like a weasel but looked like a balding mantis wearing knee breeches that crept nearly a third of the way up his spindly thighs. Gervais' narrow eyes crawled all over me—studying me, weighing me, judging me. He was not friendly or concerned for me, no matter what he said to Edgard. If anything, he was waiting to see what I would do.

And I did what everyone expected. I kept silent.

I rose to my feet and straightened myself with as much dignity as I could muster in a mud-covered, ripped dress. I kept my gaze steady, head up but not looking directly at anyone. If I didn't focus on them sneering and looking down on me, I wouldn't get upset.

"Such a submissive thing, Edgard. Yes, well done," Gervais said, giving Edgard an approving nod. "What do you think, son?"

A hand clamped down on my shoulder. Long fingers twisted into the wool of my shawl and jerked me around. The tall, slim form of Gervais' son loomed over me. He resembled his father in every way, except the wiry strands of his dull yellow hair were pulled into a tight ponytail. His sneaky, squinting eyes trailed down from my face to my shoes. An evident expression of revulsion spread wider with each pass.

"Such a dreadful sight. Why is she so filthy?" he asked.

"I'm afraid that's my fault," a timid reply drifted from the crowd.

Mathieu stepped forward, his head down, rubbing his hands together. "She was at the lake. I-I think I startled her, and she fell in. I didn't mean for it to happen."

He was lying for me. But why would he do such a thing? Edgard patted Mathieu on the back.

My lips pressed into a thin line. His excuse was not for me after all.

"Good man," the mayor murmured. "An accident," he announced loudly. "Just an accident. A little mud never hurt anyone. We can have her cleaned up for you in no time, Master Cyril."

"That sounds like a convenient lie." Cyril leered at me with lips stretching like a frog's. "I bet she did it on purpose to put me off. Why should we help such an ungrateful girl and the peasants that keep her?"

Edgard's eyes widened like he'd been stabbed in the chest. "Oh, no, I assure you, Master Cyril, we have nothing but gratitude—great gratitude—for you and your esteemed father." He glared at me. "An even if this little tart has her qualms, I promise you that it has nothing to do with the rest of—"

"As usual, Edgard, your tongue is getting salty from all the rear-licking you've been doing."

All eyes turned to the pixie-esque voice. A woman floated through the crowd like a fairy caught in the breeze. Her wide green eyes gleamed with the glory of fresh spring grass, and her cheeks flushed pink with joy. She was pale and wisplike, but vivacity seemed to set her aglow. The emerald dress she wore was once the envy of every woman in the village—fine silk and rich embroidery. That was seventeen years ago, but it was still twice as wide as it was long, and she made sure to swish the skirt out to hit as many people as possible on her promenade toward the hub.

"You. You there, Envie boy. What are you doing with my daughter?" she demanded.

"Boy?" Cyril seethed under his breath.

"Ah, Fleurette, as *enchanting* as ever," Gervais said.

Mama flicked her fiery curls over her shoulders and pranced up to Gervais like a queen. She whipped her hand out in front of him. Gasps and heated comments spread throughout the people. Gervais ignored the noise and grasped my mother's hand. He gave her a self-serving smirk before he bent down to kiss it.

"Have peace, my flower. We were only admiring your lovely daughter. There's no need to spark a fire," Gervais said with a tone as slick as grease.

Mama flicked her wrist back and gave the seigneur a suspicious smile. "And why would you be doing that? What is my Gavril to you?"

"Why, a bridge between our towns, of course." Gervais spread out his arms. "A bridge between our families, Fleurette."

Mama flounced around the lanky man, a mocking chortle fluttering past her lips. "Isn't that nice? A bridge. And how exactly do you intend to stretch Gavril's body from Nostalgie to Envie? It's quite far."

Gervais' smirk dropped, and his eyes cut into my mother like shards of glass. "Th-that's not—"

"Why don't you speak plainly for once, Ger? Your language is as gaudy as that ancient suit."

The self-proclaimed seigneur's face colored like leaves of purple cabbage. The muscles along his neck twitched.

Behind him, I could see panic lighting up on Edgard's rugged face. "See here, Fleurette—"

"Marriage," Gervais hissed at Mama, snipping Edgard off. "I'm talking about marriage, Fleurette."

My mother's eyes lit up, and she gave Gervais a flirty, sidelong glance. "Marriage, you say? I'm afraid my heart belongs to another—"

"Between my son and your daughter," Gervais clarified with a growl.

My jaw clenched. Me. It was going to be me.

Mama's eyes narrowed. "And why should we accept such an offer?"

Edgard bared his rotten teeth. His mouth opened and closed in rapid spasms while his arms thrashed around as if holding himself back from throttling Mama. Mathieu dodged a wild swing and retreated back to the crowd.

Gervais gave my mother the most incredulous look. He strode up to the Solenoid and gave it a tap. "Given your current situation," he began with another tap on the rattling metal, "I don't think—"

"What I mean is," Mama cut in, "what is your son going to do to show his undying love for my daughter? Goel acquired this Solenoid from the Paramount for me. That's hard to surpass."

"As a matter of fact, it'll be exactly that, my dear Fleurette," the head of Envie declared with a confident wave of his hand. "We intend to provide you with a Solenoid."

Excited rustling burst forth from my fellow villagers. The outpouring of emotion made me uncomfortable. My eyes flicked to the sky, searching for any movement or sign of the Phase. I heard talk of "a new Solenoid," "protection," and "great savior." The village was bursting with happiness, relief, and elation. And all it would cost was my freedom.

"Those are fancy words, Ger, and I've had my fill of fancy words. How exactly do you intend to get a Solenoid? A service must be paid to the great Suzerain, and Envie has no Résonateurs," my mother pointed out, putting a hush to all the premature celebrations.

Edgard puffed up like a balloon and jabbed a stubby finger at my mother. "Hold your tongue, woman. It's bad enough you've pranced out here to interrogate this fine man, but now you have to doubt and insult him, too?"

"Keep your temper, Edgard," Gervais said, dismissing Edgard like an unruly child. "I'm glad Fleurette is asking these questions. It is a mother's concern, after all." He swayed up to Mama and encased her hands together in his. "You see, my dear, it all has to do with Jalousie. Word through the relier is that a Résonateur—a *commandant*, if whispers hold true—is finally being dispatched to Jalousie to retrieve the remains of the dead Solenoid."

"And what does that have to do with getting a new one? Jalousie has already been purged. They won't be installing a new Solenoid. Not that there's anything to install it into after you scavenged Jalousie's siphon," Mama slipped in with distaste.

"Why let good parts go to waste?" Gervais reasoned, his tone glib. "And it's not about the dead Solenoid. It's the Résonateur. I will appeal to the commandant as an extension of the Suzerain's will. It will be much quicker than submitting a request through the Sommet. As great as our councilmen are, the government isn't known for swiftness."

"You still have nothing to offer, Ger," my mother maintained. "I suppose this commandant will be content with those fancy words of yours."

"You are right," he admitted. "I have nothing to offer . . . at the present time. You see, what I am offering is the future."

Confusion shone clearly on every face that wasn't hidden behind the pretense of prestige. Gervais obviously reveled in the attention. My mother refused to indulge him, and for once kept her silence.

"What do you mean, Seigneur Gervais?" Edgard finally prompted.

At the awaited inquiry, Gervais' lips slid into a wide grin. "Children."

"What about children, Seigneur?"

"The children of infinite potential. Fleurette's daughter is the offspring of a Résonateur, and my grandfather, as you all will recall, was also one—the savior of Envie. While Cyril and the girl may not be Résonateurs, the gift is in the blood. That is what I will offer for the Solenoid. I will pledge to the Suzerain the service of any Résonateur child born. And what if they have many children? He won't be able to refuse such an offer."

Gervais looked so pleased he all but patted himself on the back. This was his master plan? Not only was I to be shipped off as payment, but also any children I may produce would already be in servitude to the Suzerain. My whole body felt like it was still submerged in the cold water of the lake. My stomach twisted and churned. Any hope for the future drained out of me like I was being leeched from the inside out. Was this my future? Was this *hopelessness?*

I weakly inched my eyes up to look at my mother. There was no way she would go along with this plan. This whole ridiculous scheme wasn't what we needed. We needed help, not this veiled extortion.

Mama's eyes flitted to mine, and what I saw—

"Very well, Ger," she agreed with a light giggle and a smile. "Your son may marry Gavril."

The last remnants of hope extinguished.

FACE OF DESPAIR

R *apt . . . rapt . . . rapt . . .*

That was all I heard. Not the cheers. Not the applause. Not the congratulations thrust in my face. Mama placed her hand on my back and gently nudged me along. I stepped forward, feeling not the ground, but a numb pressure encompassing me from head to toe. I walked in a haze, and only stopped when we arrived before the rusty tin door of our home.

I pushed it open, and it squealed like it was dying—just like everything else in this dwindled town. I headed for the rickety table that served as our only valuable possession. On it sat Papa's relier, a rectangular dark gray metal box with a silver speaker on one side and three round tuner knobs on the other. A short cylinder jutted up from the top with a hollow opening that once held the microphone. It had been seized years ago by Edgard, along with every other useful part he could claim, including the antenna. The device had been Papa's only way of communicating with the Paramount and receiving new orders. It was useless now but of sentimental value to Mama.

A box of heat coils and loose wires on wheels that we used as an oven was pushed into the corner in case we had any visitors and needed the space.

As if visitors would brave the world to come here.

I reached out and turned the metal dial in the center of the wooden table. Light flickered and buzzed above my head. I reached up and tapped the glass sphere a few times. It stopped . . . and stayed off.

I groaned and buried my face in my hands. I could keep my emotions under control. I was good at this. *I know how to not feel. Feeling is the end. Feeling is death.*

Mama hummed wistfully. "What's wrong, little flicker? You're brooding more than usual. Are you a little melancholy? Upset maybe? *Furious?*"

I slowly turned my head to stare back at my mother. She peered at me, the emeralds of her gaze glinting, and slid a short candle on the table to light the dark room.

She was doing it again. Prodding me for a reaction. Pushing me to be as unrestrained as she was.

"Is that what this is about? Getting me to express some kind of emotion? You're going to marry me off to that—that *roach* to elicit some stupid *feelings?*"

Mama stroked my hair like she did when I was a child. "Oh, don't be silly, Gavril. You won't be marrying that pretend seigneur's boy. I'd never allow that to happen. He's too much like his father."

"Then why did you agree—"

"To shut Gervais up, of course," she answered. "That man loves to hear himself talk." She ran a soothing hand through my curls. "There's no way his absurd plan will work. Striking an agreement with a commandant over what may or may not happen? I've never heard such blather. You'll see. His offer will be refused, and I will break off the engagement because he didn't fulfill his promise. That's all that will happen."

"I'm glad you are so confident that everything will go to plan," I replied, the sour taste of her willingness to put *me* on the line bathing my tongue. "Is this all I am to you? A source for your amusement?"

Mama's eyes flashed and her smile dropped. "Watch your tone, Gavril. Do you think this is easy for me? I had a decision to make with the whole town watching. I had to act."

"You're not the one—"

"I told you nothing will happen," Mama snapped. "In case you haven't noticed, little flicker, Edgard's mouth hasn't slowed with age. We can't risk getting banished from the village." Her gaze clouded. "*I can't risk not being here when Goel comes home.*"

That's all that matters to you. "You really think this will pacify Edgard?"

"Don't be so pessimistic, Gavril," Mama scolded. "I don't know where you get that sullen attitude. It's not from me, and your father certainly didn't fear his emotions. A great Résonateur commands his own heart."

"I'm not a Résonateur like him and neither are you. No one in Nostalgie is. Why am I the only one who's worried about attracting Phases?"

"Oh, Gavril," Mama began with a dramatic sigh, "there hasn't been a Phase around here in years. Your papa—"

"My papa killed the last one," I finished, not bothering to mention the Phase the night before. "With his great Résonateur powers, he wielded his emotions like a sword, striking it down in a bright flash of light."

Mama's hand suddenly shot out and grabbed mine. "It was so magnificent," she said, her voice breathy, "to see such power. The air was like static. I could barely breathe. The way he could manipulate the air from just *feeling . . .*"

Her grip on my hand tightened, and I winced. Mama's daze broke and zipped to my sore, wire-torn hand. She turned it over to view my palm, and her lips puckered as she surveyed the deep scratches.

"I see Edgard had you playing with those silly wires again." She released my hand and turned to the window. "What a waste of time. Stupid man," she muttered. "He never did know when to give up."

I brought my hand back to my chest and held it while I cast my gaze to the floor. It wasn't easy striping old wires and threading new ones, but someone had to do it. Someone had to twist hope out of nothing.

"It's not a waste of time," I replied quietly. "It's giving us a chance." But it wasn't the only thing holding Nostalgie above water now. The village was floating on my back, pushing me under to survive.

An uneasy silence blanketed the room.

"Don't be ridiculous, Gavril," my mother suddenly burst out, giving my heart a jolt. She twirled around and fanned out her dress. "Your father brought me this from Éthéré Coeur."

I looked at the massive skirt of her green dress. Yes, I knew that. Everyone knew that. They knew that because she wore it and reminded us about Papa's generosity every day. Every day for seventeen years. It was old, worn, and as patched up as this little hovel we called home. The gold embroidery was thready and pulled, leaving large gaps in the flower pattern. Still, Mama pranced around in that dress as if it were brand new, ignorant of the concerned eyes that always followed her.

Edgard wasn't the only one who fought giving up.

"He said it matched the color of my eyes," Mama bubbled on. "I want him to see me in it again. When he comes home, I want him to see how well I've taken care of it."

I gave her a sad smile and touched her shoulder. "It's been a really long time, Mama. I'm sure Papa would be proud you've kept such good care of it, but don't you think—"

"Think what, Gavril?" Mama snapped, cutting me off like scissors through thread. "Don't tell me I should forget about Goel too! Your own papa? None of you understand. How could you? You've never felt such love. Known such devotion."

"N-no, of course not, Mama." I put my hands up to dispel Mama's rising anger. I wouldn't be surprised if the Phase was circling above us like a hungry vulture. I had to soothe Mama before her emotions stirred it into putting pressure on the barrier. "I'm not saying that. You're right," I readily agreed. "Papa is coming home one day. We just have to be patient."

For a few seconds, I allowed myself to feel hatred. Hatred toward Edgard and Gervais. Hatred toward Papa. But especially, hatred toward myself. I hated myself for lying to Mama and playing along with her delusions. But more than that, I hated that I was more afraid of those things stalking us outside than I was concerned for Mama's well-being. *I'm a terrible person. That's why I'll never be a Résonateur.*

Mama reached out for my hands. She flipped them over and kissed my wounded palm.

"Forgive me, little flicker. I know it's not your fault. You probably don't have many memories of your dear papa. He left when you were young, so young. About four, I think."

Yes, that sounded right. I didn't remember much about the man. The scent of spice, dusky skin, ivory fabric that flowed like water—the uniform of a Résonateur. And eyes the color of honeyed amber.

A gentle touch on my cheek broke my reflection. Mama's vivid green stare pierced into my eyes as though they contained the world.

"Just like his," she said with such wonder. "Like sunset over sand."

I broke away from her and turned to the side. "It's a shame that's the only thing I have."

Mama let out a little hum and reached over to touch the dial for the light in the center of the table. "I wish things had turned out differently. That you could have gotten to know him better before he left." She turned the dial a few times, but the light remained off. "He used to tell me stories, you know. Tales of how the first Phases appeared alongside the first Résonateurs. 'For every powerful heart there is a void,' he would say. 'Like two sides of the same coin.'"

I frowned. "If they are the coin, where does that leave us?"

Mama turned the switch one last time and the bulb overhead buzzed to life. I blinked, blinded by the sudden brightness.

"I've told you about what happens to people who are attacked by Phases and survive. Of the affliction they suffer from the contact. Do you remember?"

"Dampened," I replied. "They're dampened—deadened—to emotion."

"Yes." Mama nodded. "I was in Envie when Jalousie's barrier fell. I saw what happened to the people who fled to Envie for protection." She paused, frowning deeply. "What happened to the dampened and to those who were not." She once again took my hand in hers. "I know Gervais. He won't hesitate to do the same to the people here."

I looked down at our clasped hands before looking at her face. "So we do need his plan to succeed."

Mama's expression sharpened. "How little faith you have in your papa's Solenoid."

"The barrier is shrinking, Mama. I've been checking it."

"You've been slinking around all mopey," she quipped back. "You can't keep living like a corpse, Gavril. Happiness, excitement, love—you need these things. There's no greater adventure than love."

After everything I just said about the barrier, she still wanted to prattle on about giving into your emotions. I ripped my hand from hers and slammed it on the table. "How can you keep saying things like that? There's no hope."

"There is always hope," she replied. "What do you think has kept me going all these years?" She looked down at the bodice of her dress and plucked out a stray thread. "Your papa will come back. You'll see. Until then, we'll play Gervais' game."

I swallowed. Game? This wasn't a game. This was our lives. *My* life. Papa wasn't here. Did she really think he was going to magically appear after seventeen years? That he was going to show up at the last minute and save us?

I closed my eyes. Papa was gone, but Gervais was here. He was here and he had a plan. A plan that depended on me.

"What's the matter, little flicker? You look ill."

I opened my eyes and shook my head. "I think I need to rest, Mama. It's . . . it's been a long day. I've just gotten engaged after all."

"For now," Mama said lightly. "I was engaged too once," she added with a dismissive air and a wink. "Before my true love came and swept me off my feet."

"I don't think that's going to happen for me. And even if it does, I'll be married to Cyril, so it won't matter." No use longing for what would never be within my reach. And love? The most powerful emotion of all was a death sentence waiting to happen.

Mama huffed and gave me an exasperated stare. "Oh, Gavril, keep shutting out your heart and you'll end up like a Phase without any emotions at all. It will be the saddest day you can't feel."

"I can only hope, Mama. I can only hope." I stood up from my chair, my energy blown away with the wind. "I'm going to bed."

"Yes, you'll need your rest," Mama replied. "It's a long journey to Envie. Nearly a day on foot . . . or in Gervais' contraption," she muttered. "He brags about being able to outrun a Phase in that thing. His mouth runs faster."

I went to my room without looking back at her. How could I? She was going to let them take me. For the *game*.

My bedroom was just large enough for a straw-filled mattress, a table with a dead lamp, and a chest for my clothes and the books Papa brought so Mama and I could see the world. I lay on the mattress and stared at the ceiling. My body was heavy—tired and exhausted in so many ways—but I couldn't sleep. My stomach twisted. I'd never felt so nauseated.

It was really happening. I was being taken away. Leaving Nostalgie for the first time. But instead of a life of adventure, my future was sealed. A breeder. A woman whose only use was producing children of the right pedigree. I hadn't thought life could possibly become more desperate.

I was mistaken.

The noisy din beyond my walls gradually faded as Gervais' celebration came to an end. Only the wind whispering through the cracks in my walls and the siphon's hum remained, haunting me.

I sat up. I couldn't leave without visiting the lake one last time. I crept out of my room to the front door, carefully stepping over the planks of wood that creaked the loudest. I didn't want to wake Mama. She'd already spent the day brimming with excitement, and restraint was not a trait she valued.

The village streets were deserted, bare of any life but the gentle breeze and the occasional songs of crickets. A few lights shone from windows, flickering like candles about to burn out. The siphon was dark—a clear sign that even Edgard had taken solace in knowing we were saved and had retired for the night. Everyone would rest easy tonight, believing a solution was found. Their faith in Gervais was solid, complete, and encompassing.

I didn't understand it.

I continued to Lake Oublié. I never appreciated its beauty, truly the only really beautiful place I had ever known. This could be the last time. To admire the stars reflected in its clear surface and to savor the slow lapping of the water along its banks. To watch the reeds sway in the breeze. To sit on the roots of the old cork oak and dream of a life of freedom.

That dream was dead.

I could already feel the weight of Envie's chains on my wrists, the metal chafing my skin as Cyril and Gervais pulled on the links.

But if I didn't go, Nostalgie was dead.

It was my home. It was where I was born, where I spent my childhood playing with Mathieu, and where I celebrated and mourned with Celine. Where Mama waited faithfully for Papa to return. The deal may have been a game to Mama, but real to me. I would go with Gervais, because as much as I hated to admit it, as much as I hated him and his disgusting son, they were the only ones who could help us in time. Papa was gone, and Edgard had waited too long to address the Sommet, stubbornly trying to fix the problem himself rather than risk his reputation.

Our situation was hopeless.

And hopeless had only desperation to cling to.

I circled around the lake with the slow, beleaguered pace of a woman marching toward death. I'd paced around the edge so many times a dirt path had been worn into the grass.

A flash of orange darted under a patch of water lilies a few feet from the shore. A fish? But how? I thought we had fished the lake bare years ago. I stopped and leaned closer.

The little orange fish darted between the pads again, small but full of life. Life where there shouldn't have been any.

"Stay hidden," I whispered. "Or they'll drag you out to eat. Trust me, I know what it's like to be devoured."

I rounded the corner and reached the far end of the lake, looking at the old cork oak standing twisted but proud. One last time. One last time I would sit on its roots and dream. I nearly reached the tree when a warm rush washed over me. I immediately stopped.

The barrier.

The feeling tingled all the way from my head to my toes, filling me with a peace I hadn't experienced since I was a child unaware of the world's danger. All the tension unwound from my knotted muscles. I took in a deep breath, and when I exhaled, all my fears, worries, and doubts floated away. I stood in the barrier's edge and observed the cork oak.

No. Not you too old one. Not yet.

It was lost. It was beyond my reach. Beyond use and constantly having its bark torn off. It was free.

I raised my foot. Despite the warmth surrounding me, my body trembled. *Step back and go to Envie. Or keep going and never look back.*

I stepped forward, and the heat of the barrier left me as though I'd walked into a room of ice. I shivered and huddled into my shawl. The wind rustled the tall grass and my eyes darted around, taking in every movement and swaying shadow. The unease dispelled by standing in the barrier crawled up my spine. A cricket chirped next to me, and I jumped.

I couldn't stay out here. I couldn't. But before I went back, there was something I had to do. One last time. With slow, cautious steps I approached the tree. I raised my hand and placed it on the torn bark. I touched it. I touched freedom. "Goodbye, old one."

I lowered my hand. It was time. Time to accept my future—the end of my life as I knew it.

I turned around—and stood before a white-faced phantom. A scream caught in my throat.

The chill radiating from that specter's pale skin seeped through the surface of my skin and crawled to my bones. Its flesh was lifeless, the white so pure that the sick black blood flowing through tortuous veins up its neck and along its jaw appeared like cracks in a porcelain mask. I saw my terror reflected in its emotionless eyes—eyes such a deep sable that I saw myself drowning in their void.

The eyes of a Phase.

The bleached face hovered less than a foot from me. Black eyes stared right through me. My feet peddled backward until my back bumped against the cork oak. I pushed against it, trying to meld into the bark. The eyes of that creature—no, phantom—followed my every movement.

Oh, heart, what had I done? Like a fool I crossed the barrier. Staying inside was the most important rule we were taught since birth, and I broke it. That was where emotions got you. *I let my desires take control, and now I'm going to die.*

The Phase's shimmering, haze-like body rippled and floated to the grass below. From within its unnatural ebony mass, a pair of pale, black-veined feet manifested. They lowered to the ground, and two thin legs stemmed from them. When its feet hit the grass, the amorphous body smoothed out and settled into a form resembling a female silhouette. White arms sprouted from its sleek sides. The Phase didn't approach or twitch or blink. It stood as motionless as a statue.

What was it doing? Why wasn't it attacking me?

"Despair."

The silence that followed was almost as nerve-racking as that one reverberated whisper. Impossible. My heart stilled a beat with every echoed syllable that repeated in my mind. Impossible. My head swirled. My stomach tightened. My legs wobbled, and I leaned heavily against the tree. The world could fade for me at any moment. The Phase spoke. This heartless creature more savage than any beast. Phases didn't speak. They killed without ration or discrimination. What I heard was . . . impossible.

"Wha-what did you say?"

Her eyes didn't move from me. Those soulless, yet incredibly piercing, eyes seared into my essence. She didn't respond. She didn't speak. She didn't do anything. Did I imagine the whole thing?

The Phase stepped forward, and I pushed off the cork oak and darted around her. *It.* I fled back to the barrier as fast as my legs could carry me, not even pausing when the warmth of re-entering washed over me. Only when I passed the edge of the stump field did I dare look back.

I stopped, my heart racing in time with my panting.

"Gavril?" I heard Mathieu squeak. "What are you doing out here? It's late."

I turned to look at my friend and then pointed at the lake. "Did you see it?"

His eyes widened and his jaw twitched a few times before he finally replied. "See what?"

"You know what," I said, voice hard. "The Phase."

He smiled, a friendly action that didn't quite meet his eyes. "Gavril, there's no Phase."

"Liar," I replied brusquely. "I overheard you and Edgard talking about it. It's out there now."

His face turned white. "Y-you haven't told anyone else, have you?"

"I told Mama, for all the good it did," I muttered.

Mathieu stepped so close to me his chest almost bumped into mine. He grabbed my arms.

"You can't tell anyone else," he said in a low voice. "You have to promise me."

"Why? Everyone deserves to know—"

"And where will they go?" Mathieu cut in. "When everyone panics, where will they go, Gavril? Flee outside the barrier to Envie and tell Gervais about the Phase? I don't need to remind you of what happened to the last town that did that."

I pressed my lips together. I didn't want to think about Jalousie. Didn't want to acknowledge that keeping people in the dark was for the best. "So what do we do?" I asked.

"Not *we*." Mathieu tried to smile again, but the expression was stiff. "It's all on *you* now."

I couldn't bring myself to meet his eyes. It was all on me. Without me, Nostalgie would never receive another Solenoid. I was a prized goat. Nothing more and nothing less. And Mathieu was just as willing to sell me as the rest of them.

The thought left a bitter taste on the back of my tongue. "We used to be close," I said.

Mathieu's forced smile fell. "We're still close, Gavril. We've never been apart."

"Until now."

"Sometimes change is necessary, and it can be scary," he noted like he was reading a manual. Like he'd practiced the line a thousand times in the night to himself.

"I don't see you volunteering to leave the barrier," I griped. "So it's only necessary for a few sacrifices."

"You aren't being sacrificed," he replied in level voice. "You're moving to the top, Gavril. You're going to a new town to wed a seigneur's son. The best clothes and the best food. It doesn't get much better than that for people like us."

"I'll try to remember that when I'm selling my children."

Mathieu's face was grim, a reflection of how bleak the future looked. "I don't want you to go, but we're all going to die if you don't. Do you really want that, Gavril?"

I lowered my gaze and shook my head. "Never. I would never let anything happen to Nostalgie. It's my home."

Mathieu squeezed my hand, and I let him lead me back into the village. We made it to the door of my house and stopped.

"I know it doesn't seem like it, but this is the best thing for you," Mathieu said, his voice quiet, almost like a whisper he didn't want to share. "Even if it doesn't feel like it now. No matter what happens here, you'll be safe."

"That's up in the air at this point," I replied. "I still have to survive the journey to Envie with those two imbeciles."

Mathieu chuckled and shrugged his shoulders.

I opened the door and turned back to him. "But I guarantee I'll do what it takes to get Nostalgie a Solenoid."

"In that case you may want to change before they come fetch you. Cyril didn't seem too impressed by your current attire." Mathieu grinned.

"I don't recall falling into the lake on my own," I said.

Mathieu grimaced, and I smirked before shutting the piece of rusty tin in his face. I stood with my hand on the door for a few moments, chest heavy and light at the same time.

I quietly returned to my room, closed the door, and leaned against it. Morning would be here before long, and Mama would be up bright and early to get me ready. I had no doubt that she'd like to pester Gervais one more time before he—*we*—left. She'd never been too open about their history, but they'd known each other for years, even before Papa came. For someone she often disparaged, she never found herself able to leave him alone for long. Not like me. Mama rarely sought me out, preferring to wait until I returned to her. She told me it felt nice to have someone return to you. To feel wanted and needed. Now she was letting me go.

No one would speak up for me. No one would beg I stay.

I closed my eyes and clasped my hands together against my forehead. I was alone—truly alone—and it seemed so . . . so . . . *empty*.

Was that how Phases felt? They were, after all, vessels of emptiness—void of all sentiment. That was what attracted them to strong displays of emotion. It was a need, a yearning to stave off the apathy. A hunger that needed satiating. And we humans were nothing if not beings of emotion. And that was the great irony and our undoing. The apathy they sought to dispel, I clung to for survival.

I set my musings aside and ambled to my bed. I lay there, sleepless, staring at the ceiling. When Mama began rustling around, I finally arose, dreading what the day had to offer. I numbly bent over my chest and opened it. I pulled out my finest wool dress—the one with only two patches—hoping the musty odor wasn't too strong. The lace I could sew back into place.

Undoubtedly, I would be provided with more "suitable attire" in Envie. A tiny smile tugged at the corners of my lips. But ruffles? Those I could do without.

The loud squeal of the front door being thrust off its hinges frightened away any further personal thoughts. My stomach knotted up, and I bit my lip.

"Gavril? Oh, Gavril, my little flicker," Mama sang out. "It's time to depart with your new . . . ah, fiancé."

"In a moment," I replied, quickly sliding into my dress. No time to air it out or mend the lace. With a deep breath, I squared my shoulders and opened my bedroom door. I turned to give my little space one last look. My heart would never return here. All the experiences and emotions shed were now forever memories.

"Do cheer up, my sweet girl," Mama cooed, approaching to rub my back. "You are leaving to start a new life, not have it sapped out of you."

"Then why do I feel so empty?" I mumbled with downcast eyes. "My life is over."

Mama leaned in close and kissed me on the cheek. "Remember what I told you, little flicker," she whispered before she pulled away. "Everything will fall into place."

She gently tugged on my arm and urged me forward to the open door. Oh, Great Heart, it was happening. I was leaving Nostalgie for the first time in my life.

I couldn't let my emotions get the better of me. I had no choice but to sever all attachments, to become indifferent.

Like that Phase.

Only by shedding my emotions would I ever be free.

FAMILY OF ENVIE

As soon as I walked into the sunlight my legs froze. Mama looped her arm around mine and gently pulled me along. It was still early, but many of my neighbors were already up, eager to see the send-off. I spotted Bernadette leaning around the corner of her house. Mama waved to her, and Bernadette returned the gesture with a glare, her lips moving in ways that assured me the greeting was not returned nicely.

We reached the edge of Nostalgie where Edgard, Mathieu, Gervais, and Cyril waited, admiring a large machine on six iron wheels—Gervais' beloved automatram. I looked at the rusty crate and immediately wanted to run back to my room.

It was about the size of a large wagon and had a roof and glassless windows. An *opérateur* sat on a bench at the front of the automatram behind a row of levers. This was my first time seeing a person whose specific job was controlling a transport. He smirked at me before pulling a lever. The oval, clay-pot-shaped engine buzzed and whined in the back with the peacefulness of a thousand well-worn siphons. I saw a few wisps of smoke and Gervais let out a chuckle.

"Marvelous," he chirped. "Don't you just love that sound? Smooth and powerful."

"It's beautiful." Edgard nodded in agreement. "I must say I'm jealous, Seigneur. To own such a fine machine. I can always hope for the future."

Cyril sneered, an open look of disgust on his face.

"Best stick to dreams, Edgard," Gervais said. "Not everyone is meant for a life of luxury."

"And the ones who have it are rarely worthy," Mama piped in, her voice nearly drowned out by the automatram's sputtering. "Right, Ger?"

Gervais turned to Mama with a smile that could crawl. "Worthiness must be earned, my dear." He gestured at me. "Or in some cases, given."

"Then I certainly hope you earn your worthiness by taking care of my daughter," Mama replied, a cold clip in her tone. "You know better than most what I'm capable of when I'm angry."

"A tempest," Gervais said, fire lighting his cold eyes. "I remember well how wild you can be."

"Can we depart, Father?" Cyril butted in, and for once, I was glad for his lack of courtesy. Anything that put Gervais back on a leash was welcome. "I've seen enough of this hovel."

"It is a long journey," Gervais agreed. He gave Mama a heated stared as he grabbed my other arm and pulled me from her grasp. "Till we meet again, Fleurette."

"You better come back with a Solenoid," she replied. "Goel did."

"No, he didn't," Gervais said, tone mocking. "I'm glad you made a wiser choice for your daughter than you did for yourself."

I barely had time to see the dark look on Mama's face before Gervais turned around and marched me to the automatram. I looked around, desperate for someone to react . . . someone to speak out for me.

Edgard crossed his arms and nodded stiffly. I locked eyes with

Mathieu. His face was a mixture of emotions—like he couldn't decide whether to send me off with happiness or watch me depart in dread.

Gervais shoved me into the coffin-like cabin. Inside were two facing benches, one at the front and one at the rear. Gervais pushed me into the one at the front before taking a seat on the opposite bench. Cyril slid in next to me. I fought to keep my face straight and pushed against the side as far as I could to avoid his touch.

The automatram rocked forward, and my heart lurched. We rolled away, the wheels bumping over every pebble in the dirt road.

I closed my eyes and held my breath, listening. Waiting for a yell or cry. A single word of protest over the whine of the engine. None came. I took in a shaky breath. The warmth of the barrier's edge washed over me—a second of internal relief—then it was gone, replaced by sadness, grief, and . . . and hurt. My heart fell.

I opened my eyes and turned to the window, anything to avoid looking at the grotesque lord across from me. A black shimmer darted over the hills.

I sat straight up. My back was as rigid as the box I was being held in. Hours passed as I scoured every inch of the unprotected world through the open window, sitting close, but not daring to put even a finger out on the rim. The engine popped, cracking through the air like a whip. I jumped.

"There's no need to be so tense, my dear. This is your first time riding in such fashion, yes? They always make this noise," Gervais explained in his condescending voice.

I didn't spare him a single glance. "We're making too much noise. Something might hear us and attack. There could be a Phase—"

"A *Phase*," Gervais repeated with a chuckle. "My girl, a Phase hasn't been seen around this region since Goel slayed that one from Jalousie over twenty years ago. Fleurette likes to gloat. I'm surprised she didn't share that with you."

I tore my gaze away from the window to glower at the vile

man across from me. "She tells other stories about Jalousie. And about Envie."

Gervais' haughty expression chilled, no doubt picking up on my implication. His actions against Jalousie's people hadn't been forgotten no matter how much time passed. "We all do what we have to. You'll learn that soon enough."

"Yes, we do," I agreed in a hard voice. "We do what we must to survive."

Gervais' eyebrows briefly raised and he gave me an approving nod.

"You talk too freely, Gavril. We'll have to work on that once we are wed," Cyril said from beside me. He captured my chin with slender fingers. "That pretty face doesn't need a flapping mouth."

"An arduous task, my son. You've seen her mother," Gervais said.

"The madame was never taught by a husband, Father," Cyril went on smugly. "I'll set Gavril right."

The thin scabs on my palms ripped open as I clenched my fists to grind out my anger. *It's not safe.* I retreated into my mind. *I'm not in the protection of the barrier. It isn't worth it.*

The automatram engine screeched like a metal sheet tearing in two, and we suddenly jerked to a halt. I dug my heels into the floor when my body swayed. The cabin fell silent.

"For the Suzerain's sake. What now?" Gervais snarled and kicked the door open. He slid out like a snake and hissed venomously at the opérateur.

"Does this normally happen? What's going on? We can't stop here." I spun my head around to survey every inch of visible space. My stomach flipped at every shadow.

"Don't be so fretful," Cyril said. He grunted and glared at the floorboards. "The recycler engine stopped. I don't know why Father doesn't scrap this old thing and get a new one."

As if he could afford one. I gave Cyril a sidelong glance but kept my thoughts to myself.

"The newest ones at the Paramount don't even touch the ground." Cyril sighed like a wistful boy pining after a new toy. He propped his chin on his fist on the window ledge and looked out. After a few moments, he leaned through it. "Now that's interesting," he said, uncrossing his long legs.

I tried to peek around him discretely, but I couldn't see beyond the monumental head obscuring my view.

Cyril turned back to leer at me. "Do you want to do something fun, Gavril?"

Before I could answer, he plucked my hand out of my lap and pulled me out the tram's door into the bright light. Cyril dragged me across a field of wild grass.

"Wait, stop! Where are we going? What about the Phase? It isn't safe out here!" I protested, trying to free my hand. My eyes darted in every direction, registering every swaying blade of grass. People died out in the open. Killed without the protection of their barrier.

I gazed desperately at the tram. Gervais and the opérateur were bent over the engine, apparently oblivious to Cyril and me.

Cyril let out a mocking laugh. "It isn't safe anywhere, Gavril. Haven't you learned that by now?" He continued half-dragging me through the golden pasture and then stopped to point. "Look there. Just ahead."

I ceased my struggle long enough to follow the line of his finger. The angled lines of buildings rose from the top of a hill. Was that a . . . a town?

"Is that Envie?" I asked.

He let out another snicker and gazed at me as though I were stupid. I had learned that expression well during my years with Edgard. Normally, "stupid" set my blood boiling. But knowing the risk of encountering a Phase, panic easily suppressed anger.

"Of course that's not Envie," he answered with a patronizing shake of his head. "That rundown hick village could never compare to Envie. That's Jalousie."

"Jalousie!" I yelped, jerking away. There was no way I was going to that cursed place.

"Stop that!" Cyril barked. "I've played along until now, but enough is enough. You will obey me, Gavril. It's your duty." He squeezed my hand in a crushing grip and continued to yank me toward Jalousie.

As we passed the parameter of the first circle of buildings, I felt my chest tighten. Nothing remained but shells—bits of wood and metal collapsing on themselves as the town was consumed like its people had been. The Phase had ripped them apart. It tore out their hearts as it drank in their fear before consuming everything else.

No, no, I don't want to go in there. Those people . . . This place is damned! I clawed at Cyril's iron grip with my free hand, digging my chipped nails into his flesh.

He let out a strangled cry. "Stop that, woman," he screamed, desperately trying to pry my fingers away, yet still keep me enchained.

I threw my weight back from him, and Cyril tripped, nearly falling over.

"I said *stop*."

My nails raked across Cyril's flesh. He shrieked again and ripped his hand away from me. My feet slipped out from under me, and I flew backward, crashing to the ground. A dull thud echoed in my ears as hot pain spread across the back of my head like a wildfire. The bright of the noon sun dimmed. The golden grass swirled.

"Foolish woman."

Cyril's words echoed, waving in and out and all around me. The void took me.

A steady throb hammered throughout every inch of my head. My skull felt like it was about to split down the middle. My eyes fluttered open for a second, only to close against the sunlight beaming into them.

I moaned, pushing myself up to sit. I touched the back of my head and felt a sticky crust in my hair. I turned to look behind me. A spot of dark red painted the corner beam of a dilapidated house. I turned back around with bleary eyes. Cyril was gone. I was alone. He left me here.

Some future husband.

I pushed up from the ground, my legs trembling. A flash of glossy black streaked across my vision. I clenched my eyelids shut until my nose scrunched up. *I hit my head harder than I thought. It was only a vision. A figment.*

I opened my eyes—and a pale face greeted me. The one outside Nostalgie. She stared at me again with that blank expression. A face of nothing.

"Did you follow me here?" My stomach jumped into my chest, and I took a small step back. "Are you going to kill me?"

Her obsidian eyes bore into me, but she didn't move. What was she waiting for?

"No." Her lips barely parted, just enough to utter the sound.

The hair on the back of my neck stood on end at the soft vibration. "No?" I squeaked. "No, you didn't follow me, or no, you aren't here to kill me?"

"No."

"O-okay." I relented. I wasn't going to push it. As long as the Phase seemed content with that word, so was I. "Are you looking for something?"

She didn't answer me. The constant eerie stare shredded my nerves. I eased back until the wooden beam was flush against my back. "Wh-what's your name?" I asked.

"Gavril!" Gervais' shrill voice cut through the air.

I jumped.

"Gavril? Where are you, girl?" Gervais shouted again, anger

ringing against rotting beams around me.

The Phase's cloudlike body rippled, and she flew at me. A swirl of black twirled around me. The force sent my red tresses whipping around. I let out a startled cry and dove into a crouch, covering my head with my arms. *It's going to kill me now. It's had enough.*

The rush of air halted, but a whisper cut through the sudden stillness. "Morrow."

I hesitated, cautious of the quiet, before inching my arms down. The Phase vanished. But she left me something. *Morrow.* Was that her name? Did Phases have names?

Something tugged on the back of my dress and straightened me back up. I turned to meet Gervais' livid purple face. It successfully banished any further concerns about my encounter with the Phase.

"What are you doing, stupid girl?" he roared, shoving me in the direction of the road. "Cyril said you wandered off on your own. You're just like your mother. I won't have my plans ruined by the whims of a foolish brat. Get back to the automatram!"

I tripped over my feet and crashed into the ground. I slowly pushed up and rose to my feet, shaking off the pain and humiliation. I turned to give Gervais the most hateful glare I could muster. The Phase left me alone, but maybe I could call her back. I could see if Gervais was worthy of being spared.

He caught my expression, and a nasty smirk curled on his lips. "Be careful, Gavril. You wouldn't want your poor mama to be exposed to the dangers of the open world, would you?"

My scowl dropped, and I cast my eyes to the grass. My lips quivered. Gervais . . . he . . . he controlled our fate.

I didn't fight when Gervais grabbed me and pulled me along. I let him tote me back to the automatram like a lifeless doll. That's all I was. A puppet. And puppets didn't have feelings. They just let the world pull at their strings.

When we returned, the automatram was groaning and shaking

again. Gervais pushed me into the seat beside Cyril, who stared out the window like a child pretending he didn't do anything wrong. He didn't turn to acknowledge me, the woman he was bringing home to wed. The one he left bleeding and unconscious in a graveyard of a town.

I turned my head away. Away from Cyril and Gervais. Away from my heart. I could do this. I could live like this. I had to free myself from those stubborn emotions. I had to be more like *her*. Like Morrow.

Hours passed, and the black silhouette of Envie's skyline manifested in the twilight like a ghastly mirage. As we crossed the barrier, a tingle washed over me, and some tension loosened from my shoulders. I was back from the dangerous outside, safely transported from one cage to another.

Envie was definitely larger than Nostalgie. That much Gervais could claim with pride. But to say the conditions were better was Gervais flexing his greatest skill. The homes on the edge of town were no better than the shack I grew up in. We rattled our way through the gates of the outer ring toward the center. The further in we went, the larger the houses grew. The grating noise of the automatram stirred the town, drawing faces to windows and doors. A few people cried out, offering words of welcome and relief. Gervais' lips curled up, his chin raised high. There could be no mistake that he loved every second of it. He wanted the people of Envie to acknowledge his return. It gave him satisfaction to know he could disturb any second of their lives.

We bumped to a stop, and the seigneur smoothed out his jacket before easing the door open. He stepped out with those spider legs and strode around the tram with his arms tucked behind him like a king. Cyril followed his father out. He stretched out his back and then turned back to me, frozen to the automatram seat.

"It's time to make a grand entrance, Gavril. Come on now." He extended his hand.

I glowered at him and clenched my fingers into my dress. I wanted to slap the hand away, but doing so would only endanger Nostalgie. "Are you sure you won't let me fall and abandon me again?"

"Don't be so unruly, my dear. I didn't abandon you. Why, I went to get help, of course." He fixed a fake look of concern on his face. "How do you think Father managed to find you so quickly?"

"It would have been much quicker if you had come with him," I snapped. "But I guess it did take you time to smooth your feathers after squawking at me."

His caring façade dropped as though it never existed. He gritted his teeth and jabbed his finger in a downward motion.

"Come. Now," he demanded. "Or that bump on your head will be the least of your concerns."

It already was. I stood up and made for the door.

When I was close enough, he extended his arm and coiled it around my shoulders. "You will learn, Gavril," he muttered through his teeth. "It may take some time and *discipline*"—he gave the word an extra measure of oily emphasis—"but you will learn."

Cyril fixed a grin on his face and led me out of the automatram into the growing crowd.

"Today, I bring good news," Gervais began, drawing all eyes to him. "My son is bringing home his fiancé."

Hands and lips moved and twitched and flapped in rapid motions as he continued to speak. A few people pointed at me and whispered behind ratty fans. Others stared, but when I stared back, only velvet masks and faces distorted by powder greeted me. There was not one bare face in the crowd. Not one person willing to shed their façade. A different face flashed in my mind—unobscured and direct. Free of expectations. A face with black veins and eyes like the darkest shadows. My flesh prickled. Morrow didn't hide from me. She was honest.

I averted my gaze to the heart of the town. The Solenoid was almost identical to the one in Nostalgie, but the attached siphon was in much better condition. There weren't any exposed wires or circuits, and any visible rust had been scraped off. The siphon's hum was the only thing that could bring me comfort. It was the only thing that sounded like home.

". . . and we will all benefit . . ." Gervais droned on.

I didn't care about any of the announcements he was making. I didn't want to be there. I wanted no part of this nest of hornets and pretenders. How was Mama doing? I wondered if this made her happy.

"So, this is the famed Gavril. My, how different she looks."

A long face popped into my view, cocked to the side as if it were viewing an oddity. It belonged to a woman with a large blonde bouffant stacked on her head. She pranced up to me. Heavy white powder matted any flesh that wasn't stuffed into her suffocatingly tight lime corset, and her cheeks and lips were slathered with rouge. She flicked a lacy fan back and forth through the air, yet never seemed to accomplish the goal of fanning herself. She beamed with a wide-toothed smile expecting me to say something.

I preferred to let my stony expression do the talking, but she didn't allow my failure to respond deter her.

"Allow me to introduce myself," she announced. "I'm Cyril's sister, Charmant. *Enchanté.*"

I stared at her, but still held my words, refusing to put on a pretend display for Cyril's benefit. The silence ate away at any civility in the air.

"Now, now, my dear," Cyril chastised me. "Don't be so rude to Charmant. Introduce yourself."

"She already knows who I am," I argued. "It would be a waste of breath."

He glanced at Charmant with an awkward, strangled laugh. "Oh, such wit. You'll have to forgive her, sister."

"Nonsense, nonsense," Charmant dismissed his concerns with a flip of her fan. "Gavril is just tired from her journey. Her first time being in such a big place, too, I suspect. She must be overwhelmed."

I once again kept my tongue in its place. It *would* be a waste of breath.

Charmant looped her arm around mine. "That's it, isn't it, Gavril? You're overwhelmed. Come now. We are to be sisters, you and I."

Charmant ushered me away from Cyril and started for the largest house in the circle around the hub. It was a two-storied complex with plaster on the exterior instead of tin. The plaster was chipped, cracked, or missing in a few places, exposing the wood beneath, but the home appeared far larger and grander than any building I had seen before. The second floor even had a balcony with a rusty iron railing.

Cyril's sister led the way through the front door. The greeting room may have been magnificent once. It may have had ornate polished furniture, fine rugs, and colorful wallpaper. Now, it only had chipped wood, stained carpet, and peeling walls.

Charmant turned and gave me a wink over her shoulder. "You look speechless, Gavril. I know you have never seen such opulence before. This will be your new life. Aren't you lucky?"

I gazed down at the crusted carpet. Was that what everyone saw? The lucky one chosen to be Cyril's bride? The world was more hopeless than I thought.

"Oh, listen to me prattle on instead of letting you rest. Come, come. Let's go up to your room. Well, your *temporary* room," she tossed in with a giggle.

We climbed the creaking staircase and turned into the second-floor hallway. It was dim, the lights along the walls barely holding onto life. Charmant sashayed her way to the end of the hall and opened the door. The room inside was bigger than mine back home, and it actually had a full bed. The nightstand and dresser were modest compared to the furniture in the sitting room. It seemed all the best pieces were used for public view, and this room tucked out of the way received what was left. Yet it was still more than I ever had.

I entered, and Charmant stepped behind me to grab the door

handle. "Just take a nap and don't worry about anything, my dear sister." She gave me a quick peck on the cheek. "I will have Margaux bring your dinner up later. Then tomorrow," she started with an excited flare, "we will get you out of those rags and pick out your new clothes. It will be so much fun."

She slammed the door, and I could hear the click of heels traveling down the hall. I let out a heavy sigh and rubbed my temples. My head ached, and I was positive it wasn't solely from the blow I endured earlier. I trudged over to the bed and took a seat. The mattress squeaked like it contained a colony of mice. The springs must've rusted out, but it wasn't the only thing around here hiding what was inside. I lay back and tried to be as still as possible.

This was my new home. This was my new family. This was my new life. Wet trails rolled down my cheeks. This was horrible.

Rapt . . . rapt . . . rapt . . .

My eyelids twitched. That sound. *The Solenoid is making that sound again. I wish it would stop. It makes me so uneasy. It—*

"Mademoiselle? Mademoiselle Gavril?" My eyes flicked open. "May I enter, Mademoiselle? I have your dinner."

I sat up and frowned at the door, not sure what to do. Nobody had ever brought dinner to my room. I pushed up from the bed and walked to the door. I paused with my hand on the handle for a moment. Did I want to answer? I shook my head. What I wanted was irrelevant. Now I had to live by expectations.

I pulled the door open. A pretty young woman with light brown hair jumped back. A tray of dishes in her hands rocked like a boat.

"Oh, oh, Mademoiselle, no need for you to open the door for me," she said, recovering from her scare. "I could have opened it."

I glanced down at the rattling tray before looking back into her blue eyes. "It's not a problem," I assured her. "I'm used to doing things for myself. Can I help you with that?"

A strange expression crossed the maid's face—something akin to annoyance—before she straightened it out. "I could never allow the Mademoiselle to trouble herself like that," she exclaimed. "Master Gervais was very clear with his orders. I can handle everything." She walked in and placed the tray on the bedside table. "When you are finished, Mademoiselle, please call for me." She curtsied and turned to leave.

"What's your name?" I asked before she shut herself out of the room, leaving me alone in the dusty mansion-in-memory.

She twirled around and gave me a smile that stretched too wide to be natural. "I'm Margaux, Mademoiselle." She curtsied again. "*Enchanté*," she simpered in a voice that reminded me of Charmant.

"I'm Gavril, Margaux. Please, you don't have to keep addressing me as 'Mademoiselle.' It doesn't suit me."

Margaux's smile dropped and she looked me over. "You come from a humble place, Mademoiselle?" she questioned, ignoring my request.

"A very humble place. Probably even more so than you."

"But you are no longer in that humble place, Mademoiselle, so I will continue to show my respect as Master Gervais wishes," Margaux insisted with surprising authority for a servant. "You are to be Master Cyril's wife, and so you must be displayed as a woman of esteem."

My lips tightened into a thin line. I should have known. The image needed to be upheld. Even if Cyril was marrying some poor girl from a tiny hamlet, the notion of power had to stay in the mindset of the lesser people.

"Have you always been here, Margaux?" I asked, trying to change the subject. "Do you like it here?"

Margaux shook her head like I'd said something ridiculous. "Why, Mademoiselle, I am flattered you think so highly of me, but I have only been privileged these past two years. I used to live out at the edge of the barrier. It was a dreadful place—so close to the fiends outside. My papa had recently passed, so I was alone in that dirty barn." Her cheeks flushed pink, and her hands twisted into her stained apron. "That was how he found me. I was out scraping for food. Master Gervais came right up to me—*me*, a beggar—and asked if I needed a home. I was far too pretty a thing, he told me, to be wandering the streets." She let out a warbled sigh, her eyes filled with a dewy glaze. "He brought me back here and gave me my own room. 'All in return for my service,' he said. Like the Suzerain."

Margaux's gaze continued to be clouded as I regarded her. She was so bizarre, holding Gervais in such high esteem. I couldn't bring myself to share in the enthusiasm.

"I don't think I should keep you any longer, Margaux. I wouldn't want you to get in trouble," I said, indicating toward the open door. I did want someone to talk to, but Margaux was not the right person. We didn't have much to agree on.

Margaux snapped out of her daze, and the same irritated look from earlier flashed across her features for a second, like she was offended I interrupted her. She straightened her face and smoothed out her crinkled apron.

"As you wish, Mademoiselle. You should do as Master Gervais commands and eat." She walked to the door and turned to looked over her shoulder. "And do not be so concerned for me. I never get into too much trouble with the master. Unless he demands it." She winked at me.

I almost cringed. The muscles in my face were set, ready to move into position, but I overpowered them and maneuvered my mouth into a smile instead.

"Good night, Margaux."

"And to you, Mademoiselle."

I shut the door and leaned against it. The idea that anyone could be so taken with Gervais . . . My face contorted with revulsion. But it wasn't her fault. It was all she knew. All any of these people knew. Envie was just as much a world unto itself as Nostalgie. We were trapped in our havens. They shielded us from the Phases . . . and from each other. Sometimes even from sense itself, it seemed.

The dinner she brought me was nothing spectacular—some leek stew and a slice of bread. Not even Gervais' influence could make the food supply increase. I took my time with it and reflected between each spoonful of bland liquid. When I finished, I picked up the tray and exited the room. Margaux told me to call for her, but how exactly was I going to do that? It was much easier to take it down myself.

I stepped down the dark hall with cautious, quiet steps. I didn't know where I was going, but I didn't want to run into any of the family. I looked down the long stairway. Voices emerged and I held my place, careful not to let the tray rattle and give me away.

"She's quite the catch, brother. How long did you have to search the sty to root out that one from the peasants?"

"Search? They threw her at me. The town's nothing more than a stain on the landscape. The sooner it and its people go the way of Jalousie, the better."

Charmant clucked her tongue. "Tsk, tsk, brother. That's your bride-to-be's hometown. You should be more caring."

Cyril let out a malicious chuckle. "Don't worry, Charmant. I'll do my part to play the consoling husband. But the fact that those people had to beg Father for help is pathetic. They disgust me—especially that beastly mayor. And let's not forget that shameless old tart Fleurette."

My teeth clenched. How dare they say that about Mama. She wasn't shameless. And she certainly wasn't a—

"Don't forget she sold her daughter, too," Charmant crowed with a cackle. "Trying to pass on the family legacy, you think?"

"Charmant!" Cyril burst out in exaggerated offense. "That is my future wife you are talking about. Try to reserve your insults for the

peons in Nostalgie only."

"Ah, you are right, brother," Charmant agreed. "Forgive me. But there won't be much left to insult for long."

"True enough," Cyril snorted. "We can still laugh at their delusions. You should have seen it, Charmant. It was the most ridiculous thing I've ever witnessed. They expect Father to give them a new Solenoid. What would they do with it other than delay the inevitable? At least here we could double our barrier size with two."

The blood rushing through my ears drowned out Charmant's shrill laughter. What was I hearing? Gervais had no intentions of giving us a Solenoid? The tray shook in my hands and I tightened my grip. The handles dug into my scabs.

"Such a wonder, brother," Charmant said once she had calmed herself. "Only the truly destitute and miserable could possibly have such faith. To be honest, I am almost envious."

"You can keep your envy, sister. I will keep our new Solenoid."

I turned, legs stiff as wood and blood cold as ice. I couldn't remember how the door closed behind me or when the tray I was holding dropped to the floor. Or how I ended up on the bed, curled up like a wounded animal. The best thing for me at that moment was to not feel.

THE MORNING
AFTER THE RAIN

A sharp grunt left my throat as Charmant strangled the strings of the corset tighter around my ribs. I thought about confronting her or Cyril with what I'd overheard last night. The temptation to bring their deceptions to light was strong. But if I did, any chance of obtaining a Solenoid would be gone for good. I had to bear it. I pushed my nails into my palms. I had to hold my tongue until Gervais fulfilled his pledge. And if he was successful, I would do my duty to Cyril *and* ensure the Solenoid ended up in the right hands.

I glared at my reflection in the cracked mirror before me. The faded navy-blue dress had strips of white lace sown into the corset bodice from the square neckline to the skirt, which was lined with drab white ruffles. A large dark mark stained the bottom of the skirt—something Charmant laughed off as an artistic choice. Loose threads lined the shoulders of the dress, leading me to believe that the sleeves had been cut off at some point.

"Oh, Gavril, you look so beautiful in this dress. My brother is the luckiest man in Envie."

"I would have thought you'd say that about the man who holds your attention," I shot back. I didn't feel any need to pretend to be nice. Not after she mocked my village's struggle.

Charmant pulled at the strings again and I grimaced. I never looked more like a stranger.

"How wicked of you, Gavril!" She laughed off my comment, waving her hand like it was a funny joke. "You can rest easy, my sister. There is no man in Envie capable of capturing my attention."

I gaped at her. "You have no intention to marry? I'm shocked that your all-important father"—*Liar Gervais*—"Seigneur Gervais would permit such a thing." The fact he was obsessed with Cyril and I marrying to produce Résonateur children made me sure Charmant was next to be pushed in a marriage bed.

"I didn't say all that," Charmant said coyly. "Papa knows there is no man here with suitable blood. We've been saving *argent*." Her hands clapped together excitedly. "Once we have enough, Papa is going to buy me a house in Éthéré Coeur. Oh, how wonderful, Gavril. Can you even imagine living in the Paramount?"

No. And it looks like I never will. I'll be trapped here with your terrible brother and father forever. I held my tongue.

"It will be so grand," she rambled on. "New clothes, fine wines, and fancy parties. I can't wait. And before I know it, a wealthy Résonateur will ask me to be his bride." Charmant latched onto my arm and pulled me close. "Though between you and me, sister, that may not be that long from now."

Curiosity got the better of me. "What do you mean? Have you been seeing someone in secret? A Résonateur?"

"Ah, how I wish that were true," Charmant lamented. "But no. I am referring to the commandant who is being sent to Jalousie. Papa has heard over the relier that he left the Paramount about a week ago and will arrive tomorrow."

"That soon? But Éthéré Coeur is at least three weeks' journey away by automatram. You have to go around—"

"Oh-ho, Gavril," Charmant giggled and smiled condescendingly at me. "I always forget how simple a life you have led. It's charming."

I frowned at her. "Commandants don't travel by *automatram*."

"Then how do—"

"And I hear this one in particular is quite handsome, not that it makes a difference to you. Right, Gavril?" She smirked at me. "I will have that Résonateur wrapped around my finger in no time."

I sat rigid-backed in the greeting room, trying unsuccessfully to sip water from a tin cup. I couldn't bend or breathe with the cage tied around my torso. "The tighter, the better," Charmant had said. Maybe if I was lucky, it would tear open, and I'd have no choice but to wear my other clothes. But knowing Charmant, they were disposed of already. I clasped the cup close to my chest.

Charmant wouldn't rest until every bit of Nostalgie had been stripped from me. A bare slate for Cyril to deface.

"Is there anything I can do for you, Mademoiselle?" Margaux appeared in the room with a few dirty rags in her hands.

"No, thank you, Margaux," I replied.

"Very well, Mademoiselle."

Margaux continued cleaning and polishing the furniture. I watched her work for a while, still flabbergasted at how content she was at being here, while I was miserable. Why, I'd rather be at that dirty barn by the barrier. The air was better company to talk to than any of these pretenders. Or even—

The knot on the back of my head was still tender—a reminder that when I was in need, Cyril was not going to be the one I could depend on.

I could have died out there. That Phase—Morrow—could have killed me at any time, but she didn't. She stayed with me. Watched over me. Spoke to me. Why?

She showed more integrity in those few minutes than Gervais or

Cyril had since taking me from Nostalgie.

I clenched my fist, feeling my scabs crack against the cup.

The outside world was dangerous. Phases made it so. Nothing good ever came from venturing out.

But . . .

Why *me?*

"Margaux," I addressed the maid, "can you take me to the barn you used to live in?"

She turned to face me, surprised. "I certainly can, Mademoiselle, but I cannot even imagine why you would want to go to such a place. It is not for fine people."

I bit the inside of my cheek, mentally digging for a reason. "Y-you said it was close to the barrier," I recalled. "Since I am new here, I would like to see how far away the barrier is. It will make me feel more secure knowing what my limits are," I explained.

An odd look crossed her face. Her eyebrows furrowed and her bottom lip poked out like she was trying to process my request. After a few moments, she tilted her head.

"I'm not sure—"

"I have to Margaux," I insisted. "I'm scared of the outside. You know what it's like to be close to the monsters. Master Gervais is so brave. I don't want to disappoint him. You understand, don't you?"

Margaux's face unfurled and she let out a resigned sigh.

"If it will make the Mademoiselle feel more comfortable, then I can do it. Master Gervais will approve."

"Thank you, Margaux. And I have one more request. Could you keep this between you and me?" I asked before she could leave the room and start blabbing to Gervais. She gave me a horrified stare, as I expected. She would have reservations about keeping anything from her dear master.

"I don't think that would—"

"Please, Margaux," I pleaded. "It's just that—I—that I'm so

embarrassed!" I put my hands on my cheeks, trying my best to appear distressed. "I . . . I don't want my new family to think badly of me. They would think me silly, and Master Gervais is such a busy and important man. I don't want to burden him with trivial requests. He already has so much on his mind. We should sort out our own problems, don't you think?"

After my speech, I nodded at Margaux expectantly, like she should be readily agreeing with me. And it worked wonderfully.

"Oh, quite right you are, Mademoiselle. We should not trouble the master with simple matters such as this. I will take you there immediately," she said passionately.

Her eyes gleamed fiercely, and her hands twisted into her apron. For a second, she lost focus, and I knew Gervais' face was floating in her mind. A daydream for her. A nightmare for me.

Margaux shook out of her daze and turned around. "This way, Mademoiselle."

I followed Margaux out of the house and into the town center. My eyes darted all around for any sign of Charmant, Cyril, or Gervais. When we disappeared behind the first row of houses, I felt confident enough to stop looking over my shoulder.

The maid weaved around homes and stores and a rather sad, deserted bakery. Window glass had been removed, and a moldy odor drifted from within the dark store.

The further toward the outskirts we traveled, the more desolate the buildings appeared. Villagers walking up and down the streets became few and far between. Some glanced my way, trying not to stare, but at the same time, unable to keep their eyes away from the stranger who was betrothed to their most eligible bachelor. A woman with a pair of thin toddlers waved at Margaux, but she turned her nose up and kept walking.

The final ring of buildings approached, and Margaux pointed to a large structure about to collapse under its sagging roof and rotting plank siding, making it perilous for anyone to attempt to enter.

"That's the barn," she said. "It's even more depressing than I remember. I don't even want to look at it. Ugly thing." Her nose curled up like she caught a whiff of something awful. "The barrier is on the other side of the barn. There's an old post to mark the edge." Margaux looked at the barn door. "I hate this place."

"You don't have to stay here if you don't want to. I'll be fine by myself. I know you aren't worried about getting into trouble, but it's probably best if you get back to your duties," I suggested before stepping away from her.

"No, Mademoiselle, that will not do. You can't be left alone in such a place," Margaux protested hotly. "It's dangerous for a woman of your station to be out here with these . . . these peasants. If anyone sees you so close to the barrier, they will talk. Master Gervais—"

"Needs you more than I do," I finished for her. "He told me in the automatram he was expecting the mansion to be spotless for the wedding. He was bragging about how he had the best maid in all of Premier Esprit." Margaux's frown melted into a dreamy smile. "It would be a waste of your time waiting on me here. Master Gervais needs you, Margaux. I grew up in a place like this, so I'm not concerned at all. I'll be fine," I assured her, wishing she would just leave me be.

Margaux blinked a few times, her smile falling in hesitation. She glanced in the direction of the town center before looking back at the barn. Her face curled in disgust again.

"Well . . . if the Mademoiselle is so sure . . . I will return shortly." She curtsied and turned to leave.

Despite Margaux's insistence she stay with me, I knew she wanted to get away from this place as soon as possible. Whether it was because of bad memories or that she now felt it below her new standing, I couldn't say.

I let out a relieved breath and instantly regretted it. The corset showed no mercy as it continued to clench my ribs. Another reminder of how little control I had in Gervais' mansion. Finally, I was away from that place.

I moved past the barn to the open plains, glad to be free of Envie. I spotted the old post Margaux mentioned about fifteen feet from the barn's outer wall. Close. Way too close. Gervais was very confident in himself. If his barrier started shrinking at the same rate as the one in Nostalgie . . .

I took a few steps past the post and the tingle of exiting the barrier washed over me. I immediately felt lighter, as though I could float back to Nostalgie, but as soon as I took another step, the weight of Envie pulled me back to the ground, my troubles returning tenfold.

A sinking feeling pushed into the pit of my stomach. Oh, how I missed home. It was out there, vulnerable and alone, kept alive only by the people and their hope. Hope that would be betrayed by the great "savior."

Why couldn't they see the truth? He wore a mask like everyone else. A mask forged of deceit, false grandeur, and the insistence of propriety. Underneath his face was twisted and ugly.

A white face flashed in my mind. It was as white as porcelain and as smooth as marble—beautiful in a haunting way. A face that looked like a mask but held only the truth on its surface. She had no need for lies. What were lies to the heartless?

"Morrow," I whispered to the wind. I wasn't sure why, but she kept drifting to my mind like she did over the hills around Nostalgie. Perhaps it was Nostalgie's fate that kept her close. Wondering how much time it had left. Terrified of what would happen if the barrier fell and it was at the mercy of those who felt nothing.

"Morrow, are you there?"

A light breeze chilled my exposed arms and neck. I hugged my arms close.

"I am here."

My heart fluttered. I whipped my head around, my red curls sailing through the air like twisting fire.

Morrow floated between me and the barrier like an impassible fog—a colorless face in a shimmering black brume.

Her body shifted into a humanoid form again, but she kept her distance. Tangled between deep dread and awe, I licked my cracked lips and searched for anything to say. "Hello."

Silence fell between us. My fingers twitched over my scars, and I wanted to run back to the barn and let it collapse on me. What a stupid thing to say. She wouldn't be interested in "hello."

"Good morning."

Goosebumps exploded all over my flesh as her rippling voice shattered the silence. A strange emotion came over me—one I had a hard time identifying, so little had I felt it. My soul felt lighter, almost buoyant.

"Have you been following me?" I inquired, not sure if I wanted the answer. The idea of being stalked by a phantom monster didn't exactly provide comfort, but maybe if I could speak with her, get her to help me understand . . .

"Yes."

"Why?"

Morrow's eyelids slipped shut—a slow and deliberate movement. "Interest."

Interest? What could possibly be interesting about me? "Why me?"

The white slivers of skin folded back open to reveal those jet-black orbs. "Why not?"

"Well . . . well, there's nothing really special about me." I lowered my eyes. "I'm not a Résonateur like my father."

Morrow held her silence. The longer it dragged on, the more my stomach twisted. She was going to leave. I felt it.

"So, are other Phases like you?" I asked in an effort to hold her attention, unwilling to let her stray from me just yet.

"No."

"Do they talk?"

"No."

"Will they try to kill me?"

"Yes."

"What makes you so different?"

Her head tilted gracefully until her face turned nearly horizontal like an owl. "I am *original.*"

Intrigued, I stepped forward.

Morrow's head snapped back into position. "I must go." Her body quivered back into an amorphous cloud. She floated for a moment and then shot into the sky.

"No, wait!" I called, throwing out my hand to reach for the trailing wisps. "Please, don't leave me. I don't want to be alone!"

A shrill scream cracked through the atmosphere like an explosion.

I whirled around and saw Margaux clutching the corner of the barn, heaving in terror. Tears streamed down her face.

"Y-y-you!" She thrust an accusing finger at me. "Master Cyril sent me back for you, but you were t-talking to it. You were talking to that Phase. *You!* You led it here. You're trying to destroy us. Master Gervais will protect us. He'll protect me!"

Margaux blazed off before I could utter a word of protest. I raced after her with every drop of energy I possessed. I only made it past one row of houses before my breath was stifled by the corset. I slowed, ignoring the indignant towners staring at me as I huffed and wheezed, fighting not to pass out.

"Stop. Please, Margaux, wait," I gasped.

But Margaux was already out of sight.

This was terrible. I couldn't let her tell Gervais. I had to make her understand. But I knew deep down that nothing I said could account for my associating with a Phase—not in her eyes. She was loyal to Gervais, not me.

I stopped, reaching back to tear at the strings on the back of my bodice. The fabric popped and gave a little slack. I took in several deep breaths to clear my head and assess my situation.

It wouldn't matter if I caught up to Margaux. She was going to tell Gervais what she saw. That fact would not change.

Despite my ragged breath, my chest felt like ice. Gervais would know what I'd done and Nostalgie would pay the price. I glanced back over my shoulder toward the invisible barrier. I could leave. Run back to Nostalgie. Run back to the open world.

Exposed. Alone. Outside the barrier . . .

I quivered.

Even if I made it back, they would throw me out. Me and Mama. Gervais only needed to say the word to Edgard, and it would be over for us. No food or shelter. Nearby towns would never take us in. We were outsiders. The risk was too high and supplies too low.

I had no choice. No choice but to face Gervais and try to convince him not to turn on Nostalgie.

I headed to the center of town, occasionally slipping between houses to stay out of view. Getting back into the mansion was going to be tricky. The front entrance was in plain view of the hub, but I had to find a way I could talk to Gervais privately. A few townspeople spotted me and watched me closely, confused by the commotion but too suspicious to talk to me. They whispered amongst themselves and stepped back. It was just as well. I was about to be banished . . . if I was lucky.

A cacophony of buzzing squawks and jeers rose from the hub, drowning out the siphon. When I entered the Solenoid's circle, Gervais and his family were already gathered and stirring up the growing crowd. Margaux clutched onto Gervais' sleeve like a spoiled child.

A pit formed in my stomach.

"I can scarce believe it. Those dogs from Nostalgie think they can slaughter us all. I'll bet this was all Edgard's plan. He's trying to steal our Solenoid!" Gervais was almost screaming in rage.

Their Solenoid? I clenched my fists at Gervais' deception.

"Are you sure, Father?" Cyril chimed in. "I doubt that pig could come up with such a plan. I'll bet it was all that tramp Fleurette's idea."

A chorus of hoops and jeers belted out from the crowd. I looked around, horrified. The hatred at Mama's name—

"If it was Fleurette, I'll personally teach her a lesson," Gervais growled. "We'll teach them *all* a lesson."

More cheers and chants rose from the mob. I couldn't believe how eager they were to vilify us. We were all people trapped in the same circumstances. Did they mean to throw us away so easily? *This is a bloodthirsty place. Remember Jalousie—*

My hair stood on end. I looked over my shoulder and saw two large men in balding velvet tunics scowling at me. I dodged around angry bodies and slid into an alley between houses before circling back to the hub, trying to keep my head down.

"There she is!" a shriek rose above the other noise. I raised my head. Margaux was pointing at me as though I were a blighted leper.

Before I could move, the two men grabbed my arms. I jerked against the hold like a captured rabbit. I knew this was coming, but still my instincts kicked in, urging me to fight. The men tightened their grip and towed me to the heart of Envie.

"How dare you deceive us in such a manner," Charmant spat. "We were to be sisters. I treated you with such love and kindness."

"What should we do with her?" Cyril asked with a quick glance at Gervais. "I can't marry a dampened." Cyril leaned closer to his father and lowered his voice. "If she's been infected by touching that Phase, she's a danger to us."

"I say we ship her back to that pigsty with a message—and no eyes," Charmant declared.

"Wait," I protested weakly. "Wait, I can explain."

Gervais stared down his long nose at me in suspicion. "What exactly is there to explain, my dear?" his voice dripped with sarcasm and disgust. "You were talking with a Phase. There's nothing that could possibly explain that."

He was right. I couldn't lie. Margaux saw me clear as day. But there had to be some way I could get out of this situation. I just had to twist it. Tell Gervais something he wanted to hear. Give him a reason to benefit himself.

"Yes," I acknowledged. "Yes, I was. Of course, I was," I said louder. "It was the only way to get proof."

"Proof? Proof of what?" He lowered his face dangerously close to mine.

"Don't listen to her lies, Master." Margaux pulled on his sleeve. "It's all a trick—"

He held up his hand to silence her. I licked my dry lips. It was working. At least, he was listening to me. Gervais was vain, but he wasn't stupid. If a Phase was around, he needed the same thing we did.

"You . . . your plan . . . the one you want to address the commandant with tomorrow. What if it doesn't work?"

Several outraged gasps swept up from the mob around us.

"What I mean to say is, what if it isn't enough to convince a Résonateur we need a Solenoid?"

"*We* don't need a Solenoid, my dear," Gervais sneered.

My heart pounded in my chest, threating to jump up my throat. *Think. Make this about Gervais . . . about their Solenoid.*

"Not yet," I said. "But barriers don't last forever. When was Envie's Solenoid installed? Do you even remember?"

Gervais' eyes narrowed. "What's your point, girl?"

"You don't want to be like Edgard and wait until it's too late. You need to keep the Résonateur bloodline strong," I declared. "For Envie's future."

"Strong," Gervais sniffed. "So why should I still marry my son to *you?*"

I knew exactly what to say—the words Gervais lived by. "We do what we must to survive."

Gervais' chin tilted up, and his eyes flicked to the Solenoid.

I looked around at the screaming faces around us. "Think about it, Seigneur," I said, putting emphasis on the title. "Nostalgie's Solenoid started dying three years after Jalousie fell. My father was there to pay the service for a new one. Who is going to be here to pay the service for Envie?"

"Your point is well taken, girl, but I've been tricked by the words of a pretty redhead before," Gervais replied. "I know Nostalgie is your real goal."

"You're right," I admitted. "I'm fighting for Nostalgie, but if we don't have a Résonateur it won't matter which town it is." I tried to free my arms again, but the guards held me. "That Phase is real. That Phase could get us a Résonateur from the Sommet. It could get us a Solenoid, but only if we prove the threat is real."

The displeasure from the crowd grew even louder. A few threats and curses stood out from the jumbled noise.

"Throw her out!"

"Lying whore! Like her mother!"

"Low-class sow!"

I had a feeling that my proximity to Gervais was the only reason nothing had been thrown at me.

Despite the open protests to ignore me, Gervais remained silent, contemplative. He brought up the hand that wasn't enchained by his maid and rubbed his chin. "So, you wanted to get proof of a nearby Phase to force the commandant's hand?" he uttered quietly, a private conversation between us amid a rowdy crowd.

"Yes," I affirmed. "I thought I saw the Phase from the automa-tram. I needed to be sure it was really there, so I went outside the barrier to lure it out," I told him. I tried my hardest to keep a steady tone. The last thing I wanted was for him—and them—to see me squirm.

"Don't believe her, Master," Margaux whimpered and she

buried her face into his elbow. "She was telling it not to leave her. She's dampened."

"I agree, Papa," Charmant said. "It all sounds very suspicious to me."

I gathered myself, determined to stay as calm and passive as possible. I'd been loose with my emotions lately. It was time to put them back where they belonged. "That's right. I did tell it not to leave," I replied. "How else would I prove it was around?" I looked at Charmant like I was doing the most sensible thing in the world.

"That doesn't excuse your behavior," Cyril said. "You should have told someone if there was a Phase out there."

I narrowed my eyes at him. "I did tell you. Right before you left me unconscious in Jalousie."

"That's enough," Gervais snapped. He threw his arms out and sent Margaux stumbling back. "I'll have to think on this. Lock her in the storage house by the front gates." He glared down at me. "If—*if*—you are telling the truth, I will consider letting this little incident slide. We have enough to concern ourselves with. This Phase will be dealt with, and your involvement will be judged."

"Judged? By whom?" I questioned as my two captors pulled me away. "How do I know I will be treated fairly?"

"You will be tried by a neutral party—the fairest in all the land," Gervais assured me. "The crime of interacting with a Phase is a serious one. Indeed, there can be no crime more damning. Your fate will be determined by the highest order. You will be sent to the Suzerain."

The crowd roared like a den of wild beasts about to feast on flesh for the first time in years. I wanted to bring my hands up to shield my ears, but the men holding me squeezed my limbs as though they were afraid I would break free if given half the chance. It was amusing they thought me so strong. Or perhaps, fear controlled their hands.

I closed my eyes to the crowd and let my toes scrape along the dirt. Did Mama plan for this scenario in her carefully laid out scheme?

I suppose the end was as she predicted. I would not be marrying Cyril at this rate. And Nostalgie would pay the price.

How could I let this happen?

I let my desires take control. If I had ignored them and not sought out Morrow . . .

The men threw me into a little wooden shed near the entrance of Envie without the grace and dignity Margaux promised. It was just as well. This reminded me who I was. This was my true place. Envie was nothing to me, and I was nothing to it.

But just this once . . . in this little storehouse away from the world . . . I could *be*, without the world crushing down on me.

The hours ticked by, and the autumn temperature dipped with the sun. I sat on a wooden crate full of parsnips, rubbed my arms for warmth, and curled in to shield myself from the cool air. I hated this place. I hated Gervais and Cyril, and Charmant and her stupid dresses—

"Are you cold?"

The resounding voice snapped me out of my miserable brooding. Morrow. I forgot all about the chill and rushed to the boarded-up window. I scoured the wood for any crack or opening. A gap in the lower boards caught my eye, and I knelt down to peer out. A swirl of black about ten feet away shimmered in the moonlight.

The same lightness I felt earlier with Morrow returned. She was the reason I was in this situation, yet she was my only companion. How strange to think fondly about a creature I was supposed to fear above all else.

"Morrow, is that you? I was afraid you might have left for good."

"Why would you think that?" came the monotone reply, so flat and void it hardly sounded like a question at all.

"You were seen by Margaux," I replied. "The whole town knows you're here."

"I am always here," Morrow said. "I have been here for many

years. Those who think otherwise have been living in ignorance."

"That's no longer the case, Morrow. They know, and now they're afraid."

"I am a Phase. That reaction is natural. My existence is one of solitude—one people would rather not dwell on."

"Solitude," I repeated. A lump formed in my throat, and I struggled to swallow it. "Maybe we aren't so different after all."

"Those who are unique often find themselves at odds with the world."

A smile crept on my lips before I could stop it. An involuntary reaction—an emotion of happiness brought on by this creature of null. A whole town of people brought me misery. Morrow brought me happiness.

"The whole world is a little beyond my grasp," I replied. "And I told you, there's nothing special about me. Not like you."

I pushed my hands against the boards, wishing for the wood to collapse so I could see her. For the barrier between Morrow and me to disappear. I couldn't let them kill her. She was a Phase, but there was something about her. Something that stirred my being and made me want to reach for the world beyond the barrier. She wasn't dangerous; she was unworldly. And she was the only one who was here for me.

"I don't know if you're aware, but a high-ranking Résonateur is on the way. The commandant will try to slay you," I warned.

There was a pause in conversation so long that I worried Morrow had already fled.

"Do you not want the Résonateur to kill me?"

"No, of course not."

"Why not?"

I rested my forehead against the wood. That was a good question, but it wasn't one I was sure I could answer or that she could understand. I was still struggling to understand it myself.

"Be-because . . ." I struggled to come up with a way to put my feelings into words. "Because you're all I have left now. You followed me from Nostalgie. You've never tried to harm me," I explained. "You're the only who hasn't tried to hurt me or use me. I guess you're my only friend."

"Friend?"

The word came out with the same echoed flatness as everything else she uttered, but different—like a long-forgotten memory she suddenly remembered.

"You know, it may not be just you they try to kill. After what Mama told me about Jalousie, I'm surprised Gervais hasn't set this building on fire to be rid of me," I confided to her, sliding down to the ground. I turned and put my back against the wall. "Jalousie is the ruined town we passed on the way here. The one where my fiancé abandoned me. Do you think that arrangement is still on?"

No answer came, only the sound of wind drafting through the gap kept me company.

I turned and rested the side of my head against the wall. "Morrow? Are you still there?"

Nothing.

I let out a disappointed moan and curled up. Even Morrow wouldn't stay with me for long. It wasn't like I wasn't used to people leaving me behind. Papa left before I even knew there were other towns around us. He never looked back either. Never sent word. Never checked in on the relier. He left us like Cyril left me, alone and bleeding. And the sad part . . . without them I was nothing. I couldn't protect Nostalgie. I couldn't fix the Solenoid. I couldn't get a new one without an offering. All I had was my body. And now, not even that was enough to save Nostalgie.

My eyelids drifted closed. The buzzing from the town died down hours ago. There was only me and the approaching morning.

I jolted awake to an intense wind whooshing through the cracks of the storehouse boards. Flecks of dirt flew around, swirling in the rays of sunlight beaming through the narrow openings. Excited cheers swelled to compete with the loud whirring. I ran to the window crack and peered out. A few seconds later, the sunlight disappeared, blocked by an object too big to completely see. The loud noise slowed until it finally stopped.

The Résonateur.

The roar of the crowd picked up again. I ran to the door and pulled at the handle. The metal jiggled but the door didn't budge. I had to get out. I had to alert Morrow about the Résonateur's arrival.

I thrust all my weight against the door, desperate to force it open. Nothing happened. Sighing, I dropped onto the parsnip crate. The only thing I could do was wait. Judgment would soon be upon me. Morrow wasn't stupid. She would have seen whatever it was that came to Envie. She knew to stay away.

"The Résonateur has arrived," Morrow's voice drifted in.

I tumbled off the crate and scrambled to the boarded-up window.

"What are you doing here?" I hissed. "It isn't safe. Please, go."

The air was still for a moment.

"I thought you didn't want me to leave. You are fickle."

I blinked a few times, unsure if I heard that correctly. "I—I really don't want you to go, but it's dangerous for you."

"I am aware of this."

"Then why are you here?" I asked in distress. "Someone might see you."

"You underestimate me. You underestimate yourself."

"I'm not underestimating you, Morrow. I'm sure you are a very powerful Phase, but that man is a commandant—a chief among Résonateurs. Aren't you afraid?"

"I do not feel fear. I do not feel."

"You are still capable of rational thought. Surely you must know—"

"Who are you talking to in there?" came a loud bark from outside the locked door.

I spun around as the keys rattled the latch. The door flew open, and the two men in velvet tunics walked in.

"The seigneur wants to see you now. The commandant will determine whether you have been *afflicted*," the one closest to me said with a disgusted glance up and down my body. He held up his hands. A thick pair of leather gloves ran up to his elbows. "The seigneur was kind enough to lend us these."

They seized me before I could bolt past them. I twisted and struggled to free my arms. One man grabbed a fistful of my hair and forced my head back.

"You're not helping your case," he growled.

"I'm not being judged by you," I retorted. "Your opinion is as valueless as your claim to nobility."

The man shoved my head down and released my hair. "Shut up and keep walking, dampened."

As the men carted me out, a huge object with a ring of sunlight shining around it momentarily blinded me. I squinted, my eyes not adjusted from the dim light of the storehouse. When my vision finally cleared, I looked at the towering obstruction.

It was large. No, it was enormous. In the fields outside the gates of Envie was a machine I never would have believed existed in the waking world. It dwarfed the houses in both scale and grandeur. A series of vertical metal fins jutted out from the sides of the anvil-shaped carrier, four on each side, with the fins decreasing in length from top to bottom and the shortest fins resting on the ground to support the vessel. Several thick cords ran between the fins, crisscrossing in a lattice like the outspread wings of a cicada. Two cords as thick as tree trunks ran from the top fins to a giant spire on the top of the main body.

The carrier was built like a ship with a hull of polished steel and wood. The top of the hull ended in a ring of steel railing surrounding a deck which contained a massive palace-like cabin. Serval rows of glass panels lined the cabin, but the panes in the front were easily as tall as Gervais' "mansion." I never knew a single sheet of glass could be so big.

Unbelievable.

"Stop gawking at the commandant's *soulever* and move your feet," my guard grunted with a hard jerk on my arm. We turned away from the front gates toward the Solenoid.

The streets were empty. Not a soul was to be found, nor a spirit to ask for guidance. The closer we got to the town center, the livelier the atmosphere became. A tight cluster of people all dressed in their finest had gathered. They wore ruffles of every color, feathers attached to whatever they would stick to. No article of clothing was too big or flamboyant. It was a city of clowns, and this whole circus had been put together for one person—a person who was not here to be entertained.

As we approached the wall of people, a few turned to openly sneer at me. Painted lips curled, hands made obscene gestures, and tongues threw hurtful words and threats. But for all their bravado, not a single one dared come close to me. As I approached, bodies shifted and cowered out of the way, parting as though the great Suzerain himself were walking through.

We continued down the widening aisle until I could clearly see the siphon's platform up ahead. At the sight of the apparatus, my intestines coiled and squirmed. Oh, Great Heart, it was time. The feeling was much worse than I expected.

Gervais loomed tall in front of the siphon. He reached out and yanked me away from the two men. Their duty finished, they slunk back into the crowd of unrecognizable faces and disappeared.

"How nice of you to join us, Gavril." Gervais greeted me with an oily smile. "The commandant was just inspecting our Solenoid. When he's finished with that, *you* get to be inspected."

He moved aside, but I couldn't see the Solenoid. A group of people gathered around it. Along with Cyril and Charmant, there were three men—a pair of them twins—and a woman. Though sharing the same platform, there was a sharp distinction between the Envie heirs and the guests. The newcomers were finely dressed in crisp, clean uniforms—the clothing of real status, not just peasant fantasies. They held themselves as far apart from the siblings as possible.

The woman from the Paramount had round silver glasses and dark brown hair pulled in a curly bun. She glanced up at me with sharp, deep blue eyes and then jotted a few notes onto a thin metallic sheet with the tip of a peacock feather. Bright letters appeared as she wrote, briefly reflecting in her glasses. They disappeared before I could read them. She held the quill flat against the sheet and pulled out a handkerchief from her lilac dress coat to dab her forehead. It must've been quite warm in that layered purple uniform and long matching skirt. I eyed it wistfully. With no sleeves, my own exposed flesh was numb.

I heard a snicker, and my eyes moved to the twins. They had the same barrel-shaped chests, brown eyes, and hay-colored hair. Their silver-buttoned burgundy coats and slacks were a perfect match as well. One's eyes danced over me before he whispered something to his brother. The pair sniggered. One of them winked at me and pointed toward the man in front of the Solenoid.

An extremely bored look adorned the face of the third man. Unlike the others, his appearance was sloppy and unkempt. The untucked half of his white shirt dangled freely. One knee sock rumpled around his ankle. Salt-and-pepper whiskers sprouted from his chin in wild, uneven patches, and his long silver-streaked black hair was messily tied back. His lazy green eyes were glazed over and glued to the nothing of air.

Could he possibly be the commandant? Résonateurs were supposed to be masters of emotion—able to keep their composure under any circumstance. He had the nonchalance perfected. Charmant said he was handsome.

I bit the inside of my cheek and considered him. He could be if he washed once a week.

Those glossy green eyes rolled over to me, and I straightened.

"C-C-Commandant," I stuttered out, caught off my guard. "I, um, I—"

He shook his head and stepped back, jerking his head over his shoulder in the direction of the Solenoid.

Behind him, a fourth man crouched in front of the Solenoid with the tail of a long ivory coat pooled on the ground behind him. He moved his gloved hands along the metal frame before pulling one back to run through close-cropped black hair. Thick strands on top bounced back up to point at the sky once his palm passed over.

"Commandant Serein," one of the twins spoke up, "the villainous girl is here."

I cut my eyes to the twin. He and his brother chuckled. The man in front of the Solenoid rose, and the giggling twosome instantly became the least of my concerns.

"It's about time," he said with one last touch on the Solenoid. "I'm getting tired of feeling up the only exciting thing in this town."

The Résonateur turned around, and a little flutter tickled my stomach. He was indeed handsome, even with an apathetic look darkening his features. Lightly tanned skin stood out against a gold-trimmed ivory uniform. The high-collared greatcoat that had once pooled on the ground now floated above it by at least a foot. It was adorned with solid gold buttons and fine silk embroidery, saplings sprouting from split seeds. His eyes pierced through the air like a powerful gale straight to me. They were gray—storm clouds.

"Oh, how funny you are, *Mon* Commandant," Charmant flirted, fanning her face playfully. "There is something much more interesting than that ugly tube for you to feel right over here." She pushed against Serein's arm and latched on.

"Please, do not touch the commandant," the woman in lilac requested, her eyes fixed on her metallic sheet as she began taking notes again. "Résonateurs are sensitive to emotions and do not wish to be handled by common folk."

Charmant's smile faltered, but she held tight to her prize. "I assure you, *good madame*, I am not 'common folk.'"

The reflection from silver-rimmed glasses faded as the peacock feather stilled. Royal-blue eyes zipped from the blank surface and stabbed into Charmant like a saber.

Charmant giggled nervously, but still refused to free the commandant from her clutches.

"I got it, Bibiane." The rumpled man stepped behind Charmant. Without a shift in his demeanor, he reached around her and lifted her from the floor. She sputtered and flailed, releasing Serein's arm in surprise. As unkempt as he was, the man was not sloppy in his movements. He effortlessly carried Charmant toward the mass of people. Villagers brayed and scrambled, backing away.

The man stopped and dropped Charmant to the ground like a sack of grain. She landed on her bottom with an undignified grunt.

He looked down at Charmant with disinterest. "Apparently, you're not important enough for even the common folk to catch, Princess."

Charmant's eyes welled with tears, and her lips quivered. She looked around the crowd, but not one soul—not even her brother or father—stepped in to help her up. Unceremoniously, she rolled onto her hands and knees, her massive dress puffing out all around her. When she tried to stand, she caught her feet in the hem and stumbled.

As I watched Charmant struggle to her feet, I was overcome by something I had never expected to feel toward the woman: pity.

As soon as Charmant was upright, she barreled through the wall of gawkers and fled toward her home, leaving a high wail in her wake.

I glared at the rough man when he returned to Serein's side. His eyes drifted to mine. He held my gaze daring me to say something.

Bibiane pushed her glasses up, eyebrows set in a stern line. "I could have taken care of the situation, Hervé. There was no need to interfere."

"I took care of it faster than you could," Hervé responded. "The sooner we are out of this dog hole, the better." His gaze shifted toward the twins. "I'm just sorry to steal the spotlight from the commandant's guards."

"We didn't want to cause a scene, so we could get down to business. Right, Marteau?" one of the twins chirped.

"So right you are, Ciseau," his brother agreed. "But these two love making a scene."

"Scene-loving."

"Love scene."

"Will you two shut up?" Bibiane seethed. "You're making us look like fools."

She was correct in that assessment. Gervais and Cyril could only watch with their mouths pressed into thin lines. Cyril's hands and eyes twitched as though he wanted to say something but was too afraid to interrupt the bickering.

"We're all a little foolish," Serein finally stated. All chattering stopped. "Don't you think so, Seigneur?"

Gervais jumped.

Oh, hearts on fire, don't tell me Gervais actually introduced himself as the "Seigneur de l'Envie."

Seigneurs were lords appointed by the Suzerain who passed the title down through lineage. Gervais could get away with addressing himself as such among the people of Envie and Nostalgie, but a Résonateur would know better. Gervais' family was nothing more than a line of mayors who elevated themselves on the backs of those who depended on and trusted them. The fact his Résonateur grandfather had a fling with his grandmother while passing through only seemed to solidify his position.

Gervais' tongue spun and sputtered a jumble of nonsense before he finally composed himself. "How right you are, Commandant. Yes, very right, indeed. Foolish. Very foolish we are. So very foolish—"

"This is the girl you want me to evaluate?" Serein continued on, putting an end to Gervais' babbling.

The head of Envie snapped to attention at the clear objective. He flicked his hand at me like I was a stain on the floor he wanted someone else to clean up.

"That's her. That's the deceitful girl who was caught talking to a Phase. *Talking* to it, Commandant. Can you imagine? After I brought her here and arranged for her to marry my own son," he spat out in disgust. "Why, it's just disgraceful."

Serein arched an eyebrow at Gervais before turning to me. The moment those cloudy orbs landed on me, I tensed. *He's coming for me. What do I do? Is he going to hurt me?*

Serein stood over me like a mountain. His gloved hands reached out, and I flinched, closing my eyes. Fingers gently clasped my jaw. He turned my head and slowly tilted it left, then right. When I opened my eyes, his stormy gray gaze flicked briefly to meet mine before returning to inspect my neck.

"Are you sure you should be touching me? I'm common folk," I muttered.

The corners of his lips twitched up in a small but noticeable curve. "Are you? I hadn't noticed."

"I'm no better than these people."

"We've established you're a liar. You are nothing like these people," he stated, no hint of uncertainty in his tone.

"I suppose you're right," I admitted. "I'm the pariah conspiring to destroy the town."

Serein let out a little chuckle and pulled up my hands. He turned them over and studied my wrists and paused, face serious once more. I tried to close my fingers over my scarred palms, but he gently pushed his thumbs underneath and pushed them back open, exposing my ruined flesh. He touched the healing scabs. As his silk-covered fingers ran over my flesh, goosebumps tingled all over my body. It was like passing through a barrier again and again—comforting, yet unnerving.

"Did you really speak with a Phase?" he asked without looking up.

"Does it matter? They've already condemned me," I told him, not wanting to delve too deep into that topic. After all, he *was* a Résonateur.

"Well," the commandant started, releasing my hands, "your marriage is at stake."

"How tragic."

Serein turned away from me and approached Gervais, who waited with wide, anticipating eyes.

"This girl has not been dampened," Serein announced loudly. "She's had no physical contact with a Phase."

A flurry of chattering whirled up among the crowd as my innocence was declared. Some people nodded or clapped, and some even smiled. Others booed or heckled, their thirst for blood unquenched.

"That's good," Gervais commented above the noise, bringing a hush to his followers. "That's very good. But it still doesn't clear her guilt," he pointed out, as though he knew some great secret. "We've determined she never touched the Phase, but not that she wasn't colluding with it."

The villagers roared. They cheered for Gervais. They loved him. And he loved the attention.

"If there is a Phase, we'll definitely rouse it now," Hervé grumbled.

Serein glared at Gervais. "So, what would you have me do, Seigneur?"

"The answer is obvious, isn't it? I want that girl judged by the Suzerain. If she can prove her innocence to the greatest authority, I will be satisfied."

Bibiane stamped her foot and thrust her metal sheet out at Gervais. "The Suzerain doesn't have time to waste on—"

"I'm confused, Seigneur," Serein began, holding up an arm to silence his flustered comrade. "You told me you arranged a marriage between your son and this young woman yourself, yet you seem eager to send her off with a band of strangers. Are you trying to be rid of her?"

"Not at all, Commandant." Gervais gave a slick wave of dismissal. "This girl is the only one with blood good enough for my son. Indeed, I know her stock *well*. Better even than she does." His lips curled in an oily smile. "And I know that red hair isn't the only wildness she's inherited. I won't put up with recklessness. Not if it puts Envie in danger. This town is my life and I want to make sure nothing interferes with that."

Serein nodded slowly. "An understandable position. Tell me, what fate awaits this young woman if she is found innocent by the wise Suzerain?"

Gervais opened his arms widely. "Why, forgiveness, of course. Forgiveness from her papa."

"You're not my papa," I hissed. How dare this snake call himself that after he bought me like a piece of meat, forced me from my home, and locked me in a cold storage house. My papa wasn't some greasy, slick opportunist. He was—

"I was closer than you know, girl," he replied, still smirking. "And unlike some, I'm still here." He looked around the group like he was delivering a sage piece of advice. "The mark of a good father."

"I don't think a good father is supposed to marry his daughter to his son," Ciseau whisper loudly.

"And she will still be married to your son?" Serein asked, ignoring the comment.

"As I said, her blood is suitable," Gervais replied without pause. "Useful for good breeding, as I'm sure you will all agree."

A cross between a snort and a caw erupted from Bibiane.

"But that is only if she's cleared by the Suzerain," Gervais continued. "For now, her actions as a heretic far outshine everything else." He looked at me again, his distaste shining through as the corners of his lips curled down. "Though it pains me to treat her like a prisoner, I'm afraid it's for the best."

Serein looked at the ground with a deep frown, quiet for a few moments. Then he looked back at Gervais. "You know, Seigneur, I think you are right. Taking her away from here is the best course of action." He nodded in my direction. "I will take this girl to Éthéré Coeur to be judged. From this moment on, she will be in my charge."

"But, Commandant," Bibiane protested, "you can't be expected to play escort to some . . . some plebeian girl. Separate transport arrangements should be made by the seigneur if it's so important to him," she snapped. "Especially if she's being accused of frolicking with a Phase—"

"It is *because* she is accused of associating with a Phase that I must personally handle this issue," Serein replied, leaving no room for argument. "As a Résonateur, I have been entrusted with the protection of the people. Anything to do with a Phase, I must take upon myself."

"I-I still don't see why—"

"Shut up, Bibiane," Hervé drawled. "The commandant's had his word. Obey it."

She fixed Hervé with a nasty glare but kept her further objections silent.

"Finally, a new face," Ciseau bubbled.

"A pretty face," his brother replied.

"A face that's not Bibiane's."

The metal sheet flew through the air and hit Ciseau in the ear. He yelped and clutched the bleeding auricle.

"That wasn't wise," Marteau snickered. "Important information is on that *vigile*."

"We were sent here to retrieve a dead Solenoid." Serein stepped between the volcanic Bibiane and her target. "I want to collect that Solenoid and get back in the sky. As soon as possible."

"Yes, Commandant," Gervais said with a wary glance at the twins and Bibiane. "With all the excitement, I almost forgot about the Solenoid. It would honor me to take you to Jalousie. It's a few hours journey by automatram."

I almost rolled my eyes. This was going to be an experience for the privileged visitors—one that would give them plenty of stories to share among their socialite brethren in the Paramount. I could care less about their discomfort.

What concerned me was Morrow. She didn't need to make a re-appearance in Jalousie. For the first time since coming here, I hoped I wouldn't see her.

REMNANTS OF JALOUSIE

Serein sat next to me as we bumped and shuddered our way to Jalousie. The automatram was much more cramped with four extra bodies. Bibiane took one look at the tram and left for the soulever without a word. The men recoiled but all boarded out of duty. I pressed myself as close to the window as possible. Having the Résonateur's form so near made me lightheaded.

It must be the power they possess. He has a special presence.

"I'm going to vomit," Marteau groaned. "This is the worst tram I've ever ridden in. It's a bucket of sick on wheels."

"Wheeling sick," Ciseau chimed in.

Marteau's face turned green. "Sick buck—*blegh!*"

"Watch it!" Cyril screamed, scrambling out of his window-blocking seat to get away from the retching twin.

Marteau threw his head out the now clear window, his body heaving. The automatram rocked, and Cyril tumbled to the floor between the benches.

"Get up, Cyril," Gervais hissed from the other side of Serein. "You don't see the commandant squealing and rolling. Straighten up."

Through a maroon-blotted face, Cyril glared daggers at his father.

"The commandant's not sitting next to the puke duke."

"Puke duke," Ciseau echoed and burst out laughing. He kicked and wiggled, knocking Hervé. The somber man slowly turned until his dark gaze bore into Ciseau. The amused twin clamped his mouth shut and tucked in all his flailing limbs.

Cyril pushed up on his knees. He looked to Hervé and the small space between him and Ciseau. Hervé stared down at him without moving to make room. Cyril then turned back to his father and made a sideways motion with his head.

"Don't be ridiculous, son," Gervais said, quashing the unspoken request. "The commandant can't be cramped in like that."

"You can sit next to me and Marteau, my little prince," Ciseau offered. He shoved his ailing brother closer to the window and patted the space between them.

Marteau heaved out the window again.

Cyril grimaced. "I'm fine right here."

We spilled out of the automatram like it was on fire. Never had I been so glad to be in a cursed, abandoned village. I considered running away. *I'm halfway to Nostalgie,* my inner voice tempted. *I could just disappear from this place. Avoid that shaking torture box and walk home.*

A hand gently grasped my arm and pulled me back to reality. "Let's move quickly and complete our task. I'm not eager to spend the night at the seigneur's manor," Serein said, urging me along.

"*Our* task?" I repeated. "Since when am I considered part of your entourage?"

"Since you became bound to me as my charge. Until you have been declared innocent by the Suzerain, we are as one in time and place."

I glanced at him from the corner of my eye. "What makes you so sure I'm innocent?"

He didn't look at me, but I could feel his hand tighten on my arm. "Because you don't feel guilty. You don't feel like one of *them*."

We passed the dilapidated buildings one by one, and as we closed in on the town's hub, it seemed far less haunted with Serein by my side. Because he was a Résonateur, I quickly reminded myself. It was like being protected by a barrier.

"I must admit something vexes me, though," he said with an interested tone. "I understand the seigneur's interest in choosing you for his son, but I don't understand your reason for accepting. Your fiancé and you don't seem to be well-suited. He's an extremely unlikeable ass."

I smiled, something unexpected considering I'd dreaded his arrival not long ago. "That's an honest opinion."

"I'm a Résonateur."

"It's all part of the master plan," I blurted. "Seigneur Gervais' scheme to get a new Solenoid."

"A Solenoid? The one in Envie seemed fine. The barrier's held for fifty years with no loss."

"Yes, that's good for them," I said roughly, as though a rock had been stuffed down my throat. Fifty years. To imagine a place so corrupt could be so fortunate, while my own home suffered loss after loss . . . it wasn't fair. Nothing was fair. I took in a deep breath and let my anger seep down my legs and bleed into the grass of Jalousie, where so much emotion had already been spilled.

No, I couldn't think like that. As much as I loathed Gervais, his people deserved protection. They weren't in Envie by choice. Nobody was sealed from the world by choice.

"It's for Nostalgie," I told the commandant. "My home."

"What does that have to do with marrying his son?"

My mouth grew dry. How could I even answer that? He wants his son to breed me in the off chance we produce Résonateur babies he can sell to the Suzerain? The thought of telling that to a man of Serein's prestige—letting him picture me in that position—knowing the depths of how we sank . . .

But maybe he needed to know. Maybe that was what all the Sommet needed to know—to see how destitute we had become.

"It was a payment of sorts," I said at last. "I'm going to help my village by"—I coughed—"by being with Cyril."

Serein shook his head. "They expected your village to sell you into marriage for aid?" he scoffed. "This place is even worse than I thought."

"It's not the worst," I countered, surprising myself. "It's desperation. Someone who has never known true need could never understand."

"And you plan to go along with this marriage even though the whole town turned against you?" Serein asked, his voice straining.

I nodded. "I'll do what I have to for Nostalgie. Even become an outcast."

"You're very kind," Serein said, releasing my arm. "Don't let it bind you." He led me into the heart of Jalousie, where a grassy and weed-covered siphon loomed before us. It was silent, its life extinguished long ago.

He stepped onto the platform to inspect the machine. I remained at the edge of the platform, looking at the once proud siphon. Panels and wires had been pulled free and parts removed or broken. Serein scraped away clots of ivy and probed inside rusty holes. What was once a beacon of protection was now an empty shell, stripped of its power and left voiceless. The quiet was unnerving. A reminder that even machines could die.

"How's it look, Comm?" Hervé questioned, approaching the platform.

"Completely unsalvageable," Serein declared. "And by that, I mean nothing left to salvage."

"What about the Solenoid?" Hervé tapped me on the shoulder and indicated I move closer to the Solenoid ahead of him. "Can't risk you running off, big culprit that you are."

I gave him a dubious glance but stepped onto the platform and strode up to the Solenoid anyway.

Serein's forehead creased as he studied the front of the huge cylinder. "What do you think, Hervé?" he asked.

A massive gash ran down the entire length of the Solenoid, partially obscured by a tangle of ivy, which wrapped around the cylinder as though trying to seal it back together. Serein stuck his head inside the hole, careful of the jagged metal edges. He turned his head a few times then pulled out.

"It's empty," he confirmed. He shot a sharp glare at Gervais.

"That wasn't me," Gervais defended his self-proclaimed honor with an indignant cross of his arms. "I will admit to utilizing a few pieces from the siphon—just a few—but the Solenoid was like that when I came to survey the town . . . for . . . for survivors, of course."

"Of course," Serein echoed half-heartedly.

"Do you think it exploded?" Hervé theorized. "There could have been an internal issue and the whole thing erupted from inside."

"It's possible," Serein said. "What happened to the survivors?"

"They're dead," I whispered. Mama had told me. She told me everything about Jalousie.

"Dead?" Serein repeated. "*All* of them?"

"Yes, it was a terrible thing," Gervais answered before I could open my mouth again. "You see, right after the barrier dissipated, a Phase attacked. Very unfortunate for the people here," he observed with a matter-of-fact tone holding no sympathy or remorse. He had mastered the art of not concerning himself with others' troubles.

"And what happened to the Phase? Is it the same one seen here recently?"

"No, no, that Phase was slain," Gervais explained. "You can ask that girl all about it. I'm sure Fleurette shared the story with her in full, exasperating detail."

Everybody looked at me expectantly, and being the center of

attention, my cheeks burned. I hoped against hope they weren't as red as my hair. "That Phase was killed by a Résonateur. Goel. My father," I meekly replied.

"What a shame," Marteau lamented.

"Such a shame," Ciseau mimicked.

"The Phase girl's a Résonateur's daughter," Marteau put his hand next to his mouth like he was sharing a dirty secret.

"A Résonateur's daughter dallying with a Phase," his brother mused.

"Phase-dallying."

"Dally-phasing."

"You two are annoying," Cyril grumbled at the twins.

"I'm hurt, my prince," Ciseau simpered, rounding on Cyril. "I was going to let you sit on my lap on the way back."

"I would rather perch on the roof," Cyril growled.

"Suit yourself." Ciseau shrugged. "I've successfully freed up some space."

"Good work, brother." Marteau clapped him on the back.

"None of you are riding back," Hervé informed the trio. "You're all walking."

"What?" Cyril squeaked. "That's *not* going to happen."

"After all we've been through, Hervé," Marteau moaned, "you throw us away."

"I'm not throwing you away. I'm putting you to work," Hervé said. He rested a hand on the Solenoid. "That tram's got no space, and even if it did, I doubt the engine could handle the Solenoid's weight. Someone has to carry this back."

"There's no way we'll manage, Hervé. It's too heavy," Ciseau whined.

"Of course, you'll manage," Hervé said firmly. "It's just a shell. The three of you can handle it."

"Exactly! Just a shell," Cyril argued, stomping his foot. "Father, you can't let them do this."

"Even if there's nothing but a husk, the Suzerain has ordered the dead Solenoid be recovered," Serein intervened. "That is the word of Éthéré Coeur. Do you mean to defy it?" He challenged Cyril with a stern gaze.

The young lord visibly shrank—a great feat considering his impressive height—and he held his tongue behind flat purple lips.

"Do as the commandant says, son." Gervais gave Serein an approving nod. "He is the Suzerain's arm. It is not our place to question his requests."

"Hervé, take care of it properly," Serein ordered.

"I'll make sure it's done right," Hervé acknowledged. "You heard the commandant."

Serein put a hand on my shoulder and guided me toward the automatram.

"Get that Solenoid detached and warm up those legs. It's a long way back to the *Fulgurant*." Hervé's voice rang out behind us.

After we had cleared half the buildings, Serein leaned close to my ear. "What happened to Jalousie's survivors? A single Phase can't kill that many people at once. Some must have fled."

"I don't know for sure," I murmured. "I only know what Mama told me. She said some survived. They escaped to Envie, but . . ." I cast a wary glance behind me.

"You can be honest," Serein assured me. "It will not affect your judgment."

"Gervais killed them. Every single person who sought refuge. Gervais' father, the former head of Envie, was in failing health, so he left the decision to Gervais as his first act as leader. Gervais declared there was too great a risk that everyone had been dampened, so he had them executed." I crossed my arms and lowered my eyes to the grass. "It's a wonder I'm still here."

To my surprise, the hand on my shoulder gave an encouraging

squeeze. "You have nothing to fear. You are in my charge now, and I do not murder people on circumstance."

"But I'm in your charge as a heretic. Why are you so kind to me?"

"Because I see people for what and who they are. And what I see in you, Gavril, is a bright young woman who may drown if I don't lend a hand."

I looked back up at him with a small smile. "You know my name."

"I wouldn't be a good escort if I didn't."

The echo of my name with Serein's deep timbre ignited warmth in my chest. A split second later, a flash of twinkling black whirled in the distance behind Serein. My heart leapt at the sight, alternating between peaking in elation and falling in dread. Never had I been so torn between wanting to see someone and wishing they would disappear. I pulled away from the Résonateur.

How stupid of me. I should have known such a rush of emotions would catch Morrow's attention. This was the last place she needed to be.

"We should probably get back to Envie before the sun sets," I said.

"Still frightful of your own shadow, girl?" Gervais suddenly butted in from behind us. "You're with a commandant. But considering the company you keep, perhaps *we* should be afraid of *you*."

"By her company you mean your son, right?" Serein smiled at the seigneur. "They're engaged and you assured me forgiveness awaits her."

Gervais pulled at his coat, long fingers digging into the material. "Well, that might be subject to change," Gervais replied. "On the journey here, I had time to think about the situation. I've another child, and considering the drama with this one"—he bobbed his chin at me—"I'll fare better focusing on her prospects."

"That may be for the best," Serein said. "Even the purest rose can be overrun by a fungus."

"Absolutely," Gervais replied without hesitation, sneering at me.

"But it will be a shame if Nostalgie can't keep their end of the bargain. It's not surprising considering the stock over there."

"No!" I cried. "You can't do that to them." The Solenoid—and Nostalgie—were slipping from my grasp.

"You're the one who is doing it, my dear," Gervais retorted. "Your decisions compromised everything, and all I've done is try and be a loyal and reliable neighbor. Don't you agree, Commandant?"

"I see you feel yourself as innocent as the sky is blue, Seigneur," Serein replied. "As far as Gavril is concerned, she, too, has yet to be proven guilty of anything, so feel free to continue sharing your generosity with your neighbors as a great seigneur is compelled to do."

Gervais' eyebrows shot up. "My generosity has already been worn thin to acquire a new Solenoid. If that girl had—"

"And how exactly *do* you plan on acquiring a Solenoid, Seigneur?" Serein asked, his tone short. "It seems you have no Résonateurs to go with your lack of generosity."

"I'll get one," I declared.

The two men stopped their banter and turned to me.

"When I face the Suzerain, I'll plead with him. I'll get a new Solenoid," I said.

"*You*," Gervais snorted. "You're just as moony as your mother, girl, but I'll make you a deal. If you manage to convince the Suzerain to give you a Solenoid, I'll bless your marriage with a grand toast and name your first child."

My mouth curled in distaste. *The child you want to sell.*

I was determined, but still, a dark cloud hovered over me. What if pleading wasn't enough? What if . . . What if I *did* need a child to pay the service? Bile rose in the back of my throat. I needed Cyril and Gervais. There was no way to escape this engagement and save Nostalgie.

"We're getting ahead of ourselves here," Serein said. "And we still have other important business to finish. We should put our focus on that for the time being."

"Yes, of course, Commandant." Gervais bowed his head to Serein and motioned for him to get in the automatram. "Please, let's head back to Envie."

Serein offered a mechanical smile and helped me into the automatram, where I slid to the window. Serein followed, taking the middle seat, and Gervais perched himself next to the window opposite mine. Once Hervé slid into the bench across from us, the opérateur climbed aboard, and the tram coughed to a smoky start.

Hervé sat in the middle of his bench and sprawled his arms from window to window, his head bobbing up and down with the rhythm of the tram.

"I'm sure there's some room over there for the good seigneur. Don't you think, Hervé?" Serein raised an eyebrow.

"For the seigneur? No, I don't think there is," Hervé mumbled. "For the girl? Maybe."

"The girl is under my watch," Serein reminded him. "But the seigneur is fair game."

"Please, keep his lord's company for yourself, Commandant." Hervé's eyes closed. "I'm fine with being alone over here."

Gervais straightened. "I assure you, Commandant, I'm more than happy to share my knowledge and resources with you. Anything in Envie is at your disposal. Why, my beautiful daughter Charmant would be thrilled to—"

"The woman with the blonde hair?" Serein asked.

A prickling sensation ate at my stomach and crawled into my chest. *Not Charmant.* I fumed silently. *He's not impressed by her. Gervais doesn't have a chance of marrying her off to the commandant.* My chest continued to ache with an emotion I'd never felt before. It was too strong. It needed to vanish before Morrow sensed it.

"She's quite the beauty, yes? Tell me, Commandant, are you married?" Gervais asked, his tone eager.

Across from us, a smirk slid over Hervé's face. I forced a disinterested expression on my own, but my ears were wide open.

"I'm afraid a Résonateur's life doesn't make marriage easy," Serein replied, his voice strained.

Gervais suddenly cackled. "Only if the woman is difficult, Commandant. *Loyalty*"—his eyes flicked to me—"Loyalty and obedience. That's all you need for a good wife. I learned this the hard way. That's why I'm avoiding the same mistake with my daughter. She'll make a fine wife."

"I'm sure she will, Seigneur." Serein continued staring straight ahead.

I tried to think about something—anything—else. But the image of Charmant on Serein's arm plagued me. I turned my face toward the wild grass outside my window.

I felt a gentle tug on the back of my head. I eased my head around to look over my shoulder. A red lock curled around Serein's fingers. He rolled it back and forth, a thoughtful gaze in his eyes. I turned back to the window. The strange, unfamiliar sensation in my chest flared like a wildfire.

It was nearly sunset when we returned to Envie. The crowd had dispersed, given the lack of entertainment, and people went about their daily business. A few people stopped to stare at the soulever, but none dared step outside the barrier for a closer look.

"This is far enough," Serein called out to the opérateur right before we crossed the main gate. The tram stopped, and everyone but Gervais exited.

"Are you sure you wish to stop here, Commandant? We can take the automatram to my estate. No need to stay out here when I have more than enough room to accommodate—"

"No need to extend yourself so far, my good seigneur," Serein interrupted Gervais' bragging. "As soon as the Solenoid from Jalousie is recovered on the *Fulgurant*, we will depart."

"That might take all night," Hervé mused, eyes trailing down the road into the distance. "Might take all day tomorrow. May as well get a free meal while you can."

The glare Serein shot Hervé could have melted glass.

"Yes, my maid Margaux is preparing a grand feast as we speak," Gervais said.

I bit the inside of my cheek. More watered-down vegetables.

"It would be a shame to have all that food go to waste," Gervais continued.

"You could give it to the people starving near the edge," I muttered.

"What was that?" Gervais' narrow eyes dug into me.

"She said your maid cooks like a high chef," Serein told him. "I hate to see good food thrown out. Please, show us the way to your estate."

"Us?" Gervais asked, surprise in his voice.

"Of course. All of us," Serein replied.

Gervais' eyes stayed fixed on me. "Are you sure we shouldn't return the girl to the storehouse, Commandant?"

"Certainly not," Serein replied. "I need to keep a close eye on Gavril. She'll join us for dinner." His eyes zipped warily over the tram. "Why don't you go on ahead? We'll be along shortly."

The seigneur's lips puckered like he'd bathed them in lemon peel. "As you wish, Commandant. I'll have Margaux fix a place for . . . for all of you."

"Not me," Hervé said. "I don't tolerate torture as much as I used to. I'll stay here and wait for those three morons." He spun on his heels, walked to Envie's gate, and leaned against it.

Serein stared after Hervé like he'd just been told to clean the latrine. "Just the two of us, Seigneur." He raised his voice and continued.

"It seems my *adjutant* has lost his appetite."

Hervé flicked his hand over his shoulder like he was brushing off some dirt.

Gervais nodded. "Home, opérateur, and quickly."

As soon as the automatram's deafening hisses faded into the distance, I leaned closer to Serein. "I honestly think I'd rather be in the storehouse."

Serein chuckled and looked down at me. "Sorry for your sacrifice, but I'm not going in alone."

"I did it alone," I said. "One of the worst experiences of my life."

"You're braver than I am, Gavril," Serein replied.

"I highly doubt I'm a match for a Résonateur who goes into the world and fights Phases."

"You left your home and everything behind. You faced an angry mob alone." Serein grinned. "And you stared down this Résonateur who goes into the world and fights Phases. That takes courage possessed by only a few."

"But it was the same for you, wasn't it?" I pushed. "You had to leave your home to become a Résonateur."

Serein ran a hand through his short locks. The spikes bounced right back up. "There's a big difference between doing something you've been expecting to do your whole life and suddenly being forced into it."

"It still must've been hard to leave everything," I insisted.

Instead of answering, Serein pointed down the main roadway to the center of Envie. "Why don't you show me the way? I'm quite eager to get this dinner party over and done with."

"That makes two of us," I agreed and led him toward the middle of the town.

As we passed row after row of houses, people took notice of us. They watched and pointed. Soon, the air buzzed with whispers. An uneasy feeling sank into my stomach, and the hair on the back of my neck rose. I checked over my shoulder. A few towners stalked behind us, keeping their distance, but obviously creating a wall to prevent escape.

"If they come any closer, I'll deal with them," Serein uttered quietly. He placed a hand on my shoulder and pulled me closer. Warmth from his body seeped under my skin and heated me all the way to my core, like nothing I'd ever experienced.

"Better be careful, Résonateur," someone grunted out from behind us. "Cozy up to *that* and you'll catch it, too."

Serein turned back to the growing swarm. "Catch what, Monsieur? I've already evaluated this young woman and found nothing to catch but envy at her beauty and kindness."

My cheeks blazed more intensely than the sun. Great Heart, did he really think that? Or was he trying to silence the bleating sheep?

"So the rumors must be true," the man continued. "I'd heard the mother rolled out of the seigneur's bed as soon as a Résonateur swooped into town. Looks like this whore's done the same to poor Master Cyril."

"You'd do well to keep your tongue still," Serein warned in a tone that could freeze fire. "This woman may be your dame one day. Her memory of this day might outlast your life."

"It was a mistake bringing one of those Nostalgie peasants—"

"Yes, your seigneur seems to be a man of many mistakes," Serein considered thoughtfully. "What's your name? I'll be sure to share your thoughts on his shortcomings with him over dinner."

The man's face blanched so white I expected the grass to turn red from all the blood that left it.

"No-no, there's no n-n-need," the man stuttered. "S-Seigneur is—"

"Go back to your homes and sit with your families," Serein said loudly. "This situation is in the hands of the Sommet and no longer concerns you. Gavril has yet to be tried, and I expect you to treat her with the respect your young lord's fiancé deserves."

The crowd couldn't have dispersed quicker if a Phase had flown in and chased them away.

I looked down at my feet. I would never be accepted here. Even with the Suzerain's clearance, I would always be the girl caught doing the unspeakable. I was the heretic. If I married Cyril, I would always be whispered about in alleys and dismissed in the streets.

"Thank you," I said. "Nobody's ever spoken up for me like that."

"I find that hard to believe."

"No, it's true," I responded with a bitter smile. "I suppose when your father's a foreigner *and* the Résonateur who's disappeared for seventeen years, it puts a target on your back."

"Seventeen years?" Serein rubbed his chin. "You said he's paying the service for the Solenoid?"

"So we've been told. Edgard's convinced he's returned to his homeland, but Mama desperately wants to believe he'll come back. I don't think we'll see him again."

"It's not that unusual for Résonateurs to be assigned to faraway countries during the service," Serein told me. "But you can always have hope, Gavril."

"Hope is all I've had for a long time and it seems to be running thin these days," I lamented.

"It got you to me."

I smiled at the commandant. Before I'd been dragged in front of him, I was expecting the Résonateur to be a wall—a man of uncompromising stoicism and hard laws. Serein was nothing like that. He was compassionate, honest, and . . . and human. He was everything I'd been denied so far in my life.

"I think *you're* the one who needs hope now, Commandant," I said quietly.

"Why is that?"

My eyes drifted up the plaster house in front of us. "Because this is the Seigneur de l'Envie's estate."

Serein studied the house, his hand under his chin in consideration.

"It's bigger than I expected."

I snorted, and he glanced at me.

"No, it's true," he said. "I never paid attention to it when I came in this morning. After meeting Gervais, I was so focused on getting the inspection over and done with so I could get out of here that I blocked out everything else." His head cocked, and those gray eyes lingered on me. "Well, maybe not everything."

I looked down at the steps in front of us and awkwardly twisted my hands together. I could still feel his eyes on me. Every inch of me resisted the urge to squirm. I wanted to hide from his gaze, and at the same time, bask in it. "I guess we should hurry up and finish the last task," I muttered.

"That sounds good to me, Gavril."

We stepped up to the entrance, and Serein knocked lightly on the door. A dull thud sounded from the other side, followed by a muffled yelp. We waited a moment, and a shrill voice barked, "Margaux, get back in the kitchen and finish plating. I'll see to Mon Commandant."

The door swung open like a ram had butted it. Charmant draped over the door, freshly garbed in a pastel pink gown with a neckline so low it barely left room for a single error in movement. She smiled coyly at Serein. "Commandant and"—her eyes flicked to me and her smile bent backward—"you."

"And you are?" Serein asked, his tone chipper and light.

I fought to keep my expression straight.

Charmant giggled and swatted her hand. "Oh, Mon Commandant, you and your games." She took a step toward him and purred, "If you're so playful, I've got a few games we can try later."

"I'm afraid I'm on a tight schedule," Serein replied, the muscles in his neck pulling taut like he was trying to keep from gagging.

"That's a shame," Charmant pouted. "But perhaps this is not the best place for us to get to know each other. I can go with you on your big soulever—"

"There's no room," Serein said firmly. "With your father's demands, the *Fulgurant's* quite full at the moment."

Charmant's lips puckered. "None at all?" She took another step forward and placed her hand on his chest. "Not even in your room?"

Serein stepped back from her touch. "My floor's not very comfortable."

Charmant's eyes snaked over to me. "Someone else could sleep on the floor. I promise not to make too much noise if that's what concerns you." She covered her mouth with her hand, the tips of two fingers poking out from her lace gloves. "I know men of uniform like to be discrete."

"How's your rear?" Serein suddenly questioned, earning shocked looks from both Charmant and me.

"Wh-what?"

"When Hervé dropped you, it looked like you went down pretty hard. I hope he didn't hurt you."

"I'm fine," Charmant said, her voice hardening to marble.

"I'm very glad to hear it," Serein replied. "I'm also quite hungry. Can you show Gavril and me to the dining room?"

Charmant's eyes once again went to me. "This criminal is eating with us?"

"She has been convicted of nothing yet. It was your father's wish that she be kept under close supervision until she can be presented to the Suzerain. I can't keep an eye on her if she isn't beside me. However, if you would like to watch her while the seigneur and I eat—"

"Oh, no, of course not, Mon Commandant," Charmant declined, bouncing back to eager hostess. "Please, follow me. You can sit beside me, Commandant. The heretic can sit near the end."

"I'd prefer to have her closer," he said. "Just in case. It's not wise to ignore protocol."

"Great Heart, no. We wouldn't want to get you into trouble." Charmant indicated with her finger for Serein to follow. "Not yet."

She let out a loud cackle and sashayed back into the house.

I followed with Serein, trying not to roll my eyes when Charmant's hips swayed so widely they nearly knocked over a small table. I had to give her credit. She wasn't one to let obstacles, embarrassing incidents, or outright refusals deter her. Charmant was determined to get out of Envie—something I couldn't fault her for.

Charmant escorted us to a long room with a table the size of a wagon cart carefully placed in the center. It had eight mismatched chairs, three on each side and one at each end.

Gervais sat at the head of the table in the largest chair. Its tall back was lined with red cushioning, though many of the brass buttons were missing, and the arms were heavily chipped. His hand slid over the surface of the table, which had smooth dents worn into the wood from years of rubbing and cleaning. "It's an ancient piece," he boasted. "Been here since the founding of Envie."

"It's a fine table," Serein said. "With no forests around here, wood like this must be hard to come by."

"Impossible now," Gervais said. "The closest trees are about fifty miles out, and no one but me has the courage to stay outside the barrier that long."

Charmant stood behind the chair to Gervais' left. She smoothed her skirt and flicked her gaze between the chair and Serein. She brought a balled fist to her mouth and cleared her throat demurely.

Serein ignored her prompts and moved to the chair on Gervais' right. "Obviously, you must remain mindful of your resources, Seigneur Gervais."

"Oh, yes." Gervais leaned forward. "I always make sure my citizens are aware that what they have is what they have. If they find a hole in the roof, they must patch it or make do. If their house burns down, they're out on the streets. A hard lesson, but a necessary one."

"I see." Serein reached for the chair to his right, the center chair, and pulled it back. He turned to me. "Please, sit."

Charmant's nose flared.

I quietly slid into the seat, and Serein sat beside me, completely ignoring Charmant. She stiffly pulled out the chair directly across from Serein's and plopped down with a huff.

"Margaux," Gervais barked. "The commandant is waiting. Hurry up."

"Y-y-yes, Master Gervais," the maid squeaked from the kitchen.

"There's no need for that," Serein said. "If she needs more time—"

"No, M-m-monsieur Commandant." Margaux rushed into the dining room, three bowls of steaming soup sliding back and forth on the tray in her hands. "It's ready." She placed the bowls out, her arms quivering. Sloshing hot liquid threatened to spill all over the table, but Gervais remained perfectly composed, even when the tray nearly hit Charmant's bouffant.

Margaux set the last bowl in front of Serein. A large fresh burn marred her right forearm. She bowed lowly. "I hope you enjoy my potato stew."

"We're missing one bowl," Serein noted. "Gavril hasn't received her meal."

Charmant dropped her spoon as though it were a dead mouse.

"We can't start until everyone has been served," Serein insisted calmly.

Margaux's face flushed with horror and she turned to Gervais.

He flicked his hand at the maid. "You're not deaf, girl. Get another bowl for the commandant's prisoner."

"Your son's fiancé," Serein corrected.

Gervais' line of sight crawled over to me. "Yes."

"You know, Papa," Charmant said in a saccharine voice, "I really hope Gavril is found innocent. She's such a perfect match for Cyril. It breaks my heart to see this horrible business happen." She turned to me and leaned over the table, her ample bosom spilling directly in front of Gervais and giving Serein an eyeful. She placed her hand over mine. "I forgive you, sister. I know marrying Cyril has been a dream, maybe too much of one at once. I hate to see true love torn apart."

I pulled my hand out from under hers. "Ripping out my eyes and sending me back to Nostalgie as a warning doesn't tear true love apart?"

Charmant's eyes widened for a second before narrowing. "How undignified," she breathed, straightening up and readjusting her bodice. "I offer words of love and you spit venom in return. You may be pretty, but your manners reflect the inferior blood in your veins."

"Gavril's blood is that of a Résonateur," Serein said matter-of-factly. "If hers is low-class, my own is surely mud."

Charmant gasped. "Never, Mon Commandant. Your blood is like argent—rich, pure argent that should be worshiped."

Margaux strolled back into the room with the last bowl of soup sloshing messily over the tray with each quick step, but her hands weren't trembling this time.

"Here you go, heretic." She held the bowl above the table in front of me. "Extra hot, just for you."

As her fingers released the porcelain dish, it tipped. Steaming liquid poured down to the wood below, and in one fell swoop, Serein sprang from his chair and lunged in front of me. The hot soup splashed over the front of his ivory coat.

"Margaux, you stupid sow," Gervais roared, slamming his hands on the table. "You'll be punished for this."

Margaux cowered, shielding her head with the tray.

"Oh, Mon Commandant," Charmant moaned. "Oh, your fine clothes . . ."

Serein fell back into his chair.

"Commandant, are you burned?" I asked, short of breath and taken aback by how quickly he moved to protect me.

"No," he replied, looking down at his wet uniform. "Thank the heart for layers, and look, the color matches."

"You shouldn't have done that," I murmured. "You could have been seriously hurt."

"I wasn't, but you would have been." Serein pushed away from the table and stood up. "This dinner is over."

Gervais squawked and nearly tumbled out of his own chair. "W-w-wait, Commandant. At least stay the night and let us make up for this heinous offense. Margaux can wash your clothes and Charmant could—"

"We've taken enough of your time and hospitality," Serein said firmly. He put a hand on my chair and pulled it back so I could stand. "I wish you the best of luck with your endeavors."

"Wait, Commandant!" Gervais continued, distress coloring his voice. "What about the Phase? You can't just leave without—"

"It hasn't appeared since my arrival. And as you've requested this young woman be tried as soon as possible, I'm afraid I must make that my priority. Please send a message through the relier if the Phase becomes an issue."

"*Becomes* an issue? It's already an issue if it's out there—"

"Phases are always out there," Serein cut in with a voice as icy as morning frost. "Most people just don't pay attention to them until they become a nuisance." Serein escorted me to the front of the mansion and out the entrance.

"Anything to bring with you?" he asked as we walked down the steps.

"There is nothing from here I need," I said.

"Good. I never want to go back," he confided with a grin.

"Nor do I."

We walked away from Envie. The soulever seemed to expand as we drew closer to it. Rays of the sun, low in the horizon, struck the cords running between fins and made them glow like strands of a giant fiery spider web. As the massive structure loomed over us—an umbrella of wood, metal, and freedom—my legs felt weak. I couldn't inhale enough air to fill my lungs. That machine was over-whelming. Daunting. It offered the only taste of escape before my life was enchained.

Serein removed a small black cube from his pocket. He pressed his thumb on top, and a green line glowed around the center, splitting the cube in half. Serein ran his finger along the line.

Suddenly, a great clatter shook the air and rattled the ground. I ducked and covered my head. Serein put a hand on my back.

"It's just the hatch opening," he said softly.

I gathered my courage and looked up. A silhouette stood in the midst of a bright hole that opened in the center of the vessel.

Serein pulled me back as a long ladder uncurled from the opening. It hit the ground and swayed back and forth like a swing, a slave to the breeze. He nudged me forward.

"I'm not climbing up that."

"Gavril, there's no other way," Serein said calmly. "You climb up first. I'll be right behind you," he reassured me. "If you fall, I will catch you. You have my word."

My eyes darted between Serein's supportive face and the swaying doom above us. *I have to do it. The only way to be free from this place–away from these people–is to climb.*

I clenched my jaw and grabbed the closest rung. I pulled myself up and began the ascent.

"One foot at a time. One step closer to the top," I chanted through my teeth.

I kept my vision focused on one point in the horizon—a silver dot in the distance that flashed on and off like a beacon. I took another step up. It stopped.

What happened? Where did it go?

A gust of wind rushed around the soulever, and the ladder whipped around like an angry snake. It yanked forward, and my foot slipped. I cried out, balling my fists as tight as they would go around the wooden rung.

"Don't panic, Gavril!" Serein shouted. "Get your foot back up. I'm looking out for you."

As my vision darkened, I sucked in the cool air around me to push the fog away from my brain. I needed to stay conscious. *Don't fall. Get it together.*

A thin black wisp disappeared around the edge of the hull, heading up for the deck above me.

I craned my head to peer up at my destination. She was up there somewhere. Waiting. I forced my body to move. There was only one way to get to the top. Morrow was waiting for me.

She was with me like she had been when I was alone in Jalousie. Like when I stepped outside of Envie. Like when I was locked up after the whole town turned on me.

I set my pace. I kept my eyes locked on the opening above me. I was getting closer. I reached for the top rung.

I blinked. When I opened my eyes, I nearly jumped. A man with a thin black beard leaned out of the hole.

"Need help, Mademoiselle?" The man extended his hand.

Eager to get off the ladder, I took his hand. He pulled me into the hatch, and I collapsed onto the lacquered floor, still lightheaded.

I rolled on my back and lay on the wood, panting and exhausted and utterly terrified. I was up in the sky, and Envie was far below.

I brought my arm up and covered my eyes. My lips curled up and a soft, melodious laugh escaped my mouth. The longer it carried on, the louder it got, and I couldn't stop it. Envie was so far below.

DEPARTURE OF SADNESS

Serein escorted me through hallway after hallway of waxed oak floors illuminated by bright crystal lamps. Everything gleamed, bright and new and whole. Spotless white walls seemed to stretch forever with no windows to break the illusion. We ascended a staircase, walked down a passage, and climbed up another set of stairs. I never knew a journey in a sealed area could be so exhausting.

"Does it always take this long to move upward?" I asked with a puff as we climbed up another incline of steps.

"Not at all," Serein answered, throwing a grin over his shoulder. "There's a central stairwell that connects every level. I wanted you to become accustomed to your surroundings. The *Fulgurant* will be your home for the next week."

My eyes widened. "I'm free to walk around? You're not going to lock me in a cell?"

"I don't think you're that dangerous, Gavril," he replied, voice tinged with mirth. "But you could always prove me wrong."

The next corridor widened into window-lined walls, the ceiling a great atrium of glass. Star-speckled darkness pooled in the room from the night sky. The stars looked different from this elevation. I had viewed them from the same location for so long, I'd forgotten they weren't painted in place. They felt closer here. Reachable. The world and sky were reachable.

"Is this your first time on a soulever?" Serein moved to one of the windows and swept his hand across the horizon. "The view is more beautiful when you aren't fighting for your life."

I let out an abashed smile. "This is one of many firsts for me. Envie is the farthest I've been from home. I spent my whole life inside Nostalgie's barrier." I walked to the window and rested my hand on the glass—another barrier. "That must sound pitiful to you. I'm sure you've been many places—explored everything."

Serein shook his head. "It doesn't sound pitiful at all. It sounds real. Many people like you, Gavril, have never been outside their barriers. It is a Résonateur's duty to protect people," he said with a solemn gaze. "The fact that so many must spend their lives hiding only demonstrates my failure. I am the one who is pitiful. Not you."

For a moment, my heart fluttered. To think this man—a Résonateur with so much power and respect—considered his position in regard to people like me so deeply . . .

"Humility doesn't suit a commandant," I stated with an offhanded air.

His dour expression remained unchanged. The sight of it ate at my flippancy.

"I have many things to be arrogant for, but letting people suffer is not one of them."

"Commandant, I didn't mean—"

"Call me Serein."

"S-Serein," I complied, trying the name aloud for the first time. "It was not my intention to insult or belittle you."

"You'll have to do a lot worse than that to insult me, Gavril, but you strike me as the type of person who will say what you honestly think. Sometimes honesty is not kind."

"Sometimes honesty gets you into trouble," I blurted, thinking about my situation with Morrow. I realized where my thoughts were heading and clamped my jaw before anything else could spill.

Serein smirked at me. "I know."

Without another word, he turned around and carried on through the walkway. I bit my lip and followed him. That conversation came close to ending badly. I nearly said something I shouldn't have, and I couldn't grasp why. There was something about Serein—something that made me want to talk freely with him. Tell him my troubles and fears. I couldn't say that it was trust, but it was close. So very close.

We neared the end of the glass atrium and walked into a large white-walled room with a heavy silver door. Serein touched the slick surface. A yellow light glowed under his hand, and a dark gray crank creaked to life in a small cavity by the right corner of the door. It rotated around with a smooth whir. The door rose like a sluice gate in a canal, but instead of water spilling out, bright flashing lights of every color flooded around us. Serein grinned at me before entering the new room.

Taps, hums, and beeps drifted out of the entrance, striking my curiosity, but also tickling my apprehension. People were inside. Muffled chatter and the occasional laugh confirmed that.

Paramount people.

What would they think of me—a provincial girl accused of the most heretical crime? Would I be subjected to the same jeers and hisses I garnered in Envie? Suddenly, the prospect of the open world seemed less inviting. Was I ready for this . . . *adventure?*

"You may enter, Gavril," Serein called from the daunting space. "Something wrong?"

"N-n-no," I managed, attempting to gather myself. I took in a few short breaths before continuing. "I don't want to intrude."

Serein's deep chuckle teased my ears. "Trust me, until the Solenoid gets loaded on board, there's nothing to intrude upon. We're idle for now."

I steeled myself and stepped slowly toward the blinking room. I stopped in the entryway. One deep inhale, and I passed the threshold.

Pictures and words flashed over shaded metallic screens lining the high-ceilinged room. Two curved rows of consoles sat in the room flanking a central strip of polished black marble. People in beige coats and breeches sat at the consoles tapping on the screens, writing with colorful feathers, and some even talking to each other about the images projected. Beyond the console rows, silver railings ran from the walls to the marble walkway, which descended into a small set of steps to a lower-tiered deck. Towering glass panes surrounded the front half of the room and curved around the ceiling to create a dome. Through the windows, I could see all of Envie.

Serein stood on the black walkway. He motioned for me to approach. I buried my fingers into my skirt and looked around before complying. The farther in the room I stepped, the more the lower tier came into view. A large crescent moon-shaped console sat isolated from the rest in the center. Two control columns and several levers and buttons adorned the raised control panel. In the curve of the device, a leather chair was pushed back into a reclining position with a large mass of blankets and wool resting in the seat.

"You're still toting around that peasant seigneur's burden," a voice noted with a thick air. Bibiane glanced up at Serein from her vigile with a disapproving frown.

"She is not a burden," Serein said. "This is the expectation. My help was requested, so I shall give it."

"You are far too generous, Commandant," Bibiane said. "And far too lenient. You shouldn't be playing personal guard to a common dissenter like this—"

"That's enough, Bibiane." Serein sighed wearily. "We've already been through this. I made my choice. If you don't like it, you are more than welcome to leave for Éthéré Coeur on your own."

"On my own? But that would mean—"

"Walking? Yes, it would. You could ask the seigneur to borrow his automatram. That would be a journey to forget."

"I'd rather hang on to the induction lines," Bibiane spat in distain. "I'm not trying to be difficult—"

"Well, you've certainly made that very clear," Serein quipped. "I've had enough of this. I'm not going to change my mind, Bibiane. You'll have to suffer my terrible decision. Try to do so silently."

Bibiane clenched her teeth and grumbled something to herself before whipping out the vigile. For a second, I thought she might throw it at Serein. She wheeled around on her heel and stomped to the nearest window.

"Now that was a good bit of entertainment."

I turned toward the strangely accented voice at the front of the room. It originated from the lower deck near the lonely console.

The mound of blankets in the large seat stirred.

"I'm surprised you were awake to enjoy it, Deryn," Serein said to the moving bundle.

"That's the thing, isn't it?" the mound replied. "Can't sleep through Bibiane's blustering." The blankets shifted, and a ball of shoulder length blonde spikes popped out. A hand came up and pushed some of the strands away to reveal a set of dazzling celeste eyes and a youthful pixie face.

"I heard that, you little monster," Bibiane barked from across the room.

"And I can't hear nothing anymore," Deryn replied, sticking a finger in her ear. She rotated it a few times before pulling the digit free and flicking a piece of earwax to the floor.

"Ugh. Can you not do that in the opérateur deck? Filthy creature." Bibiane scrunched up her nose and scowled at the young woman.

"Where the frizz else am I supposed to do it, Bibi? I live in the opérateur deck," Deryn pointed out as though she were talking to a fool. "You know what your problem is? Your skirt is too tight. You need someone to loosen it up, right? How about that seigne-prat Serein was going on about? I'll give him a call."

"Don't you dare!" Serein and Bibiane yelled at the same time.

"Well, cow and sheep dung in your shoes, too." Deryn pouted and threw her head back. Her whole body sank back into the chair until she was slouching over the side. "You try to help someone . . ."

She locked her gaze onto my feet and trailed up to my eyes before going back down, her lips pushing in and out with each pass like she was caught between chewing on the inside of her lip and mumbling to herself. A petite, gloved finger pointed at me. "Serein, don't disappoint me by telling me she's with you."

"You'll have to be disappointed, because she's with me," he responded. "Didn't you read Bibiane's report?"

"You mean that rubbish she put on all the viewers when she came back? No. Didn't care to."

Bibiane's face flushed scarlet. "It isn't rubbish you—you—"

The corners of Serein's lips twitched upward, but he immediately straightened his mouth into a thin line before speaking. "I'll give you the abridged version, so you can understand the mission. This is Gavril. She's been accused of conspiring with a Phase, and the seigneur of the town wants her judged by the Suzerain. We are responsible for making sure she arrives in Éthéré Coeur safe and without incident. Was that more interesting for you?"

Deryn's blue eyes moved between Serein and me. "*Safe?* For a dampened?"

A hush swept over the room at a speed faster than the wind howling outside. Every eye raked over me, each burning like hot candle wax on my skin. I pulled my arms to my chest and balled my fists until my fingernails stung my palms.

"She's not dampened," Serein declared loudly. "You have nothing to fear from her. Treat her like you would any other passenger."

"Oh. That's all right, then," Deryn replied with a shrug. She looked back at me. "I'm the top pilot—er—*aérien opérateur* Deryn. Good to have you on board the *Fulgurant*. She's the love of my life, so treat her with respect," she commanded with a stern waggle of her finger.

"I will," I promised quietly, finding it hard to speak in this room of strangers. "I'm Gavril."

"I think you and me're going to be right and tight," Deryn said. "We both like scary things and getting up Bibiane's knickers."

Bibiane's vigile smashed into the back of Deryn's chair, and a loud crack split the air.

My heart leapt and I jumped to the side as the vigile clattered to the floor and bent. All beeping and rustling stopped. A great hush spread over the room that sent a chill up my spine.

The crew hunched down behind their consoles and pretended to disappear.

Deryn pulled the blanket over the top of her head with only her round face peeking out.

Serein's fists clenched. "Now we can't access the Paramount library." His eyes locked on the warped vigile, his gaze dark and his tone hard.

"That's not true, Commandant!" Bibiane scrambled to retrieve the damaged device. "Look, it will still fit," she assured him with wide eyes behind skewed frames. She attempted to jam the vigile into a console slot. It wouldn't slide in. She tried twice more without success.

"It's official," Deryn declared. "It's buggered."

"I didn't think it would bend so easily," Bibiane said, her voice laced with disbelief. She tried to push out the dent.

"And I didn't think you would do something so childish." Serein's voice rose and grew more volatile with each word. "Get those emotions under control."

Bibiane's eyes sharpened. "Childish?" She stabbed a finger at

Deryn. "What do you call her behavior? Maybe you should worry more about getting your crew under control than that little peasant harlot!"

Her glare turned to me, and the room's atmosphere shifted before I could blink.

My skin prickled, thousands of invisible tiny thorns pressing into it. Hot, stifling air singed my lungs. I pushed it out with a quick blow. As I tried to draw another breath, the sensation prickling my arms vined down my throat to my lungs. *I can't breathe!*

"Give it a rest, Serein," Deryn said, completely at ease. "Bibi's sorry. You're going to choke out the crew."

As I struggled for air, I glanced around the room. Every crew member was gasping for air. Bibiane hunched over a console desk, her shoulders jerking.

Serein's gaze darted around the room. He turned to me.

I struggled to hold his stormy gaze, the world blurring and fading fast. *I'm going to faint!*

Serein kept staring at me, and suddenly, the prickling sensation evaporated along with its grip on my lungs. I managed to suck in a deep breath of fresh air—*fresh*. It was cool and crisp and refreshing. Serein was taking deep breaths right along with me, as if he were breathing for me. At the same time, heavy panting filled the room. Shoulders rose up and down evenly, and crew members slowly straightened, the room recovering with me.

I brought my hand to my throat. Was that a Résonateur's power?

Serein turned to Bibiane. "Forgive me," he said quietly to the quaking woman. "I lectured you about controlling your emotions, but I am just as much to blame. And a Résonateur who becomes consumed by his emotions is nothing more than—"

"Hey, is anybody listening up there?" Hervé's voice sounded from Deryn's control panel. *"It's dark and cold out here, and I've only got these two half-wits for company."*

Deryn swiveled around and pushed on the screen, causing it to flash white. "Hervy, Hervy. I've got some bad news. It seems the hatch is malfunctioning down below." She turned and gave me a heavily exaggerated wink. "Guess it'll be three snuggling up for the night. Since you're with the hammer and chisel twins, I recommend tucking your head in your rear if you want to sleep."

The twins' voices crackled through the control panel.

"Do you think that was a direct jab at us?"

"As direct a jab can be."

"Jabbing in the direct direction."

"Directional jab jabbing."

"The only thing that will be happening to anyone's rear is yours getting thrown off the deck if you don't open that hatch right now," Hervé growled.

"Ooh, someone's touchier than normal," Deryn teased. "Here you go, Grumpapa." Deryn pushed a green button, and subtle vibrations rumbled under my feet.

Serein walked down to the lower deck and leaned over Deryn's shoulder closer to the screen. "Were you able to retrieve the Solenoid?"

"It's outside Envie. Ciseau said the little lord lost his head about halfway and he's lying in the road. Lazy cretin," Hervé responded. *"We'll need some cables to finish dragging it in. Lower them down."*

"Understood," Serein acknowledged. "I'm going down to help." He straightened up and looked to Bibiane, who had smoothed out her outfit and recovered her composure spectacularly. It left me with the impression this was not her first experience with Serein's strange power.

"Please, take Gavril to one of the rooms along the sky deck," Serein said.

Bibiane pushed up her glasses. "Those rooms are for people of *importance*," she objected with a stubborn huff.

"Gavril is a person of importance," Serein replied, his words sharp. A tone I recognized when Edgard grew tired of people asking about the Solenoid. "She's going to have an interview with the

Suzerain." He turned and strode out of the opérateur deck.

Uncomfortable without Serein around, I shifted from foot to foot. He was my only guardian, my sole defender against all these accusers. Without him, I was alone with what may as well have been the Paramount Sommet itself.

Bibiane marched up behind Deryn with the authority of a commandant. Without Serein around, she may have thought herself so, and no one brave enough opposed her demands.

She leaned into Deryn's face. "Get this soulever prepped for ascension. As soon as the Solenoid is recovered, we're departing."

Deryn grimaced. "You know, Bibi, I said I couldn't hear nothing earlier, but now I can't smell nothing, neither. Stop putting so much garlic in your food."

"Get to work," Bibiane snarled before honing her gaze in on me. "And you. Keep your hands where I can see them. Let's go." She jerked her head toward the door.

I walked through it without a word.

"Don't have too many laughs without me," Deryn yelled from behind us.

With Bibiane barking directions like an instructor training a dog, the trip through the glass passage lacked the comfort and majesty it held previously. We turned a few corners and finally arrived at a hallway with doors. I almost sighed with relief, but I held back. That small action might have pushed my current overseer over the edge. Bibiane was waiting for an excuse to vilify me. I wouldn't put it past her to mistake a sigh for a death threat.

She bustled in front of me and tore open a door before stepping clear so I could enter without making any physical contact.

As I walked in, my eyes widened and my mouth parted as though a priceless gift were placed in front of me. Never in my life had I seen such a richly decorated room. The fine chestnut tables were thick, glossy, and dark. A chandelier dangled from the ceiling with countless clear, gold, and silver crystals sparkling over every surface. The windows along the far wall stretched end to end, ceiling to floor. A glass door led to the top deck of the soulever. And the bed! A massive cloud of ivory silks and rich chocolate pillows.

"There are clothes in the wardrobe," Bibiane snapped, pointing at the tall piece in the corner. "I highly suggest you change, though you may not know how to wear anything inside." The door slammed, leaving a welcomed echo in place of the purple-clad shrew.

So, this was my room. *My room.* Even just thinking those words gave me a cozy, blissful feeling inside. I jumped on the bed like a giddy child. The silk coverings greeted me with a smooth caress, and I buried my face into a fluffy pillow. This was the life of a patrician. The dream of a peasant. The lie of safety. It felt so light, so comfortable—

Rapt . . . rapt . . . rapt . . .

I rolled over and pushed the pillow against my ears. Even now I could hear it. That rapping from Nostalgie's Solenoid. It was always with me. Following me. Reminding me of where my heart should be.

I opened my eyes and sat up. Heart, how could I be so selfish? While I was up here fawning over a bed and some pillows, my friends and fellow Nostalgians were still in the cold, starving and afraid. My stomach lurched. I didn't deserve such luxury or—

Rapt . . . rapt . . . rapt . . .

I jumped as the sound came again, louder and clearer. I looked toward the deck door.

Morrow's dark eyes peered at me through the glass.

I immediately sprang off the bed and opened the door. "Are you sure you should be here?" I whispered, still wary of prying ears. "I'm so glad you're okay."

"I have been watching you."

"I know." I frowned. "I saw you at Jalousie and . . ." I recalled how seeing her fly around the hull gave me courage. The recurring desire to spend time with her motivated me in a way I hadn't expected.

Why was that?

"That was dangerous, Morrow. Serein could have killed you," I said.

"I am not so easily done away with. He will not be the first to try."

"Well, I don't want him to try. For . . . for either of you," I confessed before I could think about what I was saying or who I was saying it to.

"You don't want the Résonateur to die," Morrow said.

Again. A statement that felt like a question.

"He's not a bad person," I replied. "Serein's been very kind to me, despite the accusations."

"I sensed the anger."

"You mean in the opérateur deck?"

"He hurt you."

"He didn't mean to," I said, aghast. "That's not his true nature. That's the power—"

"That is the nature and the power of a Résonateur," Morrow said. "Emotions are not meant to be contained, yet Résonateurs try. They try to harness that which must be free. Suppression makes emotions dangerous. That man spent so long burying his anger that when it does slip out, it explodes."

A subtle edge underlay her flat tone. A finality, like she didn't want to argue with me further. But I wasn't going to let her win so easily. Serein wasn't like that. He lost his temper. We all did at one time or another. And yes, his anger was different—the gift of manipulating the physical world with emotions made that apparent—but that didn't make him blindingly dangerous or reckless.

"You're wrong, Morrow," I argued. "How would you know anyway? You don't have emotions."

Morrow's body morphed back into a floating fog and retreated to the deck.

"Wait! Morrow!" I reached toward the fog.

She swirled away from the soulever and into the distance.

"I'm sorry," I called, running onto the deck. "Please, wait."

A loud pop suddenly thundered out.

The deck quaked beneath my feet as though it were about to collapse. I stumbled and fell as a series of accelerating pops exploded around me. The sounds came faster and closer together until they transformed into a steady whirring. A flash of bright light blinded me. Then another and another.

Like balls of captured lightening, sparks danced up and down the thick metal cords running between the soulever's fins. They multiplied in a continuous streaking line of brilliant white. The soulever rumbled again. My stomach lurched, and my body buckled underneath me. Wind came from every angle, whipping my hair all around me, blinding me in a curtain of red curls.

"Gavril!" A shout rose above the roar in my ears.

Someone grabbed my shoulders and pulled me back into my room. The wind released me, and I tugged a tangled mass of hair from my face.

A gloved hand gently brushed the last tendrils away.

Gray eyes pierced through me like a javelin of steel, piercing all the way to my—*Oh, heart, please stop beating like that.*

"Gavril, are you hurt?" Serein demanded. "It isn't safe on the sky deck during ascension." His voice softened. "I should have warned you. I'm sorry." He ran a gloved hand through my disheveled hair.

The action surprised me, and I wondered if he realized what he was doing.

"What were you doing out there?" he asked.

I swallowed, my throat surprisingly dry. "I-I saw the lights," I lied. "I wanted to know what it was."

"Massive amounts of *étincelle* energy shooting this star into the sky," Serein answered. "It's highly dangerous when first activated, but it stabilizes in the induction lines and allows us to elevate. There is a siphon engine on each side of the soulever."

"This vessel has siphons on board?" I closed my eyes and listened. A faint hum filled the air, a sound as familiar to me as my heartbeat. Siphons being used to create a flying transport. This was what I was missing out on. This was the technology of the open world.

"Yes, to distribute the power. These siphons are designed to take the étincelle energy from a reservoir instead of a Solenoid," Serein explained. "It's a little different from the automatrams that use energy stored in a recycler engine that continually cycles it. Étincelle energy is not as long-lasting as energy from a Solenoid, which will impact our journey. I wanted to speak with you about that."

"That's why you came now?" I couldn't hide the disappointment in my voice. Of course. It was silly of me to believe he came just to see me.

Serein smiled down at me. "And to make sure Bibiane did what I told her to for once."

I rolled my eyes. "Why do you put up with such a person?" I slapped my hand over my mouth in shock. "I'm sorry. It's not my place—"

"No need to apologize. I'm glad you still have that honesty we talked about earlier. I would be worried if you didn't." He chuckled lightly. "You haven't experienced the best of Bibiane, but she's reliable and one of the highest-rated *archiviste* in the Paramount. Being an archiviste isn't easy, since they must gather, interpret, and control all the information for the Paramount. Unfortunately, she knows that and takes the order and propriety a little too seriously."

"Just a little." I let out a small smile of my own.

"I keep hoping that one day she'll taper her explosive temper."

"Oh?"

"I've been waiting for six years." He smiled and pulled away from me, returning to the window. "Do you want to take a look?"

I followed his lead and scrutinized the darkness beyond the glass.

"You see that speck of light?" Serein pointed to an outlying spot below.

"Yes."

"That's your former home. Envie."

"Envie was never my home." I searched for any other source of light. Nothing, not the slightest glimmer, could be seen. Nostalgie was lost in the darkness.

I forced the gloomy thought away. Nostalgie's hopelessness was a topic best not dwelled on. "You came to speak to me about something?"

"We'll be making a small detour before heading to Éthéré Coeur," Serein replied, returning to business. "Deryn assures me we have enough energy to make the journey, but the last time she said that we nearly plummeted into the Paramount harbor. I told her to head for Remords, so we can replenish the reservoir. I don't want any mishaps on this mission."

"Remords?" I repeated with furrowed eyebrows. I thought back to the maps I studied with Mama. They provided our only view of the eight regions comprising Premier Esprit. Tristesse was where we were, between Colère to the south and Crainte to the northeast. "Remords is on the border between the Tristesse and Crainte regions."

"That's correct," Serein confirmed with a grim frown. "Not the most desirable area, but the closest soulever port. I'd prefer to pass over Crainte with a full energy source. Only the Bassin de la Haine presents a more treacherous path."

My stomach fluttered. I never knew I could be so thrilled to be out in the unprotected world. I was finally on my way. I wondered what Remords was like. Would it resemble Envie or something totally new? It didn't matter. As long as Serein and Morrow were around, I would be okay.

Shouldn't that be Serein or *Morrow?* a snide little voice echoed in my mind. *The two together will never happen. They will always be separate. Always splitting you apart.*

The excitement fluttering in my stomach deadened into a gnawing trepidation. They were enemies. Résonateurs killed Phases, and Phases killed everyone. They would never understand each other, but I understood and was drawn to both. I couldn't choose one over the other.

"The trip will take three days." Serein's explanation broke through my internal torments. "You are free to explore every inch of the *Fulgurant*, if that is your wish. Nothing will be restricted to you, Gavril."

"You don't have to do that for me," I said. I knew better than to be welcomed at any level of this vessel. "I'm a dissenter."

"The Suzerain has yet to make his judgment. As far as I'm concerned, you haven't done a single thing to endanger anyone."

"That's very kind of you. I wish others felt the same, but they won't be as kind as you, Serein." My face burned as I said his name. Hoping he wouldn't detect my embarrassment, I turned away.

Serein cleared his throat. "It's certainly gotten late. I better get back to the opérateur deck." His voice softened. "Have a good night, Gavril. I hope you sleep better in here than you did in the storehouse."

Serein swept out of the room like a fleeting mirage. As the door closed behind him, I collapsed on the bed's sublime surface. The deep timbre of Serein's voice resonated in my ears, and his face seared my vision. To my chagrin, the tingle of his presence lingered all over my body, and my cheeks continued to burn.

I never expected another person could have such a profound impact on me—especially after only just meeting. But Serein was different from the men I grew up with. He was different from everyone.

Tomorrow, I would return to the real world. I would take up my burdens and remember who I was and why I was here. For now, in this instant, I would revel in the sin of *feeling*. I could feel—really feel. Such freedom. Would I ever experience anything so exhilarating again?

AWAKENING OF FEELING

Sunlight streaked through the pristine glass walls and ceiling, banishing my dreams to the night. Never had I slept so well—a real surprise considering I was in such a foreign place. I sat up and stretched my limbs to chase away the sleep and stiffness. My legs slid off the smooth sheets to the cold floor below. I shivered and sprinted to the small door by the wardrobe.

A large washroom containing a porcelain tub with bronze feet, a sink, and a latrine awaited me in the morning sunshine. A small table with a neatly folded white towel and a bar of lavender-colored soap sat beside the tub. I pulled the privacy curtain across the glass wall and set about filling the tub. This was a step up from using a wash basin filled with water boiled on the stove.

Once hot water filled the deep tub, I turned off the faucet and sank into the steaming liquid. I leaned back and let the water work its healing over my muscles and worries. So, this was the phenomenon known as relaxation. It wouldn't bother me in the least to experience it once every day.

I dipped under the surface and soaked my hair. When I resurfaced, I reached for the bar of soap. I rubbed it between my wet hands, building a thick lather. The rich scent of berries filled the room. I inhaled deeply. If one could fill their belly on smell alone . . . I ran the lather through my locks and washed my body.

I must have spent nearly an hour in the tub. I savored it until the water cooled below comfort, and I pulled myself out. I pulled the cork stopper by its silver chain, and brown water swirled down the drain. Years of dirt, sweat, and dead grass flushed away in seconds. A pang of guilt hit me, like I was trying to rend Nostalgie from my flesh. My body was clean, but my heart was still encrusted in Nostalgie's rust.

I dried with the plush towel, returned to the guest room, and opened the wardrobe to reveal a plethora of bright colors and fancy dresses.

I highly suggest you change, though you may not know how to wear anything inside.

Bibiane's voice grated my ears, reminding me I didn't belong here. Letting me know these clothes were made for others—women of fortune and respectable lineage. That wasn't me. I swallowed the lump in my throat. That would never be me.

I slammed the wardrobe closed and retrieved Charmant's dress. It would do fine.

After I dressed, my hand settled on the door handle for several seconds as I worked up the courage to twist it. I opened the door and scanned the hallway. Nobody in sight. The tension in my shoulders eased, and I stepped out.

With no objective for leaving my room, and not knowing my way around the ship, I headed back to the opérateur deck. It was close, and I would likely find Serein there.

I passed through the bright glass walkway and lingered in the entrance, listening for Serein's voice. If he wasn't there, I didn't want to walk in and have to walk back out like a fool.

"Oi, Gavril. Stop haunting that door like a bloody ghost and come in."

I nearly jumped into the doorframe as Deryn's voice barreled out. Did she address me by name? I tiptoed through the threshold and eased my way to the front of the room. The hair on my neck stood up as eyes from every corner grazed over me. But nobody said anything, and for that I was grateful.

"What's the matter? You got paste in your shoes? Come on."

I picked up my pace and walked down to the lower deck. I leaned over the side of the semicircle console so I could see the opérateur. The mass of blankets usually covering Deryn had been discarded on the floor and the chair straightened into an upright position instead of lounging.

Deryn's teal jumpsuit sparkled as vivaciously as the buttons flashing under her command. Zippers, buttons, badges, *medals*—a shining display that ran from neck to knees. She leaned back in the chair and put her hands behind her head.

"Like what you see?" she asked.

"Well, I . . . um . . ."

"Just kidding!" she shouted out before tussling her wild blonde hair. "Don't tell me you're as muck-faced-humor-void as Bibi."

"No, it's not that. It's . . . um . . . I-I, well, I'm Gavril," I driveled on, not sure where to begin or what else to do.

"Yeah, I know." She plucked lint off her clothes. "You told me already, yeah? And Serein told every bugger else. Is that why you came up here? To find Serein? Don't care to get to know the rest of us?"

My cheeks flushed. "I'm sorry?" I didn't know what else to say. I wanted to say that wasn't true, but it was. And I hadn't intended on getting friendly with anyone. My status as prisoner made the effort seem pointless.

"*Pah-ha*, I'm just frizzing with you," Deryn exploded with laughter and slapped her knee. "Go on. Ask me anything."

"So, um," I glanced down at the controls and all the displays of text, maps, and landscapes. It was a visual cyclone. How Deryn managed to make sense of any of it *and* keep the soulever under control while talking amazed me. "So, you operate the entire soulever by yourself?"

"You bet those red curls I do," she gloated. "I tickle this big girl's knobs like no—and I mean *no-frizzing-bugger*—else. Don't get no sleep for it, but that's part of the fun."

"You don't sleep when we're flying?" I asked, alarmed.

"Got nobody that can keep her steady long enough for a good kip," she explained. "I did train a few poor sods to take over while I take a piss."

"That's a start," I commented, a little abashed by her crude revelation.

"How about you?" she offered with a wide grin. "Want to give it a go? Just grab that dinky-bob there," she instructed, pointing to a lever on one of the control columns.

I shot my hands up like I was caught stealing from the food stock. "No, no. Thank you, but no."

"Eh, don't know what you're missing." She slouched back in her chair and kicked her heels up on the control panel.

I glanced at the capricious opérateur before shooting my gaze to the floor. She was *different*—a rich sentiment coming from me. She was also interesting, and her accent—

"You want to ask me something else?" Deryn asked, peering into my eyes.

"You . . . you just . . . you don't sound like you're from here," I stated slowly, not wanting to cause offense. "The way you speak is different."

"Yeah? Well the way you *look* is different," she fired back.

I blanched, not expecting that reaction. But what exactly *was* I expecting?

Deryn's face squiggled up. She kicked her feet, bursting with another loud peal of laughter. "I'm just f-f-frizzing with you," she managed to say between fits of elation. "The look on your face. I could have flown a soulever into your gob. Hearts on hearts, that was good."

The corners of my mouth inched up. The sight of her so amused was infectious.

"Hang on, hang on. Let me get myself sorted," she said, fanning her red face. "I'm not from Premier Esprit. I come from some grassy little isles off to the east called Heortefeld. I was sent to Éthéré Coeur when I was younger and ended up as opérateur for this charming lady. All works out, don't it?"

"Yes, I suppose it does." And how true that sentiment was. I began my adventure intending to be married off in Envie, and now I was on my way to the Paramount. It may not have been what I had planned, but at least my horrible engagement was on hold.

"*Psst.* This is the part where you tell me something about you," Deryn whispered and she leaned toward me, cupping her ear.

"Oh, okay, I . . . uh . . ." I struggled for a moment, trying to come up with something interesting. It saddened me how hard it was. "Um, you said I didn't look like everyone else. That's because my father is from—"

"Fu'aad. Big deserty land way off west across the sea," she guessed.

I raised my eyebrows. "How did you—"

"Been there before. You've got those eyes like sweet honey. Lovely."

"You've been to Fu'aad? What's it like? Did you like it?" I quizzed out of unexpected interest.

It was different from Mama's stories. She only knew what Papa told her, but Deryn had been there in person. She'd seen it with her own eyes. Maybe she even interacted with the Fu'aad people. Maybe I could learn more about my ancestry through her. It was the closest I would come to being in Papa's homeland.

"Well, I mostly stayed on the soulever, so I couldn't tell you nothing about the culture and shite that nobody cares about. But I did get some grand views of the cliffs and gorges. It even has some water holes and lakes and rivers. Oh! And a gorgeous oasis."

My shoulders slumped. "That's great," I said. I didn't want Deryn to see my disappointment. She was already doing me a kindness just by talking to me. I didn't want her to think I was ungrateful or offend her. If I did, she might treat me like the prisoner I was. "That's really insightful. Thank you."

"No, it's not," she replied. "But keep lying so you'll get better at it. You're worse than rubbish."

"I'm not ly—"

"Keep your eyes on the sky, Birdy," Hervé's voice drawled from the top of the steps. "I don't want to walk on the ceiling again. You know how distressing it is to have glass crack under your feet over a mountain?" A loud yawn followed the question.

"Hervy, so proper of you to check on me. Did thinking about my body controlling this beast rouse you from sleep?" Deryn teased.

"It did." Hervé nodded, scratching his stubble. "I've never had a nightmare so vivid. I've still got a cold sweat running down my back."

"That's going to stink something awful." Deryn scrunched up her nose and wafted her hand around. "Worse than my knickers after a five-day flight."

"Nothing's worse than that," Hervé declared grimly. "You practically have to sleep outside."

"Only if you breathe through your nose, Hervy," Deryn chuckled. "Now get your face out of my knickers."

"That is one place my face will never be," he mumbled. "If you don't mind keeping your face on the screens, I'll be taking my leave to scrub this conversation and all its mental images from my mind. I forgot why I even came down here." The older man gave his head a good shake and sauntered out of the opérateur deck.

"Guess that means I better get back to keeping us safe and alive. Good chat, Gavril," she said with a cheerful grin. "Come back and see me. I get a little forgotten up here. Poor shape for the chief opérateur."

"It was nice getting to know you, Deryn. Thank you for treating me like everyone else." I smiled back at her, truly grateful for the kindness she showed me. It was nice to be reminded that I was still a person, even one that was soon to be thrown like diseased cattle to the highest order of the world.

I left the control room and wandered through the glass corridor, eventually turning down another hallway. At the end, sunlight poured in through a glass door to the sky deck. As soon as I opened the door, a blast of air hit me like a wall of ice. I tucked my arms around my chest and pushed on to the outside. I approached the railing and looked down. Clouds rolled below the soulever like a sea of cotton.

"You'd be warmer if you changed into some of those clothes in your room."

I turned to Serein walking along the deck. He approached me, unbuttoning his greatcoat and sliding it off.

"Oh, no—"

Before I could finish, he set it over my shoulders. In an instant, my face could've melted a glacier. The coat felt heavy, and not just from its thick fabric. I had no business wearing it.

"Thank you, Serein," I said bashfully.

"Why didn't you change? Did you not like any of the garments?" Serein asked, looking out with me.

"It's not that," I replied quickly, not wanting him to think me unappreciative. "I just . . . I didn't find anything that suited me."

Serein sighed. "Bibiane said something, didn't she?"

"N-no," I lied. "Nothing felt right for me."

"I get it. I'll let it drop," he said. "But as soon as we get to Remords, I want you to buy something you like using my argent, because believe it or not, that dress is not good enough for you."

"It's the most expensive thing I've ever worn," I informed him, straight-faced and unashamed. I knew my circumstances, and I wouldn't let people like Bibiane make me think less of myself.

"I've offended you," Serein said before looking at me. "I apologize for my lack of tact."

"It's not you," I told him in earnest. "The people here . . . they don't understand what it's like to live trapped inside your own home with no possessions. Even if I wore the finest dress in Éthéré Coeur, it still wouldn't change who I am. It would just be a façade. An act. Like those pretenders in Envie."

"You're right, Gavril, but you're also very wrong. It's true we don't know what it's like living out here with the barest of essentials. But it's not true that wearing something outside of rags would make you anything but what you are. It's the person inside that makes you who you are." His eyes gleamed with something I couldn't place, and its brilliance burned into my soul. "It's not the clothes or the argent or the titles. It's the heart birthing our emotions that makes us who we are. You are only a pretender if you lie to your own feelings."

"But sometimes lying to yourself is the only way to make it through the day."

"You're not in Envie anymore. You don't have to close off your heart."

His words opened something then—a door I'd kept shut for years. I clasped my hands to my chest. My lips quivered, and I struggled to keep tears from pouring down my cheeks. I'd spent my whole life suppressing my emotions, struggling day by day to find a way to live and find peace. It was life. A meaningless, empty existence that I clung to because there was nothing else out there for me. Emotions were nothing more than useless burdens, tricking my mind with fantasies.

Then Serein came. He talked about emotions with such passion, like they were the most important part of a person's life. I ignored that part of me for so long.

An image came to me. Mama's face with a winning smile on her lips as she danced around the house in victory. *You can't keep living like a corpse, Gavril. Happiness, excitement, love–you need these things. There's no greater adventure than love.*

I brought a hand up to wipe my eyes and smiled. I suppose Mama was right about some things.

"Your mood softened," Serein said.

I cleared my throat. "You can tell?"

"I can," he replied.

"I'm sorry if I seem ignorant. I don't know a lot about Résonateurs."

"You told me your father was a Résonateur. Did he live in Nostalgie long?" Serein asked.

"No, he was only with us a few years before he left for the Paramount to pay the service," I replied. "About a month after he left, a new Solenoid was brought in by messengers from Éthéré Coeur. They said that the Solenoid had been gifted to us from a Résonateur's service."

"And you need a new one so soon?"

"Edgard thinks the siphon may have been pulling too much energy from it. Whatever the case, we need a new one, and Papa isn't around to appeal for it. It's up to me to make sure Nostalgie is protected." I clenched my fists until my fingernails dug into my palms and fixed my gaze on the clouds in the distance. I was the last hope.

Serein placed his hand on my shoulder, and when I turned, he met my eyes. "That's very brave of you, Gavril. I don't know many people who would be willing to make the same sacrifices. But there's more to life than Nostalgie. Have you ever thought about moving to Éthéré Coeur?"

"What would be the point? I never thought I would leave the barrier to go to Envie." I would not spare a moment to entertain such an impossible thought. "I can't afford to travel, and I'm definitely not a Résonateur. There's nothing I can do."

"What makes a Résonateur?" he asked, still peering into my soul. "People talk of blood and chance and nobility, but that's not all there is to it. Your *heart*," he stressed. "A heart filled with an incredible feeling that affects you like no other. All it takes is one."

"You make it sound like anyone can become a Résonateur." I gave him a skeptical glance. "I thought Résonateurs had to keep their emotions under control. Feeling too much is dangerous."

"There's a difference between maintaining control and feeling nothing," Serein said. "The truth is we feel more deeply than anyone can imagine. Sometimes it's hard not to be consumed by those feelings, but I do feel controlling them is the secret to being a Résonateur. All you have to do is dig deep enough."

I smiled sadly. "That's a wonderful thought, Serein, but it just doesn't work that way. Some people are born with the gift, and some people are born with their whole lives planned out for them. Not everyone can be strong and fortunate. There has to be weakness for there to be strength. And I am one of the weak ones."

"You are anything but," Serein replied with a defiant tone. "I wish you could see it like I do."

"The only thing I see, Serein, is the shadow of a titan coming to crush me. I am a speck of dirt at his feet. It will be a miracle if I convince the Suzerain of my innocence, let alone to provide us with a new Solenoid."

"Desperation is a consuming emotion, Gavril. You are too strong to fall into it. Don't let it be your only weapon. You will find a way if you have the courage." Serein pulled his hand from my shoulder and turned away from me. "Have you ever heard the legend of the first Résonateur?"

I shook my head. "No, I've never—"

"Such drama," a voice breathed.

"Such passion," an identical voice followed with. We turned around to face the twins, Ciseau and Marteau.

"You better be careful, Commandant," Ciseau warned with a waggle of his finger. "This little heretic may lead you astray."

"And we can't have that," Marteau concurred.

"No, we certainly can't. It would be a travesty."

"A tragedy."

"A triviality."

"A—a—a truancy!"

Ciseau wacked his brother over the head. "You just made that up!"

"I didn't," Marteau defended, swinging his arm out. "I just didn't use it correctly."

"I'm glad to see you two are well rested after your afternoon of hard labor," Serein said with a shake of his head.

"The hardest part was before the last stretch," Ciseau remarked.

"It would have been easier if it wasn't just the two of us," Marteau complained, shooting a glare at his brother.

"The little prince wasn't much help to begin with. He was definitely dead weight at the end," Ciseau claimed.

"I appreciate your service," Serein broke in before the pair could get heated again. "Is there anything you need?"

"Oh-ho! You see there, brother? He's already trying to get rid of us," Marteau exclaimed with an appalled gasp.

"Wants to be alone with the girl, I bet," Ciseau accused and gave Serein a sidelong glance. "He's falling under her spell."

"He's spell fallen."

"He's fallen."

"Will you two shut up for once in your life," a razor-edged voice slashed through the air.

Bibiane marched up to the twins with the same air of self-importance she always carried, yet somehow seemed incomplete without the little vigile in hand.

"Stop harassing the commandant. I need him to make a thorough inspection of the Solenoid," she informed us with a stiff nod.

"What's the point of doing it now?" Serein debated. "We can't log the data into the library."

"Protocol dictates that a detailed inspection must be performed as soon as possible regardless of communication issues," Bibiane explained, pushing up her glasses. "As for the log, we'll have to do it the old-fashioned way."

"How's that?"

"With ink and paper," she stated, her face as humorless as ever.

Serein looked like he'd rather jump over the railing. "Bibiane, that will take all day."

The archiviste smiled darkly. "We'd best get started then, hadn't we?" Her gaze zipped over to me, icier than the wind. "Once you've recovered your uniform, Commandant."

Despite the warmth of Serein's greatcoat, my flesh prickled. I looked around at the eyes staring at me. Ciseau and Marteau smirked.

"She definitely found something better to wear," Marteau said.

I quickly slid the coat off my shoulders and held it out for Serein, trying to not let the tail drag on the deck. Serein opened his mouth as if he was going to protest but closed it again and took his garment from me.

Bibiane strutted to the glass door leading back into the cabin and held it open. She gestured for Serein to enter ahead of her.

Serein took a deep breath and gave me a weary nod. "I will see you again eventually, Gavril. Please, keep me in your thoughts." He trudged through the entrance.

Bibiane glanced back at me with a satisfied smirk and then followed him.

Though I'd lost the warmth of the coat, fire burned beneath my skin. I shouldn't have let Bibiane bother me. I had no right to wear a Résonateur's—a commandant's—greatcoat, but that superior look on Bibiane's face . . .

A strong jerk on my hair pulled me back to the sky deck. I twirled around, ready to deliver a scolding. Ciseau stood in front of me so close that I could feel the heat from his body. I stepped back and bumped into something soft. Another body.

Marteau leaned over my shoulder. "Lost in thought?" he asked with a knowing grin.

"Lost in Serein's lurid gaze," Ciseau breathed with a dreamy flutter of his eyelids.

"Maybe she should get lost in mine," Marteau suggested, snickering.

"Maybe she should get lost."

Diving to my right, I slid out from between them and hit the railing. I pushed myself against it in a defensive stance, the cold bar digging into my lower back as I bent my knees, ready to bolt.

"What do you want?" I asked, inching my way along the railing away from the twins. They stalked after me.

"Nothing." Ciseau held up his arms in surrender. "It was just a jest."

Marteau slapped his knee and hunched over with intense chortling. "*Just a jest*. A jest of just."

"We meant no harm," Ciseau shouted over his brother's humor. "It's some fun. A little bit of frivol and drivel."

"I don't like this type of fun," I snapped. "Go bother someone else."

Marteau stopped laughing and gave me a crestfallen frown. "Oh, dear, we've done it now," he mumbled to Ciseau. "We pushed it too far."

"Forgive us." Ciseau dipped into a low bow. "We never meant to upset you. We just wanted to be friends."

Surprised, I uncoiled from my protective shell. "I . . . I'm not sure . . ."

"No, no, it's fine," Marteau bemoaned. "You hate us. We get it."

"I didn't mean—"

"And I thought she was different than Bibiane." Ciseau gave his brother a sneaky glance. "Like two snakes in a rat nest."

"Two cats in a mouse house."

"Two dogs in a cat house."

Marteau sniggered and nudged his brother. "Two men in

a cathouse."

"I'm not like Bibiane," I argued, holding my stomach like I'd been mortally wounded. Definitely pride-struck. "I could never be like that."

"She says now that she's done ravaging our emotions and insulting our persons." Marteau stuck up his nose in a huff. "I won't have it."

"Well, I won't stand for it," Ciseau proclaimed. "Let's take our leave, brother. The commandant's no longer in danger from this heretic. We have a wig to fluff."

"And some shoes to buff."

"A stain to snuff."

The two snickered and jaunted back to the door, leaving me alone with a disturbed knot in my stomach. Those two were . . . *unusual*. They enjoyed joking and laughing, but there was definitely something dark about their humor. They loved getting a rise out of people, Ciseau in particular.

I looked through the door at the polished floors and bright lights. Everyone on the soulever seemed a little unusual. Their actions always came as a surprise. Nobody seemed familiar, yet the feeling they gave me was in a way, as though I were still in Envie. An outsider. An intruder. But given my status as a criminal awaiting trial, I suppose it couldn't be any other way.

"You are very muddled at the moment."

I snapped my head up and spun around to smile at Morrow as she glided over the deck toward me like mist over water. She'd never know how glad I was to see her after the way our last conversation ended. I feared she would have left me for good.

It still seemed strange. To have such attachment to a creature I was supposed to fear and despise. But she was unlike everyone else. The only other being who reminded me of belonging.

"This is a foreign place to me," I told her. "I'm not used to these people or their ways."

"It is best to stay that way."

"I don't know, Morrow. Some of them can be unpleasant and even rude, but not all of them. I might like to see what people from the Paramount are like. Aren't you curious?"

"No. I am not."

I frowned at the abstruse phantom. "But you'll travel there with me, won't you?" I asked hopefully. Even if the Paramount held nothing for her, I wanted my friend by my side. I needed all the support I could find.

"I will go as far as I am able."

"I can't ask for more than that."

Morrow floated over to the railing and sat on it, facing the horizon. "Have you ever been to the Paramount, Morrow?"

She didn't immediately answer, seemingly lost in the view. "Yes."

"You have?" I exclaimed. "Can you tell me about Éthéré Coeur?"

"No."

"Why not?" I stared at her back, wishing she would turn around. "I'd like to know—"

"I have never been to Éthéré Coeur."

"But you said—"

Morrow's head suddenly rotated completely around to stare at me. Startled, I bit my tongue, but hardly noticed the pain.

"The apex is not above."

"I-I don't know what you mean," I whispered when I finally regained control over my speech.

"I must go."

"No. Don't," I pleaded, stepping closer to her.

Morrow's head spun away from me to face the horizon again.

"Why do you always leave like this? Please, stay with me for a while."

"I must go. For you."

With a shimmering flicker, she dove into the clouds and vanished in a sea of white.

I put my hand over my heart and watched the tufts float by and change shape. What a gift it must be to change so easily. To be free and without cares or worries—or any emotion—to ensnare and twist your heart.

I sighed deeply and slipped through the deck door into the glass corridor.

Navigating the soulever without a guide proved even limited spaces could offer impossible challenges. Hallways with doors, doors behind doors, and hallways behind those doors created a confusing maze. Near the base of the soulever, a loud roaring led me to an intimidating door with a massive lock and steel plating, but I was too timid to investigate inside.

After that little venture, I felt it best to return to my room. As far as I knew, Serein was still busy with the Solenoid. I didn't want to disturb him, but I didn't know what else I could do without him—or if I could even find him in this labyrinth.

He and Morrow had more important things to do than be my caretaker.

"Have you satisfied your ego yet, Bibiane?" Hervé's low voice rumbled around the corner.

I pushed myself against the wall and closed my mouth. I looked down at the floor and saw the pair's blurry images reflected on the glossy surface. It was wrong to eavesdrop, but if it was between that and making my presence known to Bibiane . . .

"It's not a matter of ego," Bibiane clipped back. "It's a matter of protocol, Hervé. You should understand."

"Seems to me it's a matter of you getting revenge for that petty little opinion of yours being ignored," Hervé answered coolly.

"It isn't petty," she seethed. "Why am I the only one who can see how ridiculous and improper this whole arrangement is? That heretic should be chained up and transported at the expense of the Seigneur de l'Envie. Not living it up on a commandant's soulever."

"What's the big fuss?" Hervé dismissed. "She seems pretty harmless to me. I think you might be a little jealous of the attention she's garnered from the commandant."

Bibiane huffed and her reflection's arm slung out before something hit the wall. "I don't understand why he can't see reason. You should talk to him, Hervé. He'll listen to you."

Hervé chuckled half-heartedly. "Why would it be any different coming from me?" he asked dubiously. "I'm an ordinary man, no different from anyone else."

"Don't play the fool with me," Bibiane snapped. "You know that's not true. You—"

"It is true!" Hervé barked.

I jumped at the unexpected spike in volume. The furious rustle of cloth followed. I squinted at the reflection. Hervé held his shirt open.

"You see," Hervé said in a much lower voice. "There is nothing special. It's gone."

"It's not gone," Bibiane replied. "Things like that don't just disappear. They merely—get misplaced. It's still inside, Hervé. You just have to find it."

"I can't, Bibiane," Hervé replied, voice resigned. "I just can't. After what happened with *him*. . . I've lost touch with myself. No matter how hard I try, I can't make the connection."

Cloth rubbed together, swishing as Hervé tucked his shirt back into place.

"If I can help Serein, that's good enough. He's a fine commandant and a noble man. Better than the Suzerain deserves."

"Don't say that," Bibiane hissed. "The Suzerain is the pinnacle of life. The very heart of the world!"

"Woe be upon me for speaking ill of his divine," Hervé snorted. "Some lands seem to get on fine without him."

"Dissenters and savages," Bibiane stated with a sniff. "Traitors to law established thousands of years ago. Who are they to defy the hand that protects all—the heart that surges with the greatest power? They reject the Solenoids and the safety and order the Paramount offers. Why, they are no better than the dampened or those rogue Résonateurs who—"

"People are not dampened by choice." Hervé silenced Bibiane's rant. "There's a difference between willful dissension and having it forced upon you. Don't compare those unfortunate people to a *Fluctuateur* who gleefully abandons his cause," he finished bitterly.

"It makes no difference how one came to dissent. The point is they must be quashed for the good of us all," Bibiane declared, unsympathetic, it seemed, to anyone's plight.

"Don't ever let anyone accuse you of being a soft woman," Hervé said, following my train of thought.

"I don't have time to be soft, Hervé," she told him harshly. "I only have time for regulation."

"Then don't get so uptight when no one asks for your opinion on a matter," Hervé responded. "Because they already know what rigid-backed law you're going to spout."

Bibiane's heels clicked furiously as she walked farther down the hall.

"Say what you want," she shouted down the corridor. "But in the end, I'm the one who will be laughing when that little sweet peach goes sour."

Hervé grumbled something I couldn't make out before his own shoes tapped on the wooden surface—straight around the corner and into me. My eyes widened, and I pushed against the wall while I stuttered, trying to come up with an excuse. But Hervé's dull green eyes didn't even look my way as he passed.

I stilled my flapping lips and watched him leave in silence. Did he not notice me? I frowned. Obviously, he noticed me. He didn't want to acknowledge a heretic—one of those dissenters Bibiane disparaged.

I stayed for a few minutes before rounding the corner and following the hall Bibiane disappeared down. I kept working my way up until I finally returned to the glass corridor. Stars twinkled at me through the glass shield. Had I spent that much time wandering the soulever?

I gathered my senses and headed back to my room. Serein had yet to make an appearance, so he must've still been busy with something— even without Bibiane. I had to stop seeking him out. He had duties more important than spending every waking moment by my side.

I entered my room and sat on the bed. I wished Mama could be here. She would love being on a soulever, so venturous and free. But she would never leave Nostalgie as long as there was the slightest chance that Papa would return.

I leaned back onto the bed. Papa. He could be in Éthéré Coeur. All Résonateurs had to return to the Paramount at some point in time. Would he recognize me? Would I recognize *him?* And what would he think when he found out his daughter had befriended a Phase?

He would probably never want anything to do with me again. Mama would have to choose between us. *She'll choose him.*

I rolled over and closed my eyes. Who would choose me? *As soon as we arrive in Éthéré Coeur, Serein will no longer have a reason to stay with me.* The thought slithered out from the darkest reaches of my mind. He would move on to other duties, and I would be damned to punishment as a Phase sympathizer or married to Cyril.

I couldn't say which fate was worse. To finally taste freedom, only to have it snatched away—that was the greatest punishment they could administer. My heart—that had just learned to really *feel*—would have to be stone once more.

NUMB

I stared at the white curtains dangling against the backdrop of deep black outside the window. Every so often, the soft material would shift, swaying with the motions of the soulever. It drifted like the long coat train of a person walking away.

Papa told me he wouldn't be gone long. He told me he would solve our problems. He would keep Mama and me safe. He promised me he would take care of Nostalgie always.

Where was he now?

Rapt . . . rapt . . . rapt . . .

I sat up and looked at the wooden door. The soft taps were barely audible, almost lost in the hum of siphons. So quiet I could have imagined them. Figments of the dying Solenoid that never left my mind no matter how far from Nostalgie I traveled, reminding me of the duty I inherited.

I went to the door and touched the handle, not sure what I would find beyond. A ghost conjured from my tired mind? The mother who sent me away? The father who never returned? Or something more sinister? The hordes of Envie come to drag me back to my cage . . .

I pushed the door open to a figure shrouded in ivory and with a presence that eased the burden cracking my bones.

"Serein," I gasped.

"I'm sorry for disturbing you," he replied quickly. "I shouldn't be knocking on your door so late." He folded his arms behind his back and cleared his throat, like he'd been caught tinkering with a panel that could set the hub on fire. "I wasn't sure you'd still be awake. I don't know why I didn't wait until morning."

"I'm glad to see you." I smiled.

"I wanted to apologize for leaving you like that earlier. When Bibiane gets her mind set, it's best to get it over with so she can move on to harass someone else." Serein rolled his eyes.

"No, no, it's fine," I answered, mortified that he felt sorry. "I know you have important duties. You don't have to waste your time with me if it's an inconvenience."

"You could never be an inconvenience to me." He looked into my eyes, his gaze as striking as the étincelle running along the cords outside. "I take your safety personally. That is part of my duty. I promise I will get you to Éthéré Coeur."

I lowered my eyes, chest burning from the intensity of Serein's entire being. It emitted from his eyes, colored his every word, and surrounded his presence like a halo of positive energy. "You've already done so much for me. I can't ask any more of you, Serein."

"You don't have to ask," he said. "I'm doing it because I want to."

I shook my head. "But I'm not worth . . . I'm not anyone of importance."

A gentle hand rested on my shoulder, a touch as smooth and delicate as silk. I looked up at Serein.

"Would you care to look at the stars with me, Gavril? I know you must be tired, but I promise it won't take long."

"I'd like that very much, Serein." Even if I had been falling over with my eyelids sagging like sandbags, I would never turn down his request. Doing so felt like heresy, and I already attained the ire of a seigneur.

Serein grinned and offered me his arm. I gingerly slipped my arm around his. The fabric of his coat pressed against my skin. So few had the opportunity to touch the cloth of a Résonateur's uniform, and here I was, indulging in it once again. If fate ultimately tied me to Cyril, I would be sure to share with Charmant on a daily basis all the exquisite details of how its warmth was willingly shared with me. Maybe her envy could give me the strength to carry on living.

"You seem tense, Gavril," Serein commented. "Are you upset I disturbed you?"

"No," I replied swiftly. Nothing could be further from the truth. "I'm just thinking about the future. About survival."

"And what is survival to you?"

"My life. Being able to breath in fresh air and look at another sunrise." I looked up at him. "What else could there be?"

Serein shook his head. "I've never known someone who could find so much in so little."

My stomach tightened. "I-I know. I-it doesn't—"

"That's not an insult, Gavril." He let out a deep breath. "It's quite the opposite, in fact."

The walls around us opened to the glass atrium. Stars twinkled above. "Like diamonds," people always said. I'd never seen a diamond, but I knew it couldn't sparkle alone. It had no glow of its own. A diamond was as lifeless as a star was unobtainable. I clasped my arms close to my body.

"I could never see the stars growing up," Serein said. "There were always too many city lights washing their glow away."

"The stars *were* my lights," I replied. "And the fireflies in the grass."

"You appreciate life," Serein said. "That's more than I can say for anybody back home. Definitely more than anyone in the Paramount."

"You appreciate life, Serein."

"What makes you say that?"

"You put your life in danger for others. You've chosen a life of protecting instead of protection like all Résonateurs. Only a person who understands the value of life could make such a sacrifice."

Serein gazed at the stars. "You have far too kind a view of Résonateurs."

He thought I was romanticizing his service. I looked away, my cheeks warm. A white face peered at me from outside the glass on the other side of the corridor. Morrow tilted her head, sable eyes drifting to Serein's back. My gaze quivered left and right before finally stilling on Serein.

He turned to me and studied my face. "Gavril, what's wrong? You seem startled."

"Phase." The word tumbled out before I could think, as though the truth were drawn out by the power of Serein's gravity.

Serein's eyebrows creased. "What about Phases?"

I crushed the urge to look at Morrow. I couldn't let him see her. If he did, there would be a confrontation, a fight to the death. I couldn't lose, and I couldn't choose.

"You have to be very brave to face Phases," I stated.

"You do," Serein agreed. "But to be honest, encounters with Phases aren't as common as the Paramount would have you believe. We usually can't find them until they are ready to make themselves known. In nine years as a Résonateur, I've only seen six." He lowered his face closer to mine and whispered, "I only killed one of them."

"Did the others escape?"

"No, they were killed by more experienced Résonateurs." He frowned. "That was a long time ago. I don't need to depend on anyone now."

Once again, my mouth moved of its own accord. "You can depend on me."

Serein nodded. "I'm sure I can, but you've got enough people pulling you underwater." He straightened and pulled away from me.

"The burden of obtaining a Solenoid is not a light one."

I brought my hands to my chest and clasped them over my heart. "Do you really believe I can do it, Serein?"

"I believe you can do anything you put your heart into," he replied. "Maybe even kill a Phase."

I slowly turned my head to look out the windows. Nothing but night.

"I don't want to kill a Phase," I said softly.

"Sometimes you have no choice."

I turned back to him and asked, "Has anyone ever tried another way?"

Serein crossed his arms and set his gray eyes on me, a storm brewing beneath the surface. "Did you try, Gavril?"

A lump caught in my throat. It wedged like a ball of sand, and the harder I tried to swallow it, the drier my mouth became. "Phases can't talk," I uttered through the drought.

"No, they can't," Serein replied firmly. "They can't speak. They don't listen to pleas or reason. They don't show remorse for those they kill. They are the reason for the barriers. They are as beasts."

"As beasts," I repeated. "But what are they really?"

"No one knows," Serein replied, voice stiff. "But we do know they are a plague. One that leaves behind a dreadful disease in its wake." He looked back up at the stars. "It's time I returned you to your room," he said. "It's gotten very late."

He wasn't looking at me, but I nodded, tongue still parched and unable to curl around a single syllable. His entire demeanor had changed in less than a second, the air around us now as dense as steam. I knew better, but I couldn't keep my opinions to myself. People didn't want to talk about Phases. They didn't want to argue with a person trying to defend them. Especially Serein, whose duty was to kill them. I sought to brag to Charmant too soon.

Serein led me back down the corridor, opened the door to my

room, and stepped aside. I swiftly walked past him with my head low.

"Phases aren't people, Gavril," he muttered. "Nothing good comes from the heartless." He closed the door.

I clenched my fists and leaned back against the cool wooden door. Heart, what had I done? I took a perfectly pleasant conversation and turned it into . . . into . . .

An admission of guilt.

He had to know now. There was no way he couldn't. What sort of person said those kinds of things about Phases? Those phantoms hunted us and kept us trapped in barriers.

I brought my hands up to cover my face. It was over. The Suzerain was going to make an example of me.

Nostalgie was never going to get a Solenoid.

Rapt . . . rapt . . . rapt . . .

I slowly lowered my hands. Morrow's face floated outside the sky deck door, her white fist resting against the glass. In spite of everything, my lips curved into a small smile. I rushed to the door and opened it. Immediately, the cold night air bit at my flesh. Frigid wind whipped at me, but I pushed onward. She was worth the pain.

"You've got to stop getting so close to Serein. He's going to see you," I told her.

"Résonateurs cannot sense my presence because I have no emotions. He is blind to me."

"I should be glad for that," I replied. "Have you been watching him?"

Morrow's white limbs formed from whirling black, and she settled on the deck. "I have been observing him when he is with you. If his anger rises again, I will kill him."

Ice filled my chest. Kill *Serein?*

"You can't do that," I whispered. To think that she could say it so easily. Like she hadn't even spared a second thought to the brutal action. "Please, Morrow, leave him be. Promise me."

The Phase's dark eyes stayed on me. They peeled away my flesh and stared straight into my soul. The experience should have been unsettling, but instead it filled me with hope. She was listening.

"Promises are meaningless to those without hearts." She slowly blinked and turned her face away. "But I will refrain from taking his life for now."

I smiled and stepped closer to my friend. Without looking back at me, she glided over to the railing. She stared into the darkness surrounding us. Her shimmering body twinkled, a glow all its own.

I gradually approached until I stood next to her, but her eyes remained fixed ahead.

"You shouldn't get so close."

"I trust you," I replied. I waited, but she didn't reply. I flexed my fingers against the numbness overtaking them. How did Morrow's fingers feel? "Have you killed many people?"

"Yes."

"Do you regret it?"

Morrow's face finally turned back to me. She was so close. Almost as close as when we first met.

"I do not feel regret."

I balled my fists but couldn't feel the tips of my fingers as they pressed into my palms.

"Did you think about killing me?"

Morrow's lips parted. They closed back. She tilted her head and studied me.

"No," she finally uttered.

"Why?"

"You remind me of a memory."

I placed my hand on the railing next to her and leaned closer. I couldn't feel anything. My skin was numb. "You have memories, Morrow?"

"That is all I have had for millennia. I have seen many things.

Cities rise and fall. *His* rise and fall."

"His?"

The Phase took several steps back and her body transformed back into a cloud. I didn't reach out or try to call for her. It wouldn't make a difference. For Morrow, the conversation was over.

I stayed on the sky deck for several minutes after she departed. I finally returned to my room, my body as unfeeling as my heart had once been. Not a single sensation teased my flesh, nor stimulated my nerves.

Is this what it felt like to be a Phase? Or was it worse? The numbness of the flesh, or the absence of a heart.

Did not having a heart feel worse?

DAMPENED FROM EMOTIONS

So, we're making really good time. We should be in Remords by tomorrow morning. Gorgeous flying weather. Bit boring, though," Deryn said before stuffing a roll into her mouth.

"Will we be staying in Remords long?" My stomach fluttered as though it were about to fly up my throat. The more time we spent in Remords, the longer my judgment would be delayed.

"Nah, Serein just wants to stay long enough to top the kegs," she explained after swallowing the rest of the bread with a loud gulp. "Can't say I blame him. Remords is two steps away from wiping its bum with your best serviettes. If it wasn't for the soulever port, I doubt they would've been approved for a Solenoid. Lots of dampened stalking the area."

"If it's that dangerous, why don't we go to another port?" I asked, torn about visiting Remords. It sounded like a terrible place. And a desperate place. It sounded like *my* place.

"That's actually what I said," Deryn pointed out, waving her arms. "But Serein says, 'It's the only one en route to the Paramount.' So then I told him, 'I could have you in Anxiété before you finished scratching your bollocks.' But he was dead set on staying on course.

He's got no faith, Gavril. No faith at all. You run out of sparks midair once and they hold it against you forever."

"Maybe he wants to make sure I don't get a chance to escape before my trial." I looked down at the ground. After last night, I was surprised my freedom to walk around hadn't been revoked. "It'll tarnish his reputation."

Deryn slapped the arm of her chair and crowed out a loud, "*Kah!* The only thing Serein's worried about tarnishing with you are his trousers."

"That's what white pants are for," Hervé commented while sauntering into the opérateur deck.

"You'd know, eh, Hervy?" Deryn prodded with a cheeky smirk.

"And speaking of Serein," Hervé continued, ignoring the mischievous dig. "He would like to see our captive in his chambers."

"Oh-ho-ho, I told you. I said it, didn't I? You doubted the great me." Deryn danced in her chair.

My face lit up like a flame as she continued to wiggle and make rude gestures, but deep down a sense of dread ate at my stomach. I greatly doubted Deryn's interpretation of the request. Serein wanted to ensure I wasn't a threat.

"Where, um—" I bashfully started in between Deryn's yips and hoops. "Where is Serein's room?"

Hervé continued to stare ahead at the front windows, as though I were as invisible as I'd been in the hallway. He shrugged. "How should I know? I don't care to see it."

"It's down the hall from yours," Deryn replied. "Big blooming door right at the end." She stopped dancing and reached over to touch my hand. "Remember, Gavril, if he gives you any tosh, come straight to me. I'll ram that commandant title so far down his throat he'll be squirting alphabets."

I smiled at the opérateur with appreciation before exiting and working my way to the hall leading to my room. Instead of stopping at my door, I followed Deryn's directions and continued to the end.

A wide door lined with gold foil blocked further trespass. The air hitched in my lungs. I felt like a worm before the gate of a deity. Surely not even the Suzerain could provoke such frailty. The Suzerain didn't hold any power over me yet. *He'll never hold this kind of enchantment.*

I raised my hand, pulled my fist back to knock, and—

The door swung open of its own accord. I jumped back from it as though a vat of acid had spewed out.

"You can come in, Gavril," Serein called from inside.

I swallowed hard and walked through the doorway. Instead of being greeted by a wave of corrosion, a breeze of warm, relaxing air hit me. Peace wrapped around my body. I looked around the room. Ornate redwood tables with polished surfaces and chairs with black plush cushions furnished the room. A gold-threaded rug lay on the floor, and various sculptures were artfully placed around the room—figures of faceless people who held their arms wide in acceptance or hung their heads in shame. On the wall above the fireplace hung a large painting. Gray clouds hovered over a meadow landscape, and a lightning bolt struck down the center to a solitary tree in a field.

My gaze drifted to a huge poster bed with ivory drapes positioned before a wall of windows that opened to the rear of the soulever.

"Have a seat," Serein offered, directing me to a chair across from him at a small round table.

I slid into the chair with as much grace as I could muster. Feeling awkward and unpracticed, I probably looked like a fool, especially to someone like Serein who had no doubt seen polished ladies perform the simple task flawlessly.

"Are you doing well, Gavril?" he asked. "I want to express my shame at how our conversation ended last night. I was extremely rude."

"No more than I," I said, taken aback by the apology. What happened to the accusation that kept me awake all night? Was he so forgiving? "I know many Résonateurs have lost their lives against Phases.

You know far more than I could ever hope to learn."

"I'm not angry with you for having an opinion." He reached over the table and grabbed my hand. Blood rushed to my face as the smooth texture of his gloves caressed my flesh. But before I could tighten my fingers, Serein released my hand and stood up.

"It's actually rather refreshing to hear you voice your opinion. I'm just concerned for your safety, Gavril. Phases are deadly." He cleared his throat and turned to face the wall of windows. "Deryn expects to be in Remords by the morning."

I blinked and fought to collect my thoughts. Such an abrupt change. "She said we won't be there long," I managed to respond.

"Not if I can help it," he said, throwing a grin over his shoulder. "I hope to be back in the sky by that evening. That should be more than enough time to replenish our étincelle energy and do a quick maintenance check." He turned back to me. "During that time, I want you to feel free to leave the *Fulgurant* and explore the town. I only ask that you go with someone and exercise caution. Remords is not the safest town to get lost in."

"Deryn told me there is a lot of dampened activity around the area." I thought about the insults and persecution I had suffered—even after I was declared not dampened. "Are they really so dangerous?"

Serein placed his hands on the table and leaned toward me with a solemn stare. "Just by being there? No, in that regard they aren't particularly anything to be concerned about. The real danger is their state of mind. When a Phase makes physical contact with a person, it takes something from them. All their emotions and cares slowly dissipate until only memories are left, like a shell. They still function and remember their lives. They can even laugh when prompted to do so, but it's all a farce. They don't feel anything more than the ghost of something gone but not forgotten."

I broke my gaze away and squeezed my fists in my lap. Every rough scab in my palms pressed against my fingertips. "That sounds very sad."

Serein sighed. "Yes, Gavril, it is. But no matter how much you may pity those people, I need you to understand that there is nothing you can do to help them. They are still driven to survival—some even seek revenge—and they will kill you without a sliver of hesitation. They will do whatever it takes to *feel* again, to evoke an emotion that will never come."

"And there's no hope for them?" I was reluctant to just give up on someone. "Not anything in the world?"

"You are very kind, Gavril," Serein said softly. "But your heart will never reach them. The greatest kindness is to end their oblivion."

I took in a sharp breath. "You—just *kill* them? That's horrific!"

I couldn't believe what I was hearing. Killing people for the sake of being dampened? It was like . . . Gervais and Jalousie.

"It's not horrific. It's necessary."

"Necessary to kill people for their circumstance?"

He lifted his hand from the table and strode away from me. His back straightened like a post, posture rigid and unyielding.

"I do what I must for the good of the Paramount," Serein declared.

Even without a Résonateur's senses, I could tell this conversation was at an end. Serein kept his back turned, and if he wasn't going to speak or look at me, I wasn't going to remain in the silence of his displeasure. He told me he didn't kill people for their circumstances. He lied.

I stood up and walked to the door. When I reached the threshold, I paused. I had to know more about these people who were shunned and hated by all. "How will I know a dampened when I see one?"

"You will know," the commandant informed me in a stern voice. "Their blood is marred by apathy."

MARRED BY APATHY

I sat in the quiet and shadow of my room, still debating if I was prepared to face the world. The conversation with Serein left me shaken and cold. I knew the stigma of being involved with a Phase, but I couldn't grasp why the only solution to dealing with dampened was killing them. There had to be some way we could work together. Those people weren't just monsters without names and faces. Serein said they still had their memories. Did it matter if they didn't have emotions? I managed to get on fine while suppressing mine.

But that was different. I still had emotions. I just didn't acknowledge them. And I wondered what it would be like to lose them all now that I'd tasted life. Could Serein be right? Was it better to die than live such an existence?

No. Morrow didn't have emotions, and she was amazing. She was free of that burden. Nothing could hurt her. She was invulnerable. The dampened hurt people, but maybe they only did so to defend themselves. Maybe if they weren't so hunted . . .

I stood and approached the glass wall. The night sky shone through, brilliant and clear. Stars twinkled in the shimmering blanket, and the moon glowed like a beautiful face against the darkness.

It reminded me of Morrow. Her shimmering body was like the night sky. I bet if she were out there, I wouldn't find her if I spent the entire night searching, so well would she blend in.

To think I spent my whole life cowering behind a shield from Phases only to end up befriending one. But Morrow wasn't like the rest. She was special. She told me so. And she had been there for me as a friend. She came when I called for her in Envie. She stayed with me. She talked to me and listened. For the first time, with Morrow, I truly felt heard.

I wasn't alone when with her.

I pressed my head against the glass. It was cold. So very cold. Like the chill emitting from Morrow's skin. And this was as close as I could come to touching it. If I ever made contact with Morrow, I would become dampened.

And Serein would have to kill me. I closed my eyes, sagging against the cold barrier. He would kill me. He had to. He was bound by his duty as a Résonateur. Bound to the Suzerain. Not to me. I pulled away from the glass. It was late, but maybe a walk would do me good. I needed to get out of my room. Get away from my increasingly depressing thoughts.

I opened the door and walked into the hallway. I glanced down the corridor leading to Serein's room. Not that way. I turned in the opposite direction and let my feet take over.

Instead of staying on the top level, I found myself descending into the belly of the soulever. It was quiet, save for the familiar hum lurking in the background. It was always there when a siphon was active, though we never paid any attention to it unless it stopped. Panic and terror would soon follow.

I hoped Nostalgie never had to experience those feelings.

I hoped against hope that the siphon was still humming for them.

I found my way to the mess hall. A little water might do some good. The first time I drank water on the soulever, I hardly recognized it as the same liquid. I had been so used to sipping rainwater from an old barrel. The soulever water tasted pure and fresh. I drank until I felt my corset would burst.

I walked past the empty tables and showed myself into the kitchen. The stove was wiped and the dishes cleaned to perfection, but the light scent of braised lamb and potatoes still lingered in the air. That evening had been the first time I'd eaten meat like that, but no matter how delicious the morsels that bathed my taste buds, I couldn't eat much. A town of people living off brown cabbage leaves and weeds waited for me. Depended on me.

I fetched a glass and filled it from the faucet of the deep-dish basin. Suddenly, wood scraped against the floor in the dining room. I held the glass close to my chest and stilled. Someone was here.

"I can't keep doing this," a low voice muttered. "I don't know how long I can keep up this charade."

I peeked around the corner and saw Bibiane hunched over a table with her head resting in her folded arms. It was bizarre to see the ever straight archiviste curled up like that, vulnerable and imperfect. Human.

"Why doesn't he want me by his side?" she whispered. Her shoulders quivered, first in small jerks. Then they shook, and muffled moans arose.

I swallowed the lump in my throat. So she could feel. I smiled softly. It all sounded a little too familiar. I knew what it was like to wear a mask and pretend nothing mattered but the bare basics of survival. Feeling like I was the only one who had the fortitude and discipline to stick to the task and frustrated when no one else seemed to get it.

But I got it. I understood. Bibiane and I had a few things in common after all.

I kept my glass close and began to tiptoe out of the kitchen. I nearly made to the door when I stumbled, and the water sloshed in the glass. Bibiane's head shot up. She stared at me, eyes like saucers and her usually pursed lips slacked open. I nodded to her and kept walking.

"H-how long have you been there?" she asked hoarsely.

"Not long," I said lightly. I continued on my way, sure that was the right thing to do. Bibiane and I were more alike than either of us cared to admit, but that didn't mean she wanted my company. I accepted that. I was an outsider to her. A criminal. She wouldn't want comfort from me, and that was fine. But I would keep her secret all the same. Because it didn't matter what she was talking about or who she was talking about, her heart was in those words. And I would let her keep them close.

I rounded a corner and my heart stopped. The twins stood in the middle of the hall, blocking the way to my room.

"Little late to be sneaking around, don't you think, Ciseau?" Marteau said, grinning.

"I heard she was in the commandant's room earlier, brother," Ciseau replied, eyeing the glass in my hand. "It must've been quite strenuous. Seems she has a thirst."

"Oh, that's the worst."

"Worse than being cursed."

I swallowed and took a step back. "I told you I don't like these games."

"Games?" Marteau repeated. "We're not playing games. We're simply doing our job."

"And what is that?" I demanded. "Scaring passengers?"

"What's that, little red?" Ciseau asked with a smirk, his voice low. "You seem to have forgotten. You aren't a passenger. You're a prisoner."

"But we don't mind," Marteau said. "We like to get into trouble too sometimes."

I considered bolting back to the kitchen. Bibiane wasn't my friend, but she had these two under her thumb. One word from her, and they would be back to skulking the lower decks.

Marteau approached me, and I froze. He leaned close to my ear. "Can I tell you a secret?"

I looked at him but didn't answer, not sure I wanted to hear what was coming.

His grin widened. "I like you better than Ciseau does."

I glanced at Ciseau, who frowned deeply, clearly unhappy about not being included.

"Thanks, I think," I replied. "Should I be worried about that?"

"Oh, no, no," Marteau said. "I'd be more worried about Serein exploding. After all, Ciseau can't choke you from across the room like he can."

The blood drained from my face. "Serein would never do that."

"So sure?" he asked, voice teasing and melodic. "I've seen the commandant do things that would shock you, little heretic." He breathed deeply. "And not just violent things."

I shook my head. Serein wasn't like that. He couldn't be. He'd shown me nothing but kindness. He shielded me from Margaux's boiling soup and gave me his greatcoat when I was freezing on the sky deck and . . .

I thought back to our conversation in his chambers. How his voice and posture had hardened when speaking about the dampened, and how cold he had reacted to my questions about his methods.

"I don't know what you've seen," I said. "Now if you wouldn't mind, it's late and I would like to return to my room."

"Of course, Mademoiselle," Marteau said with a bow. He stepped to the side. "Might as well enjoy life while you can."

"Brother," Ciseau suddenly called, face red. "You know I don't like it when you leave me out."

Marteau straightened up. "So sorry, Ciseau. Just passing along some friendly advice."

"Advice?" Ciseau repeated with a high chirp. "On how to pick up diseases?"

Marteau rounded on his brother. "You're the one who insists on cheap teases."

"My cheap teases never displease . . . es."

"That's because they're usually deceased." Marteau burst out laughing.

I glanced between the two, glad they were focused on taking jabs at each other instead of me. If I could slip by unnoticed . . .

Ciseau punched his brother in the ribs. Marteau hunched over in pain.

"We've got to talk to Deryn, remember?" Ciseau said over his brother's groaning. "It's her ass you should be kissing instead of this heretic's. This is going to be our only chance."

"You worry too much, brother," Marteau replied, still gripping his side. "When have I ever let you down?"

"Never," Ciseau grabbed Marteau by his shirt collar and pulled him along past me.

Marteau blew me a kiss as he was dragged around the corner.

I grimaced and sprinted to my room before the pair could make an unexpected return. I closed the door and leaned against it, an unsettling tingle sweeping up my spine. At least in Envie, I knew where I stood with Gervais and his family. His words were obvious lies. With the twins, I was unsure. Their conversations flipped between silly nonsense and thinly veiled threats in a heartbeat.

I pressed my hands into the door, holding it closed against anyone who might try to enter.

I was overreacting. Like Gervais, the twins' mouths were their only real weapon. And if they felt emboldened to act, Serein would never let anything happen. Even if he was angry with me.

I kept pressing against the door until my palms ached.

Serein would protect me . . . wouldn't he?

My stomach plummeted. Clouds zoomed from the bottom of my window and beyond the top before I could blink. We continued our descent until a metal-framed dock blotted my view. The continuous static hum I unconsciously grew accustomed to ceased, and only darkness kept me company.

I sat for several minutes in the silence, caught between fear of leaving my safe room and excitement at venturing into the uncharted territory. I had made it to a new town, so far from home. All the way to the Crainte border. What could possibly be waiting for me outside the—*Whap!*

A mass of teal smashed into my window. Deryn pressed her face into the glass and stuck her tongue out.

I burst out laughing and staggered over to the sky deck door. I flung it open. "It's certainly a surprise to see you out here, Deryn. I thought you might be glued to that chair," I joked while inspecting the new spit stain on my window. "Thanks for the art."

"Eh, it needed a clean," Deryn said with a dismissive swat of her hand. "And I've been officially freed from my bum guardian to stretch out my legs a bit. I figured we'd go fetch Serein's dress," she added with a wink.

"Dress?" I repeated, caught off guard. "How do you know—"

"You should know that anything said in the twins' hearing range is no longer privileged information and the whole bloody vessel knows."

"Thanks for the advice," I said. I looked down at Deryn's face. Deep bags sagged under her eyes. "Are you sure you shouldn't be resting?" I asked. "This will be your only chance before we leave for the Paramount."

"Nah, I'm right. It does me good to get out every now and then. But if you think my company's a bit brash for your knickers, I can take a hint."

"I don't think that at all," I said quickly. The last thing I wanted was to send away one of the few people who wanted me around.

"Where should we get started?"

"Well, for one thing, we need to get off this big beautiful girl. They should've run the stairs to the deck by now. Let's take a look, eh?" Deryn sauntered toward the bow of the soulever.

"You mean we don't have to climb down the ladder at the bottom?" I asked.

"Not at a proper port."

Deryn broke into a skip, and I jogged after her, beaming.

At the front of the sky deck, a large winding staircase was hooked to the railing. We scaled over the metal bar and sprinted down the giant swirl of steps.

The port was larger than anything I had seen before. Soulevers were docked along two rows of rusty iron platforms, and a large aisle littered with metal scraps and dust ran down the middle of the port. Workers moved large metal carts around the aisle. Five other soulevers of varying sizes and conditions rested at separate docks. One resembled an oversized automatram. Another, an oval, had purple iris flowers painted on the side. Yet another had deep gashes along the front. None were as grand or large as the *Fulgurant*, and people stopped and shaded their eyes to study it.

"How do they refill the reservoir?" I asked when we stepped down to the center aisle.

"You see that?" Deryn pointed at the soulever with the flowers. Several men in heavy coveralls on a platform behind the soulever rolled a cylinder the size of my house closer to the vessel. "It's like a Solenoid but with étincelle energy stored inside. They roll that nasty lad into the reservoir room and hook it up. The energy is pulled into the reservoir and sent to the siphons when activated. I'd say it'll take three of those to top us off right now."

"Three?" I choked. "But that thing is enormous, and we aren't out of energy yet."

"What can I say?" Deryn smiled. "The flashier you are, the more food it takes to fill your gut. And the *Fulgurant* is one hungry lass."

I looked back over my shoulder as the men pushed the cylinder into the soulever. *What an amazing—*

"*Hmph!*" I stumbled back, wobbling on my feet after slamming into something.

"Watch where you're going," a muffled female voice said.

A set of brassy eyes stared straight at me from above a heavy scarf. A young woman in an oversized work suit and thick leather gloves blocked the way.

"I'm sorry. I—"

"Why don't *you* watch where *you're* going, love?" Deryn challenged, poking the woman in the chest. "It takes two to tumble, and *you* didn't move out of the way."

"I didn't see *you* making any effort to stop your friend," the girl replied, unaffected by Deryn's fervor.

"Because I didn't think you were daft enough to keep walking, you stupid cow!" Deryn growled.

"It's fine," I intervened, stepping between the two. "Nobody is hurt—"

"Yet!" Deryn said, waving her fist.

"—so we'll continue. Come on, Deryn." I grabbed my friend's arm and pulled her away. As we departed, I glanced over my shoulder. The other woman's gaze trailed after us, but she said nothing.

"Can you believe the balls on some people?" Deryn huffed as we exited the port.

I gave Deryn an amused grin. "Yes, I can."

Not since my mama had I met someone who blurted out exactly what was on her mind when it was on her mind. It made me a little envious. As frustrating as she could be, Mama never let anyone walk over her. She put Edgard in his place and wasn't threated by Gervais' bluster. She was who she was. Deryn was like that. Unabashedly herself. I loved that confidence.

"She better hope I don't see her in my soulever when we get back. I'll push her off the sky deck before she can feel my foot on her arse." Deryn crossed her arms and squeezed her neck down into her shoulders as far as it would go.

I surveyed the new area and shook my head. Remords was definitely not a rustic little town. Roads and buildings were constructed from yellow brick, just like the path we walked along. It gave the town a sturdy appearance, despite its disrepair. Cracked windows. Black water stains running down walls.

As we made our way through the streets, Remords' citizens ignored us—impressive, considering my companion. Such lack of concern about strangers was a foreign concept to me. If an outsider entered Nostalgie, they would be tied up and interrogated. But this was a soulever port. The population must have grown used to a steady flow of unfamiliar faces.

We took our time exploring the streets and searching for shops. Deryn ran up to windows, peeked inside, and either pointed with excitement or stuck her tongue out in disgust and declared she'd never seen such "frizzing rubbish." Proprietors glared through the glass at the rambunctious girl.

After a particularly surly-looking man whipped out a knife, I snatched Deryn's arm and pulled her to another street before she could further insult his wares.

She grabbed my arm and dragged me to another shop. A sign with a red ribbon and the words *Simone's Finery* painted on the front swung above the door. Before I could even glance in the window, Deryn shoved me inside.

A woman with a towering powdered wig and a fuchsia gown jumped as we clamored in. When she turned to us, it was my turn to jump. Makeup powder sank into every crease and wrinkle lining her face, emphasizing her age. Rouge coated her cheeks and mouth like glops of paste, and a beauty mark the size of a beetle stared at me as though she had a third eye between her brows. She slapped a smile on her face and approached us.

"Can I help you, Mademoiselles?"

"Yeah. This sailor's dream needs to get a new look." Deryn thrust her thumb at me. "And make it naughty. It's for a man."

"Oh, for a man," the old woman repeated, smiling coyly. "You've come to the right place. I am an expert on these matters."

"It's just for me," I clarified. "I need something simple for daily wear."

"Bah, you're no good for a laugh," Deryn pouted.

The woman gave me an equally disappointed and offended glower. "Mademoiselle, we do not have 'simple.' I am Simone, and I only sell *finery*. I do, however, have a few items of a subtler nature if you are insistent on shunning great beauty."

I smiled nervously and nodded.

"I'll be right back." Simone raised her nose and strutted to the back.

"You sure slapped the powder off her beak," Deryn noted with approval.

"I didn't mean to," I whispered. "I didn't want to waste time with something I'll never wear."

"You mean 'never' as in two days? Because that's where I have my argent."

"What are you talking about?" I asked, bewildered.

"My argent, right? For the bet on when you and Serein finally nix the knicke—"

"Here you are, Mademoiselle." Simone grudgingly held out a dress.

Before Serein and I did *what?* And Deryn was betting on it? With whom?

The image of the large bed in Serein's quarters flashed before me . . . and then one of him with his back to me.

"My least elegant piece," Simone continued. "A woman brought it from the Paramount years ago, begging me to sell her work."

I pushed both thoughts aside, not wanting to focus on how my stomach tickled with one and ached with the other. I studied the dress of deep charcoal-dyed cotton. Silver buttons ran down the arms from neck to wrist, and an embroidered pattern of ivy climbed from the hem to the bodice in silver thread. The dress was simple, but Simone was wrong. There was an elegance about it. The detailing was immaculate, beautiful, and when I traced the embroidery with my fingers, my heart leapt. It was perfect. I wanted it. I *really* wanted it.

"I'll take it," I told Simone with a pleased grin.

"I'm glad to hear it, Mademoiselle. You may change in the back after I've collected the argent."

My smile faltered. "Oh, yes, my—my argent." I gave the dress a forlorn gaze. I was supposed to get some from Serein. Not that I had any right after I insulted him and the rest of the Résonateurs.

"You go on and change, Gavy. I got this," Deryn said, pulling out a little coin purse.

My mouth gaped open. "Deryn, I can't expect you—"

"Sure, you can. We're mates, right?" she chirped and tossed the purse to Simone, who had to scramble to catch it.

Tears welled in my eyes. "Yes, we are. Thank you so much, Deryn."

"Don't start blubbering. Go get that bloody dress on," Deryn ordered, her cheeks blooming red.

I hugged the dress to my chest and rushed to a small room in the back.

Deryn's voice trailed after me. "Oi, old woman! I see you trying to nick some extra."

I quickly changed, loving the soft texture of the cotton and feeling truly warm for the first time since leaving home. Not sure what to do with Charmant's dress, I tossed it on a pile of ripped cloth thrown in the corner. I was sure Simone could use the fabric for something, at the very least a dish rag.

When I returned to the front, Simone turned to me with an undignified scowl. "If there's nothing else I can assist you with, the door is over there," she said between her teeth. Her piercing gaze darted between Deryn and the entrance.

"Ta for everything." Deryn cheerfully sashayed out the door.

I gave Simone a grateful nod, which she ignored, her eyes still cutting into Deryn's back, and followed my companion.

We stopped by a pastry shop and spent our time laughing, eating, and sharing stories. I'd never had a friend like Deryn before. There was something refreshing and freeing about being with a person I could carelessly enjoy the day with. Morrow and I would never be able to sit out in the open together like this. And with Serein, things were just . . . complicated.

"You know," Deryn began as we walked down another street, "you're pretty decent for a heretic."

"I hope the Suzerain agrees with you, Deryn," I mumbled. I almost forgot that I wasn't here by choice.

"He will if he knows what's good for him. Now, let's go see if they've treated my girl right." Deryn pushed a fist into her open palm and narrowed her eyes. "I may have to hammer some chisels and chisel some hammers if they bugger up that inspection. I can't believe I agreed to let those identical fools take on an important job. Guess that makes me the bloody fool."

My cheer dimmed a little at the mention of Ciseau and Marteau. Our uncomfortable encounters on the sky deck and in the corridor were still fresh on my mind. I dreaded the next time our paths would cross.

"Have you known them long?" I asked. "Are you, um, good friends?"

Deryn groaned, but the wide grin on her face told me she was anything but annoyed.

"Hate to say it, but yeah. Me and the boys have been through some pretty bleak times together. And by that I mean years of putting up with Bibiane." She chuckled. "Always good for a laugh, those two. Good for helping me stay awake."

I stared at the cracks in the brick path. She looked so happy when she was talking about Ciseau and Marteau. It wasn't an emotion I associated with them at all, but maybe I was wrong. Deryn said she had known them for years. Far longer than I could claim. I didn't know anything about them.

"Watch, Gavy." Deryn's hand suddenly flew in front of my chest, bringing me to an abrupt stop. "This is as far as we go this way."

I looked up to face the harsh reality of a more familiar world. The road ahead was in pieces and covered with grass. The buildings around it were dilapidated. Loose bricks and tangled vines barely held them together under collapsed or sagging roofs. Bushes grew freely and untamed on doorsteps.

"It's Fin Fragile," Deryn said.

"What's Fin Fragile?"

"An old part of Remords," Deryn explained. "Remords used to be much larger. A second Solenoid was located here, and its barrier overlapped with the one still humming in central Remords. When Anxiété built their port, the number of soulevers stopping in Remords decreased, so it was decided only one Solenoid was necessary to protect the poor buggers. Fin Fragile has been abandoned for about a century now."

My blood ran cold. It was decided they didn't need a Solenoid. Decided *for* them by people who didn't even live there. The Paramount forced people from their homes because enough argent wasn't flowing in. The cold settled deep in my chest, and I felt short of breath. Nostalgie didn't have *any* argent flowing in.

I looked out at the ruined buildings, broken roads, and lifeless homes. Abandoned. Left to rot. No help from those they depended on for protection.

Something caught my eye, and I found my breath. "There's a light."

"What?" Deryn snorted. "There's absolutely no energy being supplied to this part of town. The wires have been cut to avoid waste."

I pointed to a building about three streets ahead, visible through a crumbled row of houses. A tiny light twinkled from a window.

Deryn shifted her head to follow the line of my finger. She took in a sharp breath. "Frizz of frizzing frizzes," she hissed. She grabbed my upper arm with a grip so tight my arm numbed. "We're going back to the port. Now."

I started walking with her, but I turned to look back. "What's wrong?" I asked, confused by her sudden need to leave. She seemed worried. Scared. Definitely not Deryn. "It's just a light, Deryn. Someone is living out there."

"*Someone's* a bit of a stretch," she replied, her voice tight. "That's a bleeding dampened."

"A dampened?" I tried to look again, but Deryn pulled me around a corner. "Would they really attack us in the daylight like this? I'm sure if we just keep our distance—"

"Yeah, we should keep our distance. At the port," she said decisively. "You don't understand, Gavril. They don't care if you don't make the first move. They'll attack if they think you're a threat to keep you from spilling their location. And unlike Phases, dampened can follow you inside the barrier to finish the job. We shouldn't be here. Not without Serein."

My throat tightened. If Serein found out a dampened was living nearby . . .

"Are you going to tell him?" I asked.

"Frizz, yeah," Deryn replied. "He's got to know."

I stopped short, and Deryn, who was still gripping my arm, nearly tumbled back. She rounded on me, her expression a cross between surprised and furious.

"Gavy, what the fu—"

"I don't think we should," I said.

Deryn's eyes nearly popped out of their sockets.

"They haven't harmed anyone," I added quickly. "Serein doesn't need to know. We shouldn't go to him."

Deryn pursed her lips and tilted her head like something dawned on her. "Did something happen between you two?"

"What?" I blurted. "What makes you think that?"

"You're turning down a chance to throw yourself into his muscled arms and stare at his handsome visage as you pour your troubles into his heroic ear. If that's not a bull's eye on the horse's arse, I don't know what is."

"We had a . . . a disagreement," I relented. "I really . . . I don't want to put this on him right now."

Taking this to him after everything I said . . . Whoever that light belonged to wasn't a problem, dampened or not. Serein didn't need to make it his problem.

Deryn put her hand on my shoulder. "It's part of his duty, Gavy."

My face fell.

She gently squeezed my arm. "But there haven't been any complaints since we arrived. I guess I can wait until we get back to the Paramount and make an official report."

My whole body felt lighter. I smiled. "Thanks, Deryn."

"Save your thanks. I'll be taking a favor"—she winked—"when you least expect it."

I laughed and placed my hand on hers. "It's a deal."

We started walking again and headed for the port as sunset kissed the horizon. Serein said he wanted to be out of Remords by the evening, so our time was nearly over. I would not forget it anytime soon, but there were still many things I didn't get to see. Places I would never go. Places in Fin Fragile.

"Who do you think was living there?" I asked my companion. I couldn't help it. I was curious. Were they dampened? Could we find some way to live together? "It was very strange."

"The whole blooming thing was strange," Deryn replied as we walked into the port entrance. "Could have been anyone, but like I said, probably a dampened. I'll admit it was impressive getting the lights on that far out. Probably had to build a tiny engine, but that's not the point." She stopped and frowned. "What's all this fuss?"

A large cluster of people had gathered around something in the center of the docks. Some were whispering. Others frowned or looked confused. Deryn shoved her way through the mass of bodies, and I followed in her wake.

In the heart of the crowd, two people faced off. Serein commanded the atmosphere as though he could steal your soul with but a breath—and after experiencing his anger on the soulever, I knew very well that he could. I wiped my forehead. The air was hot and oppressive, and people pulled at their collars, obviously uncomfortable but unwilling to leave. Some workers even unzipped their coveralls in a bid to find relief. Only one other person occupying the space remained untouched. The girl I had tripped over, the one with the scarf, faced the Résonateur without a trace of fear.

"I bloody knew she wasn't right," Deryn muttered.

"Remove your scarf and show your face," Serein ordered in a voice as hard as stone.

"No," the girl replied, not intimidated in the least. Her bravado impressed me. Not many people would openly defy a commandant like that.

"Then you bring this upon yourself." Serein grabbed the girl like a hawk seizing its prey. She struggled to pull away. He reached for her face and ripped the scarf away.

Gasps and hisses flooded the room as loud as any raging mob. Her face was perfectly normal, but her neck . . . Dark gray, deadened veins branched up its flesh like a withered tree. I stared at them. The color was so lifeless. It was hard to believe, but blood flowed through those vessels. Blood marred by apathy.

Despite the angry crowd with all its eyes on her, she expressed no dismay. She showed nothing.

"Dampened." The whispered word resounded around the circle like a chanted curse.

Serein released the girl and stepped back. "Are there any others here? If you show me to the other dampened, I may offer you mercy."

"I have no need for your mercy, Résonateur," the girl said, voice as emotionless as her expression. "In the end, it will make no difference to me. I know your mercy is short-lived and meaningless."

"Then it ends here for you."

Serein couldn't be serious. There had to be some other way. "No, wait—" I held up my hand.

The atmosphere instantly cut into my flesh like a thousand razors slashing across my body. Crimson spewed into the sky, and a dull thud sounded from the floor.

I ran my hands over my arms and torso for tears or gashes.

Nothing.

A stream of red liquid oozed past my foot. I followed the trail and—

A scream caught in my throat. I clapped my hands over my mouth. Trembling, I shot my gaze to Serein's motionless back, then Deryn's unconcerned face. I surveyed the disgusted and *satisfied* people in the circle around me. And I ran.

"Gavy, wait!" Deryn's voice trailed after me.

My feet pounded into the spiral staircase as I fled back to the *Fulgurant*. I wrenched open the glass door to my room and collapsed on my bed. Even the silk felt coarse.

How could they? How could *he?* And not a single one of them felt sorry. That poor girl. She never harmed anyone. She did nothing wrong. She worked on the docks. She carried on with her life like everyone else. *It's not right. It's not fair. Why must the helpless always suffer?*

I curled up. Not even the soulever's jerky ascension bothered me. And that was fine. I just wanted to lie here—unbothered.

Moonlight illuminated the planks of the sky deck like a frozen lake. It was beautiful, like walking on a field of ethereal white, but at the same time, haunting.

I wandered to the bow, watching my shadow lead the way and wishing it would come to life as Morrow. Only she understood. A hint of warmth skimmed my flesh, and up from my shadow, my gaze drew to a spirit in ivory standing at the bow, his back against the railing.

Serein. He stood as a marble statue—still, straight, and imposing. For the first time, he struck me as *frightening*. I stepped back.

"Gavril, please don't go," he pleaded.

My heart ached, and I stopped. Despite what I had witnessed that afternoon, I did not want to believe he was cruel. Someone so kind and generous couldn't be a monster.

"I know what you must think of me," he began as if reading my thoughts. "And I wish I could take that away. I wish I could go back and remove that image from your sight. But I can't." He looked tired when he said that. Like the thought had been eating away at him. "All I can do is speak and hope my words reach you."

I pulled my arms against my chest. I didn't reply, but I didn't turn away, either. I would stay and listen. It was the least I could do after all he'd done for me. I wanted to believe in him. I had to try.

"You think I'm spoiled. That I have never experienced one ounce of sacrifice in my life," he said steadily. "And for someone who has known true need, I can't blame you for forming that opinion. I'm from a town in the Bonheur region near Éthéré Coeur with three Solenoids, while you struggle to obtain only one. Calme is like a paradise compared to Envie. Why would you feel anything but spite toward someone who comes from such a place?"

A frown pulled on my lips. Spite? I could never feel spite for Serein. Is that how he saw me? Did I show bitterness so easily?

"I'm descended from an old Résonateur family in Calme. At least one Résonateur is born every generation. For my generation, it was me. For the previous one, it was my uncle. We were two of a kind, my uncle and I, and it irked my father."

That seemed familiar. Edgard never tried to hide his distaste for the pedestal Mama put my father, the Résonateur foreigner, on. Often, I faced Edgard's jealousy and retribution because I looked like my father.

"I was still training to become a Résonateur when representatives from the Paramount Sommet came looking for a candidate, someone to pay the service to the Suzerain and establish a new village. Being an ambitious youth, I readily volunteered for the task." Amusement flickered across his face and then fell. His expression grew grave. "I told my uncle what I did, but I didn't receive the reaction I expected.

"He was angry—even afraid. I was confounded. When I asked him what was wrong, he shook his head and told me to report back to my training. He would take care of everything. 'The service is a duty for an old Résonateur, not a young one just starting out,' he told me. And take care of it he did. My uncle was Commandant Suprême. The head of all Résonateurs."

Serein cleared his throat and gazed out into the darkness. I let him have the moment to himself. I couldn't fathom what must've been going through his mind, but I knew the importance of memory. The importance of nostalgia.

"I never saw my uncle again. When I became a Résonateur, a . . . an *acquaintance* of mine used his influence as a commandant to inquire into his whereabouts with the archiviste library. Bibiane informed me that he was sent to the new remote village, Agacement, in the southern Colère region, and that it was a strictly confidential mission. Against orders, I went to that village. Do you know what I found, Gavril?" he asked, resting his tempest eyes on my face.

I shook my head. Colère was the southernmost region of Premier Esprit. The elders told me it was a place of dirty deeds and black-market trading. A place the worst places looked down upon. Any mission there was surely a perilous one.

"I found absolutely nothing." He swept his hand at the open sky. "The mayor informed me that a Résonateur had never set foot in the village—not even when the Solenoid was delivered. I couldn't believe it. Either the archiviste was wrong, or my uncle did not fulfill his duty. That was something I could never believe.

"When I returned to the Paramount, I demanded answers from the archiviste library. The next day, the head of the Sommet came to see me. He told me that news of a Résonateur's death was reported at the time my uncle was dispatched to that village. He said the report was kept silent to avoid panic. The Résonateur was killed by dampened." He scowled. "The Commandant Suprême was dead, and no one was told why. The Sommet covered it up later by saying my uncle died in a soulever accident on his way home.

"My uncle was killed trying to fulfill his duty to those people. He wasn't killed for *who* he was, but *what* he was. And he hasn't been the only one. Many others have fallen to Phases and dampened. Innocent people like you, Gavril. I can't accept it. That's why I must do everything in my power to protect those around me. You may hate me for it, but I do not feel sorry for killing that dampened if it makes the difference between you being here with me or martyred by the condemned souls who will only repay your kind heart with death. The thought of living such an existence—"

I ran forward and threw my arms around him. I squeezed as though I were holding onto his life force, desperate to keep it close to me. He tensed for a moment before his hands gently held my shoulders.

I looked up at him, and he stared down at me.

His breath warmed my face . . . his intense eyes stole my heart . . . and his lips . . .

I felt light and dizzy. Such a feeling. A thousand soft feathers kissing my flesh. My heart raced, emotions tumbling and blurring together until one burst out from the tangle. It was one I had buried deep long ago. An emotion as powerful as it was dangerous. The costliest emotion of all.

Love.

I stood on my toes and leaned forward, light enough to fly away.

Boom!

My feet left the floor and I careened sideways. I hit the metal railing. Pain lit up my whole side. I rolled back into the air—nothing beneath me but open sky.

A gloved hand seized my wrist, and I whipped to a stop, dangling above a valley of bottomless black. The *Fulgurant* listed heavily to the left. Smoke and fire erupted from the side of the vessel.

I looked back to my savior.

Serein clutched the railing with one hand and held me with the other. His face was red—strained—and sweat poured from his brow. The storm in his eyes raged like a hurricane.

"I'm not going to let you go, Gavril," he rasped through clenched teeth. "I can't . . .let . . . you . . .go . . ."

A sad smile crossed my lips. "You may have to," I whispered.

Another explosion shocked the soulever. Metal, wood, and glass rained from the sky. My eyes widened as a large panel rocketed down.

The sharp edge glinted in the firelight as it hurtled straight into Serein's back.

A strangled cry ripped through the air. Wind lashed out at me—at my back and in my face. I couldn't breathe. I descended to the void below. Darkness overcame me.

ORIGIN OF RESONANCE

I coughed and sputtered cold liquid from my lungs. Loud rushing filled my ears. My side felt like one huge bruise—a pain intensified by a heavy weight resting on my back. I crawled out from under the mass along slick gravel, and it slid to the ground, emitting a low groan.

I rolled over and gasped. Serein lay face down in the gravel. Dark red stained the entire back of his coat. A steady flow of water ran over his feet, the edge of a wide river that shimmered in the moonlight and extended far into the darkness. He must have pulled me from the water onto the riverbank after we plummeted into it.

Tears poured down my cheeks. "Serein!"

I scrambled to Serein. I grabbed his shoulders and pulled with all my might, ignoring the pain shooting up my side. He slowly rolled over, his face twisting as he let out another moan. I cupped his face. He was freezing. And all that blood . . . We couldn't stay here. We needed shelter.

"Serein, I need you to stand," I whispered. "Please, stand. We need to get some help."

Serein wheezed and moaned but managed to climb to his feet with my support. He sagged against me.

I steadied myself and scanned the ground and the sky. Roughly a mile in the distance, wisps of smoke swirled in the moonlight. A fire. I swallowed hard. It was too close and small to be the *Fulgurant*. It could be a town. That's where we would go.

It was difficult to keep my balance given our difference in height, but I forged on, leading him through thick grass toward the smoke. I had to keep going.

The valley was mostly flat with waves of grass and some sparse trees, but tall moonlit mountains rose in the far distance. We limped inches at a time. Serein swayed, and I used every bit of strength to hold him up. My body ached and I struggled to keep moving. I focused on the smoke. The moon behind it slowly descended to kiss the mountains before we finally reached the source. A dying fire gripped onto life in a patch of dirt. It wasn't a town, but the best I could hope for. I gently lowered Serein to the ground beside the fire, careful to keep his wound from touching the dirt. I rushed off and scoured the area for any twigs or dried leaves. When I obtained my bounty, I returned to the fire and blew on it. I worked and worked until vigor returned to the flames.

Waves of heat radiated over my chilled body. My joints and muscles reveled in the new temperature, but I resisted the temptation to relax and give in to my exhaustion. I lightly touched Serein's forehead. He shivered violently. I helped him sit up and pulled off his soggy, blood-stained coat. The back was shredded, a soiled wad of red and rags. I threw the coat to the side and undid the buttons on his shirt from his chin down.

When I pulled his shirt open, my eyebrows shot up in surprise. A ring of pure white veins bloomed in the center of his chest. Thin vessels branched from the circle and curved over his chest to his neck. They ran down his arms and down the sides of his abdomen.

"Unnatural, isn't it?" Serein slurred, swaying.

"It's not." I held him steady and inspected his wounded back.

"It's beautiful."

He let out a rough chuckle and hissed when I touched the border of the large gash running diagonally from his left shoulder to his right hip. That nasty wound needed tending. I tugged at my skirt.

"No." Serein grabbed my hand and stopped me. "Not your dress. Use the coat. It's a useless rag."

I bit my lip and shifted my gaze to the tattered ivory greatcoat. It didn't seem right to reduce the symbol of a Résonateur Commandant to bandages. It had more gold on it than Nostalgie and Envie possessed combined. But it was irreparable now.

I nodded and tore at the bottom of the coat where the fabric was cleanest. I pulled off a large strip and wrapped it around Serein's torso to stem the bleeding. When that was done, I led Serein closer to the fire and helped him lie down. As I started to pull away, he curled an arm around my waist and hugged me against his chest.

"Stay close to me," he rasped in my ear. "The dampened are near. They're getting help from *him*."

"Him?"

"Betrayer," he groaned. "Lost control . . . friend. Fluctuateur. Fluctuateur helping dampened against me."

"Serein . . .?"

His panting slowed into a steady rhythm.

"Stay close to me."

"For as long as I am able," I promised.

I settled into Serein's arms and closed my eyes. Even in this terrible situation, his hold remained warm and comforting and safe. Like being held in a private barrier that only we could enter.

"Gavril." A whisper skimmed my ear, and a hand gently shook my shoulder. "Gavril, wake up."

I opened my eyes to blinding sunlight. With a groggy yawn, I stretched out my arms. Ugh, my whole body ached.

Serein knelt beside me. He was fully alert, but his complexion was pale and dark lines drew under his eyes. He was hurting.

"You should be resting." I frowned. "That's a very serious injury."

"That's why I can't rest," Serein replied. He pointed over to the nearly extinguished fire. "Gavril, did you start the fire?"

"No." I furrowed my eyebrows. "It was already here."

"That's what I feared," he said, scrutinizing the site. "Did you see anyone?"

I shook my head. "I never saw a single person. Do you think whoever started the fire is still around? Maybe they could help us."

"Most likely they saw the *Fulgurant* fall and left to investigate." He stood up and held out his hand. I took it, and he helped me up. He winced, and I snatched my hand from his, not wanting to put more strain on him.

"It's not that bad," he said.

"You have a huge gash running across your back," I replied. "Serein, you lost so much blood."

"I know," he replied, nodding stiffly. "I'm using my powers to bolster myself and fight through the pain, but I don't know how long I can last." He looked at the dying embers. "I don't want to concern you," he continued, "but 'help' might not be what those people offer. We're in the Vallée de la Solitude, and it's a well-known area for dampened. Look there." He pointed at a line of pristine white peaks in the distance. "It's enclosed by mountains. There are few ways in, so it's a great place for a stronghold. There's one possible entrance—a small pass in the mountains. The village of Panique guards it."

"Then there are people around," I said, relieved.

"Not exactly," Serein replied. "The Solenoid at Panique died about ten years ago. They weren't able to pay the service, so the village was left to defend itself, much like your Jalousie."

"What's the point of going to an empty town?" I wasn't eager to enter another cursed place.

"Panique may still have a relier," he explained. "If I can find it, I might be able to patch it up and contact the nearest town. And Gavril"—he grabbed my shoulders and gazed into my eyes—"it may not be as empty as you think. I want you prepared in case we have to defend ourselves."

I averted my gaze. I couldn't understand why the dampened automatically posed a threat. But I knew his personal feelings on the matter, and now was not the time to start a debate. Serein was seriously wounded, and I was just a rural girl lost in the big open world. We needed to stick together.

"I'm ready," I declared.

He smiled down at me, a beautiful and reassuring sight. "I'm glad. We need to get to the pass as soon as possible. The river, Le Solitaire, should guide us. If we don't make it before nightfall, we'll have to bed down somewhere hidden for the night. Let's go before whoever started that fire returns."

We trekked through tall, lush green grass toward the northern wall of mountains. The Vallée de la Solitude was beautiful. Despite the autumn season, all the trees, flowers, and foliage were blooming and splendid as if it were the height of spring. It deserved a better name than the "Vallée de la Solitude."

"I have to thank you, Gavril," Serein said. "I was the one who promised to protect you, but you ended up saving me."

"You did the saving," I replied. "All I did was tear your coat and relight a fire."

"And keep me from bleeding to death," Serein added. "Your courage shines. I don't remember a lot about last night, but I remember you guiding me through the darkness."

Despite my aches, joy uplifted my tired body.

"I wish I could take you where you need to go," he whispered, his tone soft and remorseful. "I won't get you to Éthéré Coeur as easily as I promised. I'm sorry, Gavril."

"I'm not concerned about that," I said. Truthfully, the delay relieved me, although I would have preferred far better circumstances. "I hope everyone else is safe."

"I don't see any smoke or signs of the *Fulgurant* in the valley, so they must have successfully cleared the mountains," Serein assured me. "If there's anyone in the world who can land a soulever with one functioning siphon, it's Deryn. I imagine they're in a much better position than us."

"I hope you're right," I murmured, worried for my friend.

"Don't fret about it, Gavril. I'm sure they're sending the repair list to the Suzerain as we speak."

I frowned and clenched my fist. Back to the Suzerain. The time for us to come face to face crept closer, and even this hitch wouldn't stop it. My fingertips grazed the scabs on my palms. They were peeling off.

"What kind of man is he?" I asked.

"The Suzerain?"

I nodded. "Just the thought of him alone is frightening. What type of man can control nearly every land known to us?"

"Well, ah . . . " Serein reached as if to scratch the back of his head and released a sharp hiss.

"Serein—"

"I'm fine," he said firmly. "You wanted to know about the Suzerain." He studied the sky, his eyebrows furrowed. "The, ah, the Suzerain is a man of . . . of a . . . well, he is a unique character. He has a presence that is truly his own."

"He's strange?" I asked.

Serein chuckled. "Yes, you could say that. But the cup of the Suzerain is a heavy chalice to bear. Some have prospered under the weight—like Amarante, who extended her heart's reach to Heortefeld and Himinnhjarta, or Gaubert, who successfully conquered and made a treaty with Fu'aad. Others preferred a moderate approach. However they choose to rule, the blood of the first Résonateur runs in their veins."

"The Suzerain is a Résonateur?" I asked.

"Yes, but you won't see him running around slaying Phases unless that's something he really wants to do. I don't think a Suzerain has been in battle for nearly two hundred years."

Even the Suzerains felt it was safer to stay inside a barrier—despite all that power. They were sacred, revered throughout the lands. Mama told me the death of a Suzerain was akin to losing a piece of the sun. A time of great mourning that struck the hearts of everyone under Premier Esprit's rule. Perhaps that was why they stayed locked away while people like Serein had to put their lives on the line instead—and push themselves to the limit.

I glanced at Serein. His shoulders sagged and beads of sweat dripped down his temple.

I stopped. Sensing my lack of movement, Serein turned to me.

"Tell me about the first Résonateur, Serein." He once told me anyone could become a Résonateur. "I want to know how it all started."

"Getting bored with our long walk already, Gavril?" he teased. "I thought you liked me."

"Of course, I like you," I said quickly. My face burned, probably matching my hair. How could he possibly question that after what happened on the sky deck? I nearly kissed him. And it awakened something in me. "I . . . I just thought it might be a fascinating story. I'd like to hear it."

He scoped out the valley. "We can take a break." Serein grabbed my hand and led me closer to the river. My chest swelled with a rush of warm emotions. We found a dry spot of gravel and sat down. Serein didn't say it, but I could tell from the deep, relieved sigh he was glad to be off his feet.

"It's a tale that has given me a great deal of inspiration, and I hope it gives you something, too," Serein said, squeezing my hand.

I took a deep breath. If it gave me anything like the wonderful stirring inside my chest, I'd consider it the best tale in history.

"About four thousand years ago, there was a man born to a land that we now call the Île de l'Amour. The man was strong, cunning, and brave, and it didn't take long to amass an army of followers. But it was not his wit alone that attracted people to him. The man had a gift more special than any other. He could draw on his emotions and influence the physical world. Some say he could even make them as corporeal as flesh and blood—create incredible manifestations that could be seen, heard, and touched. And it was this gift that enabled him to conquer the world and unite the people under one heart."

To be united under one heart. I held my hand to my chest. Was such a miracle even possible? Even now, the Suzerain held dominion over several nations, but others rejected him. Edgard called them people barely aware of their own existence. Primitives. From what I'd overheard Bibiane say on the soulever, he wasn't alone in that opinion.

"But the man did not want to stop there," Serein continued. "'Why,' he thought, 'should I be the only one who possesses this gift?' He wanted to share it. He wanted others to experience the same wonders. Eidolon wanted others to feel his heart." Serein grinned at me.

"Eidolon consulted with the best scientist in Premier Esprit, and together they constructed a city called Athánatos Kardiá—Immortal Heart. He began conducting experiments to draw out the power of emotions. From these experiments, his closest friends and companions transformed into Résonateurs. Eidolon was now a legend." Serein's voice flared with excitement.

"Like any legend, we don't know the full truth, but it's said that Suzerain Eidolon ruled for over one hundred years before some great tragedy struck his city—a terrible event that took the life of his queen. Then the first Phases appeared. Eidolon was so devastated, as the legend goes, that his sudden surge of powerful emotions drew the Phases out from the earth beneath his city. Athánatos Kardiá fell into complete chaos. Citizens became dampened and massacred each other in droves. Left with no choice, Eidolon was forced to use his power to bring the city down in the hopes of killing the Phases, sacrificing himself in the process.

"Only Eidolon's son, the scientist, and a handful of new Résonateurs managed to survive. Not wanting his father's legacy to die, his son constructed a new city, Éthéré Coeur, and a dynasty was born," Serein concluded.

An uneasy silence fell over me. "That's a pretty sad story," I finally said. Eidolon achieved what he wanted, but to what end? His entire city was destroyed by Phases, and he lost his life.

"Yes, in some ways, but even though Eidolon was never seen again, he left a great legacy. Thanks to his effort, we've risen to where we are today. We still use the technology they discovered in the Solenoids. And as for the Résonateurs, why, we wouldn't even exist if it wasn't for Eidolon's experiments," Serein explained. "You asked why I thought anyone could become a Résonateur. If they were able to pull out that power from ordinary people thousands of years ago, the potential must still exist."

His eyes gleamed. I had never seen Serein like this. He was excited and proud, like a boy who received a new toy. The air around me felt buoyant and lively, and I couldn't help but share in his good cheer.

"And have they?" I asked with a smile. "Been able to produce new Résonateurs with the technology?"

Serein's grin faltered. "No," he replied. "No one has been transformed into a Résonateur since Eidolon died. But that doesn't mean it couldn't still happen," he added quickly. "I believe Eidolon was just a catalyst. Instead of relying on his power, it's possible for someone to unlock the power on their own. You have to look deep enough into your own heart."

Serein's idea was wonderful, but how was it possible? You were either born a Résonateur, or you were not. But I wouldn't share my thoughts. I didn't want to crush his passion. It inspired me to see him so animated.

"We should continue on," said Serein. He looked at the sun. "We only have a few hours of light left."

I studied his face. He was still pale. "Are you sure you don't need longer to rest?"

"I can't, Gavril. The longer we wait, the harder it will be." He went to grab his left shoulder but stopped, his mouth twisting. "If it wasn't for this damn injury . . ."

My gaze fell to the gravel. If he had let me go, he wouldn't have been hurt.

"It's not your fault," he said.

I looked back up at him, surprised.

He buried his face in his palm. "You wouldn't have been on the sky deck in the first place if it wasn't for me," he continued. "That dampened girl . . . I shouldn't have . . . not in the middle of the port."

I pulled his hand down from his face. He looked at me, eyes tired. The girl's mangled body flashed in my mind. I closed my eyes and willed the image away. She was dead. It was done. He did his duty.

"You did what you needed to protect everyone," I said, not wanting him to punish or doubt himself. I opened my eyes. "Just like you're doing now. I don't know what it's like to be a Résonateur and have to make those kinds of decisions, but I would be dead if it weren't for you."

"*I* would be dead if it weren't for *you*," he replied. "Fate couldn't have put me in better hands."

I blushed and averted my gaze to the river. "We should drink some water," I said, trying to hide my embarrassment. "We don't want to be dehydrated on top of everything else."

I helped Serein scoop some mouthfuls of water from the river, which he drank greedily. Our thirst satiated, we set off. We walked in silence for a small stretch, just enough time for me to dwell on my impending fate—and the fate of Nostalgie.

"Serein," I broke the quiet, "do you really think it's possible for me to convince the Suzerain to send a new Solenoid to Nostalgie?"

Serein placed his hand on my back. It was a small touch, but a reassuring one. "You're positive he will find you innocent of conspiring with a Phase, then?"

"Well, I'm n-not p-p-positive," I stuttered.

"I'm glad to hear your confidence." His fingers lightly grazed my shoulder blade as he moved his hand to squeeze my shoulder, and my locked muscles nearly turned to jelly despite the tense topic. "The Suzerain is an unusual man, but if you lay your heart bare before him, if you let him see the honesty and integrity behind your words, he may be moved."

Serein stepped in front of me, and we both stopped. A sober expression flashed across his face. "But, Gavril, remember what I told you about desperation. Don't let it become your only option. If you let it consume you, you may destroy all other paths."

"I'll try to be strong," I vowed, staring deep into his cloudy eyes. Such a storm of strength and knowledge and power. Oh, how I admired him.

Serein beamed at me, and we began walking again. "I know you will. Let's keep going. We don't want to be caught out in the open during the night."

I surveyed the field around us. There was no shelter, just a few small patches of trees here and there, but no groves large enough to hide in.

"If the dampened are so ruthless, why don't they come for us now?" I asked.

"I can't say for sure," Serein said. "Dampened typically prefer to move at night to avoid detection, but that wouldn't matter in a place like this. To be honest, Gavril, we've been lucky. They must've gone looking for the *Fulgurant* and missed us. They can't sense our emotions like Phases do, so perhaps they are still unaware of our presence."

I looked up at the sky and felt a tug in my heart. Morrow. If she were here, she could help. At the very least, she could protect us until we found our way out. My gaze returned to Serein. It pained me, but he was too injured to fight.

It might be the perfect time to tell him everything. To let him know I'd been lying to him the whole time. To see if he would still feel the same about me though I had befriended a Phase.

My insides curled and I felt sick again. He would reject me, and Morrow would kill him.

"Should we be worried about Phases around here?" I dreaded the answer, but I needed to know.

"You should always worry about Phases," Serein replied grimly. "But again, fortune may be in our favor. Dampened don't attract Phases as they possess no emotions. Since this area has been void of emotions for so long, it's unlikely Phases are nearby. But in case something happens"—Serein placed a hand over his heart—"I promise I will protect you with my life. I will give everything I have, Gavril."

I felt it again. Something in the air, radiating from Serein, that put my mind and body at ease. It was warm and reassuring. Every boulder of worry I carried disintegrated to sand.

We walked for another hour or so. The closer we drew to the narrow black gap in the silver rock of the mountain, the more a sense of foreboding grew. It soon overshadowed Serein's warmth.

I had to be brave like him. I couldn't rely on him for everything. Only the Great Heart knew why he put himself in danger to save me. I thought back to those moments before the *Fulgurant* went down. That blissful feeling and how it emboldened me to act on my desires. My cheeks flushed again, and I prayed Serein wouldn't notice.

I never knew such a feeling could exist for anyone, let alone someone like me. Were happiness and security achievable together? With

Serein, everything seemed possible. As long as he stayed with me, I could open my heart to the world. But if he left . . .

Unease gnawed my stomach. He hadn't said anything about my nearly kissing him. Now was not the time to bring it up, but . . .

Did his evasiveness mean he didn't feel the same way? Was he purposely pretending nothing happened in the hopes I would let it go?

Serein's pace slowed and he took in several deep breaths. The air around me cooled as though flames were doused.

Serein swayed. I threw my arm around his waist, afraid he would pass out. "Serein, what's wrong?"

"I'm sorry, Gavril." He rubbed his face, sweating profusely. "We're so close, but my energy is draining fast."

"You need to rest. We've pushed too hard." How could I have let him push his limits?

I helped the unsteady commandant to a downed log by the river's edge. Serein dropped onto the wood and swayed backward. I threw my arms around him, swiftly latching onto him. My hands pressed into his back, and he hissed.

"I'm s-sorry." I snatched my hands away from the deep gash.

"No, no, it's fine." He spoke between clenched teeth. "I just need to sit for a minute."

"You need more than a minute, Serein," I replied. "We're not going anywhere."

I put my hand on his cheek. It was hot and damp. His eyes rolled, but he shook his head and stayed upright.

"You need to lie down," I told him. "Here." I pulled on his arms until he sagged to the ground in front of the log, rolling onto his side. "We need something to eat. I'll see if I can find some berries before the sun goes down."

"Gavril, no." He grasped my hands. "I'll come too. It's dangerous."

"You can barely stand, Serein," I argued. "You'll grow weaker if you don't get some nourishment."

Serein groaned and muttered under his breath. I took that as a reluctant agreement and pulled my hands from his. I turned toward the thick grass and shrubs surrounding us. There had to be something edible growing wild. I ran from bush to bush, racing against the twilight, desperately searching for anything familiar. Many times in Nostalgie a wild weed made the difference between filling an empty belly and not seeing the next day. Learning how to discern toxic from edible was one of the first things children learned. I squinted, trying desperately to spot any color among deep green. A little thicket next to a group of trees caught my eye as the sun dipped below the mountain range. It could be my last shot.

My dress snagged on a low bush, but I tore it free, not wasting a moment. I dove into the bushes, the thin branches scraping at my hands. Blackberries! I pulled thorny branch after thorny branch until something soft fell from the tangle and hit my foot. I dug deeper. There were more. I knelt and piled as many of the deep-colored fruits as I could into my skirt. When I emptied that side of the bush, I careful cradled the berries and crept to the other. Something bumped against my knee. I looked down. A basket. What was it doing out here? I picked it up. It was tightly woven and in great condition. Almost new.

My stomach dropped. I put the basket down, hoping it looked undisturbed. I surveyed the area. Nothing moved in the growing dark—not the wind or the potentially dangerous owner of the basket. I rose, carefully securing the blackberries in my skirt, and followed the babbling flow of the river back to Serein.

Serein was sitting up when I returned, one arm slung over the log as though he was about to topple over. "I was about to go after you," he rasped.

"I hope you like blackberries," I replied.

"Right now, they're my favorite food in the world."

I sat next to him, and he grabbed a handful from my skirt. "You eat the rest," he said.

"Serein, no. There are lots, and you need them more than I—"

"I'm a hindrance right now, Gavril," he said bluntly. "If we get attacked, I'm finished. But you have a chance to run. Eat and keep up your strength."

"I'll never leave you, Serein." I swallowed, my throat burning. "No matter what happens, I'm staying with you." I held my skirt over his lap and poured the berries into it. "So you better get your strength back or we can't run together."

Serein lowered his head, hiding his expression. "You should have been a Résonateur. They say *we're* supposed to have the purest hearts. It couldn't be further from the truth."

"That's not true, Serein." I cupped his cheek, and he slowly raised his tired eyes to me. "Anyone else would have shipped me to Éthéré Coeur in a crate. Your heart is as noble as they come."

"Only because of your influence." He placed his hand over mine, still on his cheek. "Do you know what I saw in Envie?"

I shook my head.

"The moment I stepped foot into that town, I was surrounded by negative emotions, like walking down a dark, frozen corridor with no sign of the end in sight. I've been in places plagued by unrest, but Envie was so . . . so consuming. It burrowed under my skin. I wanted nothing more than to escape that pit. I set my focus on the Solenoid and blocked out the dark hearts around me. But then something happened. When the seigneur told me a girl accused of having contact with a Phase was being brought before me, I turned expecting to see a void. Instead, I saw this glow. And I felt this warmth, a tiny ray of sun peeking through the clouds. The only light or warmth in that miserable place."

My eyes prickled, but I held the tears back to stay strong for him. But what he said about Envie . . . it was a hell for me, too. I tried to remain apathetic, tried to bury my despair for the sake of Nostalgie, but deep down I was so . . . so . . .

"It's okay to be sad, Gavril. Sorrow lets us know we survived."

I buried my face into his chest, tears pouring from my heart. It was all so awful. Watching Mama's life and sanity slowly dwindle away over a man who'd been gone seventeen years. Growing up with Edgard's hateful speech echoing in my ears. Being sold—by both of them—to a family that turned on me faster than an argent collector turned on compassion for the poor. Wanting to save them all anyway.

And through it all, the one creature they despised as a monster was the very being who kept me going. Morrow, the creature with no heart, led me to this man so I might finally find mine.

I pulled back from Serein's chest and gazed into his eyes. "Serein, there's something I need to tell—"

A sharp snap pierced the air.

Serein pulled me down against the log. I stared at the river ahead as we lay there in the night, barely breathing. Grass rustled and crunched in a slow, steady rhythm behind the log. The sound paused. Serein tensed against me, his clenched fist pressing against my stomach.

The footsteps started again and gradually died away. Serein continued to hold me, rigid and silent. "You should get some sleep," he finally whispered. "We'll stay hidden here for the night. I'll keep watch."

"You need to sleep more than I do," I responded softly. I watched the river flow over some black pebbles. They glinted in the moonlight. "Do you think it was a . . . a . . ."

"I'm fairly certain," Serein replied. "And I don't know how many more are out there. We need to get out of this valley. We'll reach Panique tomorrow."

And then what? What if they didn't have a relier? How were we going to reach someone then? We'd be trapped here, and there was no barrier to protect us from Phases for miles and miles.

"We can do this, Gavril," Serein whispered. "Do you believe in me?"

I turned and met his brooding gaze. "More than anything."

HOME OF THE LOST

Weeds and ivy grew around Panique and gripped it in a living shield. It looked like Jalousie. It sounded like Jalousie. It even smelled like Jalousie. And the atmosphere felt like Jalousie—an echo left to rot in solitude.

"I don't like it, either," Serein said, tuning into my worries. "But we have nowhere else to go. We need to find the former mayor's house. The relier should be there."

It had taken nearly the whole day to get to the town. Serein straightened and put on a determined face, but his pace grew slower and more cautious. We stood just outside Panique, our shadows growing tall in the late afternoon sun. About a dozen buildings still stood, shielded by the mountain walls on each side of the town. We needed the light and time was running out.

We searched through the buildings with care, but the more fleeting sunlight became, the harder it was to see into all of the small closets and deep corners. When I tripped over a broken chair, Serein suspended the search until morning.

We returned to a small single-roomed house with one entrance and two windows.

"The fewer rooms to keep an eye on the better," Serein explained.

We cleared the broken furniture and pulled a dusty mattress from a collapsed bed into the center of the floor.

"We'll try again at dawn." Serein carefully lowered himself to the mattress. "If we don't find a relier, we may have to continue through the pass. If we are lucky, the *Fulgurant* will be on the other side of the mountains."

"Do you think they managed to find help?" I sat next to him. "I hope Deryn didn't get hurt trying to land the soulever."

"You two have really become good friends in such a short time," he said. "I'm glad you've found someone to connect with. Both of you. Deryn puts on a brave face, but being confined to the control room takes its toll."

I smiled. "I'm jealous of her if I'm being honest. She's free and uninhibited. She says what she feels and isn't bothered by what other people think. I wish I could be more like that."

"There's nothing wrong with being considerate and tactful," Serein said. "You have respect for others' feelings and care about their well-being. That's a desirable trait. I wish people could be more like you."

"I think I've got you fooled." I chuckled. "I've been known to let out some tactless comments."

"Only honest ones, I'm sure." Serein let out a short laugh of his own before grimacing and grabbing his chest.

My smile dropped. "Serein, you're getting worse." I glanced at the pitch-black doorway. An eerie chill ran down my spine. "I could keep looking for the relier while you rest."

"No," Serein said firmly. "It's too dangerous."

"I'm not afraid."

Serein's lips pulled into a tired smile. "I know you're telling yourself that, but I'm afraid it's hard to fool a Résonateur." He gazed at the floor. "You're afraid and you should be. I've failed you in so many ways." He paused for a few seconds and licked his cracked lips. "There's something we should talk about. Gavril, before the explosion on the sky deck—"

"I'm sorry," I spat out. "I don't know what came over me. It was very forward. You're a commandant, and I'm—"

Serein grabbed my hand and turned the palm up, studying its scars. "To tell the truth, I wasn't sure how to feel about it at first."

My heart fell, knowing what was coming. Rejection. He was about to drop me.

"I could tell kindness wasn't something familiar in your life, especially after seeing the way the seigneur spoke to you," he continued. "I wanted to show you some warmth, but I must admit, I was afraid of overstepping my bounds. You are engaged, after all."

"Not by my own choosing," I said bitterly. Envie's first family wasn't even here and they managed to keep me bound, from getting what I wanted.

"I told you what I saw in Envie, and I can't deny that ever since that moment—through our conversations, and even our disagreements— there's been a connection. A growing bond. At least for me." He held my hand between his. "I thought I could ignore it. Résonateurs are good at pushing their emotions aside. But after watching you nearly die, seeing how you risked your life for mine, I can no longer stay silent. I know it's inappropriate. I have no right to feel this way. I don't want to put you in an awkward position, but the affection I have for you extends beyond my duties."

The air around me warmed, humid and palpable.

Serein leaned forward slowly.

My whole body burned—my flesh all the way to my core—as though I were transforming into living fire. My heart danced and flashed and flickered wildly, bursting through the last of the chains I had wrapped around it.

I crashed my lips into Serein's and pulled him down with me. Hot pulses of static ran all over my body. Serein's mouth caressed mine. His hands ran over my sides. Every place he touched was being blessed with pure, unfiltered *life*.

He pulled back. "I take it you feel the same way."

"I didn't think I ever could," I said, cupping his cheek. "But you've freed my heart." I grabbed his hand and moved it to the buttons along my neck. "I want to feel it all."

"Gavril, are you certain? Like this? With me?" He stared into my soul, igniting my heart.

"I can't imagine being with anyone else," I replied.

Even if I did end up marrying Cyril, at least he couldn't have this. This was my choice—the only one I had ever been given. And I would make sure it stayed in my heart forever.

Serein kissed me again, and I closed my eyes, trusting my entire being to him. He pulled away and—

Cold.

I felt very cold. The torrid touch extinguished into bitter chill.

"Serein, what—"

I shivered and opened my eyes. And I screamed.

A large man held Serein by his hair, a long knife pointed at his throat.

The man wore rags, barely enough to cover himself, and gray grit covered much of his skin. In the center of his chest lay a ring of dark gray veins. Thin vessels branched from it up his neck and down his limbs. He stared down at me with empty eyes. Dull, sparkless eyes.

A dampened.

"I knew someone was in the valley," he stated without a change in inflection. "I saw my fire reignite, so I waited here for the trespassers. It was a good idea. I've captured a Résonateur." He pressed the knife against Serein's skin, and a thin trail of blood trickled down his neck.

"Stop!" I shrieked.

The dampened released the knife's pressure. "We move. Tell your woman to follow silently, Résonateur. If she makes a sound, I will slit your throat and hers."

"Do as he says, Gavril," Serein said coolly. "Everything will be fine."

"No, it won't. Start walking." The dampened shoved Serein in the back.

Serein drew a sharp breath, and his jaw clenched.

I bit my lip and nervously followed, trying my best to keep even my breathing silent.

The man led us from the house to the mountainside along the edge of Panique. A small cave entrance hidden in the rock wall appeared in the moonlight.

"Inside," the man said.

Glowing torches lit up the space. Boxes, crates, and baskets of supplies littered the floor along with tools, food, and some mechanical equipment. There were other dampened too. People dressed in the scantest of clothing. Did they feel no modesty?

No. They don't feel anything.

The dampened dropped what they were doing and approached as we stopped in the middle of the cave. The dampened holding Serein looked at me.

"Over there," he said, pointing the knife at a spot about ten feet away. I silently complied and turned around to face him and Serein.

A woman with wild red hair tied Serein's hands behind his back with a length of coarse rope. I blanched. We could have been sisters.

"What do you want?" Serein growled at the man with the knife.

"We do not 'want,' as you know, Résonateur," the dampened replied, walking around to face Serein. "But it is important to our survival that you and your fellows leave us alone."

"Then let us go, and you'll never see me in this place again," Serein said.

"I do not believe you, Résonateur." The man pointed the knife at Serein's chin. "I know a Résonateur is willful and cannot leave duty behind. You have decided you must kill us, so you will return with allies."

"Fine. Keep me here, but let Gavril go," Serein said. "She's not a Résonateur. She poses no threat to you."

"On the contrary, she is a threat by being here with you. I cannot let her leave, knowing what she knows."

I held my hands to my neck. So, I would die here with Serein. Such an end I could bear as long as we were together. I just wished I could have done more with my time. Nostalgie would never get a Solenoid. I would never see Mama again. Never see Morrow. My heart clenched. I wanted to speak with Morrow one last time.

"If you're going to kill us, then get it over with," Serein spat. "But don't think I'll make it easy for you."

The air prickled around me, and the man with the knife struck Serein across his wounded back with his fist. Serein grunted and fell to his knees.

The air cleared.

"We won't give you the chance to use your power, Résonateur, so save your emotions," the red-haired woman said. She pulled a rusty stake from a wooden crate and held it up.

"It isn't enough to just kill you, Résonateur," the man said. "We must send a message, a warning for others to stay away. We are going to dismember your body, piece by piece, and stake your remains outside the entrance. No trespasser will dare disturb us again."

He grabbed Serein's hair and yanked his head back.

The redhead raised her arm . . .

"No!" I screamed. "What are you—"

. . . and she thrust it down.

A shrill cry echoed throughout the cave, and I couldn't tell if it was from Serein or me. Someone seized my arms and pushed me down.

"No," I sobbed. "No, no, no . . ."

I looked up as the redhead stepped back, and Serein's face came into view. Blood streamed down his right cheek. His eye . . . oh, Serein's beautiful eye . . .

The man released Serein's hair, and his head sagged forward.

"I meant to pluck it out," the woman said. "I'll get the next one."

"No, please," I begged. "I'm sorry. I'm sorry for what's been done to you. Please, don't hurt him anymore."

The woman approached and crouched before me. "Your apologies mean nothing to us. They cannot nourish our bodies or provide protection. What good are your words?"

"I-I know but . . ." I looked at Serein, and his suffering tore me apart. As did theirs. I understood. I had to make them see. "I know," I choked. "I know what it's like to live every day in fear and to long for nothing more than protection from the outside. But this isn't the way. Killing us will not bring safety. It will only bring others to hunt you."

She titled her head as if mulling over my words. "We shall only know what it brings when it happens." The red woman turned around and went back to Serein, towering over him with the stake clenched in her hand.

Bile rose in my throat. This couldn't be happening. These people—these *dampened*—how could they possibly do this? We had done nothing to them. *They're going to kill him for what he is, not who he is. It's just like Serein said. I shouldn't have questioned him.*

The woman raised the stake again. I closed my eyes. I jerked against the dampened holding me. I couldn't take it. I couldn't. Fear welled in me. It rose from my stomach and erupted out my mouth. *"Stop!"*

I opened my eyes.

The shout reverberated off the cave walls before the loud crack of wood breaking boomed out and pieces of crates scattered across the floor.

An uproar of shouts ensued as the dampened scattered throughout the cave.

"Phase."

"There's a Phase."

"Why is a Phase attacking us?"

The red-haired woman and the man holding Serein dove to the floor as a swirling vortex of black luster launched at them.

Morrow!

"It must be after the Résonateur," the woman said, slowly rising to her feet. "Let's retreat to the town until it's finished with him."

"I agree," her associate replied, voice still flat despite the danger. "Hurry. It's coming again."

The dampened clamored for the exit with Morrow on their heels. As soon as the cave was clear, I raced to Serein's side. I untied the rope binding his wrists and rolled him over. A deep gash ran through his left eyebrow. The eye below it was fine, but his right eye—

"Commandant!"

I whipped my head up. Hervé ran toward us. He knelt down and grabbed Serein's shoulder, taking a long look at his battered form.

"I've got to say, Comm, you've definitely been in better shape." Hervé hauled Serein up and slung him over his shoulder. "Come on," he grunted to me.

I scrambled to my feet and sprinted after Hervé. As soon as we got out of the cave, relief swelled in my chest. A small gray soulever waited in the field outside the edge of Panique, a ladder hanging down the side. When we arrived, two men in beige uniforms leaned out the hatch and helped Hervé bring Serein on board. After I climbed in, Hervé yanked up the ladder, and the soulever ascended.

I followed Hervé and the men carrying Serein down a central corridor to a room with a bed, jars of different colored liquids, and a strong acrid smell. A short balding man with a thick mustache promised to "patch what's left," and ordered everyone out.

The door to the medical bay closed.

I stared at the door for several seconds before looking at Hervé.

"How did you find us?"

"It was easy," Hervé muttered, stretching his neck. "There's only one main entrance to the Vallée de la Solitude. And then we followed the Phase."

"You followed a Phase?"

"Yeah. Led us right to you. Guess I should send it a note of gratitude next time I'm in the area. Which will hopefully be never." Hervé set off down the hall. "The crew rooms are on the floor below this one," he said as he went. "Help yourself. Henri's a skilled medic, but Serein's going to be in there for a while."

I turned back to the medical bay door with a heart full of conflicting emotions. Happiness, sorrow, relief, mourning, dread. How could so many feelings exist at once? I took in several breaths, trying to settle my nerves as best I could, and left for the lower deck. My head and body ached, and I yearned for rest. I located a vacant room and sat on the bed.

Rapt . . . rapt . . . rapt . . .

I turned to the window, and a porcelain face peered in. I shot to the window and pushed it open.

"Morrow, I'm so glad to see you," I said.

"Are you injured?"

"No, and it's all thanks to you." I offered her a tender smile. "I can't thank you enough. If there's any way I can repay you, Morrow, please name it."

"There is no need for 'thanks.' I did what needed to be done."

"You saved our lives," I insisted. "I'm so grateful."

"I saved your life. The Résonateur is not my priority."

I lowered my gaze. If that was the case, then she could have waited until they finished with Serein before starting on me. "I'm still in your debt," I said. "I missed you."

"I had a task to attend to. I did not realize how incapable in danger the Résonateur is."

"He barely survived the fall, Morrow," I defended my protector, but left it at that. If I got too far into the topic of Serein, she would fly away. "Were you able to complete what you needed to?"

"I was not. Many things have changed. The ruins sealed. I am abated."

"What are you trying to do, Morrow? You can trust me," I assured her. "I won't tell anyone."

"It is not time for you to accept the knowledge."

"Knowledge?" I repeated.

"Yes," Morrow replied. "Knowledge that has been buried for thousands of years. For now, it must stay buried."

"Why?"

Morrow's dark eyes continued to stare at me, unblinking. Despite her expressionless face, I swore I saw something in her gaze. She was thinking. Weighing her options.

"You have a mission," she said quietly. "Something important to you."

"I do." I nodded earnestly. "I'm going to save Nostalgie."

"There isn't much time left."

My eyes fell. "I know. I'm not sure I can do it, Morrow . . . do you believe I can?"

"I . . ." she sighed.

I looked back up.

Her gaze remained on me, unwavering. "I believe you can save Nostalgie."

I smiled. I didn't expect her to say it. She probably didn't believe it, but she said it anyway.

"It warms my heart to hear you say that," I said. "Will you stay around until we reach Éthéré Coeur? I like knowing you are with me."

"I will watch over you while you are in the sky, although the dangerous element has presently been removed."

"I appreciate that, Morrow. You're a true friend."

"You need rest," Morrow said abruptly. "The dampened were merely a nuisance. True trials await in the future." With a flash, she disappeared from my window.

I sighed and closed the glass. One day, I would invite her inside where she couldn't vanish.

I lay back on the bed and closed my eyes. The long day of exertion and mental strain dropped on me in an instant. My breathing evened out, and darkness swept in.

PRIVILEGE OF CALME

Serein's torso and face were clean and freshly bandaged. I'd overheard the medic telling Hervé that he'd done all he could, but some things were beyond repair. I looked at the bandages covering Serein's right eye and squeezed his hand. What a terrible loss.

Hervé leaned against the wall in the corner of Serein's room, ignoring my presence.

Serein groaned, and his left eye fluttered open. I sat up straight as his lone dark pupil trailed over to me and then to Hervé.

"I take it you rescued us," his voice cracked, dry and hoarse.

"Most of you," Hervé quipped. "We're on the *Scarabée.*"

"What about the *Fulgurant*? Did everyone make it out?" Concern tinged Serein's voice.

"Well, Deryn's wearing more silk than she ever has in her life with those full-body bandages. Our Birdy refused to leave her chair throughout the whole thing, even with all that glass raining down on her. Bibiane took a nasty spill into one of the console desks. She was out for half a day, and her forehead swelled about twice the size—if you can believe that. Both have already gone on to Éthéré Coeur with the rest of the crew. And Ciseau . . ." Hervé broke off and rubbed his chin. "Overall, we suffered three casualties. Two unlucky sub-opérateurs who happened to be in the storeroom above the siphon. And Marteau."

"Marteau? What happened?" Serein's eye narrowed.

"He was down near the siphon when it exploded. Probably went down to grab a bottle of liquor after Bibiane chewed him out for drawing a few bosoms on the inspection sheet. Ciseau's likely the only one who knows for sure, and he hasn't said a word since it happened. Shock of losing someone dear, I know."

I placed my hand on my chest. My heart went out to the remaining twin. I couldn't imagine what it must be like to be parted from your brother and best friend.

"Why did the siphon explode?" With great effort, Serein pushed himself up on his elbows. I held my hand out to stop him, but he ignored it and continued until he was sitting. "Have you any idea?"

Hervé shook his head. "Not a clue. Deryn didn't detect anything in the *Fulgurant's* systems, and all the sub-opérateurs say everything was in normal limits. I've requested the Paramount send some carrier soulevers to recover her and conduct a detailed review of the siphon. Maybe that will give us some answers."

"Thank you, Hervé. I'll be eager to hear the results of the inspection."

"So will I." Hervé pushed away from the corner. "I'll leave you to it, Comm. I came to make sure you still have some wits left."

"Just a few," Serein replied with a grin. "I'll be back to top shape in no time."

"You hope," Hervé said and left the room.

When the door closed, Serein grabbed my hand and pulled it to his lips. "I'm glad you're safe, Gavril," he declared, kissing my hand repeatedly. "So glad."

"I'm fine, Serein. But you . . ." Tears pooled in the corners of my eyes. "Your eye. Oh, your eye is—"

"I have a spare eye, Gavril," Serein said with a gentle smile. "I don't have a spare *you*."

"It's still horrible what happened."

Serein nodded. "Was I imagining things when I heard a Phase flew in the cave?" he asked slowly. "Wouldn't have been a friend of yours, would it?"

The blood in my veins froze, and a thousand panicked questions swirled through my mind. *What should I say? Does he know? How can he possibly know?*

"I'm kidding, Gavril." Serein chuckled. "It's been a stressful few days. Why don't you take a break and get some rest?"

"But, Serein, you just woke up. I don't want to leave you—"

"Not a lot of places for me to go," he countered. "Please, I know it's been hard on you. I want you to be well-rested before we get to Éthéré Coeur. Once we arrive, sleep will be the last thing on your mind."

"If that's what you think is best," I said numbly, lowering my eyes. I walked to the door, glancing back at Serein. He smiled encouragingly, and I shut the door behind me.

Outside, I pressed my ear against the door and listened. Moments later, I heard a muffled grunt and a sharp intake of breath. It wasn't personal. It was pride. We weren't alone anymore. Serein didn't want anyone to see him struggle as he kept his emotions under control.

I quietly returned to my room. If only Serein trusted me enough to let me into his heart. I wanted him to share his pain. He could open his emotions to me. He didn't have to bear the burden of being a Résonateur alone. He didn't have to spend so much of himself maintaining control.

I winced as Serein's hot, damp fingers squeezed my hand. He thrashed and kicked, unintelligible sounds rasping from his cracked lips.

"It's not good," Henri muttered to Hervé. "The infection's spread like wildfire. I don't have enough *tonique* on the soulever to fight it back."

"It's three days until we reach Éthéré Coeur," Hervé replied. "Do you think he can make it that long, Henri?"

"It's risky—"

"Then we won't chance it." Hervé turned to the door. "I'll tell the opérateur to head for Calme. We can be there in half the time, and they have a decent clinic."

"I'll make a list of medicines to stock up on," Henri said, following Hervé out.

I held Serein's hand to my chest and bowed my head. Calme was Serein's home. We were taking him home, where he would be able to rest and get the medicine he needed. And he could see his family again. Home was important.

Home would heal him.

I glanced at the bandage over his wounded eye. A thin trail of yellow crust below it stuck to his cheek. The red-haired woman who took his eye . . . what was she doing now? Was she upset we got away? Did she regret not killing us on the spot?

She felt nothing. No upset, no regret. But still, despite not feeling anything toward Serein, she and the others tried to kill him. The dampened were hopeless. They were beyond help and beyond heart. They were monsters. They were real monsters, and a Solenoid couldn't stop them.

Serein tried to tell me. Instead of listening, I showed him just how much of a foolish peasant I was. I argued with him in their defense, and they nearly killed him. The dampened nearly killed the man I loved.

I looked down at my hand intertwined with Serein's. To think I almost touched Morrow.

I stayed with Serein all day. I dabbed his face with a cool wash-cloth, whispered softly to him through his fits, and averted my eyes when the medic changed his soiled bandages. I sat and waited and watched, and when my head felt heavier than the moon, I curled up next to him, trying with all my might to pull the pain from his being. *Let me be your siphon. Let me take your burden.*

The bed jumped beneath me, and I sprang up. All was quiet. Serein uttered a barely audible moan.

Hervé entered the medical bay and stared at Serein for a moment. "He's gotten weaker." He beckoned for me. "You're coming with me. We've got some errands to run."

I stared back at him, eyes wide. "I can't. If I leave him—"

"Listen, girl, as far as the Paramount is concerned, you're still a criminal awaiting trial. Since the commandant is currently unable to keep you under his supervision, the responsibility falls on me."

"Then chain me here," I replied. "I'm not leaving him."

"That's still a problem because Henri and the boys are going to take Serein to the clinic. Someone's got to keep an eye on you."

I placed my hand on Serein's forehead. He didn't respond to my touch.

"They'll take care of him?"

"Better than you and I can," Hervé replied.

I sighed and pulled my hand back. "What do we need to do?"

"*I* need to get in touch with Éthéré Coeur to let them know Serein's still alive and to see what's happening with our crew." Hervé stroked his stubble. "There's also the matter of the dampened in Panique to report."

I stared at the floor. So they were going to be hunted after all. Perhaps it was for the best. There was no saving those souls, but we could protect any unfortunate travelers who found themselves lost in the Vallée de la Solitude.

"*You* are going to stay where I can see you at all times and keep your head down," Hervé continued. "I don't want to draw any more attention to myself than is necessary."

I looked back up at Hervé. "Is Calme not a safe place?"

"It's safer than the Suzerain's garters," Hervé muttered. "And that's part of the problem. They aren't used to . . . well"— his eyes trailed over me—"people like you and me."

"Heretics?"

"Those in want."

"Oh." I glanced down at my dress—the dress I had only days ago been so proud and pleased with. Traces of mud from the river streaked the hem, and shrubs had snagged the cotton in a few places. Even in its original condition, it wasn't good enough for here. Not for Serein's home.

"Let's go," Hervé said. "Best get it over with."

I nodded and gave Serein's hand one last squeeze. I followed Hervé to the soulever's hatch and climbed down the ladder to the smooth pearly-gray floor of Calme's port. The port in Remords was rough. It was old, well used, and had never seen a broom in its life. This port was not rough. Or dirty. Or cheap.

The ramps and platforms were glossy, polished steel instead of rusted iron. No clutter or junk to be found. The docks were neat, arranged in lines with the smaller soulevers on one side and the larger ones on the other. Workers in clean uniforms pushed the energy cylinders onto flat-topped automatrams and easily maneuvered the refueling tanks to each dock in wait.

"Birdy hates this port," Hervé stated. "Said any maintenance floor you can lick and come back with a polished tongue is focusing on the wrong—what's that word she likes to throw around? Shite."

I smiled. "Yes, that sounds like her."

I followed Hervé out the port, keeping my head down and eyes focused on the spotless floor. It was true. There wasn't a single scuff.

The smooth gray suddenly stopped at the top of a large ramp.

From that point forward, down the stairs and beyond, light sand-colored square paver stones led the way into a marvelous town surrounding us in uniform rows. The buildings were all at least two-storied and had smooth stucco walls in vibrant pastel colors. Houses fronted with decorative shapes and bright painted patterns lined the streets. They were so close together that balconies from adjacent windows nearly touched. Small patches of grass and flower gardens framed each doorstep, wilting in the crisp fall air.

As I studied each new door, one opened. A man in a velvet top hat and long overcoat stepped out. He met my gaze. He frowned at me and turned to Hervé.

"Is that you, old prickle?" the top-hatted man said. "I know you've gotten used to slumming it in the Paramount, but these sorts of activities won't stand here." He nodded his chin at me. "Especially the exotic ones."

Hervé stopped short, and I nearly ran into his back.

"Mind your own business, Noam," Hervé grunted. "We actually have something important to do. Not all of us have the luxury to dick around with our minds in the gutter."

Noam swept one hand down his coat and cleared his throat. "I see culture is still not your strong point. Even now that you've fallen and had to rely on the charity of others—"

"Is there a point to your annoying chatter other than to hear your own voice?" Hervé barked. "Like I said, some of us do things of importance, while others take up barrier space."

"How's your son, Hervé?"

Hervé's expression sharpened. He gripped my arm firmly and stalked off with me in tow, growling threats and heated insults.

We rounded a corner and entered a bustling street lined with shops.

"Who was that?" I asked.

Hervé released my arm. "A man soon to have his house burned down."

I knew that feeling. Though our interaction was brief, Noam reminded me of Gervais, all pomp and no substance. It seemed no matter how high, the upper class still needed someone to look down on.

"I've met a few of those," I said. "More than a few."

Hervé slowed and rubbed his forehead. "I hate this place. It's full of old acquaintances who know too much and won't shut up."

That's how it was in a barrier. There were no secrets. Everybody knew everybody's business, and it wasn't until something more scandalous came around that other missteps were temporarily pushed aside. Your life and decisions were always judged. There was no moving on.

"We better pick up the pace," Hervé said. "Now that clown knows I'm here, we haven't much time. If I'm here, he knows Serein is here, and he's sure to inform Seigneur Rodrigue. I don't feel like lasting an interrogation today."

"Serein knows the seigneur?" It shouldn't have been surprising. As a commandant, Serein was likely familiar with many of the patricians in affluent towns.

"More than he cares to," Hervé muttered. "The relier hub is up ahead. Don't make eye contact with anyone."

The shops were packed. I didn't realize so many people could exist in one town without complete chaos. But Serein did say there were three Solenoids. Was Calme split into sections like Remords?

"How big is Calme?" I asked. "The houses were set out in straight rows. Do they have the Solenoids stretched out like a line?"

"All three are together a few rows down that way," Hervé replied, tilting his head to the left. "The barrier is one giant sphere, but the locals like to keep things square. Limits growth." Hervé stuffed his hands in his pockets and slouched. "Bigger, more *important* towns like this have certain privileges with the Sommet. If the population becomes too large for the established housing, the seigneur can appeal to the council and have selected families relocated."

"To where?"

"Wherever they can get in. But the newest arrivals aren't always sent away first. Sometimes an old family falls out of favor and gets a shiny boot in the ass." His dull eyes narrowed. "No matter what sacrifices they've made."

I glanced at the shoppers meandering without a care. Sacrifice. That was something only a few could make and even fewer appreciated. A gift of the heart that was always taken for granted.

My eyes drifted back to Hervé. But for him, it sounded very personal.

A large circular building with several wide windows formed the relier hub. A thick antenna about twenty feet high sprouted out of the top. Inside, several small stations with vigile docks honeycombed around a separate room at the building's core. A solitary woman stood in front of the door leading to the central room.

The woman—clearly an archiviste—wore a lilac jacket and skirt identical to Bibiane's, and her short auburn hair was neatly tucked behind her ears.

"I need to communicate with the Paramount on behalf of Commandant Serein," Hervé told the woman. "It's urgent."

"For a commandant, of course." The woman responded with a smile that didn't quite reach her eyes. "We'll send the bill to the Sommet."

Hervé nodded and grabbed the door handle. He stood there for a moment, then turned back to me.

"Wait out here," he ordered. "If anyone asks who you are, tell them you're a witness to a gruesome murder or something. Don't try to run."

"I would never leave Serein."

"So you say." He opened the door. "Desperation has a way of breaking our 'nevers.'"

Hervé disappeared into the round room. I stared at the closed door. Serein said something similar to me when we first met. He warned me not to fall into desperation and let it be my only weapon.

The archiviste cleared her throat, and I turned to meet her gaze. She stared back at me with the same false smile still stuck to her face. It chewed at my nerves.

"We don't get too many lesser people in here," she said. "Try not to touch anything."

"There's nothing here worth touching," I retorted, glaring around the room before returning my gaze to her. "People included."

Her brown eyes subtly shifted, but her face remained masked with a grin. "Touching people isn't in my work description. I prefer to leave that to the professionals." She looked me up and down. "Like you. That's how the plebeian girls make their argent, right?"

"Actually, we know how to work hard and make do with what we're given. You wouldn't last a day in my home," I said, my voice hard. "You wouldn't last a day outside this station. It must be hard to be so pitiful."

The archiviste's lips flattened into a scowl. "As soon as your monsieur is done with the relier, I want you to leave and never dirty my floor again." She stepped away from me. "I'm going outside for some fresh air. The stench has become overwhelming. And don't think about sneaking in with your man. I like to keep the seats clean."

I glared at her as she walked away. Her attitude toward me shouldn't be so shocking. People like her were always looking for someone to lord over. Nearly every person I'd met since leaving Nostalgie thought of themselves as "better" and talked down to me. Everyone except Serein and Deryn. Even Hervé in his own cynical way.

"I'm done," Hervé announced, returning from the relier room. "I hate talking to those vigile fumblers. They want every little detail laid out. They've got no imagination. Like Bibiane."

"Imagination takes passion," I replied. "It's easier to live a life pushing facts."

"And I see you pushed that fake-faced archiviste out the door. Got to admire that fear of peasants. Never found a patrician who didn't believe poverty was contagious."

"Do you believe it is?" I asked.

"Maybe once," he said.

Hervé struck me as a man caught between two worlds. He was from privilege. I could tell that much. But he didn't speak like others of privilege and didn't keep up his appearance like the rest. What could force such a change?

"Argent can't save you from pain," he said. "It can only coddle you into thinking you're above consequences." He glanced to the crowded street beyond the windows. "We should get to the clinic. Serein will receive priority because of his title, but a little prodding never hurts."

I nodded and followed Hervé outside. As we passed the archiviste, she held her nose high and wafted her hand as though a bad smell drifted close.

I smiled. This would be where Deryn loudly made a gas comment. I missed my friend and her wit. She never let anyone get her down.

The clinic wasn't too far from the port. That probably made getting medical supplies in and out easier. The sky-blue rectangular structure had no windows and only one entrance.

The pungent smell of alcohol permeated the clinic interior. It held no tables or chairs, just a white wall with an arched doorway.

Henri walked out from the archway, furiously rubbing his bald head with a yellow cloth.

Hervé let out a deep groan. "Why do I get the impression you're not going to tell me anything I want to hear?"

"It's the medic here," Henri hissed. "He won't let us take Serein back to the *Scarabée*. 'Keeping him out of the hands of an amateur,' he said. Amateur!" Henri snapped the cloth down. "That pompous posterior hasn't seen half the injuries I've dealt with. He's just trying to win points with the Paramount by treating a commandant like he's on death's doorstep."

"Well, he was looking pretty dead when we flew in." Hervé rubbed the back of his neck. "Where's this guy? I'll talk to him."

"Bay five." Henri pointed through the archway. "I'm going to finish restocking the soulever's cabinet. Let me know how you get on with the great anus."

"That's my favorite thing to talk about," Hervé replied. "Let me find out what's going on. Don't let the opérateur leave without us. If he does, he'll find himself without a soulever or his left hand."

Henri stomped to the door. "I'll pass the message on."

Hervé released a heavy sigh. "Have you ever felt that all the dung in the world only drops on you?"

I tilted my head. "I wouldn't know how it felt any other way. But it's okay."

"Falling dung is okay?"

"Yes," I asserted. "Because when you're covered, you can truly appreciate the moments when it stops."

Hervé snorted. "I can see how you've managed to develop that small ounce of hope, but I have to disagree. When it stops, it's just a trick—a cruel temptation to show you how life could have been. But it always returns in the end, deeper and fouler than ever."

He set those sparkless eyes on me, and my shoulders tensed.

"It's stopped for you, heretic girl. Don't let it bury you when the tide comes."

I balled my fists. "When that time comes, I won't be alone. I have Serein—"

"You don't," Hervé said flatly. "Serein is a Résonateur and a commandant. You're his prisoner. Don't forget that."

My chest burned. "No, we're more than that. In the valley—"

"I don't care what happened in the valley. I don't care what happened in Envie or Remords or in his bedchambers. You'll never fit in with his life. And his family—"

"I could try," I burst out. "His family is here in Calme, right? I could meet them and bring—"

"Don't," Hervé snapped. "Don't even think about it."

Tears welled in my eyes, and I held my hand to my heart. For a moment, I had thought Hervé was different, but he was just like the rest. "Why?"

"Serein's young," he said. "He's got his whole life ahead of him and it leads up, not down. And people like us, girl, we're so far down that the damn earth is choking us."

I ran out the clinic, my eyes so blurred with tears that I bumped into people. They scoffed at me. Yelped. Threw insults at my retreating back. Not one person asked what was wrong or if I needed help.

Memories of Envie's citizens merged with the Calme crowd. Fine silks deteriorated. Masks frayed. Fancy hats shriveled and grew holes. Faces distorted, twisting together into one hideous creature.

Once again, I was on trial. Lost. Where was Nostalgie?

I stumbled down one street of tan brick and colorful blocks after the other, twisting and turning. When the sun set, bright balls of étincelle sparked to life on wires strung between the buildings, casting a light so bright that the night sky glowed. How could they tell it was night? Did the town never slumber? Did they not want to see the stars? Or were the stars so close that they didn't need to reach?

Sore from pounding against stone instead of soft earth, my feet slowed, and I came to a solid white curved wall about the same height as a shrub. It blocked my path, a caution that the edge of this town's world was near. I placed my hands on the edge and vaulted over it. The outside world called to me. I had tasted it, and now I was addicted.

Grass sprang through my worn soles. It felt wonderful, fresh. Alive. So alive was the world beyond barriers and walls and towns. A brand-new horizon waiting to be discovered.

I took another step, and a soothing rush spread over my body. The tingling lingered, and I debated turning around and stepping back through the barrier, reveling in its warmth. Bathing in it was the closest feeling to being with Serein I could get.

I looked up at the night sky. Still cast with the brilliant light of Calme. I walked toward the darkness. It wasn't so scary. Not when you had a friend out there.

"Morrow," I called. "Please, tell me you're out here somewhere."

Something flitted in the corner of my vision. I whipped my head around to face it. In the distance, a faint shimmer snaked in the air, twirling around like a flag in a gale.

I smiled widely and chased the ethereal cloud, longing to speak with Morrow. She would listen and not judge like the rest. She was good. She was nothing but good.

The Phase darted toward a grove of tall trees. A sight not common near Nostalgie or other small towns as they had been cut down for housing, but Calme didn't have to scavenge for resources. The Sommet took care of them.

"Wait, Morrow." I raised my hand. "I'm right here."

The swirling vortex stopped, the waves of its body stilling like a dead calm over water. A white head with black veins twisting along its crown slowly rose from the ebony cloud.

"Morrow . . ."

The Phase slowly turned toward me with an expression as neutral and non-threatening as a newborn baby's.

But this Phase was male.

Eyes the color of slate focused on me, and the alabaster visage chilled my blood.

The Phase's mouth opened—a great black maw—and I paused. Waited for it to speak, to say anything. To show me that it was like Morrow.

A screech louder than a flock of screaming owls exploded through the air, and my heart leapt into my chest. Calme's lights called me, and I ran, my feet barely hitting the ground.

The barrier. The barrier. The barrier. Get inside the barrier.

Even as sweat poured down my forehead, a cold breath swept over the back of my neck, biting my flesh and crawling down into my spine.

The warm rush of the barrier whooshed over me. Behind me, a warped crack shattered the night air. Pulses of white streaks danced along the barrier from the point of the Phase's contact, rippling along like lightning coating the surface of a bottle until they faded. The streaks crackled a few more times before disappearing into the invisible shield that protected us.

I collided with the white wall, the edge digging into my ribs, and threw myself over it. I slid to the ground on the other side and drew my legs in, my chest heaving.

There was nowhere to go. Inside. Outside. It didn't matter. I buried my face into my knees. There were monsters everywhere.

"What's this girl doing here?" a sharp voice asked. "Is this where it happened? Girl, what did you see?"

I raised my head. A tall gentleman in a blue frock coat and gray knee trousers looked down at me with piercing eyes colored like the silver of an aged tree. Gold buttons ran down the front of his coat and adorned the wide cuffs. White gloves covered his hands, and long gray hair ran down his back like a smooth stream.

"Are you going to stare all night like a mute, girl? I asked you a question."

I hauled myself up from the ground and stared over the wall to the outside. "There's a Phase out there."

"Not again," the man muttered. "Jacques," he barked.

A skinny boy with mousy hair ran up to the man and stopped beside him, back as straight as a rod. The look on his face was one I'd seen a hundred times on Mathieu—terrified, yet so desperately eager to please.

"Yes, Seigneur Rodrigue."

Seigneur? I clenched the skirt of my dirt-covered dress. I'd come so far that a real seigneur was addressing me.

"Go to the relier hub and tell the Sommet that our problem has resurfaced," Seigneur Rodrigue continued. "I want someone to actually kill it this time, not just scare it off. I'm tired of dealing with greenhorns. Tell them to send a professional Résonateur—Serein, if he can shake his pride long enough to come home."

"Serein?"

The moment the name left my lips, I felt it again. The sharp sting of judgment bearing down on me.

"*You* know Serein?" the seigneur asked.

Yes, I know Serein. He saved me from being martyred. He talks to me, cares for me. We even kissed—the greatest joy I've ever known.

I looked into the seigneur's eyes. There it was. Disbelief. Disgust even, shaping his cold gaze in the subtle curl of his lips and the crease of his forehead. Because Serein was a commandant. He was one of the greatest Résonateurs in Premier Esprit. He was strong, handsome, wealthy, and could have any girl he desired. He was perfect. And I was . . . I was so far down I choked on the damn earth.

"I've heard of him," I said. "He's pretty famous."

"A little too famous for his own good, it seems," the seigneur replied. "I don't know where you're from, girl, but I can tell it's not here. Our young ladies don't squat in the streets late at night."

Seigneur Rodrigue put a gloved hand on my back, not close enough to offer comfort, but a touch meant to prod me along like cattle away from the wall toward the rows of buildings. A silver automatram waited in the road with its engine humming as smoothly as a freshly tuned siphon. The design was sleek, sides rounded and smooth, not boxy like Gervais' monstrosity in Envie.

The seigneur pointed over the top of the automatram at a tall, open-roofed building in the heart of town.

"That's the soulever port," he said. "Just start walking that way, and you'll be back where you belong and ready to fly out in no time.

I'm sure one of the cargo deliverers will give a pretty girl like you a ride. Maybe make a good woman out of you, too. You'll like that. It's much better than setting eyes on a prize you can never obtain."

My teeth clenched. I couldn't speak. My tongue remained as still as it had my whole life. After all those years of being the scared, obedient child in Nostalgie, I was finally free. Why couldn't I speak up?

I know Serein. He sees me. He knows me. He needs me. He's hurt.

And that was more important. I nodded and walked numbly around the automatram. My nails dug into my palms, threatening to split the scars open.

"Seigneur," a male voice addressed from inside the tram. "I just got a message from Noam on the relier. You'll never guess who he saw today."

Noam. That slimy little toad who gave Hervé a hard time.

"That man dares show his face here after what happened with his son?"

"Quite. Noam said he looked like a peasant. Hervé's lucky he wasn't executed."

I quickened my pace back to the center of Calme and Serein. Regardless of what Hervé or anyone else thought, I planned to stay by Serein's side, and no dirty looks or nasty comments could stop me.

It was easier to move around now that the streets had emptied for the night. Serein told me Calme was like a paradise compared to Envie, and visually he was right. But the heart was the same. It was a cold heart—one that beat for argent and propriety. Serein was right to leave this place. It would have drowned him and made his good heart unfeeling.

I approached the blue building. Hervé stood by the door with his arms crossed, his expression as indifferent as ever.

"Glad you made it back. Thought I was going to have to hunt you down," he said as I approached.

"Don't strain yourself," I replied. "You seem like the type who can't handle too much stress."

"No, I'm the type that's *seen* too much stress," he retorted. "Come on. You need to stay inside where I can keep watch on you."

"I didn't escape while I could. I came back," I argued. "Why would I—"

"Serein's been asking for you."

My eyes widened. "He's awake?"

"In and out. He's been saying your name for an hour now."

I brought my hands to my chest. "And you think it's a good idea for me to go in there?"

"We've got to take you to Éthéré Coeur regardless. I've said my piece. It's up to you whether you want to hurt him or raise him up."

"Why are you so against me?" I asked.

"It's nothing personal," Hervé replied. "But I've seen a lot. I know people and know their emotions. Serein's been good to you, but it's more than that for you. He's an answer. He's your ticket to the Suzerain to get what you want. I don't want him to get tossed out like trash when he's fulfilled that role."

"Serein could never be trash to me," I said sharply. "I would do anything for him."

"Even give up Nostalgie?"

A lump caught in my throat. Give up my home? "How do you know about Nostalgie?"

"I may not look like I'm listening, but I hear things," Hervé said. "And with your obvious deflection, I'm going to assume the answer is 'no,' then."

"That's not what I'm saying."

The silence that followed disturbed me more than any harsh words could. It gave me time to dwell. Time to consider if Hervé was right.

He snorted and pointed his chin. "What happened over there? Got pretty exciting for a few seconds."

"Why do you think I'd know?"

"Call it intuition." Hervé cocked an eyebrow. "And call me paranoid, but anywhere there's evidence of a Phase, you seem to be pretty close by."

I fixed him with a sour expression. "It hit the barrier. It must have disappeared after that. And then the seigneur showed up."

"The seigneur?" Hervé's brows rose. "What did he want?"

"He said the Phase has been here before and he wants someone to kill it. He wants Serein to do it."

Hervé's eyes bore into me. "And did you tell him Serein is already here?"

"I didn't," I said, casting my eyes down. "He's already so injured. He doesn't need this responsibility thrown on him. I pretended to not know anything, and he let me know how unwelcome I was here and told me to jump on the nearest moving soulever."

"Old goat's manners haven't changed a bit," Hervé scoffed. "We need to get Serein out of here first thing in the morning. It won't be long before someone in the clinic gets a runny tongue. Having the seigneur drop in unexpectedly will put him back in a fever."

"Does Serein not get on well with the seigneur here?"

"Nobody gets on well with Seigneur Rodrigue," Hervé said. "The only one who could stand him was his brother. Still don't know how Corentin did it for so long." He nodded toward the clinic door. "Serein's in the last bay on the right. If anyone other than a medic tries to enter, tell them they'll receive a summons from the Sommet about interfering with a Résonateur's mission."

I nodded and rested my fingers on the doorknob. "They already know you're here, Hervé. I heard them mention Noam."

Hervé chuckled lowly. "Don't worry. The seigneur cares for me about as much as dove droppings. And to think I used to be the one telling him what to do."

"They were talking about your son."

"My son is dead."

I looked back at Hervé, surprised. His back faced me, his posture stiff, like a soldier.

Hardened like a Résonateur.

I pushed the door and entered the clinic.

What type of death could cause such shame?

Dampened. His son must've been dampened.

The rooms along the hall were shielded with white curtains. Soft voices or rough breathing filtered through some of them. I moved to the last one on the right and slid through the curtain.

Serein's gray eye rolled over to me, a heavy pouch beneath it. His lips were chapped. The rest of him was hidden under a thick blanket.

"Gavril."

I seized his hand. My eyes burned. "Oh, thank the Great Heart. Serein, you're finally awake."

"Have I . . . have I been out long?" he asked. "Gavril, are we still on the soulever?"

"No, you took a bad turn a few days ago. The medic didn't have enough medicine so we had to come here. We're in Calme, Serein. You're home."

The color drained from his face. His lips parted, the strangest expression crossing his features—a mixture of horror and surprise. "And does anyone know I'm here?"

"Not yet." I squeezed his fingers reassuringly. "Hervé wants to keep everything quiet. But if you want me to find your family—"

"No," he burst out.

I stared at him, eyes wide.

"No," he repeated levelly. "We should leave them out of this. It's none of their business."

I looked down at his hand clasped with mine. "Are you talking about you or me?"

"Both. It's for the best, Gavril. They won't accept a girl like you."

I pulled my hand away. "I see the medicine's letting you speak your mind."

"That didn't come out right," he replied, reaching for my hand.

I turned away.

"You're not like them, Gavril. You're kind and good. I don't want to see you hurt."

"I've already had a meeting with the seigneur. If I can survive an encounter with that charming lord, your family should be a piece of cake."

A raspy laugh sounded out. I spun around.

"What's so funny?"

"Nothing," he replied, struggling to stifle his laughter. "But I want you to know, Gavril, that I've never met anyone like you. You're fearless."

I cupped his cheek and looked him dead in the eye. "I'm not. I've been scared my whole life. But that was nothing to how terrified I was when I thought I might lose you."

Serein smiled wryly. "The great Résonateur Commandant done in by infection. Has potential to be a surprising story. Better than getting torn limb from limb by dampened."

He opened his arms, and I gently curled into them, careful not to jolt him. "This is turning into more of an adventure than I planned. Closer to a nightmare, in fact. I bet you wish you were back home."

I rested my hand on his chest. "Some part of me, yes. But another part couldn't imagine being anywhere but here."

"And which part is bigger?"

The tip of my index finger traced a thin white vein on his chest. "I'm feeling pretty comfortable right here for the moment."

"Then I hope this moment never passes."

"So do I," I whispered, placing a light kiss on his skin.

Please. Last forever.

CITY OF ETERNAL HEART

Hervé had us loaded on the soulever before the first rays of dawn finished lighting the horizon. I would like to say I would miss Calme. It was Serein's home—a concept I treasured—but the town left little in the way of a pleasant memory.

Approaching the Paramount made time and travel spin faster. I spent most of the day visiting Serein, and during the late hours of evening, I gazed out of my window for Morrow. She'd been absent since our rescue. Memories of my encounter with the Phase in Calme lingered, and so did my questions about the nature of Phases and why Morrow was so different. I had so much to ask her, but her answers would be vague at best.

Serein made great progress. He was up and moving around in only two days, though I worried how much of a show he was putting on.

"I'm well enough to dress myself," Serein said, reaching his arm back to slip into the sleeve of a white shirt. His smile tightened and his form tensed for a moment before he jerked his hand through. "See?"

"I see you've been properly healed in the hands of an anus," Hervé muttered before stepping out the medical bay.

Serein turned to me, eyes wide. "What?"

I bit my lip, not wanting to find humor in the situation, but the bewildered expression on Serein's face . . .

"What exactly happened when I was feverish?"

"He's talking about the medic in Calme," I said. "Henri didn't have a high opinion of him."

And Henri wasn't the only one holding a grudge. When we were outside the medical bay, Hervé ignored my presence, not a word about our conversation uttered between of us.

But no matter how hard I willed time to stop, my days of shining freedom were short, and it wasn't long before the shadow of the Paramount cast over me.

When the day came for our arrival, Serein wanted me to witness our approach to Éthéré Coeur. "There's nothing like it," he insisted. But a thin sheet of white obscured the blue sky.

This would be yet another experience I missed out on.

"We should be able to see the Paramount skyline any minute now," Serein mumbled, looking out the large window of the control room with me. He adjusted the leather eyepatch covering his lost eye.

I tried to smile despite my jumbled stomach and leaned against him. Serein looked less formal in the plain ivory coat Hervé managed to procure in place of his lost Résonateur's uniform, but he was still stringent when it came to wanting things to turn out perfectly.

A shadow darkened the clouds. I squinted as a massive stone wall manifested in front of us—a great barricade larger than even the *Fulgurant*. My heart leapt into my throat. *We're going to hit!*

The soulever tilted to the side, and I lost my balance.

Serein pulled me close. "It's just one of the pillars," he reassured me. "The opérateurs know to look out for them."

"*Pillars?* That was the size of Remords."

"It has to be to hold up the city."

My stomach dropped. How big—

We broke through the wall of clouds and sunlight poured from the sky like golden rain. I didn't think my eyes could get any wider.

A disk as large as a mountain's base was suspended about a half-mile above the ground by eight arching pillars. The soulever ascended above the platform's level. Rows of buildings started at the edge of the plate and increased in size and elevation until, at the center, three dominating ivory towers surrounded a golden lighthouse.

The city's colors changed from the outside in, almost like a target. The edge was gray with green patches coating the rim and the small stony buildings. Thin streams of water poured over the edge from deep rivets cut into the stone. The middle ring was vibrant red with stacked buildings of different shapes and styles—a geometric wonder mingling ideas and architecture.

The center ring couldn't have been more different than the rest of the city. It was white—the buildings smooth, pristine, and uniformly structured with shimmering glass and tall peaks.

Soulevers and small automatrams darted over and around the buildings like bees buzzing around a hive. It was more amazing than I could have pictured. Éthéré Coeur, the Paramount of the world.

We lowered again, lining up with the edge of the disk.

"Look down there." Serein pointed down at the ground underneath the city. Crumbled stone lay half-buried in the dark ground, shrouded in Éthéré Coeur's shadow.

"What is that?" I asked with an uneasy feeling in my stomach. Just the sight of it . . . my flesh prickled.

"Athánatos Kardiá. It's the original Paramount built by Eidolon. His son wanted the location his father selected to remain sacred—even though the land was ruined. So, he literally built a new city on top of the old one and used his mother's tongue for the name. Some say the design is an homage to Eidolon's birthplace."

"That's incredible. A place such as this . . . I never could have imagined it, not even in my dreams," I marveled. How this city could exist was inconceivable. My mind whirled in an attempt to process what my eyes told me was true.

And I had thought the old cork tree at Lake Oublié was a treasure.

We circled around the base as the soulever drew closer to the Paramount. The tingling sensation of passing through a barrier washed over me.

"Feel that?" Serein asked. "It takes a hundred Solenoids to sustain the city barrier. There's a siphon system under the towers."

"What are the three towers in the center? And the golden one?" I asked, not wanting to dwell on the fact that one hundred Solenoids were right front of me, yet even a single one remained outside my reach.

"The golden lighthouse is the Suzerain's palace," Serein replied. "His heart is the light that guides us through the darkness. The towers are the three hubs of operation for the Suzerain's lands. The one with the crystal heart on top is the Résonateur Édifice, where all Résonateurs and recruits are trained, housed, and given assignments. The next one with the purple spire is the Bibliothèque de l'Archiviste. It contains the governing Sommet and all the world's information. They also monitor the relier system. And the last tower, the one with the silver Solenoid replica, is the Pylône de la Science. That's where all technology and innovations, like the soulevers and automatrams, are produced."

"And the Solenoids, too? Would I be able to see one being made?" I asked.

Serein shook his head. "The Solenoids are constructed in a specialized lab inside the city platform. Apparently, the process is too dangerous to be performed out in the open."

Deep disappointment filled me. If I had been able to visit the Solenoid production center, I could have asked for someone's advice on extending the life of the one in Nostalgie.

". . . about your father."

"What?" I asked, returning my attention to Serein. "What did you say?"

"If you go to the archivistes, you could inquire about your father," Serein repeated. "They keep records on all Résonateur locations. Maybe they could tell you where he's doing his service."

I bit my lip and looked at the pit below Éthéré Coeur. If I was being honest with myself, Papa had been gone so long that I didn't feel all that affected by his absence. But Mama . . . how elated she would be to finally know something. She would leave Nostalgie in a heartbeat to go to him. And given the current circumstances, perhaps that was the best thing that could happen.

"I want to do it." I gave Serein a grateful nod. "I would like to know where he's been all this time."

Serein brushed a stray curl from my face. "I'll have them push your request to the front of the line." He grinned at my surprised expression. "Being a commandant has its advantages once in a while."

"Serein, you really don't have to do that for me," I said. "I can't just push other people out of the way."

"Your sense of sacrifice still manages to amaze me." Serein stroked my hair. "Other people have the time and the luxury of being here in the Paramount. Your need is more dire, yet you are still reluctant to put yourself first."

"When you come from a place like I do, you never come first," I said. "You get used to waiting."

"Well, that's not going to happen this time. I don't like waiting."

"I've noticed." A titter passed my lips as I pictured Serein pacing the fields outside of Nostalgie. "You would not do well in the country."

"But you'll do wonderful in the city, so there's no need to compromise."

"You think I'll be staying here?" My cheeks colored under the connotations of his words.

"I have a good feeling—"

"We're moving in to dock," Hervé announced, his voice thick with sleep. He looked like he recently rolled out of bed. "We'll land on the outer edge. This piece of junk doesn't have Crest clearance." He rolled his eyes.

"What's that?" I asked.

"The Crest is the center of the city where the white buildings are." Serein cleared his throat. "The wealthy ring. Where we should be heading." He gave Hervé a pointed look.

Hervé shrugged. "They wouldn't take our word that we had Commandant Serein aboard."

"That means we'll have to walk to an automatram station," Serein bristled. "All the way through the Trough?"

"You got it, Comm. You'll get a nice view from the edge."

"I can't drag Gavril through there. It's the worst part of the city."

"It's fine with me," I piped in before Serein's temper could change the air. "I'm not from a lavish area myself."

"Yes, but there's a difference, Gavril," Serein insisted. "It's not an impoverished little town in the middle of nowhere. It's a slum. The worst kind of activities go on there. That is not the first impression I wanted you to have of the Paramount."

I held his hand between mine. "It may not be the impression you wanted me to have, but it's the real one. I value the truth more than any façade. Don't let this bother you at all, because it certainly doesn't bother me."

"Very well." Serein squeezed my hand. "But we aren't doing any sight-seeing. I want to get to the station as quickly as possible."

"Then you'd better hang on," Hervé grabbed the doorframe. "I can see the dock approaching rather quickly."

Serein and I leaned forward as the soulever decelerated and staggered back when it rocked to a sudden stop. He kept my hand in a tight hold and pulled me to the door.

"Make sure the crew of this soulever are properly compensated for their service," he instructed Hervé as we strode past.

"Already taken care of," Hervé told him from his favorite position against the doorframe. "I made sure the medic doesn't plan on spreading any rumors while he's counting argent, either."

"Excellent."

Serein led me to the side hatch of the vessel and opened it. He pushed out the ladder and helped me down onto the mossy stone platform below. Green algae-covered, crumbling blocks of gray stone jutted out to create docks along the outer rim of the city. Soulevers lined the docks as far as I could see. It was a busy place. Citizens in ratty clothing peddled wares along the slick docks, and workers hauled huge cargo crates back and forth. Children ran so close to the edge that it made my heart stop, and they played with loose hunks of rock. Women with heavy makeup strutted back and forth along the stones to greet new arrivals. Almost every person who glanced at Serein put their head down and rushed away. How they recognized him without his uniform bewildered me. But the air around him was thick and unmistakable. How far did it extend from his being?

Serein led me across a bridge extending over a set of dirty canals that poured rancid water down off the edge of the disk. Stone houses sprouted from the ground like chipped warts on the back of a toad. Serein rushed along each narrow street until we came to a set of stairs with a copper gate blocking the top landing. Two guards in burgundy uniforms stood on the other side with their backs to us.

"I'm Commandant Serein," he said through the bars. "Let me pass to the market ring."

The guards jumped and turned to inspect us. One's eyes darted over Serein's face. They then zipped over me.

"Playing a little rough in the Trough, Commandant? I know you high-types like a little mischief, but I'm really not supposed to let a lower resident into polite society, if you know what I mean." He winked and let out a rowdy guffaw.

It didn't take long for his fellow guard to join in.

"She isn't a resident here," Serein growled, grabbing the fence.

"Now let us in."

The guard continued to snigger, but he unlocked the gate and let us pass without further commentary. Serein continued on briskly, as though he were trying to escape a plague.

One flight of stairs created an amazing separation. The market ring was indeed much finer than the Trough. Large crowds of people bustled around the streets among shops, carts, and stacked residences. Clean red bricks and pavestones contrasted sharply with the green-dominated stone down below. As we passed, citizens openly stared at us. Some smiled, some backed up with horrified expressions, and some thanked Serein for his service.

We wove through the throng of people until we arrived at a domed building with numerous large holes around every curve from top to bottom like a big sponge. A bright red automatram levitated from a hole near the top, and I watched it speed off. As soon as we walked in, the hum and buzz of several automatrams filled the air. I saw small ones, barely bigger than a carriage, and some large enough to carry twenty people. They all appeared in better shape than Gervais' prize.

Serein approached a large desk where a man in glasses furiously jotted data into a vigile with a black quill. He glanced at several viewers and entered more data. He didn't look away from his work.

"I'll take your best tram to the Crest," Serein said with an irritated tap on the wooden surface.

The man snorted. "That's a tall order, Monsieur. Do you have the argent and the documents to back up your request? You can't get into the Crest without the proper paperwork."

"No."

"Oh, so sorry, Monsieur, but—"

"Look at me."

The man let out a cross between an irritated grunt and a huff. He threw the vigile down on the desk.

"Look, Monsieur, you see how busy—"

My hair stood on end and the air prickled my skin. The man behind the desk grabbed his glasses and leaned back, gasping for air. He stared at Serein with bulging blue eyes.

"R-R-Résonateur—"

"Commandant."

"Com-C-C-Commandant?" The man's mouth gaped so wide one of the trams could've driven through it. He scrambled for his vigile and scribbled in a few codes. "I'm sorry, Commandant. I'll have our finest automatram prepared immediately."

"Good to know," Serein said with a winning grin. "We'll wait over there on the bench."

We sat down, and Serein rubbed the top of my hand. "I'm sorry this is taking so long, Gavril. We'll get to the Crest sometime today."

"Don't worry. I'm enjoying the walk," I replied.

A few passersby stared at us and whispered to each other.

"It's nice to spend time with you, even if you did almost scare that poor man to death," I continued. "I don't think you should use your power like that."

"He should be more observant," Serein replied defensively. "Résonateurs don't come through here often, but that's no excuse to disregard vigilance. That's how dampened manage to sneak around under our noses."

I tightened my fingers around his. How many times had I squeezed his hand since we left that cursed valley?

"We're finished with the dampened," I said firmly. "We don't have to worry about them any longer."

"*You* don't, Gavril," he corrected gently. "And that's what I want for you—to never have to be afraid again. But as long as I am a Résonateur, the dampened will always be in my future. We are bound by fate to always cross paths."

"You could stop being a Résonateur and come live with me in Nostalgie," I suggested, half-joking. I wished he would take me up on the offer. That way I could have everything.

Serein chuckled and rubbed his chin. "That would be . . . that would be something. You know, I don't think anyone's stopped being a Résonateur—at least not by choice. You keep going on missions until the Sommet dismisses you or, one day, you don't return." He went silent for a few moments, his gaze lost in the distance. "Anyway," he turned to me, "we wouldn't have any of the privilege and prosperity I possess now."

"I don't need any of that," I said. "As long as we are together, nothing could give me greater happiness."

"Y-y-your tram is ready, C-Commandant." The attendant nervously pointed to an automatram near one of the arched walk-throughs.

"About time," Serein mumbled.

The tram was lavish—a long, sleek model with dark mahogany sides and large windows. Serein opened the door for me, and I climbed inside. Cyril would have a fit if he could see this. There was so much space and so many seats. I sat down on leather cushions and relaxed into the pillow behind me.

"I'm going to take a nap." I sighed and closed my eyes. "A very long nap."

"That's fine, but you'll miss the view," Serein said.

"What view?"

The automatram rose into the air like a soulever. We flew out of the station through one of the highest openings and over the market below. People and buildings dwindled down to small figurines. We sailed toward the city center, where red brick was replaced by white marble. A large golden fence ran between the two colored rings. The buildings in the central part of the city were elegant, impressive structures with walls of white, doors of silver, and balconies lined with deep bronze.

"That fence separates the Crest of the Paramount from the market ring," Serein explained. "We'll be landing near the Pylône de la

Science by the harbor."

The golden lighthouse gleamed in the sunlight as we approached the towers. Several fountains surrounded it, water flowing down in gentle waves before running through a series of elaborate channels like a glistening maze.

My breath stilled for a moment. That lighthouse contained the heart of the world.

The automatram banked around one side of the Pylône de la Science. I stared at it in awe. As large as it was from afar, it was monumental up close. The silver Solenoid at its peak was easily as large as a small soulever. A row of enormous soulevers docked at a port beside it. It was colossal, the largest port I'd seen with inlets and covered bays. We flew to the other side of the harbor and descended. Once on the ground, Serein helped me exit the tram, my feet nearly tripping over themselves as I craned my neck to take in everything.

"We'll go through the harbor back to the pylon," Serein said. "Then we can visit my archiviste friend."

As we ventured forth, I marvelled at the giants surrounding me. I thought the *Fulgurant* must surely be one of a kind—a massive oddity. But now I stood surrounded by a flock of grand vessels and titanic transports. The one at the end—

"I see you've plucked another country rose, Serein," a velvety voice floated down the central aisle ahead of us.

A handsome, lithe young man glided toward us. The tails of his commandant's coat fluttered in the brisk breeze running between the aisles, his hands resting in its pockets. He had wavy, chin-length hair as light as sunlight and eyes the color of fresh ash.

"Looks like you had to put up a fight for this one."

"And she was well worth it. Something I can't say for everyone here," Serein replied coldly.

The young commandant let out an amused half-laugh. "You're surly today. Just because you lost your eye and your soulever *and* part of your crew doesn't mean you get to be prickly whenever you feel like it." He gazed down at me with a cheery smile. "You've still got your rose." He twisted a finger around one of my curls. "For the time being."

My face flared like a torch. Serein moved in front of me and forced the other commandant to take a step back.

"What do you want, Vaskrid?" he snapped. "Your presence is neither warranted nor wanted. Get lost."

"So belligerent," Vaskrid said with a breathy sigh. "I'm merely checking on your well-being before heading out to New Heartlandia."

Serein's livid face lit up with surprise. "That's impossible. That was supposed to be my mission. I personally requested it."

"Yes, I know." Vaskrid crossed his arms. "Everyone knows. And that's the problem. This mission is too personal for you, so it was given to me."

"Don't be ridiculous," Serein snapped. "What do they think is going to happen? That I'm going to lose control and go wild?"

"That is exactly what they think is going to happen," Vaskrid confirmed. He surveyed Serein with narrowed eyes. "It's not far from happening now. Careful or you'll wilt your rose."

"I would never do such a thing," Serein snarled. "And for you to suggest it is an insult and a grave mistake." Serein grabbed my hand and pulled me along. "I'll be sure to pick up the pieces of your failure."

Vaskrid chuckled behind us.

Serein muttered to himself the whole way down to the end of the harbor.

Despite my curiosity about the other commandant and his mission, I kept my silence. Now was not the time to probe Serein for information. His dislike had never shown so clearly.

"Oi, oi, oi! When's my girl coming in? You lot better pick up the pace and get her back together, or I'll gas in your air tanks!"

That voice. A figure covered head to toe in bandages shook her fist at a group of port workers about twenty feet ahead of us.

"Deryn?"

The wrapped person wheeled around to face me. Blue eyes peeking out from cloth sparked with elation. "Gavril! Oh, Gavy, I'm so glad you're okay." She ran to me and threw her arms around me. "I'm so—ouch, ouch—glad—ouch—you're not dead."

She released me and turned to Serein. "Serein, you look bloody awful. But not as bad as I expected considering you fell from a soulever."

"Thanks, Deryn. That makes me feel better about the whole ordeal," Serein replied, voice as dry as sand.

"You do realize you're supposed to wait until we've touched ground to disembark a soulever, right? Or you'll end up looking like shite," she badgered. "Frizzing heart, you look terrible."

"Well, Deryn, at least I'm in good company. You aren't looking so good yourself," Serein fired back.

"I got sliced up in the line of duty," Deryn retorted. "Your stupid arse fell off a moving transport."

"I was on the sky deck when the siphon exploded! People died in the soulever!"

Deryn suddenly looked away. Her voice softened. "Yes, they did." Moisture gathered in the corners of her eyes. "I keep dwelling on that moment, wondering if somehow I missed something or was too busy picking my nose . . ."

"Hervé already told me that nobody detected any abnormalities beforehand," Serein assured her. "Nothing was missed by you or anyone. It was a bizarre accident."

Deryn wiped her face and nodded. "I still feel awful for the chisel twin. He hasn't spoken to anyone. He went straight to the archiviste tower when we returned, and I haven't seen him since."

"I'll try to find him later. We are heading that way. Gavril's going to make an inquiry about her father."

"Sniffing out the old man, eh?" Deryn said, wiping her nose on a bandage. "You better be chuffed Bibiane's out of commission, or she'll block you before you can belch."

"How is Bibiane?" Serein asked, walking away from the harbor along a smooth walkway.

I looked up. The Pylône de la Science was right beside us. It was even more incredible from the ground, like staring up the side of a cliff. I turned my head toward the center of the city. The other towers appeared to flank the golden lighthouse, but they stood as far away from it as I was now. The three towers marked the points of a perfect triangle and would easily take twenty minutes to walk from one to another.

"Demented cow keeps yammering on about how her 'past flashed horrifyingly before her eyes' and she needs to complete her life's work instead of being everyone's pass for information. That blow to the head really frizzed her up. She's gone bonkers."

Serein grimaced.

Deryn latched onto my arm and snickered in my ear. "How was the private tour in the valley?"

"Not so private." I frowned in return. "There were dampened living in the town."

"Ugh, those dampened manage to pinch their way into any crack," she groaned. "So, what you're telling me is that you and dear Serein didn't manage to tumble through the flowers? I mean, I know he looks like dung on shite and probably had a hard time moving, but he's still got lips."

Flashes of our time in the abandoned house darted before my eyes. His lips. His hands. That wonderful feeling. That intense heat.

"Hah, your face is absolutely blistering!" Deryn exploded. "Something naughty did happen. Tell me. I want to hear all the nasty little details."

"No! I-I-I mean nothing happened. Not really. The dampened showed up and tried to kill us," I recounted in my flustered state.

"Ah, that's a shame. Was looking forward to some juicy tales of knobs and bobs, if you catch my saucy say-so."

"N-not really."

"We're almost to the pylon's tram stop," Serein announced over his shoulder. "From there we'll catch a *voietram* to the archiviste tower."

"What's a voietram?" I asked, confused.

"It's like an automatram, but it follows a specific path set by tiny lights between the buildings," Deryn answered. "An easy way for people to get around without going to a station."

Serein led us past the pylon entranceway to a small area with two rows of benches and raised flower beds. He approached a panel on a pedestal and tapped on it. A green light blinked on the panel and zipped down the pedestal in a thin line.

"It should be here soon," he said, escorting me to a bench.

"Don't bet your knickers on it," Deryn grumbled.

"You don't have first-class clearance," Serein boasted. "I get priority routing."

"Good for you. Slick basta—"

A tram whizzed in front of us, coming faster than anything I'd ever seen before. It was about the size of the twenty-seat automatram from the station, but tall enough to stand in and there was no opérateur.

"Is it safe to have no one controlling the tram?" I asked, while Deryn opened the door.

"Don't need one with the light path." Deryn smacked the side of the voietram with her palm. *"Ouch!"*

"It's perfectly safe, Gavril," Serein assured me. He gave Deryn a doubtful look. "Maybe even safer than opérateur-controlled vessels. They automatically check for low energy levels."

"Hah! I'd like to see this piece of rubbish fly over a mountain sideways while picking glass out of its bum."

We entered the tram and I looked at the leather seats lining the sides of the tram. Deryn plopped in one at the back and Serein took a seat in the back corner, leaving an open space between him and Deryn. The tram suddenly sped up, and I stumbled into it. Serein helped me straighten up.

"Are you okay?" he asked. "These things have a little kick when they start. I should have warned you."

"I'm fine," I said, laughing. "I'm probably the only person in this whole city who's never ridden one. I feel like such a bumpkin."

"You're not a bumpkin," Serein said. "You're new. Sometimes that's better."

"I don't know. I kind of like bumpkins," Deryn said. "Well, I like one bumpkin. The others can sod off." She gave me a thumbs up.

Serein rolled his eye. The tram sped around a curve until we pulled up near the entrance of the Bibliothèque de l'Archiviste. This ivory tower was almost identical to the Pylône de la Science, except a purple spire extended from the top. I craned my head back to get a better look. It looked like it was about to pierce the heavens.

"It's the biggest relier in the world," Serein said. "Capable of sending and receiving thousands of messages at once. I don't envy the archivistes who have to discern each one."

"I hate this place," Deryn grumbled when we stepped out of the tram. "This is where they make you submit reports and detailed re-counts of stuff you did. Gives me a headache."

"It's also where we will find information on Gavril's father. Let's go in." Serein proceeded through the door.

A guard in a burgundy uniform glanced at us when we entered, but Serein breezed past as though he didn't exist. No one said any-thing, so Deryn and I followed. We passed several rooms with more screens than I could count and shelves full of metal vigiles. Little black boxes, like the one Serein used when we left Envie, sat in piles on tables.

We entered a large room where numerous people sat bent over consoles vigorously entering data. Every person wore a lilac suit.

Serein walked up to a young, rotund man with wispy brown hair and freckles isolated in the back corner.

"Bedell," Serein called.

The man nearly flipped out of his chair. He locked his gaze on Serein and patted his chest a few times. "Oh, oh, Commandant. It's just you. I surely thought it was Jean-Louis come to scold me again." He leaned forward and whispered, "I got caught sneaking into Commandant Erzulie's file again. Did you know she's gone through three husbands? I wonder how they keep dying off. I bet it's messy."

"I didn't know that, Bedell, but I'm sure she has her reasons for being discrete." Serein gave Bedell a generous, almost pitying, smile. "But I've something *I would* like to know, and I can't ask Bibiane's favor on this one. She's a little upset with me."

"Bibiane, Bibiane," Bedell sang with a dreamy look and a goofy grin. "What a stunning lady. Top of the ranks. I can't wait to ask for her hand." His expression sobered. "Wait. If she's mad at you, won't helping you hurt my chances? I don't want to do that."

Serein put a friendly hand on Bedell's shoulder. "Not at all. If anything, it will prove what a skilled archiviste you are. Not everybody can pull from the restricted Résonateur archives."

Bedell leaned in again, his body quivering with glee. "How restricted are we talking? Personal biographies or mission assignments?"

"Solenoid service."

The archiviste clapped a hand over his mouth.

Deryn snickered.

"The most secure of secure," Bedell breathed from behind his palm. "Oh, the challenge. Bibiane will love this." He dug in his pocket and pulled out a thin piece of graphite and a scrap of paper. "What's the name of the Résonateur and location of the Solenoid?"

Serein glanced at me and nodded once.

I swallowed my nerves before stepping closer. After all this time, an answer. "His name is Goel, and he's originally from Fu'aad. The

Solenoid is in Nostalgie of the southern Tristesse region," I said.

"Nostalgie, hmm? That's almost to the Colère border. Not a lot of living it up going on down there. You know, with whosits holed up in New Heartlandia across the sea."

"That'll be dealt with soon enough," Serein replied sharply.

"I sure hope so." Bedell clucked his tongue. "Bad image for the Suzerain." He folded up the paper and stuffed it under a vigile. "I'll get started on this right away. Give me a day."

"You're a good man, Bedell." Serein patted him on the back. "We have an appointment with the Suzerain coming up. I'll make sure you receive a nice bonus—and put in a good word with Bibiane."

Bedell's cheeks tinged pink. "Do you think she'll speak to me now?"

"Not a blooming chance—"

Serein clapped a hand over Deryn's mouth. "Absolutely." He pulled Deryn along as he backed up. "Thanks, Bedell. Good luck."

When we were clear of the room, Serein released the flailing Deryn and continued to the main atrium as she barraged him with curse after curse.

A woman with a silvery-white face and luminous yellow eyes stepped into our path.

Serein stopped dead.

"Commandant Serein of the city Calme," she said in a stiff, mechanized voice. "You are required to give an official report on your time in the Vallée de la Solitude."

"I'm aware of my duties," Serein snapped. "But as you can see, I am escorting this young lady. I will return once I have her situated in my residence."

The woman's face remained as blank as a canvas. Dark lines ran from the corners of her mouth down to a pointed chin, and in place of hair was a wig made of fluffy white feathers. She looked odd for a person in a crisp Résonateur's uniform—or for a person at all. I would have likened her to Morrow—something strange and unreal about her—but Morrow had a fluidity. Her body was alive. This woman was stiff.

"You will report immediately, Commandant Serein of the city Calme. These orders come straight from the Sommet," the woman returned, unaffected.

The air around me stung. Serein's hands balled into fists.

"I can take care of Gavy," Deryn offered, jumping between the two. "Go let the old farts know you're safe and sound. They probably took one look at you on the viewers and thought 'Suzerain's bollocks, he's frizzed up good,' yeah?"

Serein tossed a glare at Deryn before staring at the strange woman. "Let's go, you clock. I want to be done with this as soon as possible." He stormed back down the hall toward the heart of the archiviste tower.

The silver woman marched after him with stiff, heavy steps.

Deryn and I left the building. I waited until we were a good distance from the door before speaking. "Who was that woman? She had a Résonateur's uniform, but she seemed peculiar."

Deryn's mouth popped open, and she turned to me, shocked. "Gavril, I can't believe you said that. It's so offensive and . . . ha . . . and . . ." She beamed at my horrified face. "And I'm—*haha*—just—just frizzing with you!" She cackled all the way to the tram stop.

Several people stopped and glowered at us. I trailed after Deryn, disturbed and embarrassed. Deryn flopped on a bench and gasped until she finally caught her breath. She sat up and patted the spot next to her. I sat down.

"That fine piece of machinery is a product of the research department. We can't turn people into Résonateurs anymore, so I guess they figured they'd have a go at making one. It's called the *Projet de Marionnettes*, and it's based off some old research notes scientists have been arousing themselves over for centuries. Gear-lass is known as

'Vide,' as in 'empty.' Research types got no creativity."

"So she's not a person at all," I deduced around my shock. "But how can she . . . how can something that has no emotions possibly be a Résonateur?"

"I'm glad you asked." Deryn pointed up. "Solenoid energy."

"You can use the power from a Solenoid like that?"

"Oh, yeah. It lasts way longer than étincelle energy, but there's a limited supply," Deryn explained. "The Suzerain's soulever uses ten Solenoids to function, and that bugger can stay in the air for a year. Shame he only takes it out for an annual bum-scratch to Île de l'Amour."

My stomach burned like lava bubbling up to my chest. "Ten Solenoids wasted on a docked transport vessel?" I asked with a stiff jaw.

"Eh? Yeah, I guess you could put it that way—Oh, Gavy, I'm sorry," Deryn squeaked, biting her tongue. "That must be a horrid thing to hear when you're busting your bum to get one for your home."

The atmosphere around us stilled, becoming stale and uncomfortable. My companion's eyes darted around.

"You were telling me about Vide," I said. "How does that woman use Solenoid energy to ward off Phases?"

Deryn's shoulders relaxed and she let out a relieved sigh. She returned to her usual boisterous form in a flash. "That's the real trick. It obviously can't pull from emotional stimulation, so it distributes stored Solenoid energy in a barrier-like fashion. Vide's essentially a strolling siphon with a gob."

"That's incredible," I admitted despite my frustration. "When such things are possible, it makes you wonder how places like Nostalgie are still so isolated and in need."

The tram pulled up. Deryn snatched my hand and tugged me off the bench. She rushed to it, nearly knocking a couple out of the way. "You know what's so exciting?" she asked, a mischievous grin lighting her face.

"No?"

"Deciding where to put you so Serein will have an easier time sneaking in during the wee hours of the night."

My blood rushed. I stared out the side window and turned my mind away from *that* subject. The three ivory towers gleamed in the afternoon light.

Deep down, I was a little disappointed. Arriving in the Paramount was the experience of a lifetime, yet it wasn't as wonderful as I expected. When I was in Nostalgie, the Paramount seemed like a dream—something I could imagine and vision, but never touch. It was perfect. Now that I knew the reality of the place, I wasn't sure it was much better than my small village. This city had spectacular structures and amazing inventions, but it also lacked something.

It lacked heart.

GRIEF

I know you probably can't wait to start moving into Serein's gigantic castle, but I was wondering if I could run a little errand first." Deryn leaned forward and then pushed back against her seat with enough force to lightly rock the voietram. The other passengers shot her disgruntled looks.

"Of course," I replied. "If you have something important to do, let's go. It's not like I have any personal plans."

Deryn snickered. "I wouldn't tell Serein that."

"You know what I mean," I muttered, refusing to let her get me flustered again so soon. "I'm not exactly here to enjoy the city."

"Sorry, I'll stop. I'm just real frizzing glad to see you, Gavy." Deryn put her hand on mine. I looked at her, but her eyes were focused on the floor, refusing to meet mine.

"I was really worried," she said. "*Really* worried. Serein's capable and tough as steel, but surviving a fall from a soulever? I thought you were—"

I placed my other hand over hers. "I was worried about you, too."

Deryn pulled her hand back and wiped her eyes. "Frizz, I hate this mushy shite. Been years since I've gotten this soppy."

My own eyes prickled with sorrow. I pushed the tears back. If I started, we'd both bawl our eyes out, much to the annoyance of our fellow passengers. Not sure I could speak without my voice cracking, I settled for putting my hand on Deryn's shoulder and giving it a gentle squeeze.

She sucked in a deep breath. "I've actually got a huge gash there, Gavy."

I jerked my hand back, horrified. "Heart, I'm so—"

"No, no, it's fine," she said, still puffing air between her teeth. "It could have been worse. It's not like I lost an eye or anything. So how did *that* happen?"

"The dampened did it." My voice cracked, thinking about our time in Panique and remembering Serein's pained cries, his bloodied face. The memories would haunt me forever. There when I awoke late at night, descending without warning. I swallowed. "They wanted to tear his body apart and place it outside the town."

"Shite," Deryn hissed. "Thank the Suzerain's knickers Hervy went looking for you, eh?"

"I suppose," I replied, feeling distasteful over crediting Hervé. "He got us out of there." After Morrow saved us. She was the one who scattered the dampened. She was there when I needed her. My heart twinged. If only she could be here to guide me through this strange place.

"Hervy's a great guy to have when your arse is on fire," Deryn said. "Even after all that's happened to him, he still always comes through when it counts."

"Serein really trusts him." I didn't want to shower praise on the man who accused me of using Serein for my own gain, but I would admit, he did everything he could to save Serein. He protected him, spoke up for his best interests, and put himself in danger for Serein. He treated Serein like a son.

"Well, he and Serein've got a lot in common." Deryn's mouth

twitched in disgust. "Got screwed over by the same bloke." She drew in a deep breath and closed her eyes. "And I got my bloody mouth running like diarrhea again." She breathed in again. "Don't think about arseholes," she muttered. "Think good thoughts—like flying way up in the sky."

I glanced out the tram window at the automatrams and soulevers buzzing above the city—free of walls and roads and mountains.

"I'm really sorry about the *Fulgurant*, Deryn," I said.

"Why?" Deryn replied. "I was the chief opérateur, Gavy. I'm the one who should be sorry."

I shook my head. "That's not true, and that's not what I meant. You said she was the love of your life. I'm sorry you can't—"

"Tickle her knobs anymore." Deryn broke into a cheeky smile, but her eyes lacked their usual gleam. "I guess I better get used to having my feet on the ground." She groaned and held her hands out. "That seat had the perfect impression of my arse."

The tram slowed and we rocked to a stop.

Deryn looked out the window. "Here we are." She stood up. "Come on, Gavy. I've got to get my legs back in ship-shape."

We exited the tram and I gazed at the large tower in front of us. I could barely make out the crystal heart at the top, glinting in the sunlight. This was the Résonateur Édifice. My chest tightened. Deryn couldn't be serious about going in there. I was an accused heretic.

"The only place worse than the archivistes' nest," Deryn said with a sniff.

My face must have shown my worry because Deryn waved her hand. "Don't worry, we aren't going in. I'd never make it past the front door anyway." She pointed to the side of the tower. "We'll follow the path around to the guard barracks. That's where the non-gifted folks get training and housing."

"Guards? Like the ones at the gate between the rings?" I asked.

"Exactly. Anyone in a burgundy uniform is a Paramount guard.

They keep order in the city and some of the larger towns with ports. A select few get chosen for Résonateur support and travel around with them. Help them deal with riffraff and people who get a little too touchy. It, uh . . . it isn't a good look for Résonateurs to use their abilities on ordinary people."

"That's why the twins are with Serein," I blurted. I grimaced at my mistake and it did not go unnoticed.

Deryn sighed and looked at the ground. "*Were*," she said. "Yeah, Ciseau and Marteau got assigned to Serein's command when he became a commandant. That's actually why I'm here. I want to try and talk to Ciseau if he's here."

An uncomfortable knot formed in my stomach. I felt bad for Ciseau. His loss was substantial—perhaps the greatest loss of his life. He needed comfort and a friend. The knot twisted. That wasn't me. The twins and I didn't have the best relationship. I was an outsider, and they delighted in reminding me so. But Deryn was their companion. She was Ciseau's friend.

"You should talk to him, Deryn," I said. "I'm sure he could use some company. I can wait for you here."

"Oh, I don't think so." Deryn crossed her bandaged arms, wincing. "Serein would have the rest of my skin if I left you here alone. You're coming with me."

I cringed. "Deryn, I really don't think Ciseau wants to see *me*."

"You don't know that," she said, grabbing my arm. "It may cheer him up that people care enough to check on him."

I forced a smile like I had lockjaw. "If you think so."

The tangle in my stomach twisted tighter as Deryn dragged me down the white walkway around the tower. It wasn't a short walk by any means. The base of the tower easily exceeded the size of Envie, but the distance shortened quicker than I would have liked. *Everything will be fine.* I'd just poke my head in, excuse myself, and let Deryn talk to him in private. I wouldn't have to see him for long. I wouldn't have to listen to his drivel anymore because . . . because . . . he just lost his brother.

The growing knot made me feel nauseated, and I was overcome with something else. A feeling I often felt about Nostalgie as I ate tasty meals on the soulever or enjoyed my luxurious room.

Shame.

What was wrong with me? The man just lost his brother—his other half—and here I was, loathe to offer him a kind word. I wasn't the right person to go with Deryn. I trudged on anyway.

A long oval building four stories tall was attached to the Résonateur Édifice by a glass corridor. Two guards in burgundy stood at attention next to a gate at the center of the interior of the corridor. Though everything was visible through the glass, there was no entrance from the outside. I looked back at the oval building. It was the same ivory as the tower, but without doors or even windows. Deryn kept strolling toward it, seemingly unabated by the lack of entrances.

We curved around the building until the pathway met the building's outer wall and stopped. I stared at the wall, not sure what to do.

Deryn rummaged in the pockets of her jumpsuit. "Bloody thing's here somewhere," she mumbled. "Ah-ha!" She pulled her hand out and opened her fist. A little black cube lay on her palm, like the one Serein used to access the *Fulgurant* when we left Envie. She grinned at me.

"I'm not supposed to have this. The twins smuggled one out so I could drop in and have drinks."

"What is it? Serein has one as well."

"Well, his is as useless as toes on a fish now that the *Fulgurant* is out of commission. It's a *dévoiler*, but I call it a box key. Each key is matched to a certain access door. Serein had a master box key to the *Fulgurant*. He could access every hatch and even lock me out of the opérateur deck if he was feeling stupid. This one," she held up the box, "grants privileged access to the barracks. Only head guards are supposed to have them."

She pressed her finger on top of the box key and a little red light glowed under her finger. A thin red light appeared on the wall in front of us. The wall vibrated, and a series of clicks followed. A rectangular panel slid back a few inches before slowly raising upward, exposing an entrance.

Deryn stuffed the box key back in her pocket and stepped into the opening.

My mouth felt dry. I didn't want to go with her. I felt bad for Ciseau. I did, but the memory of how he behaved toward me—the comments he made at my expense—left an uneasiness that I couldn't shake.

I'll do it for Deryn. This was important to her. I had to stop being selfish. People did things they didn't want to all the time, and avoiding Ciseau was the least of my concerns. I had my innocence and a Solenoid to fight for.

I followed Deryn into the barracks. About fifteen feet ahead, another gate blocked further entry. A guard sat in a chair by the gate. He covered a wide yawn with his hand.

"Cecil," Deryn said loudly. "Better get a good kip in before tonight. They'll bust your bollocks if you fall asleep outside the Crest gate again."

"Not my fault, Deryn," Cecil said in return. "I'm not even supposed to be out here. Damn Serge asked me to cover while he ran off to the brewery for a restock. He better have my ale when he comes back." He rubbed his eyes and took a long glance at Deryn. "I figured you were back when Ciseau turned up, but damn, you guys really took some bad hits." He leaned over and rested his forearms on his knees, hands clasped. "Heard about Marteau. Awful way to go, siphon blowing up like that. Damn sub-opérateurs should have been doing their jobs."

Deryn tensed, and I could practically feel the ice from her breath when she hissed, "They *were* doing their frizzing jobs."

"Dead bodies say otherwise," Cecil replied. "But nothing can be done now." He stood up and unlocked the gate. "I take it you're here for Ciseau." He glanced at me. "He could use some cheering, but I think she's more your type than his."

"This is my friend," Deryn snapped. "And she's engaged to Commandant Serein, so you better watch your frizzing mouth."

I shot Deryn a wide-eyed stare. Serein and I weren't—well, technically, I was engaged, but not to him. My heart fluttered. If only it could be him.

Cecil's eyebrows rose. "Beg your pardon, ladies. Please, don't let me stand in the way of your privileged boots."

Deryn brushed past the guard with heavy steps and I rushed after her. I felt Cecil's eyes on my back as the gate clanked closed. Heart, that was going to start a rumor. And with me shortly going to trial and Serein being my official escort, I wasn't sure that was a good thing.

Serein hadn't ignored me in public. He'd been more open than I expected, but there was a big leap between handholding in the Trough and being engaged, especially to someone accused of heresy. I wanted to be with Serein. I reveled in his attention, but I didn't want that attention if his reputation were to come into question.

I followed Deryn through the brightly lit barracks. The gray stone floors of the hallways were clean but marred with scrapes and cracks. No paintings or banners hung from the walls. No decor of any kind. It was a place of strict purpose, not pleasure.

We passed a large open room where several guards were exercising and sparring each other with wooden batons. I feared we would get stopped and questioned, but no one gave us more than a passing glance.

"Is it really okay for us to be here?" I whispered to Deryn.

"We got past the gate, didn't we? Lot of these meatheads owe me some argent over lost bets. They wouldn't dare call me out."

She pushed a heavy silver door open. Over her shoulder, I saw the hallway split into three directions. Doors spaced about ten feet apart lined each of the corridors. Deryn took the corridor to the right and continued on.

Each door had a placard on the front with an ink drawing on it. One had an owl, another a tomato, and a third a rose. Pictures of wildlife and flora and everything you would find outside the barrier. They were very professional, each one imitating life in every way but breathing. Whoever drew them truly brought the only semblance of life they could to the barren building.

Deryn stopped and turned to face a door with a hammer and chisel displayed on the placard, their handles tied together by a fraying rope. This was their room. Ciseau's room.

My stomach lurched.

Deryn grabbed the handle and pushed the door open without knocking. I took a step back, horrified, as she barged in.

I froze, listening to the voices on the other side of the door.

"Go away! I told you I don't want to talk," Ciseau barked.

"That's one frizzing way to greet your best bud and chief defender from Bibiane," Deryn shot back.

"Deryn?" Ciseau's voice softened.

"Bet your sorry arse on it. Though I don't know why I bothered. You should have come to me, you stupid lout," Deryn scolded. Even in the hall, I could hear her voice shake. "I'm here for you."

"I know. I kno-ow b-but it—" He sobbed loudly.

"Come here, you daft fool," Deryn murmured.

Heart, I wanted to sink into the floor. I had no business listening to this obviously private conversation.

"Why was it him?" Ciseau wept. "It wasn't suppose—it wasn't—"

"I know." Deryn sniffled. "It's hard. It's going to be so, so hard. But we're here for you. Me and Serein and Gavy."

The weeping stopped. Silence echoed down the hall.

"What?"

"Yeah, remember Hervy told us not to give up hope until he found proof? He found them, Ciseau. Serein and Gavril are alive," Deryn chirped. "And Gavy's here with me."

My legs jerked and, for a moment, I thought I would bolt. I pushed my heels down and held my place. I took in a deep breath, set a small smile on my face, and stepped into the room, giving Ciseau a tiny wave.

Ciseau glared at me. His left eye twitched before he bared his teeth. "Get out."

"Oi, there's no need for that," Deryn jumped between us, putting her hands on her hips. "We came to—"

"Get out!" Ciseau roared. *"You."* He pointed at me. "It's your fault! My brother is dead and it's all because of you."

I stepped back, mouth opening in shock. Me? What had I done?

"Come on, Ciseau. You know that's not true." Deryn put her hand on Ciseau's arm, but he ripped it away. She stood with her hand still raised for a moment, then her fist clenched.

Ciseau continued glaring at me. He thrust his finger toward the door.

Deryn slowly brought her fist to her face and pinched the bridge of her nose, eyes clenching shut. "Okay, Ciseau," she said, lowering her hand and opening her eyes. "I can see . . . maybe this was a bit much. I'll—I'll check in on you later, mate."

Ciseau gave a stiff nod but kept his heated glaze locked on me. He wasn't a Résonateur, but every ounce of resentment in his eyes raked across my flesh. I was used to dirty looks and glares, but this? This was pure hatred.

Deryn let out a deep sigh and finally moved toward the door, her eyes red and glistening. I backed out of the way and followed back down the hall. As we neared the end of the corridor at the split, I glanced over my shoulder. My heart dropped into my stomach. Ciseau stood outside his room, still casting that hateful stare.

I quickly turned back around and sped to the door ahead of Deryn. I held it open for her and followed, closing it tightly behind me. Any barrier between Ciseau and me was welcome.

Deryn remained silent all the way back to the entrance gate. Even then, all she did was bang on the metal to get Cecil's attention so he could open it for us. He tried to speak with her again, but she grunted in response and kept walking.

I couldn't tell which was more unnerving, Ciseau's gaze or Deryn's silence. It wasn't like her, and I had no idea what to say.

Heat welled in my chest. She should have listened to me.

I pushed the bitter thought away. Deryn didn't know he would react like that. *I* didn't know he would react like that. She was trying to do a good thing. Be a good friend.

We made it to the voietram station. Deryn jammed her finger down on the pedestal, and it lit up. She stalked to a bench and dropped on it with a low grunt. She stiffly pulled her legs up and wrapped her arms around them, burying her face in her knees. I stood beside her.

"I'm sorry," she mumbled, face still buried. "I'm really sorry."

I took in a deep breath and stared into the distance. The white buildings of the Crest surrounded us like the mountains of the Vallée de la Solitude.

"You didn't do anything wrong," I finally replied.

"I thought it would be good for him to see some friendly faces. I guess he wasn't ready."

"That makes two of us," I said, that smoldering fire igniting before I could stop it.

"Gavy . . ."

"He accused me of murdering his brother, Deryn."

Deryn lifted her face. "No," she replied. "He didn't say that. He . . ." She shook her head. "He's trying to find somewhere to place his anger. He's trying to find a reason for what happened. And since we were taking *you* to the Paramount—"

"Naturally, I get to be his scapegoat?" I crossed my arms. I spent my entire childhood being Edgard's whipping girl. I didn't need to be someone else's. I clenched my fists and felt the scars on my palms. "I'm the root of everyone's problems. I'm so honored."

"You know that's not true." Deryn shot to her feet. "It's not about you. I mean, he just lost his brother and—" Deryn gulped and muttered to herself for a few seconds. "Look. I frizzed up. I never should have taken you there. I admit it. I'll talk to him later and make bloody sure he apologizes." Deryn looked at me, a sad frown on her face.

The sight of it ate away at my anger.

"I'm sorry," she said.

The remnants of heat left my body, replaced by shame. Deryn was right. I didn't like Ciseau, but the man did just lose someone important to him. I took his tragedy and made it about myself.

"It's fine, Deryn." I looked down. "I'm sorry, too."

A pair of arms wrapped around me. I stared down at Deryn.

"I hope we're done rowing because this really hurts," she said, her voice muffled against my arm.

I closed my eyes and started giggling. Even after all that, she managed to say the right thing to cheer me up.

"That's not helping," Deryn mumbled. "Ouch."

SHADOWS OF THE CREST

Paramount houses loomed over me like rectangular mountains of wealth. White monoliths with stained glass and spotless porches and bronze balconies. I felt very, very insignificant.

Deryn marched through the streets like she owned every pebble.

"Does everybody who works in the Crest live here?" I wondered as I took in every fine detail.

"Not everybody. Only the elite like commandants, brilliant archivistes, scientists, and Sommet councilmen get priority housing. The rest are owned by prats with enough wealth to afford the house and make a totally not self-serving donation to the Suzerain. A guy up the next street owns three shops in the market ring. Gives about thirty percent of his earnings to the Sommet's 'library preservation' charity."

"How many other commandants live here?"

"There's Erzulie the manslayer, Commandant Tosser, Commandant Bigger Tosser, Vaskrid the Valiant—"

"I met that one," I piped in, "in the harbor." The image of the handsome Résonateur came to me. Although he appeared dashing, he had quite the air of arrogance, yet Deryn called him "valiant."

"Frizzing heart, I bet that really twisted Serein's nips," Deryn exclaimed with glee. "Coming eye to eyes with his tormentor."

"What do you mean?"

"It's a nice, juicy story," Deryn said. "Vaskrid came from Himinnhjarta for Résonateur training at the same time Serein started. The two have been competing ever since. Vaskrid's a natural talent and got promoted to commandant shortly after becoming a full Résonateur—the youngest there's ever been. Serein didn't get promoted until that nutter—" Deryn broke off and spat in a flowerbed. "Well, it doesn't matter how. The point is Serein was named a commandant." Deryn let out a loud laugh and smacked her bandaged knee. "*Ouch!* The two of them used to really have a go at each other." She rubbed her knee. "We often joked they'd get married."

"Married?"

"But Vaskrid's not the type for it. She's—"

"She?"

"So you see where I'm going with this." Deryn clapped me on the back. "There's nothing to fret on. Vaskrid's not interested in your man. Not in anything in his trousers, at least."

"I still can't believe it," I breathed, holding my cheeks. "She looks just like a—like a—"

"Prince," Deryn finished for me. "And it's not just that lovely face, either. She may knock Serein's bollocks around, but Vaskrid's as noble and brave as they come," Deryn gushed. "I wanted to be just like her."

"But you *are* noble and brave," I declared. "I don't know of any other opérateur who would have put their life at risk to land that soulever."

"You don't know any other opérateurs," Deryn countered. Her face darkened with a blush. "But ta for the compliment."

My friend pointed at a five-storied house with several balconies and ornate flower boxes filled with violet orchids. It dwarfed any house I'd ever seen. The whole population of Nostalgie could have fit in the dwelling.

"That's Serein's modest home. I stagger in from time to time after pissing the night away with chaps at the harbor or barracks. It's closer than my place."

"Where do you live?"

"In the market ring. I like the color and liveliness. Reminds me of home," she said, a faraway gaze in her eyes.

"That's a little far from here," I said, concerned. "Do you take a tram?"

"Nah, I usually just puff my way down. Got two legs, so might as well use them while I'm on the ground." Deryn shrugged, dismissing my worry.

Deryn pranced her way to the door and put her finger on the black panel beside the handle. She traced some small symbols—a series of raindrops in a precise pattern—and the lock clicked open. She bustled in without pause, and it was obvious she'd done this plenty of times.

While Deryn breezed through the foyer nonchalantly, my mouth fell open. I was walking into a palace. In the atrium, a large crystal chandelier with golden arms dangled like a jeweled spider over the polished hardwood. The draft from the door stirred silver curtains until they flowed over windows like silky water, and the walls held beautiful oil paintings—landscapes I'd never seen, even in Papa's books. This one room contained everything Gervais aspired to have, but never would.

This was the magic they attempted to create in Envie. But that was fake—a cheap imitation built on what used to be. This was real. This was the world of a true noble.

"Oi, we're going up. Serein's room is on the top floor," Deryn purred, quirking her eyebrows up and down.

I followed her up the marble staircase. It gently curved around the foyer in a large spiral all the way to the fifth floor. When we reached the final landing, Deryn swayed down the hall with exaggerated hip movements.

"It's right—*ouch*—down here," she teased. "The door to your future." Before two large black doors at the end of the hallway, she opened her arms in a grand gesture. "All you have to do is go inside," she whispered breathlessly.

"You're enjoying this too much." I smiled.

"Maybe a tad," she replied stiffly. "I think I tore all the scabs down my sides."

"Are you okay?"

"No—yes—no," she lowered her arms and staggered down the hall. "I'll see myself out . . . before the blood runs through."

"Deryn, I—"

"No, no, nope! You stay right here and await your destiny," she sang in a mystical voice before wobbling down the stairs.

I watched her leave, and the corners of my lips pulled down. Alone again.

I turned back to the "door of fate," bit my lip, and reached for the handle. When my fingers touched the shiny gold metal, my fingertips burned. Like a trespasser, I sought to barge into Serein's room uninvited. Would he want me in his personal space? Did he find me worthy? I dropped my hand and walked away.

I ventured back down the hallway and found a single gray door. There was nothing else in the hall except vases of long-leafed plants and paintings. Intruding was not my goal, but I didn't see anything else for me to do. I opened the door and relaxed my shoulders when a simple bedroom revealed before me. This would do.

I curled up on the soft surface of the bed pushed against the right wall and gazed out the large window opposite the door. If Serein wanted me, then he would let me know. Until then, I wouldn't invade his privacy.

The light of the setting sun bathed over the city and transformed white to gentle amber. Like sunset over sand. A burst of life before darkness. It was beautiful. So beautiful . . .

Creak.

I opened my eyes and squinted into a stream of light. My body felt drowsy, still hanging onto sleep. A silhouette loomed in the doorway. I blinked, trying to adjust to the room's brilliance. "Serein?"

The figure walked to me—slow and steady. My heart pulsed rapidly. *He's here for me. Time for me to get what I want.*

The silhouette reached the edge of the bed and leaned over me. Warm breath cascaded over my face. I waited for the warmth of his presence to bask over the rest of my body. Goosebumps tingled on the back of my neck.

A hand squeezed the front of my neck. "Hello, red dread."

The hand tightened. "Crimson vixen."

I clawed at the fingers.

"Scarlet harlot."

Ciseau's brown eyes gouged into me like a chisel. He yanked me up and slammed me back on the bed.

"It's you. It's you. It's you. *It's you.* It should have been you! All you had to do was die! Fall into oblivion! But it didn't go as we planned. It didn't explode on time and Marteau . . ."

Ciseau's hand loosened, and he crumpled over me, his tears dropping on my face.

"I told him not to go," he sobbed. "I told him to leave it be—that we would find another way. But he couldn't . . . He said that it was our . . . our special mission. Our specialty . . . our . . . our . . ."

The hand clenched again. I fought for breath.

Ciseau snarled. "'Watch the commandant,' they said. 'Keep him from asking anymore questions. Keep him from any aberrant influences,' they ordered. And that's exactly what you are! A very"—he jerked me up—"bad"—he shook me violently—"influence."

A splash of warm liquid struck me, and a high screech pierced the air. The vice grip on my neck disappeared, and I sucked in air.

Ciseau rolled on the floor, deep gashes along his arms and legs. Splattered blood covered his clothes, the bed, and the carpet below. A tall figure darkened the doorway.

"Serein!" Ciseau shrieked, scrapping to his feet. "Serein, you stupid, naïve fool! Don't you see I'm trying to save you?"

"I'm looking very hard, Ciseau, but that is *not* what I see," Serein answered gravely. "Are you hurt, Gavril?"

"I'm not," I rasped.

"Then Ciseau can thank his lucky heart." Serein pointed at the wounded man. "You are coming—silently—with me to the Résonateur Édifice. I want to know exactly what you were doing and why you're trying to kill Gavril."

"I can't tell you all that if I'm to remain silent," Ciseau gibed. He limped toward the window. "But I see you've made your decision. I hope you're happy with the friends you've chosen and the ones you've thrown away."

"Ciseau, wait—"

"Brother, I'm here."

In a burst of speed, Ciseau threw himself forward. Glass shattered and shards launched in all directions.

"Ciseau!"

Serein ran to the window and peered down. His shoulders sagged, and he turned around. The bleak expression on his face . . .

I crawled off the bed. Serein rushed to hold me. He crashed his lips into mine before pulling away and inspecting every inch of me. "Are you sure you aren't injured?"

"I'm fine," I reassured him, placing my hand on his chest. "What about you?"

"Of course, I'm not hurt. I—"

"That's not what I meant."

Serein pulled my hands up and kissed them. "I—" He stepped backward and pulled me with him to the door. "Let's get out of this room. I need to use the relier and report Ciseau's . . . I need to report what happened here."

I nodded.

Serein led me down the hall to the great black doors of his room. "Please, wait inside for me. I don't know how long this will take, so use the room as your own and get some rest." He opened the door and ushered me inside. "I will return as soon as I am able." He gave me one last kiss and closed me inside.

I stared at the black wood in front of me for a long time. My neck ached, and the skin was sore against the cotton of my dress. He tried to kill me. That man actually tried to kill me.

I dropped to my knees, lightheaded, scared even. But there was nothing to be afraid of. The threat was gone. I just . . . I . . .

I leaned my head against the wood and closed my eyes. My chest hurt—a gnawing throb that took my breath away. White stars flashed inside my eyelids. And then, black.

ONE DAY INTO THE SKY

G avy. Hey, Gavril. Wake up."

I groaned against the intrusion. A soft nudge on my shoulder forced me further from the land of dreams. I pushed up from the hard surface I leaned against, my back popping out of a stiff curve. Finally, I opened my eyes. A pair of celeste orbs greeted me in the soft moonlight.

"Deryn?"

"Don't know how you managed to sleep on a frizzing door," she said with a grin that didn't look as natural as the cheery girl's effortless smiles. "Serein sent me a message. He wanted me to come get you before the *Enquête* arrives to . . . to clean up. He thought it best you weren't in his room. Your status hasn't exactly been cleared, and you may get more of a drilling than anyone wants."

I nodded slowly. "O-okay. Serein's not here?"

"Got called to the edifice. It's messy business when someone—" she paused and swallowed. "When something like this happens."

"Deryn, are you all right?"

"Me? Yeah, yeah, I'm right as rain," she answered quickly. "Let's get the frizz out of here before the probe-party shows up, right?"

"Yes, let's go," I agreed, standing with the other girl. We walked out into a dark and eerily silent house. The gray door to the bedroom where everything happened was closed, hiding the damage inside.

Deryn gave it a quick glance, shook her head, and silently continued toward the stairs. Seeing her so reserved and pensive reminded me of how our visit with Ciseau ended.

Her friend just died.

Yes. He may have tried to kill me, but that was not the man she remembered. That was not the fellow crewmember she laughed with and ate with and shared stories with. Ciseau was dead, and she had to wrap her mind around that.

And the fact that he was an attempted murderer.

The Crest was noiseless, something unexpected in such a large place. Small lights shone from wires strung along the white roads, guiding the way.

The farther from the center of the city we walked, the more noise rose in the distance. Laughing, yelling. People staying up late to have a good time. When I was younger, I had thought the whole world slept at exactly the same time—so silent were the lands around Nostalgie. But when I grew older, Mama explained that time was different the farther away you went, and some lands woke up to the sun just as we settled down with the moon. My pulse quickened and my breath grew short as I tried to fathom anything that far away. An existence beyond my village . . . Mama had to hold me close all night to calm me down.

A large golden gate blocked the continuation of our journey. A guard sat propped against the bars, his chin pressed against his chest, head bobbing up with each slow breath. I recognized him. Cecil from the barracks.

Deryn walked up to the sleeping Cecil and reached down to his waist. She fiddled with something for a few seconds and then pulled back a large key. She fit it in the keyhole and pushed the gate open. The guard slid to the ground, snorting once before settling back into his deep sleep.

"Told you to watch the ale," Deryn muttered. She walked through the gap, and I followed after her.

"Is it okay to leave him like this?"

"Wouldn't dream of it." With a hard shove, Deryn forced the gate back, pushing it into Cecil until his head bent back and his torso twisted at an odd angle. She tossed the key in his lap.

"Sorted. He'll have one hell of a crick in the morning, but the old alky won't lose his job." Without another word, Deryn turned on her heel and strolled on.

Great spheres of étincelle energy burned bright from the tops of the market ring's red brick buildings. Peopled strolled through easily, meeting friends outside taverns and entering shops with dark curtains obscuring the windows.

A handsome man with a glass of red liquid smiled at me as I walked by. "Care for a taste, Mademoiselle?"

"Not interested," Deryn gruffly answered for me, pulling me along by my wrist.

"Was that wine?" I asked.

"Wouldn't bet my knickers on it," she replied. "And that's exactly what he wants. Don't take nothing from anybody, Gavy. You'll end up in an alley with three hairy blokes in no time."

"And nobody does anything to stop it?"

"Everywhere's got their dingy parts, Gavy. Even the hoity-toity Crest has some nasty deeds going on in their polished palaces. Not everyone lives in some sheltered, morality-pure bubble."

I wrenched my arm out of her grasp. "Not by choice."

Deryn stopped and pinched the bridge of her nose. "Look. I didn't mean it that way. It's been a long night, right? Can we get out of the frizzing street before we become the next items on the Enquête's list?"

I sighed. "Fine. Let's keep going."

I followed the shorter girl down several more streets, nothing but awkward silence between us. Deryn turned down a narrow alley between two long rectangular residential buildings. At the very end, a cube-like house no bigger than my home in Nostalgie stood separate from the housing blocks. She stepped up to the cerulean door and traced something with her finger along the panel next to it. The door cracked open.

Deryn slipped in through the narrow opening.

I bit the inside of my cheek. "Welcome" was not the feeling emitting from the crack, but there was nowhere else for me to go. I walked into a small bare space with no pictures or lamps or rugs, only a small foyer with brick walls that led to a windowless room. A small étincelle bulb dangled from the ceiling, and underneath it sat a round table with three chairs. A green chaise lounge was pushed against the far wall, and a pile of colorful blankets covered the top of it, wadded up like a soft hill.

There was nothing else but a door to what I assumed was the washroom. This place had even fewer belongings than what I had in Nostalgie.

"Just take a seat," Deryn said. "Probably going to be here a while."

I slowly walked to the table and pulled out a chair. The wood looked nice, barely scuffed from use at all.

The other girl dropped into the opposite chair, hissing and letting loose a sharp curse. She gently lowered her arms to the table and rested her forehead on the cool surface.

I stared at her, waiting for some start to a conversation. Deryn always had something to say. But she just lay there, head down where I couldn't see her eyes. "Deryn, are you sure you're okay?"

"Smashing," she replied in a flash, raising her head, but not looking at me. "Just got a message in the middle of the night saying my crewmate for the past six years tossed himself out a window after trying to off someone, but I'm right as an angle."

Off *someone*. I bit my lip. "Do you think I'm to blame?"

Deryn's sky eyes darted to me. She didn't answer immediately—and that disheartened me—but she didn't give an abrupt confirmation, either. The more she stared, the more watery her gaze became.

"No," she finally whimpered, lowering her head again. "I could never . . . But it's hard, Gavy. It doesn't make sense." Her voice quivered, and she wiped her nose with her sleeve. "Why? Why would he do this? Something so frizzing stupid. Gavy, he must've said something." She looked back at me expectantly.

My throat tightened. A bad influence. That was what he called me. That was why he attacked me in the dark of the night as I lay helpless.

Your friend was a coward. He feared me, a girl being held as an accused heretic. A girl with nothing. Yet somehow, getting rid of me was worth his life.

"He mentioned his brother, and . . . um—"

"I knew it." Deryn's face crumpled and wet trails dripped from her cheeks like rain. "I should have kept him company. Bibi told me to leave him alone to mourn, but that's the last thing I should have done. I should have visited sooner. I should have gone back after I took you to Serein's. He was hurting so much without Marteau. Oh, Gavy, it must've driven him mad. He was in so much pain . . . so horrible . . ."

I watched the opérateur, unsure of how to follow that up. If I told her the truth now—

"What else did he say? He blamed *you*. There must've been a reason."

"I . . . h-he said . . ." The longer I looked into Deryn's sorrowful eyes, the harder it was for the words to come. Never before had the truth felt so heavy and dismaying. Would she even believe me if I told her? Deryn had known me for only days, but she'd known Ciseau for years. He was part of her crew. He was her friend. He wasn't an outsider like me. He belonged. She needed to hear the truth from someone who belonged.

"It's still kind of hazy for me," I said. "Still in shock, I guess. I think Serein would be able to tell you more. You should ask him."

Deryn reached across the table and grabbed my hand. "It must've been pretty frizzing scary for you."

I tightened my fingers around hers. I opened my mouth, but my throat tightened and no words came out. I shook my head violently, eyes burning.

"Oh, no, no." Deryn leapt out of her seat and threw her arms around me, tucking my head under her chin. "I'm such a great daft cow. I'm sorry, Gavy. Here I've been blubbering about *him* when you're the one . . . it's so hard to wrap my head around it all."

"He was your friend," I sobbed.

"But you're my friend, too," she murmured in my curls. "And you're still here. And, Great Heart, if my head doesn't feel like it's about to blow my brains out my blooming nose."

Despite my tears, I giggled. "Maybe you should lie down."

"We both should. It's been a long night, and that's coming from someone used to sitting through five of them in a row."

I looked over to the chaise sitting so lonesome against the wall, the only possible place to lie down other than the floor. "Are you sure it'll hold both of us?"

Deryn flicked her hand. "Oh, that old thing's held two on it plenty of time—" Her face turned beet red. She drew her hand back and fiddled with her badges. "Well, not plenty, just a few and—you forget all that rubbish. It'll hold two people fine."

I grinned behind my hand. So many times she'd teased me about Serein. It was fun to see her flustered for once. "Should we be expecting anyone, Deryn? Someone special?"

"I told you to forget all that shite," she huffed. "No, there's no one like that. Never has been."

My smile fell. "There's never been anyone? Not in a city this large?"

"Not everyone has this supercharged, divine sexual connection like you and Serein," Deryn replied, much to my mortification.

"There's really no point to it anyway. Hard to keep a good relationship when you're off flying heart-knows-where ninety percent of the year." She cast a glance around the room. "No point in buying furniture, neither."

"It quite surprised me," I admitted, settling onto the chaise near the wall.

"Ha. You thought there'd be a mountain of shite to climb over, didn't you?" Deryn stabbed her finger at me, smiling. "Well, I'm not spending good argent on rubbish I'm not here to enjoy. Better off putting it to something useful." She launched to the chaise and flopped down beside me.

"You're saving up for something?"

"Yeah. Can't keep cruising the skies for the Paramount forever." Deryn reached for the top of the pile of blankets and threw a wad over us. "I would like to see home again before it's over."

I smiled. That was a wish I knew well. "I'm sure Heortefeld is beautiful."

"You want to go with me one day?"

I turned my head and stared up at the chipped plaster ceiling. Me? Crossing the sea and going all the way to another country? I still hadn't seen half of Premier Esprit. And it was just one of many lands and many adventures. "Is it far?"

"Yep." Deryn raised her arms and folded her hands behind her head. "You've got to cross a body of water that stretches over the horizon and fly over the peninsula of Huǒ Jīn."

"Hu-huwa Sheen?"

Deryn chuckled. "Yeah, that one's kind of hard. We could make a quick stop if you want to check it out. Shite, we could even go on past Heortefeld. Himinnhjarta, Starkherza, Fu'aad . . . we'll do the whole round of the world and come back here to fill this empty box with our treasures. It'll be amazing, Gavy."

My head swirled. So many places . . . a world so big. Flying across seas and exploring new countries. The swirling stopped, and the shadows of doubt crept in. I couldn't. Not me. I was Gavril of Nostalgie—a town so small it was barely a dot on the map. I felt so small. Insignificant. Nostalgie was so insignificant despite what it meant to me.

"We could start small," Deryn quickly threw in, sensing my troubles. "Just dip our toes to start with."

I nodded, trying to pull myself from the depths of unease. "I'm sorry."

"Nah, it's nothing," she said. "Plenty of people have a hard time grasping it. I've been here for so long, I guess I take it for granted that I get to bum along with a Résonateur between barriers. It makes me feel bad about putting it that way."

"You shouldn't feel guilty for having freedom," I told her. "It's an amazing thing. I'm sure you worked hard to get where you are, Deryn. You should be proud of that."

"Well, actually I got where I am by being really bad at something else, but I'll take the compliment." Deryn loosed a deep sigh and closed her eyes. "You could do it, too, you know. It's not that hard."

I shook my head. "Being an opérateur looks pretty hard to me. I don't know the first thing about engines or controlling soulevers."

"Nobody does until they start apprenticing. Think about it. You could go to that seigne-prat that had you locked up and tell him to piss off before flying away on your grand soulever. It'll be frizzing brilliant."

I pictured Gervais, Cyril, and Charmant standing inside the gate to Envie, slack-jawed and immobilized like statues catching pigeon droppings.

"That would be amazing, but . . ." My smile slipped. "But I wouldn't get to see Mama as often. Or Serein."

Deryn moaned dramatically and cupped her cheeks. "Oh, no, Serein. What will I do without your strong arms embracing me to your chiseled chest all day? And the bed is so cold without your intense, smoldering—"

"So you've felt it," I broke in, putting an end to her vivid storytelling.

"Not with *him*," she replied. "No matter how hard he and Hervy try, I'm just not interested." She rolled on her side to face me. "A Résonateur's power isn't just limited to attacking Phases and dampened. It can show itself during any intense burst of emotion." She smirked and tapped my nose with her finger. "And that includes passion. Blistering, eh?"

"What about the emotions from others? Can they feel them just as intensely back?" I asked, my face flaming.

"Oh, yes. Some better than others, and the more tuned into a person they are, the deeper the connection."

"That's incredible."

Deryn poked her tongue out. "Sounds like soppy mess to me, but whatever blows up your skirt."

"Maybe so," I whispered, looking back up at the ceiling.

Deryn yawned loudly. "Oh, I can't get used to breaking my routine. Up one second, down the next. Night, Gavy."

"Good night, Deryn," I replied. I rolled on my side away from her as she snuggled into the blankets.

I knew Résonateurs were sensitive to strong outbursts, but I had no idea the depth of their perception. Had Serein always been aware of my feelings, or did that only happen when we grew closer? Did he feel my fear in Envie? I brought a hand up to my neck. Or tonight?

And what about every other time? Did he know when I was lying to him? Or when I longed to see him? All those times we were alone and I secretly admired him . . .

"Stop thinking about Serein and go to sleep, Gavy," Deryn slurred sleepily.

"I am."

I closed my eyes and forced my mind to clear. It had been a long night, and I was very tired. But the more I lay there, the more another emotion crept in to haunt me and keep me on the cusp of awareness. Worry. Worry about Serein and worry about the future. Worry about being attacked again. Worry about what would happen in the end . . .

RESONANCE

The crack in the ceiling wasn't quite a foot long. Five thin lines grew from it, each less than a hair's width. They were small now, but over time those barely-there lines would extend and become an eyesore. They may have grown a tiny bit in the hours I spent studying them. Staring at that black crack in the white plaster. It reminded me of black veins on white flesh, but it was curved slightly. Almost looked like a mouth. And if I pictured two obsidian eyes and a round nose—

Rapt . . . rapt . . . rapt . . .

Knock-knock.

My gaze drifted toward the door.

Knock-knock.

I looked at the blonde sleeping deeply by my side. One arm was thrown above her head, and a thin trail of drool dribbled down her chin. She looked so peaceful, and she didn't get to sleep like this often.

Knock-knock-knock.

Deryn's steady breathing never broke rhythm. Gently, I pushed the blankets back, slid to the bottom of the chaise, and stood. I would have to tell whoever was knocking that Deryn was sleeping and to come back later. I didn't even know what time it was.

Knock-knock–

I pulled the door open. The figure on the other side swiftly stepped back and stared at me, surprised.

"Serein," I breathed, eyes widening.

A heavy bag drooped under his bloodshot eye, and his shoulders slumped. But as weary as he looked, his new commandant uniform was pristine.

"Gavril," he said, "I'm glad Deryn kept you safe. I was worried about the two of you walking here in the middle of the night. Is she here?"

"She's asleep," I said, taken aback by his cordial tone but smiling at him nonetheless. "She could sleep through a thunderstorm right now."

"She's used to catching her rest in a room full of beeping consoles, so I'm not surprised." Serein rubbed the back of his neck. "It's fine. I'll leave her a note. Wait here for me."

He marched past me without a word.

A cool breeze flitted over me, and I shivered. My lips dropped, and I stepped out of the doorway and into the alley.

So cold . . . was he not glad to see me?

Bustling sounds from the nearby market assured me it was sunset, not sunrise, bathing the buildings in a soft orange glow. Several clouds slowly floated by, casting large, creeping shadows over the walls.

The door clicked shut behind me. I turned.

"It's been a long time since you ate," Serein said. "Why don't we get something? There's a great restaurant close to here."

I put my hands on my stomach. It had been a long time, but that was nothing new to me. "I'm fine if you don't feel like it, Serein. I know you've been up all night, and going this long is—"

"Something you're used to. I know," he cut in. "But you're not in the country anymore, Gavril. There's no need to keep punishing yourself."

"Being in the country isn't a punishment."

"No, but purposely starving yourself because you feel guilty *is*," he replied. He grabbed my hand. "There's no need to keep denying yourself things because you think you deserve to share Nostalgie's pain." He lifted my hand and opened the palm, displaying all the calluses and scars. "You've already had your share of pain. There is nothing to be gained from torturing yourself."

"Serein, it's something—"

"And I'm hungry myself." He smiled. "So why don't you indulge me and give me the privilege of taking you out to our first real dinner together?"

My inner defenses went on full alert. Something was wrong. He was pushing this dinner, but why? What was going on? "If it means that much to you."

He continued to hold his smile, though it appeared forcefully locked in place, and clasped our fingers together before striding down the alley.

Serein definitely wasn't himself. He said we should enjoy our first dinner, but his strained demeanor made it seem like our last.

Shops and taverns of the market ring glowed with a different aura as evening approached. Families strolled about, and store windows remained open, fully displaying the goods for sale. Dress shops with elaborate gowns, jewelry stores filled with gold and silver, and carts loaded with fresh produce dazzled me. The selection dwarfed even the wares available in Calme. There was no shortage of competition, either. Around the curved central road, merchants waved people over and shouted their offers with promises of quality.

Some even had the courage to approach Serein.

"How about some pearls for your lovely lady, Commandant?"

"I've the perfect dress for Crest parties, Commandant."

"I've special spices from the West, Commandant. Guaranteed to put some spark in your evening."

While I tilted my head in interest, Serein didn't acknowledge any of the merchants and walked past as if they didn't exist. But it didn't matter. As soon as we departed from one, another appeared with a new offer.

The commotion of it all made my head spin. How did anyone know what to buy or who to buy it from? Just shopping for vegetables could take hours.

"I don't think I could live here," I announced over the din of the crowd.

Serein turned to me. "Why not?"

"It's so busy. I can't keep up with what's going on."

"You'll get used to it. All it takes is some practice, bit of trial and error to figure out who the thieves are."

"What if I don't want to get used to it?"

Serein's eyebrows furrowed. "The restaurant's around this corner, Gavril. Why don't we talk about this there?"

I nodded. It would be easier to hear each other outside the marketplace bustle. But there was nothing to discuss. I didn't have a place in this city. That was obvious.

Serein led me to a cylindrical building with three layered stores, each one a little smaller than the one below. Brick composed the bottom story, but the second had several oval windows, and the top floor was constructed of clear glass panes separated by narrow brick rows.

Inside, on the main floor, we approached an older gentleman in a red velvet dress coat. He gave Serein a quick once over, and his hand jumped to his thin mustache, plucking at its few remaining hairs.

"My lord Commandant," he said with a low bow. "What a pleasant surprise to have such a guest. My name is Pierre. Will you and this beautiful mademoiselle be dining with us this evening?"

"Yes, and I'd like the top floor," Serein replied. "The whole floor. I like to dine in private. You'll be compensated for the unavailable tables."

"But of course," Pierre replied. "Please, give us a moment to clear the area for you. We'll have everything set up perfectly."

Serein gave the man a quick nod, and Pierre disappeared up a curved set of steps behind the foyer.

Silence again descended. I didn't know how to break the ice creeping between us.

"What did you mean by that?" Serein asked suddenly, making me jump.

"By what?"

"That you didn't want to get used to the market?"

I shifted my weight and stared at the ground. "Well, it's so different and loud around here. I don't think I could adapt to the pace. This place isn't an easy adjustment for a girl used to simple things."

"Just because you were born somewhere, it doesn't mean you have to spend your whole life bound to it," Serein said gruffly.

"No, but such a big change isn't easy. It's unsettling and . . . and . . ."

"Scary," he finished for me. "Going somewhere new is scary. So is starting over, but life isn't life if it doesn't make your heart race every once in a while."

I raised my head to look at him, but he turned to the wall. He shoved his hands into his greatcoat pockets and studied a landscape painting. A thin, jagged pillar of stone sprouted from the shadowed dirt like a flower, but that was all that could be seen. What was at the top of the column creating the shadow was beyond view. A secret only the artist knew.

"Have you considered what I said about coming back to Nostalgie with me?" I asked.

"I can't, Gavril. I'm a Résonateur."

"My papa stayed with us for four years," I said. "It's possible."

Serein sighed. "He wasn't a commandant. I have more important duties to fulfill."

My tongue suddenly felt like sandpaper. "More important than protecting the people of a vulnerable village?"

Serein turned, meeting my gaze, peering right into my soul. "Yes,

Gavril. There are more important things in the world than Nostalgie."

"The room is ready, Commandant."

Serein turned to Pierre. "Please, show us the way." He took my elbow, but I pulled it away.

Pierre's lips pursed like wadded cloth and his gaze zipped between us.

"Ladies first," Serein said. He stepped back, allowing me to follow Pierre up the stairs.

The host nodded vigorously. "Very good." He spun on his heel and began the ascent.

I stiffly stalked after him, not caring if I appeared uncultured. I wasn't cultured. I was just a peasant. A dirty, ill-mannered plebeian.

The top floor was beautiful. Cherry floors gleamed with light cast from the wall of windows. Even the ceiling was glass. A solitary round table with a red tablecloth waited for us in the middle of the room. A pair of black candles stood in the center between the place settings of chinaware and silver-rimmed wine glasses. Pierre pulled my chair back, and I sat.

"I hope it's not too bold to make a suggestion," he began.

"Depends what it relates to," Serein replied sharply.

"The food, Commandant. Our chef would like to prepare a special meal for our esteemed guests."

Serein nodded, taking his seat. "That's fine. I'm sure it'll be delicious. Do you have any wine?"

"For a commandant, nothing but the best." Pierre bowed once again and retreated back down the stairs.

Once more, all was silent. I looked at the sky. Clouds continued to build, puffing out and up into the heavens.

"Are you going to ignore me for the whole dinner?" Serein asked.

I blinked, continuing to stare upward. "Why would you say something like that?"

Serein's chair squeaked, and the table gave ever so slightly. "I thought we'd have a little more time to prepare, but we don't, Gavril."

I lowered my gaze. He was leaning over the table on his elbows, head down.

"What do you mean?"

He raised his head. "When I made the report about Ciseau, I had to tell them about you. Who you are. What your connection to Ciseau is. And why you were in my house. I had to tell them everything." His frown deepened, the lines of fatigue on his face becoming more pronounced. "Gavril, the Sommet was not pleased to hear that a young woman set to be tried by the Suzerain for heresy was walking free instead of waiting in the Édifice holding cells."

My stomach dropped to the floor. "You didn't get into trouble, did you?"

He chuckled and shook his head. "No. Fortunately, my clout holds more water than I expected. They were reluctant but trusted my judgment."

I reached across the table and took hold of his hands. "Oh, thank goodness. I couldn't bear it if you ended up getting punished because of me."

He squeezed my hands and stared at our locked embrace. His jaw twitched a few times before he spoke. "There was one condition. To keep you out of the cells, I had to agree to it." He swallowed. "Gavril, your trial has been expedited. You'll be before the Suzerain first thing tomorrow morning."

My fingers froze. Ice pulsed through my veins to my chest and down to my feet. My thoughts whirled.

"Gavril, it's going to be okay. We knew this was coming."

"I hope I'm not interrupting." Pierre approached the table with a wine bottle in hand. Behind him, a young lady followed his shadow with a bowl balanced on each hand.

Pierre poured the wine, and the young lady placed a bowl of thick, creamy white stew in front of me.

"You can leave the bottle," Serein told him. "We'll need it."

"As you wish, Commandant."

The soup's steam swirled through the air. It danced and twisted like a . . . like a Phase. A white Phase. A pearly fog the opposite of Morrow's shimmering black cloud form. There was a greater chance of seeing one of those than there was of saving Nostalgie.

"Eat, Gavril," Serein urged.

"I can't," I muttered. My stomach felt like a boulder.

"You have to," he pressed. "You need to be at your best tomorrow. You can't think well on an empty stomach." He raised my hand and slipped a spoon into my fingers. "Please, Gavril. If not for yourself, do it for Nostalgie."

I licked my dry lips and nodded dully. Yes, the town was counting on me to give it my all. I had to be strong for them. The moment the thick liquid hit my tongue, my resistance melted into a puddle. It defrosted my veins and bathed me in a blanket of pure warmth. And the flavor—such a taste of perfection.

"What's in this?" I asked.

"Scallops, I believe," Serein told me.

"Scallops?"

"From the sea. They come in shells." Serein grinned and winked at me. "Way better than Margaux's gruel, huh?"

"I've been spoiled. I'll never be able to eat her cooking ever again—if I don't end up wearing it first."

"Do you really anticipate repeating that pleasurable experience?"

I slowly stirred my stew, watching the cream split and reform. "I don't know."

Serein cleared his throat, and I looked up from my bowl.

"You know when I said I told the Sommet everything, I wasn't being completely honest. I had to leave out one notable part. Do you know what it was?"

I hummed lowly and thought for a second. "I have a pretty good idea. If the Sommet didn't like the idea of me not being in a cell, I don't think they'd be thrilled that you and I are . . . we're . . ." We're what? Close? Involved? In . . . in love?

The warning Hervé offered in Calme rang in my ears. *Serein's young. He's got his whole life ahead of him and it leads up, not down. And people like us, girl, we're so far down that the damn earth is choking us.*

I didn't have Serein. He wasn't mine. Why should he tell others about us?

"You're right," he answered, grabbing his wine glass. "I thought it might lead to something neither of us want thrown in our faces at the present time."

A dull ache pressed against my breastbone. "So how did you explain why I was in your house?"

"I told them that instead of treating you like a criminal, it was my duty to provide you with guidance and lead you toward a path of noble purpose and humble devotion to the Suzerain. I said that anyone who disagreed with guiding strays back to their shepherd was a heretic unto the Great Heart's teachings. I've never seen the Sommet agree to anything so readily."

I smiled. "Such a dedicated and selfless calling for you, Commandant."

"I know. It sounds even worse now that I'm having to explain it." He held my glass out for me. "But that's the last time I want to lie about us. After tomorrow, I want to start anew. No more keeper and prisoner. Will you toast to the future with me, Gavril?"

The ache in my chest transformed into a wonderful flutter of joy as I took the glass. "I'd like that very much."

My stomach had never felt so full. I was satiated. The city disk below my feet could have crumbled, and I would have rolled off without a care.

"You have a beautiful glow about you tonight," Serein said as we ambled down the Crest road side by side. We were heading toward his home—returning to a haven where the world was for us alone.

"It's the food," I replied. "I never realized how enjoyable indulgence was until I tasted that exquisite cherry tart. That chef should receive a medal from the Sommet for his noble purpose and humble devotion to good food."

"And the touch of wine didn't hurt either, I suspect."

"Are you saying I'm a lush, Commandant?"

"I'm saying it's good to see you relax." He wound an arm around my waist and nuzzled his nose into my neck. "You deserve a little pleasure."

I curled my fingers in his short hair. A low rumble of thunder rolled in the distance. To my disappointment, Serein pulled away. He grasped my hand from his hair and held it.

"We should quicken our pace. I got this uniform today, and I'm not ready to see it meet the same fate as the last one."

"You mean the one I pulled off you and tore to shreds?"

"Actually, I meant the good drenching. A little pulling and tearing I can tolerate."

I laughed and gazed up at the sky. Dark clouds churned and rolled above the city skyline like a sea of dark enchantment.

"Is this what the coast looks like?"

Serein leaned into me. "I'll show you every coast in Premier Esprit. We'll swim in the waves and scoop up a barrel's worth of fresh scallops."

"I'll never go hungry again."

"No, never again."

A tiny drop of water hit my cheek, and I blinked in surprise.

"Guess that's our cue." Serein chuckled. He pulled my hand, and we took off jogging.

"I didn't realize Résonateurs were so afraid of water," I teased.

"Oh, it's our worst enemy," he replied. "Nothing musses pomp and arrogance faster than dripping, clear liquid."

"There's nothing scarier than losing your pomp."

"You say that like it's a joke." He pushed me against the door of his house and encircled his arms around my waist. "But it's very serious business."

At that moment, the sky opened, and a torrent of water came crashing down on us.

I chortled loudly while Serein scrambled for the security panel by his front door. The lock clicked open, and we tumbled back on the polished wood of his great atrium.

"Great Heart, that was a river. How close to the sky are we?" I said, picking myself up from the cold surface.

"Not close enough." Serein took my hands and walked backward to the stairs. "To touch the stars, you have to climb higher."

Together we ascended, smiling and whispering sweet nothings to each other. Never in my life had I thought it possible to feel like this, so buoyant and alive. This was my eve. Possibly my last chance to set my heart free.

And I was going to seize it.

Only when we entered the threshold of Serein's room did we finally break contact.

"I'll light a fire," he said. "Why don't you get comfortable?"

I nodded and wandered farther in the room. Straight ahead, a balcony awaited behind a pair of wide glass doors. Rain cascaded down over the Crest, covering the houses below in a cloud of steamy white.

A little higher and we would break through those clouds to the stars. Finally reaching the impossible I spent my whole life grasping for.

Serein ran his finger over a thin green line in the middle of the fireplace mantel, and bright flames jumped to life. They cast a warm glow on the surrounding black marble.

"That would have been handy in the valley," I commented.

Serein grinned. He stepped toward the balcony and peered through its glass doors. A bolt of lightning struck across the heavens, illuminating the city all the way to the golden lighthouse.

"I love lightning," he said. "It's powerful and destructive, but undeniably beautiful. It makes me feel safe, as bizarre as that sounds."

Another bolt arced down like a crack in a glass globe.

"The barrier," I whispered. "It's like the barrier when it's been hit by a Phase. It reminds us that we're protected."

"Maybe so," he replied. He turned around slowly, facing me head on. A streak of light zipped behind him, surrounding him with an aura of pure white. Like a cloak. Like a white ghost waiting for me.

Serein *was* lightning. Powerful, deadly, and the most bewitching creature I'd ever laid eyes on. And he was like the rain too—gentle and soothing or harsh and raging. He was a storm. He was the storm that broke down the barrier around my heart.

I took one step forward, then another, and another, afraid he would disappear with the lightning and leave me alone in a world filled with darkness.

I raised my hands to his uniform, slowly, timidly, waiting for rejection. But he stood still. Didn't pull away. I reached up to his buttons. Buttons of gold and buttons of pride. I undid one, then another, and another.

When the last button slipped free, the ivory cloth parted to reveal the ring of white on his chest. I leaned forward and pressed my lips into its center and traced my fingers over the vessels branching out to his neck, his arms, and the sides of his abdomen.

Such a precious treasure, this man.

Serein slid his hands up my arms to my shoulders, and his fingers grazed the buttons along my neck. He hesitated, his fingers lingering on the silver, running over the surface but not pulling.

"Go on," I whispered with another kiss to his chest.

One by one, silver buttons loosened their hold, and my dress opened. Instead of chilly night air, I felt heat.

Serein tangled his fingers in my curls and tilted my head back. His lips pressed against mine, slaking the building thirst. He grabbed my waist, and my feet left the floor. I circled my legs around him. I clung to him as he moved, my lips dancing with his until the smooth caress of silk sheets met my back.

There was so much to touch, so much to feel. Serein moved his hands over my body hungrily, blessing me with rapture, introducing me to new and exhilarating sensations.

My heart beat so fast and full and loud that I was sure the world could hear its thunder. Again and again and again the walls shook around us as my body exploded with its own raging storm—one that touched my core.

Finally, I rested my head against his chest, my breath slowly returning to normal. Who knew being struck by lightening could feel so good?

Serein gently traced patterns below my ribs, his gaze locked on the storm outside. The rain eased to a steady flow, and the thunder rumbled far beyond.

"I said it for a reason," he murmured.

I tilted my head to look at him. "Said what?"

"At the restaurant, I said there were more important things in the world than Nostalgie."

I sighed, the wonderful heat of our storm cooling fast. "Please, Serein. Do we have to talk about this now?"

"Your trial is tomorrow, Gavril. There's no other time." He cupped my cheek and ran his thumb along my lips. "I said it because I need you to believe it."

A hard lump formed in my throat. "I can't, Serein. Something like that—"

"You have to." His voice cracked, brimming with an urgency that

I'd never heard from him—not even when we were surrounded by dampened. "Listen to me, Gavril. The Suzerain is not like the rest of us. His decisions can be unpredictable, and they are *final*. If you can't convince him of your innocence, the chance to plea for a Solenoid for Nostalgie will never come about. You have to put yourself first, Gavril. Please."

My eyes filled with tears, and before I could take in another breath, they descended to his chest in waves. "But I'm not innocent. I did it, Serein. I was talking to a Phase."

He held me fast. "I know."

I pulled back to stare at him. "Ho-how l-long? How could you possibly—"

"Since the beginning. The moment I asked you and you avoided answering, I knew the truth."

"Then why?" I sobbed. "Why did you fight for me and bring me here?"

"I already told you," he said softly. "There was only one source of light in the whole town, and you were it." He kissed my forehead. "You may have left the barrier, Gavril, but you were not guilty of what they accused you of. To think you a heretic capable of plotting to bring ruin to a town? That seigneur's head is so far up his backside he can see his teeth."

I giggled through my tears. "What's left of them."

Serein settled back down and stroked my hair. "I don't know why you sought out that Phase, nor tried to reason with such a creature. I'm sure you'll tell me one day in your own time. And to be honest, it's the least of my concerns right now. I'm afraid, Gavril. I'm trying not to be, but I am. That sounds so selfish compared to what it must be like for you."

I placed my hand on his chest and felt his heartbeat. "I've been afraid my whole life. I thought that surviving was the only thing that mattered in life, but tonight you've shown me something wonderful—a treasure worth leaving the barrier for. I promise, Serein. I promise that I will fight with all my heart tomorrow."

"For *you*, Gavril," he said, voice rough. "Don't worry about the rest. I want you to leave Nostalgie behind."

I averted my eyes from his face and rested back down next to him.

Leave Nostalgie behind.

The people I grew up with. The fields that I loved. The lake and the old cork tree.

I clamped my eyes shut.

Nostalgie wasn't a place. It was . . .

I can't.

PLEA OF DESPERATION

I pushed my face into something firm and sighed contentedly. It smelled good. It *felt* good. I could stay here all day, resting against this heavenly chest.

"Gavril," a divine spirit whispered in my ear. "Gavril, it's time to wake up. You have an appointment with the Suzerain."

My eyes snapped open like a gate caught in the wind, and it all came back to me. Nostalgie. Envie. The Paramount. Ciseau. I tried to sit up, but an arm held me in place.

"Calm down," Serein shushed in my ear. "There's nothing to panic about."

"I'm not sure I agree with that," I replied, heart in my throat. "I've had more near-death experiences in the last week than I've had in my entire life. But this may be worse."

Serein cupped my cheek and turned my head so he could gaze into my eyes. "Gavril, I-I don't know what to say. I never meant for any of this to happen."

I tangled my fingers in his hair and pressed my lips against his. "No, but I'm glad it did. If it hadn't, I wouldn't be right here with you." I'd never bared my heart like that before. Not with anyone. Not even Mama.

"It doesn't matter what happens with the Suzerain today," he murmured into my hair. "You're coming back here with me."

"It does matter. Lives depend on me." I released a quivering breath. "I have to get ready."

Serein helped me slide out of the massive bed, like the one on the *Fulgurant*. If only we could still be there together, safe in the sky.

"The washroom is over there." He pointed to a door along the left wall. "I'll put a dress out for you."

"No." I picked up my dress from the floor. "Mine will do."

"Gavril, it's covered in dirt and blood."

"I know. It shows what I had to go through to get here."

Serein smiled down at me. "Yes, it does."

With shaking limbs, I set about cleaning up. My entire body twisted in knots that left me feeling sick. *I have to do this. I can do this. I can do this*, I chanted softly to keep from vomiting. After I finished drying, I dressed and headed for the main floor.

Serein waited at the bottom of the stairs. He wrapped an arm around my shoulders. "You should have something to eat."

"I can't." My voice cracked. "It'll join the blood and dirt on my skirt."

"Wouldn't that be something for the Suzerain?" Serein chuckled.

He led me out the house and onto the street. The roads were still damp from the storm, but the sky was crystal clear—a calm sea after turbulent waves. "I want to show you something before we leave for the lighthouse," Serein whispered in a voice as soft as flower petals. "I don't know if it will give you any courage, but maybe it can soothe your heart."

I nodded. Wave after wave of nausea tore through me. Courage or no, I could use any type of help available.

We followed several streets until the buildings opened into a small grassy area. A few people sat on benches or strolled in the cool morning air. Serein led me around the field. I remained silent, waiting for him to explain his intentions.

After another lap around the park, I touched his elbow. "What exactly are we doing, Serein?" I asked gently.

"What do you mean?" His brows knotted. "I thought it might help you to be surrounded by trees and grass."

I glanced around the little park. "It's—it's very beautiful, Serein," I said. "Is it special to you?" If it was, I didn't want to offend him by being unimpressed.

"To me? No, I thought—" He scratched the back of his head. "I know you love the country, and I thought if you could see this . . ."

My heart leapt.

He looked around the park. "It's kind of stupid . . ."

I pressed my head against his chest. That's what he meant by soothing my heart. He wanted to comfort me with familiar sights and sounds. "Thank you," I breathed into his coat. "It's perfect."

"No, it's not." Serein voice sounded oddly strained. Was he embarrassed? "This is nothing like the fields in Tristesse. I don't know why I thought it would be."

"That doesn't matter." I pulled back to look into his face. "You want to help me, and that means everything. Thank you for trying to put me at ease."

"Listen, Gavril." He cupped my cheeks, and his gaze shot right into my heart. "I want you to give everything in your might to the Suzerain today, but I don't want you to surrender your heart to him. No matter his judgment, believe that everything will be okay. I need you to believe in me. There is always a way to save what really matters."

I released the breath I was holding. "I believe in you, Serein," I whispered to his heart.

"We have come so far together, Gavril. I have faith in you."

I tried to smile, but I couldn't. He believed in me. He truly believed in me, and nothing could be worse than failing him and everyone else.

How could he put such hope in me? I couldn't fail. I would do whatever it took to get a Solenoid for Nostalgie. Anything. No price was too great.

Serein ran a hand through my hair. "What I wouldn't give to know what you are feeling right now," he murmured. "So many emotions blurring together. It's against my training to live so unrestrained. Maybe one day, I'll feel that freedom."

I looked down at my feet. "You don't want to," I rebutted. "They're not good emotions."

"There's no such thing as good and bad emotions, Gavril," Serein expressed. "There is only your heart. It's a power greater than any other." He rested a hand on my chest. "Just believe in it, Gavril. All you have to do is let it guide you."

As we left the safety of the park, I spiraled into doubt. *I can do this. Serein believes in me,* I chanted silently. The walk to the tram and the ride into the center of the Crest blurred together in a haze. I repeated my chant over and over, until I could almost believe the words were true. They had to be. Nostalgie was counting on me.

We rode past the tall ivory towers straight to the golden lynchpin in the heart of Éthéré Coeur. Several people gathered and moved around the elegant, curved golden legs connected to the elevated base of the lighthouse. I saw guards, Résonateurs, workers, patrons, and archivistes. People were free to mingle outside their stations, the only place where all life converged.

Serein escorted me through a row of guards and into a large chamber below the lighthouse. An enormous throne of white marble with thick black cushions stood on a platform at the head of the room. Rubies, amethysts, and pearls encrusted the throne's arms and legs in swirling sprout and seed patterns. At the top of the tall back, a single heart-shaped black diamond the size of my fist rested inside a large oval indentation. A crack splintered the stone's center.

"That's Le Trésor d'Eidolon," Serein informed me. "The stone was a gift from the Great Suzerain's wife. Legend says that when she passed, Eidolon felt so much grief that the diamond split in half."

"And all of Athánatos Kardiá felt his pain," a deep voice added.

A man in rich purple robes walked up to us—a thin, tall, straight-backed figure with long golden hair that nearly reached his knees. The gentleman's mane was streaked with silver, but nary a wrinkle touched his face. When he looked at me, his maroon eyes sparkled.

"Chancelier Fabrice." Serein's voice was laced with surprise. "I didn't expect to see you here."

"That is the beautiful thing about life, Serein." The man smiled, twirling a white cord attached to his robes. "Sometimes things don't go as you expect."

"Well, to have you present is certainly an honor."

"There is really nothing honorable about my being here," the chancelier said. "I merely saw your request for a trial by the Suzerain, and my curiosity got the better of me." He studied me. "Is this the, ah . . . accused?"

"Oh, yes," Serein replied. "This is Gavril. Gavril, this is Chancelier Fabrice, the head of the Sommet and right hand to the Suzerain."

A rush of mortification and anxiety swept through me. I curtsied as low as I could without falling over. "Chancelier, I—I, uh—"

"There is no need for such formalities," he said kindly. "Serein gives me far too much credit. To say that I have anything to do with the Suzerain's decisions is a great overestimation."

"Forgive me for disagreeing, Chancelier, but if it wasn't for you, I doubt anything would get done around here," Serein said.

A weary look briefly crossed the chancelier's face. "Yes, unfortunately, that is true." He leaned in close and smiled at me. "It's a good thing I'm so old. I've much experience in the matter of getting nothing done."

I returned his smile despite my nerves. *Please, don't throw up on him.*

Chancelier Fabrice straightened and put a hand on Serein's back.

"I'm afraid I lied when I said curiosity was my only gain. I believe there was an incident at your home. I'm sorry I was not able to attend the report hearing, late as it was."

Serein's fists clenched. "One of my crew broke in and tried to kill Gavril," he growled through his teeth. "He threw himself out the window before I could capture him."

"Do you know his motive?"

Both men turned to me.

I had lied to Deryn, but this was the Chancelier of the Sommet. He wasn't Ciseau's friend, and after the hours of questioning Serein no doubt endured, the least I could do was tell the truth to support a thorough investigation.

"He blamed me for his brother's death and said I was a bad influence on Serein," I replied softly. "He said something about being sent to watch Serein, their special mission."

"Oh, I don't doubt that," Fabrice responded. "I'm sure he said many strange things in his derangement. It's a sad thing, but the mind of a mourning man is not rational. I will oversee the investigation into the issue, so you can put your minds and hearts at ease."

"We greatly appreciate it, Chancelier, but with your workload—"

"My work is for the people of Premier Esprit," Chancelier Fabrice insisted. "I'm just glad our young lady friend wasn't injured in the ordeal."

"You may not have that opinion when the Suzerain is through with me," I said gloomily, clutching my skirt.

"I wouldn't worry so much about him," Fabrice said. "The only thing people are truly defeated by is themselves. Now, I hate to be rude, but I'd better see to the delay."

"No doubt the Suzerain is finalizing his preparations." Serein grinned slyly.

"And his appearance." Fabrice rolled his eyes and turned away. "The Suzerain is a man of great eccentricities."

Serein waited until the chancelier left before leaning closer to me. "He's a good man to have on your side. Well done, Gavril."

"Me?" I said, floored. "But I didn't do anything. I hardly said anything at all."

"Yes, you did," he countered. "You'd know if you didn't."

"Peace! Peace in the chamber!"

All activity in the room came to a halt. It was so quiet I could hear the blood pulsing through my veins.

"Please, bare your hearts before Suzerain Ambroise, divine heart of the world and ruler of all emotions."

Every person in the room knelt on one knee, so I followed suit. Heels clicked across the marble floor, echoing throughout the chamber. I thought someone snickered behind me, but I dared not raise my head.

"*Oui, oui, oui, mes enfants*," an exuberant voice rang out. "Raise your heads so I might look upon your petite faces."

I furrowed my brow but followed the instructions and took my first look at the almighty Suzerain.

The Suzerain was a man of many colors and *accoutrement*. A powder-blue wig the size of an oval beehive perched atop his head like a wad of candy. Pure white makeup covered his face, and his hooded, ebony eyes were covered with vivid green eyeshadow.

My gaze cut to Serein, who held his lips together like a clam.

As the Suzerain extended his arms to the crowd, beaming widely, his golden jacket and knee breeches glittered. He slid onto the throne. When he crossed his legs, a shiny black heel kicked into the air.

"You may rise, children," he sang.

Everybody stood up, but other than the shuffle of shifting bodies, the room remained silent. Someone pinched my arm, and I turned around to see Deryn and Hervé standing behind me.

Deryn hugged me. "Came to wish you luck," she whispered. "Snatch the knickers right off him."

"Please, don't." Hervé shuddered.

"Gavril of Nostalgie from the Tristesse region, please step forward," Chancelier Fabrice demanded.

My heart tumbled into my stomach and then sprang into my throat. I froze. Serein gently gripped my shoulders and guided me to the front. I clopped along on wooden legs.

The Suzerain's eyes rolled over me, and I wanted to curl up on the floor and cry.

"You can do this," Serein encouraged me. "Remember what I told you."

I nodded dumbly, my brain frozen.

Chancelier Fabrice addressed the crowd again. "For the first order of business, Gavril is accused of conversing with a Phase and conspiring to attack the town of Envie."

Gasps and hushed comments swept through the room.

"*Conversing* with it," the Suzerain repeated. Skepticism colored his tone like a prism. His gaze moved to me again. "Fabrice, have you ever heard of a Phase that converses?"

"No, Suzerain," the chancelier replied.

"Neither have I. Innocent. What's next?"

My chest heaved with disbelief as the crowd exploded with applause. I felt . . . Oh, Great Heart, I didn't know what I felt exactly, but it was good. I was free to help Nostalgie. *Oh, Mama—*

"Wait!" I shouted, and a shocked hush swept through the chamber. "Please, your—your divine, most excellent . . . um . . .Suzerain." I swallowed hard as the Suzerain's dark eyes pierced into me, but his gaze felt less threatening than it had earlier. Almost like looking at a friend. "I have one more issue to raise. Please."

He rolled his tongue around a few times as though he were picking his teeth. "I'll hear it."

I clasped my hands over my chest. "Thank you. It's about the Solenoid in my home, Nostalgie. The Solenoid is dying, and we need a new one."

"Do you have a Résonateur to pay the service?"

"No, we—"

"Then I'm afraid, *mon petit enfant,* that I simply cannot gift one to you," he said.

Bile rose in my throat. "But if you don't, we'll die—"

"My little girl," the Suzerain addressed me as though chastising a child, "take a look around you. What do you think is more important? Éthéré Coeur or your tiny speck in the fields?" He splayed his arms again. "The Solenoids are not limitless. Why, if I gave one to everybody who asked, there would be none left for the Paramount. If you have nothing to offer for the service . . ."

Their faces flashed before my eyes. All the people of Nostalgie. Mathieu. Celine. Mama. Even Lake Oublié and the old cork tree. They were all counting on me, and I was failing them. The ruins of Jalousie and Panique haunted my memories. The dampened left behind.

An ivory coat flashed in the corner of my eye. I turned to see Serein. He stared at me, begging. Pleading with me to stand down and let it go. He rested his hand over his heart.

I couldn't.

"I have something to offer." My words hitched, and light-headedness swept over me. "I have . . ."

Just say it!

"I have a . . ."

Do it!

"I have a fiancé."

"So?" the Suzerain demanded.

"There isn't a Résonateur now, but there may be one in the future." I forced the words over my numb tongue. "We're both from Résonateur lines, so there's a chance . . ."—*I'm disgusted with myself*—" . . . there's a chance we may produce a Résonateur child. I pledge that child to you." *I hate myself.*

The Suzerain slouched over the arm of the throne and propped his chin on his fist. "Do you know how many times I've heard this?"

I clenched my fists so hard my fingertips grew slick. "I—"

"Oh, how hundreds of people have come to me with this grand scheme of future offerings," he said with a bored wave. "But a Solenoid does not magically appear from the future. It must be created *now*. I cannot help you, my child. I cannot work with frivolous promises."

My eyes prickled. I covered a sob with my hand.

"Oh, *non, non, non, non*," the Suzerain shushed. "I cannot stand the sight of tears. It breaks my heart."

"Such a magnanimous ruler," someone uttered. "She makes demands with nothing to offer, yet he still speaks to her with kindness."

I turned away from the Suzerain and walked back into the crowd. I wiped my eyes and rushed toward my friends. Deryn's lips were pulled back into a wide grimace. Hervé glared at me, a spark flashing in his dull eyes. And Serein . . .

"Where's Serein?" I asked.

"Outside," Deryn croaked.

I pushed my way past the wall of people and ran out the exit. I had to find Serein. I had to find my heart. I failed so miserably, but at least I still had my heart. I searched around, pushing through the crowd. Out by one of the pillars, I finally spotted him. He stood with one hand on the pillar, his head down.

"Serein?"

"You couldn't let it go. You gave into it," he murmured.

"What are you talking about?" I asked. "Serein, what's wrong? I don't understand."

He rounded on me like a bolt of lightning. "What's there to understand? You just offered the Suzerain your future children by another man. That seems clear to me."

"I had no choice," I retorted. "You saw how quickly he dismissed me. Everyone in my hometown is going to die!"

"Did you honestly think I would let that happen?" he bellowed.

I stepped back.

"Did you really think I would leave those people exposed to attack? We could have found another way—moved them to another town. You didn't even spare a thought to that possibility. And why? Because you don't believe in me." His face crumpled. "And worse than that, you don't believe in yourself. I warned you about giving into desperation. I pleaded with you, and still you let it consume you."

All the fight left my body in an instant. Serein would have helped my village without the Suzerain's approval? *Oh, Great Heart, I've been such a fool.* I was so determined to save the village itself I never stopped to consider asking Serein for help in moving her citizens—the true heart of Nostalgie. The fear of failure . . .

Serein covered his eye with his hand. "I told you there were more important things than Nostalgie. It's just a piece of land. But to you it was worth sacrificing everything—even me."

I raised my hand, eyes brimming with tears.

"No, Serein, I—"

"Oi, oi, oi," Deryn sprinted up to us. "I know it was bad, but I've said plenty of dumb shite, too. You two are—"

"Gavril of Nostalgie?" An old man with goggles in a beige jumpsuit strolled up. "I'm one of the Paramount aérien opérateurs. Chancelier Fabrice sent me to deliver a message on behalf of the Suzerain."

"From the Suzerain?" I looked at Serein, but he turned away, refusing to meet my gaze.

"He said it was regrettable that he could not help you with a Solenoid, and it pains him to see one of his children so distressed. He's ordered me to return you to your fiancé so you may find happiness and love."

I didn't think it possible, but my heart dropped even further into the ground.

"Now wait just a tick," Deryn jumped in. "You're taking her back to Envie? Not a chance." She looked at Serein. "You aren't going to let her go, are you?"

Serein's eye darted between Deryn and the opérateur before flitting to me. It was only for a second, but I caught it—a different kind of storm in his gaze. One fueled by uncertainty, indecision, and pain.

"Not to step on the commandant's toes," the opérateur began, "but these are orders from the Suzerain. I'm afraid he doesn't have a say in it."

"Bloody rubbish," Deryn barked. "Serein! You aren't going to let them squeeze your balls like this."

"That's enough, Deryn," Serein replied, his voice hard. "I'm your commandant, and you will speak to me with respect. You arguing like this isn't helping."

"I'm not helping?" she bristled. "Fine. If she's got to go back, I'll take her myself."

I felt like the sky was falling on me. This couldn't be happening. It was all a joke. Any second now Deryn was going to slap her knee and start laughing, and Serein was going to take me into his arms and never let go.

"And how are you going to do that, Deryn?" Serein fired at her. "You're the chief opérateur of the *Fulgurant*."

"The *Fulgurant's* in a hundred bloody pieces, isn't it?" Deryn yelled. "She's grounded!"

"Precisely! As long as that soulever is grounded, so are you."

"That's shite!"

"That's protocol," Serein responded darkly. "Something we've become very lax on as of late."

"I can't believe this!" Deryn screamed and ran off.

The goggled opérateur looked between Serein and me. "So, am I taking her now?"

"I—" Serein's gaze moved over me. Then it fell. "If that is the

Suzerain's wish. She has a fiancé to return to." He took a few steps forward before pausing. "I would have given you everything. Protection, argent, the world . . . my heart."

Tears streamed down my face as Serein's back got further away from me.

Stop him! A voice screamed in my mind. *Tell him! I love you! I love you!*

Nothing but silence escaped me. The girl from Nostalgie always suffered in silence. She wasn't brave enough to leave the barrier on her own, wasn't brave enough to accept her home was lost. Wasn't brave enough to call out to the man she loved—a man who held her heart like the stars held impossible dreams.

She was Gavril of Nostalgie. She would always just be Gavril of Nostalgie. Fallen and forgotten.

Serein disappeared.

I hate myself. Serein hates me, too.

GHOST OF NOSTALGIA

A re you ready, Mademoiselle?" the old opérateur asked.

I couldn't speak. I had nothing left to say. Words were as useless now as they were in the Suzerain's chamber. I simply nodded.

"Let's head to the harbor, then," he said.

I followed him, my legs moving of their own accord, because the rest of me—my mind, my soul, my heart—was rooted in the Crest. With Serein.

"Wait! Wait, Mademoiselle!"

I turned to see Bedell, the young archiviste, sprint toward me.

"Wait, Mademoiselle," he panted, bending over to catch his breath. "I have—I have the information you requested. On the Résonateur Goel."

At least I could return to Nostalgie with *something*.

"It was very peculiar." He pulled a piece of paper from his pants pocket. "You see, his last mission was posted seventeen years ago and is still active. The location is listed as Nostalgie."

My entire body numbed. Edgard was right all along. Papa abandoned us. He ignored his family and shunned his duties as a Résonateur. He left us to die. He turned his back on us like everyone else.

I turned away from Bedell without thanking him and started walking again.

The tram ride to the harbor seemed like a nightmare I couldn't wake up from. And when the soulever ascended into the sky, I was forced to acknowledge that my harrowing vision was real. One day. Two days. Three days. I couldn't tell how long I was aboard the vessel. A constant rainstorm raged outside my window like a cruel joke. Morning? Noon? Night? Meaningless words. There was only the rain to remind me of my sorrow.

As the last day dawned, the clouds finally broke and sunlight bathed over Envie like a blessing. It made me sick. The soulever landed in front of Envie's gates. I disembarked and set foot outside Gervais' town for the last time.

A crowd of people clamored behind the gates, curious about the soulever but too afraid to exit the barrier for a closer look. I used to be like that.

Never again.

I turned and marched away, following the road home.

"You!" Gervais' voice cut through the wind behind me.

I stopped.

"You . . . how dare you show your face back here after leaving with those monsters."

I listened, but I refused to turn and look at him. If he wanted that, he'd have to come to me.

"They killed him." Gervais' voice quivered. "They left him face down in a pool of his own blood. My son . . . they killed my Cyril!"

I turned around. Tears descended down Gervais' face. So even he could cry. His world was filled with sorrow like mine.

"Aren't you going to say anything?" he sobbed. "Those men . . . those twins . . ."

Ciseau's voice rang in my ears from a time that seemed ages ago. A time on a soulever's sky deck as we soared among the clouds.

The little prince wasn't much help to begin with. He was definitely dead weight at the end.

Ciseau and Marteau killed Cyril. They killed him. Like they tried to kill me.

I threw Serein away for a dead man.

"I was found innocent," I said. "Stay away from Nostalgie."

Gervais' face purpled. "Innocent? My son is dead," he snarled.

"I'm sorry," I whispered. I turned around and left Envie behind. There was only one place left to go.

The sun and wind beat at me as I trekked on. On past the fields. On past the ruins of Jalousie. On to the village I held in my heart. Even when nightfall obscured the road, I kept going. I knew the way, though I'd only traveled the road once. I was nearly to the village when the subtle splashing of water caught my ears. The banks of Lake Oublié. I left the path and followed the sound to a place I knew as well as my own heartbeat. I passed the reeds and the patch of pink water lilies. I went straight to the old cork oak. I sat down on its roots and stared at the village in the distance. Once, I would have been too frightened to sit outside the barrier like this. How much my life had changed since that time.

This was where I met Morrow. I hadn't seen her in so long. I wondered where she was.

Isn't it obvious? She doesn't want anything to do with a coward like me. If she could hate, surely she would hate me.

I stood up and gathered my misery before heading to Nostalgie. The town was as quiet as Jalousie. An eerie coincidence or a hint of the future? Only fate knew the answer.

I trudged through the worn scraps of metal to the Solenoid. The dull hum of the siphon haunted the air like a dying breath, though I had yet to pass through the barrier. Its voice was comforting, as present in the village as ever, but weaker. Even as I closed in on the hub, the hum didn't penetrate the air as it once had.

I was almost to the platform when I felt the warm rush of the barrier around me. Had so much time lapsed since I last stood here?

Rapt. Rapt . . . rapt . . . rapt. Rapt. Rapt . . . rapt . . . rapt.

That sound . . . the strange pattern. I placed my hand on the Solenoid's metal surface. Was it about to explode like the one in Jalousie? A wry smile crossed my face. That was fine. I would stay here until the end. I had nothing left, including fear. I had nothing to lose. I'd failed everyone that mattered to me. My heart was . . . it was . . . I rested my forehead against the cold metal. Tears rained down on it. My heart was broken.

A low whir broke the hum.

Silence.

I stared at the Solenoid panel less than an inch from my face. My breathing stilled. The familiar hum was gone.

The Solenoid's metal panels screeched. Something cold and hard clamped onto my jaw. A—a hand. Sharp pricks sank into my cheek, and a chill seeped under my skin, flooding to the center of my chest. From there, it spread throughout my body like a creeping explosion of icy veins.

A second set of clawed fingers pulled back the Solenoid panel like paper. As the hole in the opening stretched and lengthened a white face appeared, pushing out of the hole. Black veins vined up its neck to its temples. The creature's honeyed amber eyes held my gaze. Honeyed amber—like sunset over sand.

Like mine.

This face. The last time I saw it was seventeen years ago. He promised me a Solenoid.

"Papa?"

The creature's mouth opened with a nerve-shattering screech.

I kicked my legs against the bottom of the Solenoid. As I thrust away, the creature's sharp nails slashed across my cheek. I scrambled back in horror. A mass of shimmering black crawled out from the split

316

in the Solenoid.

Footsteps clomped behind me. "What in the world is going on out here? What have you done to the Solenoid?" a familiar voice roared.

Edgard. I turned to look at him.

"Don't think I haven't heard from Gervais about you—"

"No, stop!" I held out my hands.

An alabaster hand plunged into Edgard's chest. His eyes bulged. Blood dribbled down his face and shirt, pooling on the ground. He gaped at the bleak face in front of him. "Phase," he choked, coughing up red. "It's a Phase."

"Phase!" someone shouted.

"A Phase. Run!"

"Phase! Phase!"

As the word ricocheted, panic ensued. Shrieks, sobs, and curses unfolded in a cacophony of terror.

"Gavril?"

I turned to see Mama crouching by the siphon, her long green dress splayed out like a pool of fairy grass. A bewildered look adorned her face. "Gavril, what's going on? Why are you here?"

"No, Mama," I hissed in panic. "Go back. It's not safe."

"What in the Great Heart are you talking about? Why is everyone running around? I thought I heard someone scream Pha—"

"Mama, behind you!"

I watched, aghast, as that white face rose from behind my mother's head like the moon claiming the night sky. She slowly turned, unsure and confused. As soon as her eyes met the Phase, every muscle in her back tensed.

The Phase looked down at her, and for an instant, it was tranquil. It raised its hand and touched the front of her dress.

Mama trembled. "Goel?" Her voice wavered. "Goel?"

The Phase opened its mouth, and another deafening screech rang out. It pulled its hand back, razor nails poised to strike.

"No!" I leapt forward as the claws surged forward, aiming straight for Mama's heart.

I will be her shield. I am her barrier!

An intense rush spread through me. A warm, comforting feeling that I associated with two things: the barrier and—

Something sharp stabbed into my shoulder. A pained howl echoed in my ear. A streak of white danced across my vision. And through it all, I could only think of one thing.

Serein.

SPHERE OF EMPTINESS

A damp cloth dabbed my cheek, the flesh burning with every touch. I twitched and coughed, deluged with images. A shredded Solenoid, a ghastly face reminiscent of my father, claws reaching for Mama.

My eyes snapped open. What happened? Where was I?

An echo of pain thumped in my heart. Serein.

"Gavril."

I turned to Mama. Her green eyes glistened with unshed tears.

"Why do you look so sad? Has death claimed us?"

"No, little flicker," she whimpered. "We aren't dead."

"Then what?"

I reached up to touch her cheek. I caught a glimpse of the back of my hand and stopped. The veins . . . marred by . . .

"The only reason you're still alive is because you somehow managed to kill the Phase." Mama sniffled but her eyes shone proudly. "It was amazing, Gavril. A white light surrounded you and the Phase split apart. But you, Gavril . . . it was hard, but I convinced them to spare your life."

I lowered my hand. "Mama, about that Phase . . ."

Her eyes sharpened into emerald spears. "It was just a Phase, Gavril. Nothing more."

"It was in the Solenoid."

"No, it wasn't."

"It was *him*."

"No."

"It was Papa."

A sharp slap echoed off the tin walls. My face stung worse than the shock of being struck by my own mother. A part of me ached at that revelation. Mama pulled her hand to her chest and stood up with a guarded expression, tears streaming down her face.

"It's time for you to leave, Gavril. You can't stay here. You—you don't belong anymore." She collapsed to the floor, sobbing.

I stared at her, the words sinking in.

"You're right." I sat up on my hay mattress and stood. "Goodbye, Mama."

Oddly at ease, I left my home and glided into the morning light. Heads turned to stare. Some people cowered. Others ran away. Still others spat and hissed.

I saved their lives.

I circled the twisted Solenoid. It was an empty, torn shell now. Like the one in Jalousie. Just like everything else I had fought for.

I made my way to the edge of town toward Lake Oublié. I wanted to admire it one last time. I wanted to remember its marvel.

"Gavril, wait!" someone called.

I turned. Mathieu ran toward me, stopping well beyond my reach.

"I wanted to thank you," he said. He looked at my face and his eyes lowered, crestfallen. "This isn't how I wanted things to end up. But you saved us from the Phase. I'll never forget it."

I nodded and looked back at Nostalgie. "What will you do now?"

"I honestly don't know," he admitted, rubbing the back of his neck. "I suppose Envie is our best option."

"I would be careful with that venture. After Jalousie—"

"I know. I've heard the stories," Mathieu said. "We have no intentions of letting Gervais know a Phase attacked us last night." His face grew somber. "We'll tell him Edgard died trying to save the Solenoid from rupturing and got caught in the blast. Don't worry."

"I'm not worried."

Mathieu gazed at me sadly. "I know."

I studied him. Before, I always saw my childhood friend. Now, I saw a mayor. The last mayor of Nostalgie. "Goodbye, Mathieu. Please, take care of everyone."

He nodded and tried to smile, much as he had done before I was taken to Envie. "Take care of yourself, Gavril."

I turned away and circumnavigated the lake until I reached the old cork tree. Leaning against the trunk, I stared down at the clear water. This was where I had stepped outside the barrier for the first time. I had been afraid, then—terrified of every shadow. And a shadow had come to me that night. Not a phantom come to steal my heart, but a being who set me on a path that changed my life forever. A friend I could trust, even now, as I could trust no longer.

A cloud of whirling black reflected in the lake's shimmering surface, almost as if it had been called by my thoughts. I turned to face it as it settled near the ground and took shape.

"Morrow," I said. "Did you know what was in the Solenoid?"

"I knew."

"Why didn't you tell me?"

"I—" she paused, and silence followed for a few seconds. "I knew it would bring you pain."

I looked back over Lake Oublié. "I suppose it would have." A flash of orange darted below the water's surface. A fish. Nothing more. "Now I am dampened."

"I did not intend for you to become dampened."

"It doesn't matter now. Do all the Solenoids contain Résonateurs?" I asked.

"Yes."

"Why?"

"Only the most ardent of hearts can produce a power strong enough to create a perfect sphere of protection. What results is the final phase of giving your heart for others forever. The phase of eternal emptiness."

I studied her blank face. "You were a Résonateur once."

"For a time," she replied. "Before that, I was a queen. The first queen."

I stared at her, the pieces slowly falling into place. "Eidolon's?"

"Yes," she said. "I wanted to feel his heart as strongly as he felt mine, so I volunteered to use the Solenoid to pull out the power of my heart. That was their original intent—a marvel meant to transform the world. How foolish we were to try and manipulate the power of emotions when we understood so little of the consequences." Morrow stared across the lake to Nostalgie. "I was promised going into the Solenoid would free my heart. The Solenoid stole it instead."

"And you remember?" I asked. "The other Phases . . . Morrow, why are they so savage?"

"The process was sudden—so quickly was my heart drained by new technology that not even Eidolon understood," Morrow replied. "I was trapped inside for mere hours. The others—they suffer much longer. For years, they are locked in the darkness and pain of the Solenoids. That is the siphon's true purpose. It slows the process so only what is needed to power the barrier is siphoned away. Over those slow, agonizing years, their minds decay with their hearts. They do not remember themselves. All they know is hunger and emptiness."

We fell into a period of silence. It could have been an instant. It could have been an hour. It was enough for me to dwell on everything that changed for me. For memories were all I had now. I left the barrier. I flew in a soulever. I explored the Paramount. I went on an adventure.

I met Serein and found the one who could open my heart. I fell in love. And just when I thought I had it all . . .

"I've lost so much," I concluded with a dull twinge in my chest. "Tell me, Morrow, have I gained anything at all?"

"Your freedom."

The corners of my mouth curved up in recollection, something called a smile that I didn't feel, an expression drawn from the ghost of nostalgia.

"I suppose I have." I looked up at the open sky. It looked like rain. "Do you think he will know what happened to me?"

"He will."

"Is there any hope for us?" I asked despite no longer feeling the need to know. Perhaps what was once curiosity. Perhaps what was once hope.

"Hope is beyond us," Morrow replied. "But as long as we live, there is always possibility."

A point of silver flashed in the sky, descending from the clouds like a star falling from the heavens—the only star in the sky.

I reached out and touched Morrow's fingers. Her flesh was perfectly smooth, but not cold. I curled my fingers around hers.

Goodbye, Serein.

"Let's go, Morrow."

Together, we walked into a field of golden grass. As long as Morrow was by my side, we would survive. I had to keep that one thought with me always. It was all I had left.

This was the saddest day I couldn't feel.

ACKNOWLEDGEMENTS

Eight years is a long time to be working on a novel, but sometimes stories, like fine wine, need time to mature, and ideas, like delicious meat, need time to marinate.

I'm hungry while I'm writing this, but enough about food. It's been a long journey, and there are some people I would like to thank for putting up with me on the way.

First, I'd like to thank my family. My daughter, Elise, while not the most patient of angels, understood that some nights were for writing and editing. She's always been the biggest reason for continuing to pursue my dream, so I might add a little magic to the world. My husband, Nick, has been there since the beginning, supporting me through the ups and downs and grass-covered traps filled with spikes. I'd also like to mention my parents, siblings, and grandparents for keeping me alive with shelter and entertainment for the first half of my life so I could write this book.

Now on to my furry kiddos—Juniper, Needle, M&M, and Gizmo. Thank you for being there to provide cuddles and for keeping me company during those long hours in front of the keyboard. Some of you are no longer with us, but memories of you are always with me.

I'd also like to acknowledge the Indigo River Publishing team for seeing my potential and giving me that "yes" after many, many, many rejections. I must give a special mention to Deborah Froese for helping me jump some unexpected hurdles and for stepping up during editing. Without her pushing, poking, and prodding, this story wouldn't have the heart it has today.

Lastly, I would like to thank Google Translate for helping with my gratuitous French.

AUTHOR'S NOTE

This book is for anyone thinking about giving up on their dreams. It took fourteen years to achieve mine, and while life may not always turn out the way you want, there's always hope if you believe in yourself.

Ghost of Nostalgia has changed so much from the first draft. The title changed at least three times, the word count nearly doubled, and the characters have transformed in unexpected ways. As cliché as it sounds, a dream inspired this story, and it has been evolving ever since. Life changes. Dreams change. People change. But always keep faith in yourself. Don't give up.

GLOSSARY

Terms French (English)

A

aérien (air)

aérien opérateur (aerial operator)—an operator for a soulever. Larger soulevers require a chief opérateur and sub-opérateurs.

archiviste (archivist)—a person responsible for gathering, interpreting, and controlling information for the governing Sommet. Archivistes have a ranking system with higher ranked archivistes being responsible for more confidential information and data.

automatram (automatic tram)—vehicle for transportation. Classic automatrams have wheels and can only be used for ground travel. New models can levitate for short air travel.

C

Chancelier (chancellor)—the head councilman of the Sommet and right hand to the Suzerain.

Commandant (commander)—high-ranking Résonateur.

D

dévoiler (unveil)—a cube-shaped key for revealing and unlocking doors and hatches.

E

étincelle (spark)—electrical energy.

Enquête (inquiry)—the specialized investigative branch of the Sommet. The Enquête are responsible for investigating crimes, conspiracies, and acts of rebellion against the Suzerain.

F

Fluctuateur (Fluctuator)—a Résonateur who has lost control of their emotions. Fluctuateurs are considered highly dangerous.

O

opérateur (operator)—a person who operates a transport or device.

R

relier (connect)—devices used for communication between towns. Reliers can be small with a microphone, speaker, and antenna for basic communication or large and complex for long distance data transfers.

Résonateur (Resonator)—special individuals who can utilize their emotions to affect the physical world. Résonateurs are trained to maintain control of their emotions to combat dampened, Phases, and defend the Suzerain.

S

Seigneur (lord)—a person of noble birth whose family has been granted control of a town by the Suzerain or Sommet.

Sommet (summit)—the governing body for Premier Esprit. The Sommet is comprised of councilmen selected by the Suzerain or Chancelier.

soulever (raise)—an airship. Soulevers are the preferred method of transporting goods and people between towns due to their speed and ability to avoid danger.

Suzerain (overlord)—the supreme ruler of Premier Esprit and the countries under its rule.

T

tonique (tonic)—medicine for infection.

V

vigile (vigil)—a thin metallic device used by archivistes to record information and access data. Vigiles are the size of a small sheet of paper.

voietram (path tram)—specialized self-operating automatram that follows a designated light path.

ABOUT THE AUTHOR

Joanne Hatfield started life in the city of Barrow-in-Furness, England, but ended up stateside as a baby, growing up in Monroeville, Alabama. As a result, she takes her tea a good many ways. But the adventure didn't stop there. She eventually ended up in Birmingham—Alabama that is, not England. And despite being raised in the "Literary Capital of Alabama," it wasn't until after college she discovered a true passion for writing. She has a Bachelor of Science in Nuclear Medicine, a Master of Science in Management Information Systems, and a deep love of crafting new and exciting worlds, which has nothing to do with those degrees. She enjoys drawing inspiration from video games, classic and obscure science fiction movies, and those weird dreams that happen after going to bed caffeinated.